Sinners

Sinners

ELIZABETH FREMANTLE

MICHAEL  JOSEPH

PENGUIN MICHAEL JOSEPH

UK | USA | Canada | Ireland | Australia
India | New Zealand | South Africa

Penguin Michael Joseph is part of the Penguin Random House group of companies whose addresses can be found at global.penguinrandomhouse.com

Penguin Random House UK,
One Embassy Gardens, 8 Viaduct Gardens, London SW11 7BW

penguin.co.uk

First published 2025
002

Copyright © Elizabeth Fremantle, 2025
Images on pp 5, 149 and 247 © The Trustees of the British Museum

The moral right of the author has been asserted

Penguin Random House values and supports copyright. Copyright fuels creativity, encourages diverse voices, promotes freedom of expression and supports a vibrant culture. Thank you for purchasing an authorized edition of this book and for respecting intellectual property laws by not reproducing, scanning or distributing any part of it by any means without permission. You are supporting authors and enabling Penguin Random House to continue to publish books for everyone. No part of this book may be used or reproduced in any manner for the purpose of training artificial intelligence technologies or systems. In accordance with Article 4(3) of the DSM Directive 2019/790, Penguin Random House expressly reserves this work from the text and data mining exception.

Set in Garamond MT
Typeset by Falcon Oast Graphic Art Ltd
Printed and bound in Great Britain by Clays Ltd, Elcograf S.p.A.

The authorized representative in the EEA is Penguin Random House Ireland, Morrison Chambers, 32 Nassau Street, Dublin D02 YH68

A CIP catalogue record for this book is available from the British Library

HARDBACK ISBN: 978–0–241–70516–2
TRADE PAPERBACK ISBN: 978–0–241–70517–9

Penguin Random House is committed to a sustainable future for our business, our readers and our planet. This book is made from Forest Stewardship Council® certified paper

This one's for you, Jill

Bring on Medusa! With her aid we'll make
This man a stone!
                       Dante, *Inferno*, tr. Clive James

Prologue

Convento di Santa Maria, Montecitorio, Rome, 1586

'No soul is beyond redemption.' Mother Superior's wimple is stiff and folded sharply, like a paper bird. 'But we have tried to curtail your daughter's impulsiveness and curiosity, to no avail. I'm afraid, Conte, I am forced to consider the other girls and the bad influence this is beginning to have over them. There are already signs –'

'Are you saying,' Father talks over her. Normally no one dares do that, not even the bishop, 'that my daughter is no longer welcome in your establishment?'

I am sitting on a bench to one side while she and Father discuss me as if I am not here. I have never seen Father quite so close up, or not that I remember. He is a large man, with cold blue eyes and coppery hair like mine.

She is wearing her pretend smile. 'With all respect, I feel she might thrive better at home, under the auspices of her new stepmother.'

Stepmother? It is the first I've heard of this. I run the beads of my rosary over the pad of my thumb, not because I am praying but because I like the smoothness of the polished wood against my skin.

'And the large donation I made to the convent?' He places his elbow on the table, chin on his fisted hand.

'For the Lord's work.'

He laughs – not the kind of laugh you make when something is funny. 'I see. You want to keep the money and be rid of my girl.'

She tips her head. 'The difficulty is that other girls have begun to ask questions. And we can't have that. All those malleable little minds.'

I am trying to think about when the questions began to press at me, remembering a time, two years ago. I was seven then. We were in the oblates' dormitory, shifts hiked up, examining each other's navels with hot pudgy hands. Most of the girls had neat little cavities but Simonetta's stuck out like a tiny balloon and Carlotta's had the appearance of a knot. Mine was twisted, like the inside of a snail shell.

'What does it do?' I asked.

'It is where we were attached to our mothers,' said Fiammetta, who knew more than the rest of us. She was older and her father was a horse breeder, so she had witnessed the birthing of foals. 'Its proper name is the umbilicus.' She explained the cord that must be severed to separate infant from mother.

My last memory of my own mother drifted to my mind. It was a hug, her middle vast and taut, pressing into me, then a great slosh, and a sudden commotion, the maid crying, 'Your waters!' Everything was wet. And she disappeared. I thought she had been turned into a stream, like the girl in a story told by my nurse.

The memory made my chest feel tight. I burrowed a seeking finger into my navel, causing a strange, sharp tug at the bottom of me, surprising as the suck on a slice of lemon.

I heard my name, cut into parts: 'Bay-a-tree-chay!' and looked up to see Sister Maddalena, hiding her eyes, as if the sight of my naked belly might turn her blind.

The others had whipped down their shifts before she saw. So, it was only me who was hauled out into the cold corridor to kneel before the Holy Virgin, 'To set your mind on the path of purity.'

I held out my hands, palms up. Sister Maddalena's punishments were soft compared to some. I found a pinprick of comfort in the sting of the ferrule. It told me I was alive – not dead, like my mother.

'Pray that the Holy Virgin will deliver you from a life of shame,' she said, leaving me alone with the Madonna weeping in her niche. The candle at her feet made her tears shine. I touched them once. They felt cool and smooth like glass.

Pressing my burning hands tight together, I did my very best to pray: *Hail, Holy Queen, Mother of Mercy, our life, our sweetness and our hope, to thee do we cry, poor banished children of Eve* . . . But my mind was full of questions about why a finger in the navel was worse than a finger in a nostril or an ear. Was it because the navel sat in a part of the body that was always to be kept covered and perilously close to those other parts that must never be touched, ever? A finger slipped into *that* place, I had discovered, was another kind of furtive comfort.

As time passed, my wondering only increased.

A visiting bishop came to talk to us about the Book of Genesis. He hung a large painting on the refectory wall, showing scenes of the expulsion of Adam and Eve from Paradise.

He droned on for an age about the loss of innocence and Eve's part in it. I had questions about this that I knew better than to ask and drifted off into the painting: the naked figures of Adam and Eve, hunched in shame beneath the tree, where the serpent coiled.

The bishop quoted passages we all knew off by heart: *And I will put enmity between you and the woman, and between your offspring and hers; he will crush your head, and you will strike his heel.*

A few girls stifled yawns, but I was alert with a new and pressing query.

When he finished, he asked if there was anything he could clarify for us.

My arm shot up.

'Yes, my child. What can I explain?'

'I cannot understand,' I said.

'Speak up. Or, better still, come to the front.'

He seemed enormous, towering over me, placing his great gnarled hand on my shoulder. I looked up at him. Wiry hairs spilled from his nostrils.

'That's better,' he said. 'Now what can I help you with?'

I pointed to Adam's torso. 'If Adam was the first man and made by God, why does he have an umbilicus?'

Red spots sprang to his cheeks and his eyebrows drew together. 'Have you learned nothing from the story of Eve, how her thirst for knowledge led to her fall?'

'But how does anyone learn of God's great works without seeking answers?'

I knew I should have held my tongue. I shrank under his flinty look. 'A child of your age should be a silent vessel to be filled with the scriptures.' He brought his face close. It took all my resolve not to shrink back. 'Curiosity leads to sin just as sin leads to damnation.'

It was this incident that led me to be here in Mother Superior's receiving room, listening to her list my failings.

She still wears her smile. 'It seems to me that Beatrice has been given more than her fair share of original sin.'

I slump, the breath forced right out of me. My heart sticks in my throat, a hard lump. Curiosity is one thing but . . . *More than her fair share of original sin. What has she seen in me? A wickedness?* I imagine the place where my soul resides, a cleft deep inside me, a demon squatting there, licking its lips.

Am I one of the damned?

PART ONE
The Lovers

I

Palazzo Cenci, Rome, twelve years later

I scrub myself hard with the stiff bristled brush and harder still until I am pink and sore, but I can't scrub the terrible crawling feeling from beneath my skin.

Sliding under the water, I drift, weightless.

The bathtub's linen lining floats around me, like the medusa I saw the year I left the convent, when we travelled to Naples by sea. It spilled from a net onto the deck, a mound of iridescent nothing, as if a puddle had gathered into an invisible pouch. Its tentacles wound and curled over the wet boards. My brother, Rocco, prodded it with his foot.

'Don't touch,' warned one of the crew. 'It's deadly poisonous.'

After a few days the sun had transmuted it to little more than a vague stain, an evaporation, the memory of a creature.

I found an etching of a medusa in Father's library and learned it shared its name with a once beautiful Gorgon, raped and cursed with snakes for hair, who turned all who looked on her to stone. It made me wonder which came first: the myth or the sea creature.

The book it was in, *Historiae Animalium*, containing all the extraordinary and marvellous animals that roam the far corners of the earth, is on the Pope's index. Soon, they say, it will be banned. Rumours circulate about the *Index Librorum Prohibitorum*. Will Dante be on it for his criticism of the Church, or Ovid for his paganism, or Copernicus for daring to see the universe in a new way? His Holiness would have us read nothing but the scriptures as his grip tightens on Rome.

I discovered on that voyage, though I have never since been to sea, that I had a special affinity with the water. Its surge and sound exhilarated me as did the way, in a giddy upside-down sensation, I couldn't see where it ended and the sky began. It gave me a sense of limitless possibility, of the vastness of the world and my smallness in it, which was strangely comforting.

Apart from Father, I was the only one of our party – my brothers, my sister and my stepmother – who wasn't afraid, even when the waves began to chop angrily at the bow, rising, forming and re-forming, into great cascading cliffs, their force enough to splinter our ship into a thousand fragments and suck us down into its quiet depths. I gripped the rail, elated by the salt slap on my face, feeling life throb through my every pore, until Father ordered me into the hold.

Beneath the surface of the water my heart throb echoes through my ears, hair coiling and writhing. I am held suspended. The bathtub is big. Everything at the Palazzo Cenci is big – soaring painted ceilings, endless corridors, reception rooms the size of cathedrals – all to accommodate Father, a large man, and Father's idea of himself, which is even larger.

I push Father from my thoughts. He hovers in the gloomy wings of my mind, always there, always watching, waiting, for any trivial misdemeanour. Father is an intimidating man, not just in physical presence.

I am small. My body displaces so little of the water. It is easy to imagine that, like the medusa, I am almost nothing, uncontainable and will spill from the pocket that holds me to become part of a limitless world.

I surface, inhaling deeply. My hair clings to my throat and

shoulders, like a net. Climbing from the tub, I rub myself dry, coil my hair in a towel and shrug on my thick woollen robe, fastening it tight so no part of me is exposed.

As I leave the bathhouse, steam billows out into the chill February air. Virgil, my hound, is waiting for me. He draws himself to his feet, huge and sleek, and falls into my slipstream as I make my way along the arcade that runs around the courtyard. He has followed me everywhere, like a shadow, since I rescued him from drowning as a pup.

Exhaustion hangs heavily over me. I haven't slept all night. It is barely daybreak, the light cool and shivery, the shadows deep and quiet. It rained heavily in the night, leaving the gutters dripping, the flagstones slick with wet, and petrichor hanging in the air. The great fountain at the centre of the court is still. Neptune presides over the scene brandishing his trident, huge against the dull white of dawn. Father had him modelled in his image. His dark marble skin is pocked with white birds' mess. The windows of the palazzo are all shuttered. Nothing stirs, no one about to ask me why I am bathing so early, why I can't sleep. 'If you can't sleep, you must have a guilty conscience,' my nurse used to say. If that was the case, Father would have died long ago for lack of rest.

My anger springs up suddenly. Father should still be in prison. He was released yesterday. I wrote to the authorities begging them to keep him there. We have had three months of peace. I hoped against hope, naively perhaps, that if they had an idea of the kind of regime we, his family, were subjected to, someone among their ranks might find an iota of sympathy for us and argue our case. But I see now how the pleas of a young woman, however desperate, would fall on deaf ears when her father can pay a vast sum for his release – the kind of sum that could set the prison's governor up for life. Money talks here in Rome, and women must remain silent.

Something is on the main steps – a sack of grain? It can't be. All provisions are delivered to the back entrance. Virgil, curiosity sparked, trots ahead to sniff at it. As I near, its form takes the shape of a man sleeping, slumped face down. Nearer still, and it is my brother. If I know Rocco, he will have been too drunk to make it inside. I approach on tiptoe, wanting to surprise him, to tease him for his debauchery. When I prod his back he doesn't move.

'Rocco!' I shake him, his shoulder wet from the rain. His arm unfurls, exposing an open hand. 'Wake up! Rocco, you'll catch your death.' I pull at that chilled hand and he unrolls, exposing his front. A scream explodes from me, then another. His doeskin jacket is ripped and soaked with blood, dark and congealing. I feel for a pulse, for a breath. I shake him, yelling at him to wake up.

A note is pinned to his collar. All in capitals it says, 'NO ONE CROSSES THE ORESTESI.'

My screams have roused the sleeping palazzo, shutters banging open. 'What's going on down there?'

The gate guards arrive first, weapons out, bleary-eyed, horrified to see Rocco dead on the steps. They become jittery with nerves. They will be the ones to face Father's wrath for allowing the Orestesi to gain entry to his impenetrable palazzo.

How *did* they get in?

Everyone is here all at once, clamouring, confused. Father is storming.

Lucrezia, my stepmother, tries to pull me from my brother's cold corpse. She has to prise my fingers from his bloody jacket. 'Come away, sweetheart.' But I grip tighter. 'Bea, please.'

Father rips the note from Rocco's inert breast. 'The Orestesi can burn in Hell. A curse on every last one of them.'

Lucrezia coaxes me away. Catarina, my companion, has

joined her. They have me, one arm each, holding me up, as I can't find my feet. Once inside they lower me onto the bench in the hall, where I collapse, as if deboned. Virgil leans his head on my lap responding to my distress in the only way he knows. Catarina presses a small glass cup into my hands. 'You're in shock, Bea. Drink it. It'll settle you.'

The brandy strips the skin off my tongue and makes my head swim, dulling the terrible clang of horror, blunting it to bottomless sorrow.

'If Father was still locked up, this wouldn't have happened,' I say, once my lost voice returns.

'We don't know that,' says Lucrezia.

But we *do*. Father was in prison because of the Orestesi. None of us quite knew what exactly he'd done to them. Some said he'd raped Conte Orestesi's wife, others said his daughter, some even said his son. Many said it all started with a dispute over a parcel of land, that Father had undercut the Orestesi in a deal. Father has more land than he knows what to do with but would still fight to the death over a thimbleful of turf if he thought someone else wanted it. He maintained he'd done little more than slight an Orestesi cousin over nothing. 'That wretched family of bastards would sharpen their swords if you accidentally spilled a drop of water on one of their shoes,' he said of it.

I suspected it was more than a minor slight. If the servants' gossip is anything to go by – and usually it is the most reliable source of information – Father had been challenged by this cousin. He'd dishonoured the man's wife. Quite how was unclear. But the man had come off worst. Only a fool would challenge Francesco Cenci to a fight.

Catarina had described to me vividly the man's injuries. She knew a page in the Orestesi household, so she had it from the source. He was still walking with a stick three months on.

It was said to be unlikely he'd ever be able to father any more children. And the Orestesi aren't the only family Father has trouble with. A vendetta has been simmering with the Rientini since before I can remember.

Now Rocco is dead. Last year it was Cristofero. It had taken three weeks to find his body shoved behind one of the old Roman ruins, half eaten by rats. Two brothers out of four gone – in the name of honour.

'When will it stop?' My voice is a croak. 'Men with their weapons and their honour that they would dishonour themselves to protect.'

2

I am on Aquilino, a spirited chestnut with a white star between his eyes. Father insisted we ride the best of our horses. Father's horses draw attention and envy, even in Rome where everyone has fine horses. He is deeply fond of one or two of them, though not Aquilino, who is too capricious. He prefers his horses, like his family, acquiescent.

Rocco's bier is pulled by four of our tar-black, high-stepping Neapolitans, their quarters brushed into chequer-board patterns, hoofs oiled, tails plaited, inky ostrich feathers bouncing on their bridles. A drummer walks at the front, marking out the time, just behind the *monsignore* in his brocade robes brandishing a gold-dipped crucifix. A boy walks on each side of him, bearing pennants with the Cenci arms. Other clergy follow in black, carrying an assortment of holy items, the lock of Sant'Agnese's hair, a plaster statue of Our Lady, her robe painted in lapis, which costs more than gold, and a garish painting of San Rocco, baring his chest to show his cross-shaped birthmark.

The rain has held off today, in honour of my dead brother, and a thin February sun gilds our cortège. We move along with excruciating slowness beside the Tiber, passing the makeshift huts where families dwell, forced south by famine in the north to scratch out a living in Rome. Weekly, I distribute food to them. Father calls them vermin, mocks me – 'Trying to make God smile on you, are you?' – for helping them, but they are good people, dealt a bad hand by Fate.

Aquilino pulls at the bit, desperate to break into a trot. I keep him in check. His hoofs scrape at the cobbles. The Cenci colours are draped over the coffin and sway with the lugubrious motion of the bier. I can't look. Beneath it, the walnut casket is a thing of beauty. The carpenter worked all night to have it ready in time. It is polished to a high shine, black grain perfectly matched to make butterfly shapes and symmetrical whorls that can be imagined into faces and creatures. It is said they beat walnut trees with heavy chains to encourage the grain.

Rocco is dead.

Everything has happened so fast that my grief has barely had time to brew. It is sharp and raw and bitter.

Father, Lucrezia and I ride, three abreast, behind the bier. My married sister, Antonina, is too heavy with child to ride and Bernardo, my younger brother, remained at home. Father doesn't like him seen in public and, besides, we can never be sure how he will behave, so it's better this way. Giacomo, my eldest brother, should be here with us but he is not. Catarina is behind, on foot, with the rest of the household and a great parade of mourners. Everyone wanted to be Rocco's friend – wild, infuriating, reckless Rocco.

Memories of him swill through my mind. Swimming at the river pool near Mother's old summerhouse, the Villa Paradiso, flinging ourselves from the high rock, the giddy sensation of flying, our shrieks of laughter in the air, the sharp cold shock of hitting the water, sinking into the fizz of bubbles, floating in the green echoing depths, losing sense of which way was up, firm hands drawing me to the surface, finding myself in Giacomo's arms. Giacomo, already then a man of twenty, berating Rocco for endangering me. At only six, I could not swim but Rocco, two years my senior, hadn't thought of that. His face drifts before me, his enthralling smile that would light the darkest of corners.

Oh, Rocco!
My heart is shattered.

We pass the Tor di Nona, the prison where Father was held. It is a shabby place, small, square barred windows watching us. Crowds line the streets to see us pass. I spy a group of Orestesi boys skulking outside the Feathers Inn. They will return home and tell of the Cenci splendour, how we paraded like royalty. This spectacle is not for Rocco, not really. It is to show the Orestesi that the Cenci will not be cowed – not ever. The funeral mass could have been held in our chapel at the Palazzo Cenci, with our family confessor, Don Esposito, presiding. But no, Father insisted that the *monsignore* in his brocades hold the mass and that we process through all of Rome to the vast church of Santa Maria del Popolo for the service and back again, so Rocco can be laid in the chapel vault. A dozen guards ride alongside us, armed and drilled for the worst kind of trouble. But Father's watching enemies won't make a move today, out of respect for the dead. Why respect the dead, when they have no respect for the living? It makes no sense to me. None of it makes sense, all those beautiful boys, ours and theirs, struck down in their prime. I secretly, sinfully, wish it was Father I'd found on the steps instead.

As we enter the Piazza del Popolo, we pass a street preacher standing on a box bellowing to a gathering: 'Corruption is a cancer that has blighted the very fabric of our city. Rome was once great but now she is in the grip of depravity and vice' – he waves an angry fist to his audience – 'corruption and exploitation, by those who claim to be our betters. They drown in riches and titles.' He has worked himself into a puce-faced fervour and he prods a finger towards our cortège. I resent his angry intrusion into our mourning. 'While the ordinary man works the shirt off his back to put bread on his table, the nobles sup with Satan. Fortune may favour them, but our Lord will not. Remember His word, when He said the rich man ...'

Our drummer drowns his words and his audience, distracted, turn to watch us go by, removing their hats and crossing themselves. A loud crashing sound spooks Aqualino. He skitters sideways scattering the throng, iron shoes clashing and sliding. It takes all my focus to draw him back into line. Father gives me a scowl. Soon the bells of Santa Maria flood the piazza, drawing us inexorably towards the vast carved doors. The pallbearers have gathered there: a quartet of cousins and Rocco's two closest friends, Davide Forlani and Girolamo Grassi, boys I have known all my life, men now. Yet they still seem so young, faces drawn in grief. Twenty-five years is the blink of an eye.

The bearers manoeuvre the heavy casket off the vehicle. It sways and pitches as they heave it onto their shoulders, the sinews in their necks protruding with the effort. I can see Davide, his face bunched tight, determined to keep tears at bay as they slowly mount the steps. He and Rocco were thick as thieves. I have a flash of memory – the three of us galloping across the river field, racing fast, faster, fastest. I can feel my hair flying out and ribbons of wild laughter trailing behind me. I reach the post first. Rocco sulks to be beaten by his younger sister. Davide laughs and says it is only because of Aquilino.

The quiet interior of the church is a sigh of relief after the racket of the piazza, a momentary eye in the storm that lulls me until I am lashed by the reason we are all here. The choir chant in low voices that vibrate gently through the space, where candles spread their shimmering light and the air is sweet with incense. We slip into our seats. Father insists Antonina and I sit either side of him. He is stiff, jaw clenched, mouth set tight, staring relentlessly forwards, no hint of grief on display. Antonina is awash with tears, hands clasping her huge belly, as if she thinks she might birth her child there in the pew. Her husband, on her other side, comforts her. I envy her the marriage that took her away from our unhappy house.

In disbelief, I watch as the bearers remove the banner from the coffin and lift its lid to reveal my dead brother. He lies in a bed of satin the colour of blood. His hair has been oiled and combed back with a sharp parting to one side, styled in a manner he would never have worn. I hear his voice: *I wouldn't be seen dead looking like that. Oh, God!* I want to ruffle that slicked hair – desperately. They have painted his face, which gives him an unreal appearance, ashen against the sheeny crimson of his pillow.

Davide slumps beside me, starched with distress. His hand is tightly fisted, scraping back and forth against his leg. I take it, prising his fingers open, enveloping it in both of mine, as a mother might a child. Everyone had once assumed Davide Forlani and I would eventually marry. We shared a secret kiss once, chaste and dry. Father began negotiations but they petered out when the Forlani came on hard times. I have lately heard their fortunes have taken a turn for the better. If I can find a way to make Father think it is his idea, perhaps a new arrangement can be struck. To become a Forlani cannot be worse than being a Cenci. Escape spools through my mind's eye. But Father has shown no inclination, lately, to wed me off.

My brother's death looms.

Father swoops in with a smile, taking my hands for himself, incarcerating them in his. I know that smile. My stomach tightens. His boot, hidden beneath my skirts, pushes down hard on my slipper. A spasm of pain bites. I steel myself, holding my expression as if nothing is out of the ordinary. Father wants a reaction. I will not give him one.

The choir sing. It is an impossibly glorious, soaring sound that fills the vast space, reverberating off the arches and pillars.

But I am numb to its beauty. I sit and stand and kneel like a clockwork creature.

We take communion. When I return to my seat I see, in the gloom far to the back, half hidden by a pillar, Giacomo. I smile, a wisp of joy flitting through my grief. I haven't seen him for three years. He draws a finger across his lips and, in response, I nod my understanding. I wouldn't dream of telling Father that his eldest son, cast out and ordered never to return, has come to say goodbye to his brother.

When the service ends, the congregation mills, moving slowly towards the doors, and Father is caught in conversation with the *monsignore*. I take my chance and slip quietly over to Giacomo, whispering, 'The Foscari chapel.'

It is tucked away to one side in the dim recesses of the church. I light a candle, kneeling at the prayer stand, and Giacomo slips in beside me. 'I've missed you, Giaco – so much.'

'And I you.' We fall silent. He is nervy, strain showing in his hooded eyes, and he holds his gloves crushed tightly in his fist. As a child I looked up to my handsome eldest brother as if he was a god. I remember overhearing Father's rant to him: 'Imagine the disgrace you will bring on us, if they burn you like they burned those perverts at San Giovanni.'

I was standing unseen at the crack of the door.

'What does he mean?' I asked Giacomo later, distress simmering through me. 'Why would they burn you?'

I was young then, too young to understand. He sat me down and explained that some men love men, told me that half the clergy in Rome were of that disposition.

'And you are one of those men?'

'I am, but you must promise never to let Father know I have told you, or he'll accuse me of trying to corrupt you and . . .' He left the potential consequences unsaid.

'But is it true' – fear forced its way through me – 'that you will be burned like those, those . . .' I didn't want to say the word, wasn't sure of its meaning but knew it was something terrible.

'No, Bea. You don't need to worry for me.' He put an arm about my shoulders. 'Those men Father spoke of were conducting marriage ceremonies to wed each other. It was the sacrilege that was the crime.' I learned later that this wasn't quite the truth. I came eventually to see that what goes on between two people behind closed doors is hard to prove, that there is one law for the rich and another for the poor. There is an age at which one comes to an understanding of hypocrisy, and I hadn't reached it then. 'Besides . . .' Giacomo continued explaining about the eight poor men who were burned at San Giovanni, and why he, the most beloved of my brothers, was not destined for such a fate. 'It was years ago, Bea. Nothing will happen to me.'

'It's not worth the risk, though, surely.'

'One day you will learn that you can't choose who you fall for.'

Giacomo briefly touches my hand, bringing me back to the present. 'I can't believe he's gone. I hope he didn't suffer.'

'It was I who found him.'

'Oh, Bea.' He pauses. 'One day one of his enemies will kill him and then . . .'

We are silent again for a while, lost for words, his firm presence beside me more comfort than he will ever know.

'I should have come to you while I had the chance.' Giacomo had written to me when Father was locked up, suggesting I go and live with him. 'It's too late now.' Something had stopped me. Fear, I suppose, awareness that Father wouldn't be held indefinitely, that he would take me back and things would be worse than before.

'Domizio and I have been thinking about getting away overseas, out of his reach – taking you with us.'

A cautious filament of hope rises through me – I have had my hopes dashed before. 'When?'

'Don't know yet. It'll take careful planning.'

It is hard to envisage a place distant enough.

I glance back. Father has finished talking to the *monsignore*. 'I must go.' I prise myself from him.

'I'll write,' he says. We have always corresponded in Greek. I picked up that dead language from loitering about my brothers' lessons. The tutor disapproved but Giacomo insisted I stay. The convenience of Greek is that Father doesn't understand it. Our little secret.

I leave him in the shadows.

We process back to the Palazzo Cenci, in all our grim splendour, to receive the guests who have come to pay their respects with tipped heads and wan little smiles. I notice that Father is simmering with anger directed at me.

'What do you think it's about?' I whisper to Catarina.

'I saw you with Giacomo in the chapel. If I saw, then he might have. You're too reckless, Bea.' Concern spreads over her face. Caution is her *modus operandi*, and it has served her well but I am not like her – I am driven by my will. 'Is it worth it?'

'I *won't* be his caged pet. It's not a life.'

'I worry for you.'

'Don't waste your worry on me.'

She looks hurt. I apologize.

Despite my bravado, disquiet seethes in me as the palazzo empties, the mourners taking their sad smiles away with them. I show Davide to the door, saying quietly, 'Once you are alone, give vent to your tears. It will help.' He kisses me chastely on the cheek and descends the steps. I watch his departing shape silhouetted in the evening light and try to imagine him as my husband but can only conjure a blurred sense of what it might be like. It is that, or Giacomo's proposition, which seems equally indefinite, as something to which I might moor my future. Returning into the hall, I hear Father berating one of the servants and slip away upstairs.

Catarina is already in the bedchamber we share. A fire is blazing and the room warm. Virgil scratches at his bed circling round and round before settling. I kick off my slippers.

'What's that?' Catarina points at my foot, where a black bruise is flowering.

'I caught it in my stirrup as I was dismounting.'

She looks at me sideways and helps me out of my clothes. I am like a moth emerging from the tight tomb of its chrysalis, wings papery and crumpled. My dress is so stiff it can stand on its own. Hers is easier, fewer laces and pins and buttons and struts. We pull on our nightgowns and plait each other's hair, coiling it beneath our linen caps, a ritual that has become entirely automatic over the decade since she arrived in our household, an orphan. I sometimes see a flash of my mother in her quick smile. She is a second cousin on that side of the family – the better side.

'I can't bear the idea of someone else doing this with you,' she says.

'Are you jealous?' I tease, so I don't have to think about the fact that she will be married after Easter. We generally try not to talk about her imminent departure, but it is on my mind a good deal, or it was before Rocco's death usurped my thoughts.

'I suppose I am.'

Her serious tone makes me stop, one arm in, one arm out of my robe. The light from the fire flickers over her pale skin, catching the shine in her dark eyes. Catarina, with her oval face and inherent poise, is a beauty.

'So am I. I'm jealous of *him*.' I have met her Spanish intended only once, she only twice. I look at her then, seeing her dejection, the usual smile absent from her lovely face. 'What is it?'

'I don't want to be married, Bea.' The words spill from her. 'I barely know him, yet I have to spend the rest of my days with . . .' She makes a sound, half sigh, half groan, and wraps her arms tightly about her torso to add, 'And the afterlife.' An expression of horror crimps her face.

I take her in my arms and she sobs quietly. Father had arranged the marriage. He'd talked of it as 'an opportunity far above the station of an orphaned girl of little consequence, cousin or not. She should be on her knees with gratitude that I'm putting up such a generous dowry for her.' I hadn't told her that.

'I'm dreading it.' She pulls a small lace handkerchief from her cuff and dabs at her eyes. Even in tears her poise remains intact.

I try to think of something to make the situation seem less grim. 'At least he's young.'

'And rich.' She emits a wet laugh. I know being rich is very low on the list of things Catarina cares about.

'And he will be away a great deal, won't he? Don't merchants have to travel all the time?'

She nods with a wry smile. 'I suppose so.'

'When he's away we can be together.' I say it but doubt it.

Catarina and I had decided, as besotted twelve-year-olds, after a rare summer at the Villa Paradiso, that it was the place we would spend our whole lives together. It is a modest house on a hill above a river, with a view of the sea, just a morning's ride from Rome – I think of it as my lost Eden. We have only occasionally been since Mother died. It becomes mine in a month when I turn twenty-one.

I sit on the edge of the bed, stroking Virgil's ears, watching Catarina fold her clothes in the careful, methodical way she has. I feel already the wrench of her departure, intensified by the loss of my brother. The idea of being separated from the person closest to me in the world, the companion with whom I have shared all my days for a decade, makes my heart buckle.

A tap at the door reveals one of the pages. 'The conte has asked for you, Signorina Beatrice.' He makes a nervous little bow.

Catarina jumps to my side. 'I'll come with you.' She grabs her favourite shawl, the one she never lends, wrapping it round my shoulders. 'It's cold and this is thin.' She pinches the lapel of my robe between thumb and forefinger.

We follow the page through the corridors without speaking, Virgil's claws clicking on the cool marble. Trepidation weighs silently over me and I search for all the mettle I can muster.

'I'll be here,' she says, as we arrive at the door to his chambers. She takes hold of Virgil's collar, so he can't follow me inside.

I re-tie my robe and wrap the shawl tighter, tucking its ends into my belt, before knocking.

'What took you so long?' My resolve collapses. I want to turn and run, run as fast as my legs will carry me, as far as I can.

He is fully clothed, lying on his bed, a monstrous piece of furniture carved with gargoyles and draped with velvet. His beard has grown from his time in prison, which gives him the look of a satyr. Lucrezia had ordered the barber here on the day following his release last week, but he turned the fellow away. Unlike most men his age he still has a full mane of hair, no sign of baldness. It is now almost white yet his beard still holds the original coppery colour that was passed to me. He is a big man but has lost weight, has a new gauntness that makes him strangely unfamiliar, though his eyes haven't changed, sharp and crystalline as if they can penetrate rock. It pleases him that my eyes are pale like his. We are throwbacks to his noble northern ancestors, he likes to say.

He looks at me in a certain way, a blankness in his gaze, horribly familiar. My guts shrink.

At the foot of the bed a table displays a number of objects, artefacts collected over the years. A miniature bronze maquette of the vast Minotaur that graces our entrance is one of them. He threw it at me once, a long time ago.

I draw a deep breath and collect myself. 'You called for me, Father.'

He lurches to his feet and pitches towards me. He stinks of funeral wine. As he grabs my upper arm, I hold steady.

He is smiling, I think, or baring his teeth.

'Beatrice.' He removes my nightcap and strokes a paw over my head. 'My girl. My favourite.' His ring catches in one of my plaits. He tugs it out. I hold firm.

Show no weakness.

'Do you think you did us proud today? Were you a good girl?'

I say nothing, look at his satin slippers, embroidered in gold thread with the Cenci arms. His grip on my arm tightens.

'I asked if you were a good girl.'

I know I must reply. 'I believe so, Father.' It is little more than a mumble.

'You believe so?' He tilts my face up, so I have no choice but to look at him. My gaze skitters over his face, avoiding his eyes, landing on the mean, pink, wet mouth embedded in his beard.

'I saw you. You and him.' He spits out the word 'him' as if it is poisonous.

'Who, Father?' I dissemble.

'I saw you all over him in church,' he rasps, so close to my ear I can feel the heat of his breath. 'Behaving like a whore at your own brother's mass. Kissing and whispering to him for all to see. I don't even know you, you filthy little bitch.' His thumb and pointing finger pinch hard on my chin.

Not Giacomo. It is falling into place. He means Davide. I cry, 'No, you're wrong.' I shouldn't have said that. He won't tolerate being contradicted.

He raises his voice, face reddening, grip tightening. 'My daughter, a slattern for all to see. My own daughter.' I can feel the force of his rage. He is shaking with it. He raises his other fist. I slide into an imagined watery sanctuary, transforming into that deadly medusa, tentacles sprouting, and wait for the blow. But it doesn't come. He strokes something cold over my cheek. 'You belong to me, and now no one else will want you. Mine for ever.'

I don't know what he means.

I feel wetness on my face.

I bring a hand to the place.

I look at it.

It is red, covered with blood, my blood.

It doesn't hurt.

Why doesn't it hurt?

My stomach shrinks.

I think I might vomit.

My legs give way.

I am on the floor, blood spattering over Catarina's favourite shawl, dripping onto the marble slabs. My small dreams of marriage and escape drain away.

'What have I done?' His eyes are wide with shock. 'What

have I done to you? My sweetness. My girl. My Beatrice.' He pulls an enormous handkerchief from his breast and presses it very gently to my cheek. 'I didn't mean it.' His expression seems to shift, as if he is someone I don't know. 'It was an accident. A terrible accident.'

I gaze at the red pool spreading on the pale floor. Will the stain come out? It is the best marble, from Carrara. Only the best for Father. I can hear Virgil scratching frantically at the door. He has smelt my blood. The little Minotaur stares at me from the table. I wonder what my face looks like. I had heard that knife injuries are not painful, had never believed it. But it is true. Vengeance boils up around me silently, entering me, a vast menace reaching every last hidden corner of my being, an invisible charge that makes me strong, a secret monster that makes Father's rage nothing. I will tame this creature. I will make it mine.

3

I wake sluggish from the tincture the surgeon gave me last night to dull the pain – the best surgeon in all Rome. Father's words swill round my head: 'Only the best for my girl.'

Catarina holds a pot of ointment. She is saying we must change the dressing. It smells strongly of herbs I don't recognize.

'Your favourite shawl,' I say. 'I'm sorry.' The garment is draped over the back of a chair, red stains now russet.

'That's the last thing on my mind.' She carefully unwraps the bandage and peels away the linen wadding.

Now it hurts.

'What does it look like?' *Do I really want to know?*

'The surgeon has done a good job. Very neat. Like the best black stitch on a wedding shift.' She smiles, her lovely smile. 'It'll heal well, as long as we keep infection away. And most of it will be hidden behind your hair if we style it loosely.'

'Pass me the mirror.' Her expression says, 'Are you sure?' 'I'll have to look at it sometime.' I sit up. My head throbs and the wound smarts. My monster smoulders.

She holds my hair back so I can see. It is a clean line, of about a thumb's length. Catarina didn't lie. It is exceptionally neat. The skin around it is pink and swollen. I count six knotted stitches, embedded in congealed black blood.

The maid enters. I turn my face away to spare her the embarrassment of seeing my undressed face and not knowing what to say.

'I'm sorry for your accident, Signorina.' She bobs a curtsy. 'I hope you are feeling better under the circumstances.'

Catarina and I share a look. The whole palazzo, from my stepmother to the boy who empties the jakes, will know it was not an accident. But no one will dare say so. Accidents have happened before. I have an image of that miniature Minotaur flying towards me. Though this is one of the worst – certainly the most visible. I wonder how far he will go next time.

'Much better, thank you,' I say. 'It's not as bad as it seems.'

'Do you mind if I start packing your things now?' she asks.

'What things?' Catarina articulates what I am thinking.

'The conte says you are all leaving Rome this morning.'

'All of us?' Catarina asks.

'I am told you are to stay.'

'That can't be right.' I look at my friend. 'We go everywhere together.' My mind wheels over all the possible reasons why Catarina might not be coming. He thinks she is a bad influence on me, he wants to spite me, but I realize, with a sinking sensation, that it is most likely because she is to be married after Easter, and that means we will be away from Rome for some time.

Lucrezia sails in, like a ship's figurehead, wearing a grave look, insisting she inspect the damage. 'You poor darling. Is it very painful?' She strokes my hair gently and slowly shakes her head. She doesn't need to say anything. She is married to him, after all.

'So, we are to leave Rome,' I say.

'Yes. There were reprisals last night.' I don't want to know what those reprisals were but can't help imagining a dead boy on the steps of the Palazzo Orestesi. 'Your father says we need to leave the city for our safety.'

'And not Catarina?'

'A new girl is to join us. Ilaria. I haven't met her yet. She's the daughter of one of your father's lawyers, fallen on hard times.'

'Are we going to the Villa Paradiso?'

She shakes her head. 'Too close to Rome.' When she is sad it is still possible to see the shadow of her lost loveliness. At the time of her marriage to Father, she was known as a beauty, famed for her haunting eyes, deep velvety brown, framed by the thick golden hair that hung in ripples to her knees. She was often compared to a Botticelli Venus, and artists clamoured to immortalize her. It was the disparity of a woman so refined being matched with a man like Father that lent her the air of tragedy that was irresistible to painters. But strain has stolen her looks and she has grown stout, eating for comfort, her fine dress pulled tight across her ample breast.

'Where, then?'

'One of the hunting lodges, La Rocca. It's somewhere in Rieti, to the north-east near the mountains in a village just over the border – Neapolitan territory. I couldn't find it on the map.' She forms a false smile: 'I'm sure it will be lovely. Spring in the countryside.' Her tone fills with forced cheer as she makes to leave the room. 'Think of the flowers.'

I shove a few treasured items into a bag, my favourite books, my writing things, and sit to scrawl a note to my brother in Greek, passing it to Catarina. 'Will you make sure Giaco gets this?'

'Is it a good idea?' She looks fraught. 'What if he finds out?'

'He's never found out yet.' I search for my copy of *Metamorphoses*, unable to find it. 'Besides, I think he shocked even himself with this.' I point to my face. Usually the scars he makes are hidden. 'It gives me a certain amount of leeway, a period of peace, for now, at least.'

Her expression is sceptical. 'You shouldn't . . .' She stems her advice – knows me too well.

We go to the library, still searching for *Metamorphoses*. The room is vast and bright with four large windows facing south.

Books cover its walls from floor to ceiling, and a gallery runs round three of its sides, housing yet more books. Father claims that he owns a copy of every volume ever written, yet he is not much of a reader, so it seems to me an empty boast. Some of the rarer ones are worth more than their weight in gold, he has said, but to me their true value is the knowledge that lies between their covers. If the Villa Paradiso is my lost Eden, this library is my Heaven on earth. I am coming to believe that books other than the scriptures also offer an understanding of the workings of the world. Most people have tried to drum into me that God's word teaches us all we need to know, but I have found truths in the writings of Ovid, Aeschylus and Sophocles that are absent from the Bible.

'There it is.' Catarina points to one of the tables where my book lies open, face down, its spine broken. 'You shouldn't treat it so badly.' She picks it up carefully, handing it to me.

'Don't lose my place.' Taking a scrap of paper, I mark the page. I gather a few more books, ones that are rumoured to be on the Pope's proposed list, those I couldn't bear to think of being burned, and put them into my bag. Who knows if the Vatican orderlies will make a search in our absence?

'And this one. You'll surely want this.' Catarina is holding up my well-thumbed volume of Dante's *La Vita Nuova*.

I take it and sit a moment unable to resist scanning a few lines. 'It's said he only saw his Beatrice twice. They barely exchanged a word and then she died, yet he loved her for all his remaining years.'

Catarina is looking over my shoulder at the text. 'I wonder how his love persisted, how it didn't fade over time.'

'It's easy to love someone for ever if you never see their flaws. She wasn't a real person to him.' My tone is bitter.

We return to our rooms where I stuff the bag of books at the bottom of my trunk, fastening the lid, and two of the porters come to take it down. Dejection clouds Catarina's beautiful face – she was never good at hiding her feelings.

'I'll be back in time for your wedding.' The wedding she doesn't want. 'I promise.' I make it sound sure as death.

The yard smells of dung and straw. The luggage cart is loaded to capacity and the horses are being harnessed. Four men I have never seen before loiter – our protection, I suppose, given they have rifles slung over their shoulders and swords on their belts. Aqualino dances a jig, tossing his head as a leading rein is attached to his bridle.

I thread my elbow tightly through Catarina's, feeling now the brutal severing of our last weeks together. I don't know what future Father has up his sleeve for me but if last night's actions are anything to go by, he intends to keep me for ever. I won't let that be the extent of my life. I can't. I will be a woman of property soon – that must count for something. A dim beacon smoulders in a vague distance.

Father appears on the steps in his riding clothes. 'What's the hold-up? Why aren't you in the carriage?' He takes my shoulder roughly, propelling me towards the waiting vehicle.

'Aren't I riding Aquilino?'

'Certainly not. Not after your accident.' He pushes his face to mine. 'Get into the carriage and behave like a lady for once.'

I consider pressing my petition, but the stony set of his expression warns me off. Perhaps my injury has given me less leeway than I'd hoped. My monster smoulders silently, deep in my breast, fuelled by the throb in my cheek. Virgil jumps into the carriage. I clamber in after him to find my four travelling companions: Lucrezia; my youngest brother, Bernardo; Don Tomassino, a priest new to our household – some distant relative of Father's – and a morose, timid-looking girl, who must be Ilaria. Even with her sulky expression she is strikingly beautiful, with a head of tight, hay-coloured curls, a bee-stung pout and eyes like grey moths – the image of a *putto* on a church ceiling. I tell myself I mustn't hate her. It's not her fault that she is to replace my beloved companion.

I offer her a smile as she slides towards Bernardo to make space for me. She can't meet my gaze.

'I don't know her,' says Bernardo. 'I want to sit beside you.'

We swap places. The girl seems surprised that neither Lucrezia nor I tick him off for his rudeness. She will learn the whims of my brother in good time.

Lucrezia holds a half-eaten pastry out of Virgil's reach. Flakes of it have caught in her embroidered collar. She shoves it into her mouth, closing her eyes, chewing, then fishes a small phial of tincture from the bag on her lap, dropping a measure under her tongue. 'Appalling headache.'

'What happened to your face?' asks Bernardo.

'She had an accident,' says Lucrezia.

'What kind of accident?'

'Never mind.'

Don Tomassino, judging by the way he shrinks from Virgil, doesn't like dogs, which makes me instantly suspicious. I tell Virgil to lie under the seat, which he does obediently, tucking his long legs up to his angular body and laying his head on his paws. Bernardo reaches down to stroke him. He prefers the company of animals.

Catarina peers through the small window in the carriage door. I press my hand to the glass. She does the same, walking along as we trundle off, palm to palm. We pass through the gates, leaving her behind, sadness settling over me. We have barely spent a night apart in a decade.

I stare disconsolately from the carriage as we move along the riverbank, passing the hovels where flags of bright washing flap, sending us on our way. Over the river sits the new dome of San Pietro, so vast it renders all the nearby buildings in miniature. We pass through the Piazza di Popolo, the church of Santa Maria looming to our left, and the cabin of the carriage seems to tighten around me. As we trundle out through the city gates my two dead brothers drift into my thoughts, and Giacomo, who now seems as far from reach as they.

4

It is said that in fine weather, and with a good horse, the journey from Rome to La Petrella can be ridden at a pace in a single day. But we are a great lumbering party, the month is March, and the route is mud-bound. The cart has had to be dug out twice already. Besides, for our safety, we must take a circuitous route.

The smallholdings of the city's outskirts make way for open countryside scattered with villages, where the locals halt their labours to wave at us as we pass. We stop for refreshments at a rural inn and to water the horses, which people wander over to inspect, curious, I suppose, as to who we might be with such an array of beautiful animals. The grooms evade their questions. Everyone has been told not to mention the name Cenci, as our enemies might well be in our wake.

Father seems in more amenable spirits, so I ask once more if I can ride Aquilino, the thought of being trapped in the carriage again almost too much to bear. I receive another firm refusal. I wonder if it is truly for my safety, as he says, or if he fears I will bolt. How he thinks I would do so with our accompaniment of four strapping guards, I don't know. They are two great straw-haired German brothers called Oskar and Jakob who speak almost no Italian, and two men, soldiers, I think, one younger than the other, both coincidentally named Lorenzo. One has asked to be called Renzo to differentiate him from the other, but none of us can remember, yet, which is which.

We are jolted from wall to wall in the carriage, where I sit opposite Don Tomassino. He is a narrow-eyed young man with a thin, bitter mouth. His cassock is threadbare at the elbows and a little too short, exposing bony ankles. My first impression is that he will not be easy to warm to, unlike the benevolent Don Esposito, who has heard my confession since childhood. Ilaria is apparently a nervous traveller, emitting a stifled little cry with each bump in the road and running her fingers through her rosary until she might wear away the beads. I swap raised eyebrows with Lucrezia. We are both wondering how a girl as nervy as she will cope with a family like ours.

All I have managed to glean about our destination is that it is a mountainous region and the house has a view of one of Rieti's most beautiful valleys. It might not be so bad, I tell myself, picturing a fine country villa with umber stucco walls, a portico and ornamental gardens, a fountain and even perhaps a lake. There will surely be a library.

On the first day a wheel comes loose on the luggage cart, one of the horses loses a shoe and Bernardo has a fit, a bad one, eyes rolling, body lurching. One of the German brothers has to hold him down, a thumb pressed into his mouth to prevent him from swallowing his tongue.

Lucrezia is, as always, turned out beautifully, her fine lace collar bursting in ripples from her high-necked brocade. She smells of orange blossom and, faintly, the lemon soap she likes to wash with. Lucrezia is a woman who enjoys the luxury her status affords. She doesn't wear her jewels for the journey, though, not even her rings. We both remember, only too well, the Corsini woman who'd had a hand cut off for her rings only a year before, when she was travelling to her husband's country estates for the summer.

With the going so slow, our plans are thrown awry and everything must be rearranged at the last minute. So, the inn where we spend our first night is unprepared for our arrival.

It is a seedy place, unused to housing demanding clients, and they have barely enough provisions to feed our large party. The grooms have to sleep in the barn and the beds, even those in the best rooms, are alive with fleas.

As we are leaving in the morning an elderly woman tugs on my cloak, forcing me to stop. Her face is dark and creased like leather, her eyes milky, her hair a nest, and, pointing to the dressing on my face, she says something in a dialect I don't fully comprehend.

'I don't understand you,' I say, offering her a coin, which she refuses, repeating her unintelligible words with an urgency that makes me uneasy. I am glad when the innkeeper shoos her off. She casts her cloudy eyes back at me with a look that sends a shiver up my spine.

As we travel deeper into the countryside, our surroundings become increasingly wild and remote and I am forced to revise our imagined destination – the villa in my mind's eye becomes smaller, the gardens less formal.

We stop on a riverbank to rest the horses and eat a meal of bread and cheese. The weather has turned balmy and warm for early March. When Father drops off in the grass, hat over his face, snoring loudly as a hog, I tell Lucrezia I am going to relieve myself and take the opportunity to slip away into the trees with Virgil.

I find a shaded glade, upstream, dappled and verdant, where I pull off my shoes and stockings and walk into the shallow water, scooping it over my skin to wash off the dust and sweat of the journey. The temptation to undress, to wade in up to my waist, up to my armpits, my shoulders, to feel the brisk bite of the cold, to feel the sensation of being held in the water's embrace, is hard to resist.

Hearing Ilaria's tentative call, I clamber out hurriedly, persuading my sticky stockings back on. I find my shoes beside a patch of blackened earth, where a fire has recently been lit. I pick them up, and as I stand, something brushes my head. I swipe it away, thinking it a branch, but it becomes tangled in my hair. I tug it out. It is not what I'd thought. It is a small doll-shaped thing of feathers and sticks, knotted together with thread, suspended from the tree on a length of twine. *What is it?* Its eyes are crosses carved into the wood. Disquiet crawls into the pit of my stomach. I fling the thing away, running as fast as I can in the direction of Ilaria's calls, relieved when I see her, not quite able to shake off the jittery feeling.

'Your stepmother sent for you. Your father's woken.' She looks at me quizzically. 'What is it?'

'Nothing.' I am breathless. The image of that strange toy dangles in my mind. I push it down and lead the way back.

Aquilino has wandered away from the group, to where the grass is longer and thicker. He whickers as we approach. I stroke his nose and scratch his white star, where the fur grows outward from a single point. 'Shall we take him – go back to Rome? I shall fight off the bandits and you can navigate by the stars.'

Ilaria is dumbstruck as if I meant it, and still looks concerned even after I explain I am only joking.

'What age are you?' I ask.

'Fifteen.'

'Not so much older than Bernardo.' An awful age for a girl, I think. Old enough to draw the attention of men but not old enough to know how to deal with it. I wonder again how she, with her anxious disposition, will fare in the Cenci household.

'How old is he?'

'Thirteen.'

'What's . . .' She stops. 'He's . . .' She is searching for her words.

'He's not made like the rest of us. You'll get used to him.'

Father's mood brightens as we travel deeper and deeper into the Sabine hills and further from his enemies, while I feel a creeping unease. We pass strange shrines tucked into nooks by the wayside, dedicated to obscure saints I've never heard of. The field workers and villagers no longer wave but stop to stare and pull their children close, crossing themselves, as if we pose a threat. In our finery we must appear as characters from a comedy who have inadvertently stumbled into a darker play. That strange doll hangs in my mind.

It is dusk by the time we arrive at the edge of the hilltop town and the inn that will house us for the night. It is a large square building, with two rows of tall cypresses leading to the door, flanked by yew bushes clipped into the shape of what seem, from a distance, strange beasts or gargoyles. The toll of a bell greets us before we turn into the driveway, and we are obliged to stop to allow a funeral cortège to pass. We dismount from the carriage to show our respect, removing our hats, to dip our heads and cross ourselves. My mind immediately turns to Rocco, grief, hot and stringent, washing through me once more.

A priest leads the procession in a slow march, holding his plain wooden crucifix. An ungainly plough horse pulls a cart behind him. On it sits the coffin, open, a young girl lying in it, hair dark as tar, skin white as cod fish.

I am struck with sorrow by her youth, still showing the softness of girlhood. Her head lolls with the movement of the vehicle, as if she might spring up at any moment and announce it all an act. It is no act. Behind comes a throng of black-shrouded women, one racked so profoundly by her weeping she has to be almost carried by the others. The mother, I suppose, my heart reaching out to her. The men follow, faces firmly down, reminding me of Dante's hypocrites, marching endlessly round their hellish ditch, hunched in lead-lined capes so heavy they can barely stay upright.

Later, when the innkeeper is serving us at supper, Father asks what the circumstances were of one being taken by the Lord so young.

'It was a terrible, terrible business,' the man replies, and goes on to tell of how the girl had, in his words, 'given herself' to the local notary. He says it with a disapproving purse of his lips, as if the girl had chosen to do so, when it seems more likely to me that the man forced himself on her – she so very young, younger than Ilaria by my assessment. Certainly, the expression of dismay on Lucrezia's face reflects my thoughts.

'When her father, Signor Cappaldi, went to the man's house demanding he wed his daughter,' he continues, warming to his topic, 'the varlet slipped from a window and scarpered into the fields. He was hunted down and beaten. Trouble was, he died overnight. A bad blow to the head can do that, you know. And he was not a young man. One moment you're eating your bread and cheese, the next you're meeting your maker.' He pauses for his words to sink in. 'It left a predicament no father would wish on his worst enemy.'

I notice Don Tomassino cross himself ostentatiously.

'The girl was ruined,' the innkeeper goes on. 'I would have balked at carrying out such an act myself, but he had no choice. His honour was at stake.' He draws his big hands slowly down his face and, meeting Father's eyes, shrugs and says, 'Daughters!'

The horror of the story settles over our party, rendering us silent, all locked in our own private thoughts. Even Father is quiet. The dead girl's pale face passes through my mind, rage rising in me at the injustice – men and their wretched honour.

'What was she called?' I break the silence. 'You never said

her name.' I have an urgent need to know her name, for her to be more than someone's anonymous, inconvenient daughter.

'Oh . . .' He pauses a moment, as if trying to recall. 'I believe her name was Lucia.'

'And what was she like?' I am compelled to bring Lucia back to life in my imagination at least.

'Like? I don't know.' He appears confounded by my question.

'What did she like to do? Did she sing, play an instrument? Did she like animals? Could she read?'

'I doubt she could read.' He seems put out. 'I don't know. I never saw her, except at church. I didn't know the family well.'

Father holds up a hand to silence me. 'Enough, Beatrice! Leave our host to his business.'

That night I share a bed with Lucrezia and Ilaria. Lucrezia is pleased with the arrangement. She seems exhausted, shadows dark as bruises beneath her eyes, and sinks into the featherbed with a sigh. Ilaria falls asleep instantly. I join them, careful to lay my face on its good side. My wound seems to be healing well. The swelling has diminished and there is no sign of infection.

'Could Lucia not have taken the veil?' I whisper, when the candles are blown out. The girl's terrible fate has crept beneath my skin.

'I suppose she might have. Even without a convent dowry, she could have entered as a servant. It would have been up to her father.' Then Lucrezia says quietly, as if to herself, 'These country people. It's as if the last two hundred years never happened.'

We fall silent. I consider reminding her that city people aren't so different, that her own husband isn't so different, but think better of it. Let Lucrezia hold on to her illusion. We all cope in our own way.

The thought circulates in my mind relentlessly that we girls live hand in hand with the risk of ruin. How did he do it – her father? Did he hold a pillow over her face? Did he slit her throat? Did he poison her? I can't shake off my thoughts, and when I finally drop into sleep, she haunts my dreams. She is ahead of me walking backwards, laughing, and turns to run away, black hair streaming, whipping her head back, holding out that doll of feathers and sticks. *You can't catch me!* I wake in a sudden panic and get up to distract myself by looking from the window awhile at the shadowy shapes of the distant mountains, where there is a storm – sheets of silent lightning illuminating them momentarily.

By the third day the route is mostly uphill, winding and slow. The temperature drops as we climb, and a breeze picks up, squealing through the gaps in the carriage doors. The scenery becomes wilder, craggy peaks silhouetted against the pale sky and dark, wooded valleys. We slow to an interminable pace and the road folds back on itself again and again as we climb, its bends sharpening further as we snake our way down the steep ravines.

As the road becomes more treacherous Ilaria's prayers become increasingly urgent, the beads of her rosary clicking as she mutters the incantations. Don Tomassino is watching her. I know that look. There is something unpleasantly lascivious about the way he wets those thin lips with the tip of his tongue and slides his eyes over her. I balk at the thought of him hearing my confession – *Have you had any impure thoughts, my child?* – and long for Don Esposito. Even with him I don't confess every sin. Does anyone? I wonder. Surely it is impossible to keep track of all those small, wicked thoughts, the moments of greed or disobedience. Sometimes, too, certain sins cannot be explained and must be left to fester.

*

We arrive in La Petrella, exhausted, just as the compline bells are ringing. The village is nestled in a cleft beyond the river we have been following. A large simple brick church sits at the heart of a small piazza, where a gibbet stands as a warning. A single dirt road runs off it, lined by whitewashed houses with terracotta roofs, a few more scattered through the wooded hillside. A small herd of goats wanders over to inspect the newcomers, long faces peering over a fence, chewing. The light is fading and I scan the outskirts for signs of our destination, the stucco villa in my mind, but find nothing, no set of ornate iron gates, no lake, no avenue of trees or a perimeter wall, no sign even of a stone hunting lodge tucked into the trees.

People on their way to church in groups throw suspicious looks at the large entourage invading their sleepy village. When they realize it is the master of the place, they remove their hats and dip their heads, but a certain hostility remains in their expressions. It must be where Father comes to hunt in the autumn, when he disappears for weeks at a time and we at the Palazzo Cenci have some respite. The local women huddle together in whispering groups as they walk. They wear their skirts tucked up, ankles and clogged feet visible, and their faces, burned umber by the sun, are half hidden in hoods and scarves.

'Will we join the service, give thanks for our safe arrival?' says Lucrezia.

'We've not arrived yet.' Father is firm. 'We must press on if we're to reach La Rocca before nightfall. There's a perfectly good chapel up there.' He waves an arm upwards. Craning, I follow its direction, my heart caving in at the sight of the ancient fortress, a vast and rugged tower that rises, slightly off-kilter, topped with crenellations and tiny black openings – you could scarcely call them windows – squinting in the grey stone. It clings to a shelf of rock above the village, precipitously high – more prison than palazzo.

'Good Lord! That can't be it, surely.' Lucrezia, too, looks crestfallen.

The grooms are organizing the transfer of luggage from the carts onto mules and I, at last, have my chance to ride, Bernardo sitting pillion, slumped, half asleep, arms wrapped around my waist. Deft as an acrobat, Aquilino picks his way up the mountain. As we near it, the fortification seems to increase in size, scaling ominously into the darkening sky, making me wonder if its precipitous walls are designed to keep enemies out or to keep us in.

5

By the time we reach the great oak doors night has fallen. A gibbous moon is suspended above the high tower, casting all it touches in a vaporous light. Servants are already waiting in the yard to deal with the luggage. I wonder if they tracked our convoy's steep climb from La Petrella, watching our row of torches, like fireflies, between the trees.

A pack of hounds is making an almighty commotion from the stables, barking, howling, scrabbling at the doors, desperate to witness our arrival.

'My wolfhounds,' says Father with relish. 'They've missed me, the bloodthirsty beasts.'

While the others dismount, and Bernardo is helped down from the pillion seat, I remain on Aquilino. I have the terrible sense that once I am beyond those iron-strapped doors there will be no return. That line from Dante circles my head: *Abandon hope, all ye who enter here.* It is Ezro, the head groom, who coaxes me to the ground, where Virgil tucks himself in beside me, sensing my apprehension.

The interior is cavernous and a fire blazes in a hearth big enough to accommodate an entire family. Weapons and helmets from another age hang from the walls, dozens and dozens of them, halberds and axes and hammers and pikes and rows of pistols and several long-muzzled arquebuses. Enough to hold off a besieging army for months. I suppose that is the idea.

Bernardo, who has a fascination for arms, is inspecting them. He is able to name the region and the year each of them was forged simply by their shape. 'Look at this one, Mother.' Lucrezia has joined him. 'It's from Bologna. See the curved hilt.'

Without fabrics or hangings or any concession to luxury, every sound reverberates through the hall. I wonder what shape our days will take in such a forbidding place, with only ourselves for entertainment, without the pleasant distractions of Rome, the afternoon visits, the dances and festivals and plays and regattas and, however vague, the possibility of marriage. Though my memory throws me the image of Rocco's body slumped on the steps to remind me of Rome's other, darker, face.

Sensing someone behind me, I turn abruptly to find a tall, broad-shouldered man standing a thumb's length too close to me.

'I know you.' A small charge detonates in my gut as I meet his gaze. It is the face that once inhabited my adolescent dreams – those strange pale, lozenge eyes, foreign in the dark planes of his face. My breath quickens. I am caught by something urgent and intoxicating, a hand that has reached into my ribcage and is palpating my heart.

'Yes.' A smile flickers over his mouth while those eyes consume me, dragging briefly over my bandaged cheek with a question. I would have given a thousand *scudi* for a smile from him once. I have grown older, sharper and wiser – more cunning, those who don't like me might say. The only thing I'd pay a thousand *scudi* for now is my freedom. Or that is what I tell myself.

He folds into a deep formal bow, appropriate deference for the daughter of his employer. Some five years ago, Olimpio Calvetti was in service at the Palazzo Cenci. He was friendly with Giacomo. They used to spar together on the river field. One day he was gone. I wondered in what way he had slighted

Father, to be dismissed so suddenly. I never thought to see him again but here he is, not dismissed but having been elevated to the position of *castellano* of this remote place. So, he must be one of Father's loyal circle of vassals. A small spark of wariness ignites in me.

He smells of musk and hay and faintly of tobacco smoke. I hold out my hand, for him to place a kiss on its back. His lips are soft and damp and leave a burning trail that slides right to my core.

Father steps close.

I draw in a steadying breath, reclaim my hand and lower my eyes for fear that Father will see my pupils dilated with desire.

'It's good to see you, Olimpio.' Father pats him on the back. It is rare for him to be so convivial. 'You've prepared well for us.' He waxes on about the good state of the place.

I watch them talking, wondering why Father likes him when he likes so few. The other men, the strapping Germans and the two Lorenzos, the older one to a lesser degree, are a little intimidated by him – I know the signs – but not Olimpio. He is relaxed, undaunted as a feline. There is something about his confidence that reminds me of the spotted cat Father had acquired once. It was said that the Duke of Florence had one, and Father didn't want to be outdone. It was a kitten when it arrived and wore a gold collar set with emeralds. My siblings and I would play with it and it would knead us, sheathing and unsheathing its large claws, purring like a mill. Soon it was as big as a wolf and developed a sauntering, easy elegance – entirely un-afraid. That – its innate confidence – was what Father liked about it. But it mauled one of the servants and was consigned to its cage, where it would pace and stare. Every few days a carcass was thrown in, which it would set upon with alarming viciousness, displaying its great crimson maw.

Olimpio looks at me again, hard and serious, making me wonder if the smile I'd seen only moments before, the penetrating look, the kiss still burning my hand, had been generated in my imagination. *Be careful.*

'Your dog can be housed in the stables,' he says, reaching out for Virgil's collar.

Virgil growls at him.

'He stays with me.' I stroke the ridges of his spine with the tips of my fingers. 'Where might I find food and water for him?'

'I'll see to it.' Olimpio seems amused. I assume it is because indoor dogs, women's dogs, are usually small and pointless, and Virgil stands as high as my waist.

Undaunted, he scuffs Virgil's head. Now my hound is meek as a kitten, waving his tail, seeking approval. *Traitor.*

A feast has been prepared on a long table, candles already half burned down, dripping stalagmites of wax onto the cloth. My stomach growls, hunger all at once overcoming my exhaustion. Our last meal was at midday, when we'd stopped at a tavern with a shaded terrace, and the patron had proudly produced some kind of tasteless nondescript stew, a delicacy of the region, he'd said.

Lucrezia wolfs down a plateful of food and asks Olimpio where she might find the chapel. Don Tomassino, stifling a yawn, makes to accompany her. Olimpio catches me staring at him. I look away abruptly, feeling a flush unfold over my breast, willing it to stop before it reaches my face and gives me away.

'No, Lucrezia,' says Father. 'You will stay here with me.' He grabs his wife's wrist, holding her back. Don Tomassino looks unsure of himself.

'I wanted to give thanks for our safe arrival.' Lucrezia's voice is small.

'You don't need an altar and a priest for that.' He pulls her onto his lap. 'It's not the Lord you need to thank for our safe arrival but *me*.' He lets out a guffaw, pleased with his blasphemy, pleased by the young priest's mortification, pleased with himself. 'I want you all to myself tonight. The good Lord wouldn't want to keep a wife from her husband, now, would he?'

He begins to feed her morsels from his plate, which she accepts obediently, like an infant being weaned. Don Tomassino slinks away to the far end of the table and gulps his cup of wine in one, refilling it when he thinks no one is watching.

Bernardo scoffs his food voraciously. Despite it being Lent, everything is delicious, flavoured with herbs and spices. I savour each mouthful while Ilaria takes minute sips of broth through a trance of exhaustion.

'Where am I to sleep? Will you show me?' I ask Olimpio, masking the want that squats in my ribcage. Standing, I take Bernardo's hand and indicate to Ilaria to come with us.

'You baby that boy,' says Father. 'He shouldn't be bunking down with you girls.'

Bernardo's grip tightens round my fingers. 'He can't sleep on his own.' My words contain the bald fact that all his older brothers are gone.

I hold Father's glare, preparing to mount a defence but he seems too tired to spar and drops it with a scowl. He knows that otherwise Lucrezia will be up for hours settling her troubled son, and he wants his wife for himself tonight. My actions are not as saintly as they might appear, for I gain something by keeping Bernardo close. His loyalty to me is singular and fierce. He would never let anyone harm a hair on my head.

*

Our room is large and spartan, its window barely bigger than an eye, and it is furnished with great bulky lopsided objects that have come from another age. A fire sulks in the large grate, making a vain attempt to heat the furthest reaches of the space. A stale smell hangs in the air, as if the room is unused to habitation and I wonder when a woman had last slept here. I imagine Father's raucous hunting parties, men pissing and vomiting in the hearth, then falling drunkenly into the vast bed fully clothed. Virgil sniffs every inch of skirting, before settling onto his blanket beside the fire. I tuck Bernardo into the couch at the foot of the bed. Exhausted by the journey, he falls asleep before I have finished the bedtime ritual in which he insists upon the same lullaby each night, repeated until he drifts off.

Having locked the door, Ilaria and I, dog-tired, haul ourselves into the huge bed, closing the curtains around us. It is a far cry from the luxury of Rome. The sheets are as chilled as cold cuts of ham, the mattress hard as a slab of stone and the bolster heavy as a corpse. Ilaria clings to the far edge, acres away. I miss Catarina all the more. We would have cuddled up to each other for warmth.

Muffled sobs reach across the space.

'You'll get used to us,' I say.

'I have a vocation. I was going to take the veil.' She sniffs.

'Why didn't you?'

'It turns out that my convent dowry was spent years ago. Father is badly in debt.'

'I'm sorry. Our house is not very much like a convent, I'm afraid.' Though I resent her for not being Catarina, I feel sympathy for my timid little bedfellow.

'I have to accept the Lord's plan for me.'

'I suppose we all do.' Sometimes I wonder about that.

Despite my fatigue, sleep evades me, dark thoughts buzzing round my head: Rocco, under the chapel floor beside

Cristofero, Lucia in the red Sabine earth, all Father's enemies gathering, seeking us out. They can't have followed us all the way out here, and we are over the border in the jurisdiction of Naples. Still, I don't feel safe, even with the perpendicular walls and the guards we've brought to protect us, not with Father in the house, playing sovereign over this Godforsaken kingdom. The skin of my cheek tightens and throbs as the wound knits – a reminder. I'm glad I thought to lock the bedroom door, and hope there isn't a second key somewhere.

I keep my attention on the regular rhythm of Ilaria's breath and my mind settles slightly. With luck, Father will strike a truce with the Orestesi and we will be back in Rome by Easter. At least in Rome there is the possibility, however faint, of escape – overseas with Giacomo, marriage to Davide Forlani – but here ... Beyond the walls I can hear strange noises, unfamiliar mountain sounds, a howl, a screech, the wind whispering round the grey tower, giving me the terrible dizzying feeling that we have fallen far into a dark past.

Olimpio tugs at my attention – a distraction. Did I really see that smile? There has been no sign of anything other than formality from him since. The painful pulse in my cheek won't allow me to forget: *Now no one else will want you.* My heart hollows. A rhythmic banging starts up from below: Father's rooms. I consider poor, weary Lucrezia having to submit to his sweaty heaving, imagine her pinned beneath his weight, subjected to his humiliations.

I press a pillow over my head, but the sound still reverberates up through the floor and into the frame of the bed, into my bones. The idea of being incarcerated in this place for months on end leaves me desolate, as if my remains might be discovered here in a thousand years. I rise, pull a gown round my shoulders against the cold, light a lamp from the hearth and, shadowed by Virgil, quietly slip from the room.

A stone staircase winds through the main tower, its steps polished into curves by passing generations of feet, those of my ancestors and the families before. It seems the place has been here since the beginning of time, as if it has grown from the mountain, cleaved out of the rock of its own volition. My lamp burnishes the walls as I pass. Through the window slits the moon casts pale phantom crosses on the dark floor, feeble reminders of God's grace and how little of it seems to have found its way to this place.

I find what must be Father's study, as it houses a vast desk stacked with papers and documents. To my delight I see a few shelves of books, pulling one out. It creaks and complains as if it hasn't been opened in years, pages rough and dry under my fingers. I bring my lamp close, squinting at the text, which is small and handwritten in a language I don't know. Someone has drawn a hanged man in the margin. I take another, an illustrated hunting manual, and another with curious engravings, strange images of naked women entangled with creatures. I slam it shut and shove it back on the shelf, only then realizing that of course they are images from the stories of Ovid, stories I know so well from the volume I have upstairs. These drawings, though, are nothing like any I have seen before: Leda and the Swan, Pasiphaë and the Bull are depicted in such a violent and unsettling manner, the women in them white-eyed with distress.

A creak beyond the door sends my stomach into my mouth. I sidle to peep through the crack, finding only Virgil waiting patiently for me on the landing. Down in the hall the vast hearth has fallen to embers. Virgil finds a bowl of water, drinking noisily from it, the gilded tag on his collar chinking against the pewter, like a communion bell. The table has been cleared and scrubbed, the candles extinguished. Dishes are stacked on an enormous cabinet to one side. It is big enough to contain a body, with shelves and drawers suspended above it, the kind of thing more suited to storing ammunition than fine silverware. I open its doors, pull out its drawers, finding knives and spoons and candles, pressed white linens, folded with lavender and rosemary. The scent reminds me suddenly, sadly, of Mother, of whom I have only a few precious guarded memories. Tears nag at the back of my eyes but I repel them, admonishing myself inwardly for my softness.

I wander about, up a small set of steps and into a large cold chamber. In the lamplight I can see that its walls are painted with yellow distemper. A pair of doors is open to the air. I go to close them, seeing then that they lead to a wooden balcony.

Inquisitiveness draws me out, boards creaking beneath my feet. It is warmer outside than in. I lean over the balustrade. A bright chip of silver moon hangs in a pewter sky. A ravine falls sharply away to a dark and indistinct place some fifty feet below, from which a dense silence emanates. I throw words out into the abyss – 'I hate you. I hate you. I hate you' – all at once beset by vertigo, moving back from the edge.

Virgil growls.

'It's only me.' A male voice.

My heart stops.

A shadowy figure is seated at the far end of the balcony, feet up on the railing.

It is him. *Was I looking for him?*

Virgil wanders over, rubbing himself up against the man's thigh, pushing his head into the large hand, like a cat. I feel the hot embarrassment of knowing he was watching me as I shouted my hate into the ravine, like a child.

In the dim light I can see he is holding out his pipe, pointing to my lamp. 'Can I borrow that? Need to light this.'

I offer the lamp, liking that he doesn't stand, bow, make a fuss of my status.

He grabs my wrist to steady the flame as he holds his pipe to it, drawing it into the bowl, inhaling in short sharp bursts, emitting a cloud of smoke with the word, 'Thanks.'

'You shouldn't touch me,' I snap, pulling my hand away. His pipe glows, a tiny furnace.

My words make little impression. 'Won't you sit?' He indicates an empty chair. I set the lamp on the balustrade, remaining on my feet.

'You've been wandering around for a while. Couldn't sleep?'

Has he been following me? Has Father assigned him to keep an eye on me?

'What were you looking for?'

I don't like the thought of him watching me secretly, as I rummaged through every cranny of that cabinet, chasing the lavender and rosemary scent of Mother, searching for something – even I don't know what.

'Nothing in particular.'

'What happened?' He touches his cheek. He is the only one to ask. For an instant I imagine telling him everything. But I can't trust him. He is Father's man. I gather my wariness and make a shield of it.

'An accident.'

He says nothing for a while.

I look back down into the dark ravine.

He breaks the silence. 'Bea – is that what people call you?'

'Only if I like them.'

'Do you like me?' He offers me a smile – wide and genial. He must have used it often, successfully, on women.

I am immune. 'I don't know yet.' *Am I immune?*

He seems to want to say something but doesn't. A fox cries in the distance – the unnerving sound of a distressed infant.

After some time, I say, 'Do you always sit out here at night?'

'Almost always.'

The dark angles of his face glow in the moonlight, framed by his inky curls. I don't want to look but can't help myself.

'Well, we are in residence here now, so you probably shouldn't.' Feeling more in control, I turn to walk away, calling my dog.

Olimpio scrambles from the chair, holding the balustrade to pull himself up. The lamp is dislodged, falling into the abyss. He curses: '*Porco cane!*'

I wait a moment to hear the crash of its landing, imagining it exploding into a million sparks, setting fire to the vegetation below. But nothing rises from the black emptiness, not even the suggestion of a sound or a flicker of flame. I shiver.

He apologizes for his bad language.

'I've heard far worse.' He holds me with a look so direct it flips me over, exposing my soft underbelly to his scrutiny. Can he read all my secrets, the secrets no one else knows I keep, the secrets I long to share but never will? I step away abruptly. 'Having four brothers has taught me that men pretend politeness in the company of women. Perhaps you could spare me the artifice.'

'Understood!' He has become formal too. 'Can I escort you back to your rooms?'

'I'm perfectly capable of finding my own way.' I make no attempt to temper my sharpness.

'It's a big place. People get lost here.'

I am suddenly daunted by the thought of picking my way back through the tangle of corridors without a lamp, but I don't respond for fear of betraying my weakness. Without looking back, I leave him, Virgil following, and retrace my path through the large yellow chamber, my eyes adjusting to the dark, down the steps to the hall and up the stairs, round and round, through the silent building to bed.

6

I write to Giacomo, a plea – in Greek, as is our habit – to find a plausible excuse to get me back to Rome. A request from one of the great painters to sit for a portrait, or my sister asking for my help when she gives birth. I know it is futile as Antonina would never dare contravene Father's wishes and no one less than Michelangelo himself, who's been dead two-score years, could tempt Father to let me return. Just to be in touch, though, makes me feel less adrift and I indulge myself a moment in picturing that future he spoke of, somewhere overseas. *Could it happen? Could we make it happen?*

I fold the letter and watch the wax sizzle as it drips to the paper, twisting my seal as I press, making it indecipherable.

I sense Olimpio's presence before he speaks, as a deer must the hunter. 'Your father would like to see you in his study,' is all he says.

I don't dare meet his eye for fear of being ensnared. Ilaria looks up from her needlework briefly. Olimpio smiles at her and I watch as she offers a small shy one in return, her moth eyes fluttering to life. It is the first I have seen on the girl. Normally she carries a permanent expression of vague alarm. I had tried to draw her out of herself when we were dressing this morning, without much success.

'Did you sleep soundly?' I had asked. 'I hope this didn't attack you too.' I made a comic face, pretending to fight with the enormous, rock-hard bolster as if it was an animal.

Without even a flicker of mirth at my antics, she said, 'You screamed out in the night.'

'I often suffer from bad dreams.' The girl had looked at me as if it might somehow be a character flaw. 'I should have warned you that I'm prone to sleepwalking, too. That's why I sleep with the door locked.' I didn't describe to her the bewildering times I had woken to find myself in strange places – once, even, on the embankment of the Tiber, having no idea how I had managed to slip past the night watch. Nor did I mention the terrible creatures that so frequently hound me in my dreams.

'I'll take you to the study,' he says.

'Still worried I'll get lost?' I am pointed. 'There's no need. Tell the groom to ready the horses, so we can go for a ride before lunch. We will be four. Two of the quiet ponies for Bernardo and Ilaria.'

The horses will need to be exercised and it might be a good way to achieve the illusion of freedom, even if I am sure we will be escorted by at least one of Father's men.

He hesitates. 'Has your . . .'

'Yes, I have my father's permission.' I don't attempt to hide my impatience. He knows I have permission. He was there at the breakfast table when I'd suggested the ride. Indeed, Father had thought it a good idea, said the mountain air would be beneficial for us.

'Very well. Are you sure I can't show you the way?'

'I know where it is, thank you.' I had spent an hour earlier acquainting myself with the labyrinthine corridors of La Rocca in daylight. It has a complicated layout with three staircases, no small number of locked doors and a way of making you think a passage is taking you to one place while leading you somewhere else. 'Oh, and would you ensure this goes in with the correspondence for Rome?' I pass him an innocuous letter I have written to Catarina, slipping Giacomo's into my pocket unseen.

'Come with me, Ilaria.' I don't want to see Father alone and I know from bitter experience that a summons to his study always has its risks.

The girl looks hesitant. 'I ought to go and get our riding clothes ready.'

'I'd like you to come with me.'

She begins to pick at her fingers.

'Is it my father? You'll need to get used to him, learn to stand your ground, otherwise . . .' I'm not sure how to explain to her the extent of Father's mercilessness to those he perceives as weak, saying in the end, 'He'll respect you for it.'

Father is leaning back in a large chair, his unlit pipe hanging from his lip. A fire burns vigorously in the grate, crackling and popping.

'You've brought the girl with you, I see. What's your name?' He addresses this to a startled Ilaria.

'She's called Ilaria. You know that, Father.'

'Yes, of course. I'd forgotten.'

'I'm grateful to you for taking me in.' Ilaria's voice is barely audible.

'Speak up, child!' he booms, causing her to flinch.

I notice her small fist gripping the rosary that hangs from her belt. 'I'm grateful for your generosity in . . .'

'Yes, yes. Better here than in a grim convent. Without a proper dowry, you'd doubtless be playing skivvy to some fat, lazy Mother Superior.'

'You asked to see me, Father?' My eyes alight on the spine of that book with its grotesque illustrations.

He looks at me straight. 'I understand you've been wandering about after dark.'

How dare he? A knot of resentment pulls tight inside me.

That turncoat – for it could only have been him – *so full of himself, so full of pretend amity.*

'It's just that –'

'No!' Father silences me. 'I don't want your excuses. I want you to know that I won't have you wandering at night.' He stands then, leaning on the desk. 'It's not safe. That goes for both of you girls. You've got to remember my men. Particularly the foreigners.' His mouth turns down in distaste. 'If they've had enough to drink, I wouldn't put anything past them.'

Ilaria looks petrified.

I wonder if he includes Olimpio in the 'foreigners' for whom he has such antipathy, or only the German brothers who like their beer.

I want to point out that, however drunk they are, they'd hardly dare ravish me, or my companion for that matter, for they'd pay with their lives. I know Father and the lengths to which he will go if anyone takes anything belonging to him. My hatred unfurls in my breast, making itself known. I really want to say that *he* is the danger, not his men. But I am no fool. I make an obedient apology and assure him it won't happen again, glad I hadn't made the excuse that was on the tip of my tongue: that I'd been sleepwalking. He might then have had our bedchamber door locked from the outside at night.

He moves to see us out. Ilaria shoots from the room as fast as she can. I follow but Father puts himself between me and the door. 'I mean it, Beatrice.' He grips my shoulders firmly and meets my eyes. 'I don't want any harm befalling my favourite girl. You're the only one I have left.' He allows a finger to hover above my bandaged cheek. 'How is it healing?' He is reminding me.

'Well enough. I'll be able to leave it to the air in a day or so.'

'Let me see.' He carefully removes the dressing, inspecting

the wound with his magnifying glass, as if seeking flaws in a diamond.

'My girl.' He plants a wet kiss on my forehead and draws me into an embrace so urgent and tight it squeezes the breath out of me, murmuring, 'My sweet little doe, my sweet, sweet doe. How could you possibly know what it's like having so many enemies, those I care for put in so much danger?' He has never said anything like that before. I'm tempted to remind him that he is the architect of his own misery, but don't. I am no fool.

I free myself enough from his suffocating hold to ask, 'How long do you think before it will be safe to return home? I don't want to miss Catarina's wedding.'

'Don't you worry your little head about that. Leave the worrying to me. Besides,' he strokes a rough finger down my good cheek, 'we should enjoy this time together. Before long some miserable young man will claim you for himself and your poor old father will be bereft. Even disfigured' – he pushes his finger to my scar just hard enough to hurt – 'someone will want you for a slice of my wealth.' I give him nothing, not a wince, not a clench of the jaw, not even so much as a stuttering breath. He is silent for a long pensive moment. 'Perhaps I will never let you wed. Lock you up here.' He gives a small snort of laughter to indicate that he only half means it and kisses me again.

As I am almost out of the door, he adds, 'You take care out riding, now. Don't go beyond the bounds – it's not safe.'

Ilaria is waiting on the stairs.

'If he ever orders to see you, make sure you take someone with you.' I sense the girl might easily be bullied and want to protect her from that. 'Preferably me. I know how to handle him.'

She gives me a grave nod.

7

Aquilino is slightly lame, so I am given one of the big black mares that pull the carriage. 'Don't ride her hard, Signorina Beatrice,' Enzo says, as he helps me mount. 'They've all had a long journey. Just need to get the stiffness out of their legs.'

'Don't worry. I'll take care of her.' I know Cala well. She is gentle as a kitten ridden in the right way but can be jumpy with a nervous rider. 'Oh, Enzo,' I pull the letter from my pocket nonchalantly, 'could you see that this goes in the pouch for Rome?' He takes it with a nod. I can trust Enzo. Simply knowing it will soon be on its way makes me feel less isolated, more connected to those I care for.

I adjust my stirrups and circle Cala round the yard. Arriving in the dark last night, I hadn't seen the large walled space, dominated by an ancient spreading stone pine. The light has a certainty about it, like the clarity after a storm, and so unlike the haze that shrouds Rome, its dust churned up by constant comings and goings. Set to one side is a well and beyond it a shallow ornamental pool, filled from the mouth of a burbling stone sea creature. To the other side, a gate leads to what appears to be a vegetable garden with several fruit trees beyond. Two piglets are penned into a corner. A lad comes out of the back door with a bucket, tipping it into the pig pen. The two creatures fall on the scraps, scoffing with alarming violence, transforming in an instant from enchanting curly-tailed things to voracious squealing monsters, a reminder not to be seduced by the apparent normality daylight has brought to this place.

Mounted on Cala, I can see over the walls to where the village spills down the steep hill. Remembering last night's interminable climb, how long it took us to pick our way up here, a feeling clutches at me, the dizzying sense that we have travelled far back in time, so deep in the past there is no return.

'What is it?' Lucrezia is beside me, on Mila, another of the tall carriage horses.

'This place.'

'I know.' Strain scores across her features. 'I barely slept.'

I remember the noises coming from the bedroom last night. Father's appetites . . . I cringe inwardly.

'Are you sure you want to come? You could rest instead. We can easily exercise Mila on a halter. Or one of the grooms could take her out.'

'I'd like the fresh air,' she insists.

I understand. She seeks escape as much as I.

Just as I am expecting Enzo to mount the bay gelding, Olimpio appears, swaggering down the steps, vaulting onto the animal. 'Are we ready?'

My heart sinks now I know that each minor transgression I commit will be referred to Father. 'The spy,' I say, beneath my breath.

'What was that?' Lucrezia turns to me.

'Nothing.' I catch her staring at him.

She leans close, saying quietly, 'Don't you think he has the look of a Moorish prince?'

'I wouldn't know.' But she's right: despite his crumpled shirt and scuffed boots, he has a regal bearing, a straightness of posture that belies his disloyal nature. I keep my eyes off him.

We take a path winding downwards along the edge of the dense forest that is slung across the valley. Virgil weaves excitedly in and out of the verges, panicking the finches and other songbirds that take to the wing, tiny feather bullets, filling the air with their alarm calls.

Before long we come to the perimeter wall, high and topped with jagged rocks. It must be what Father meant when he said not to go beyond the bounds. Even if we sought to, we couldn't breach this towering barrier. We follow it for a time, Bernardo quizzing Olimpio about the fortifications: 'Would they pour down boiling water – burn their enemies to death?'

Rather than making me feel safe from outside threats, the wall makes me feel trapped, and I am glad when Olimpio shouts from behind to turn onto a new path, climbing deep into the forest.

Tall branches meet high above the track, making for a verdant tunnel dappled with light. It is wide enough for a canter, and Cala, so responsive, seems glad to stretch her legs. The soft ground is turned up by the horses' hoofs, giving off a dank mulchy scent – the smell of fresh dug graves. Soon we turn again, having to slow to a walk, as the path becomes twisted and narrow with tangles of undergrowth and nettles to either side.

I set aside my resentment of Olimpio's presence, glad that one among us knows where we are going. It would be easy to become completely lost, even within the boundary, as one tree appears much like any other and there are precious few landmarks here in the depth of the forest. I am reminded of the story of Theseus, how he had unspooled a reel of thread behind him to find his escape from the labyrinth after he'd killed the Minotaur. I try not to think that whichever way you go, here, spool of thread or not, you will eventually find yourself at the wall.

Life is everywhere: rabbits scampering away, white tails bobbing as we approach, squirrels skittering up the trees. I glimpse the occasional deer through the mesh of trunks. They are almost invisible, standing stock still, huge glossy eyes staring, big ears flared, ready to bolt, as we pass. I hear the rattle of a woodpecker and sometime later, it swoops down across our path, a streak of impossible green, tipped with crimson as if dipped in paint, or blood.

We take a new, wider track through towering pines. The smell they give off is redolent of childhood rheums, my head, enclosed in a cave of cloth, over a steaming bowl infused with oil that stung my eyes and cleared my nose. The forest is a place so unfamiliar, so unlike Rome, with its hot open expanses and marble palazzi, its cascading fountains, as if man could create an artificial perfection that Nature could only dream of. But here Nature reigns, and I am beguiled by her dark beauty, imagining I am Diana with her bow, and that the stag I glimpsed through the trees is Actaeon, to be hunted down. Here, all the stories I have read in Ovid spring to life. This is a place where one thing can become another – a man transformed into a flower, a woman into a bird, a nymph into a laurel tree. I envisage myself sprouting wings, flying away. But those disturbing illustrations insert themselves into my mind, hooking me with their strangeness and violence.

'Halt!' shouts Olimpio, cutting into my thoughts.

Something is crashing through the undergrowth.

He has drawn his gun, loaded and cocked it, fast and efficient as a soldier, and is pointing it at the path ahead.

Then it appears, the creature, huge and low-slung, black and long-snouted, tusked like a demon, hurtling towards us. The horses toss their heads in fear, dancing nervily, scuffing at the ground. My imagination runs wild – they are rearing, bolting, bones are broken, heads are injured, someone is mauled by the fiendish beast that is almost upon us.

Ilaria lets out a blood-curdling shriek and the animal veers off, back into the depths of the forest, disappearing as suddenly as it had appeared.

Olimpio begins to laugh. 'Who'd have thought that you could scare off a boar, Ilaria?' She looks completely stunned, her eyes round as plates, mouth gaping. 'Though I would have liked to get my sights on it. The conte would have been most pleased to have boar for supper.' He is still laughing. We are not.

Cala's ears have flattened, her agitation continuing. I stroke her neck and whisper to her, noticing only then that Bernardo has a long-bladed dagger in his hand. 'What's that?'

His mouth screws tightly.

'Where did you get it?' I try to make myself sound interested rather than accusatory. I don't want to set him off.

'Looks like one of the ones from the great hall,' says Olimpio, coming up beside him. 'Did you want to protect the women?' His tone is congenial, brotherly, exactly what is required. Bernardo makes a small nod. 'Good for you.' Olimpio goes to slap him on the back, in that way men do, but must notice my brother's slight flinch and withdraws his hand. 'It's always best you tell someone when you're armed, just in case of accidents. That dagger would be better sheathed. It's very sharp. You wouldn't want to do yourself damage.'

'I understand,' says Bernardo, with great seriousness. 'Rules have to be kept with weapons. Yes. I do understand.'

'I think it best if you let me take care of it for now. Would you mind that?'

Bernardo looks from the knife to Olimpio and back before handing it over.

'I can teach you how to handle a blade safely if you'd like. Show you how to avoid being disarmed.'

'I would like that.' Bernardo looks solemn. 'Very much.'

Lucrezia rides alongside Olimpio as we set off once more. 'I can't begin to tell you how good it is to find someone who understands my boy. More than anything he needs a role model . . .'

I let the three of them go ahead, while I slide in behind with Ilaria, who is muttering under her breath.

'You all right?'

'Oh, yes!' She blushes, looking up. 'Was just giving thanks. That wasn't me. That was Him.' Her eyes flick heavenward. 'I didn't intend to scream like that. It just happened. It was the Lord's work – speaking through me. I couldn't be more sure of it.'

I hardly know how to respond. 'Well, you can light a candle in the chapel when you get back.'

She looks a little disappointed. Perhaps she'd wanted me to declare that it must have been a miracle. I had come across girls like that in the convent at Montecitorio. Girls who wanted a miracle so much they'd imagine one into being. One went as far as gouging her palms with a rusty nail and pretending the marks had occurred spontaneously. Some of the novices were taken in, declaring the marks with earnest reverence, as stigmata, but Mother Superior had seen it all before and punished the girl. She died soon after. They said her blood had been poisoned by the dirty nail. God's punishment. After that no more so-called miracles occurred for several months.

Those girls wanted to be chosen more than they wanted to live. All dreamed of being declared a saint, after death, by the Holy Father. I didn't see the point. I was too fond of worldly pleasures and secretly, quietly, reading books other than the scriptures. It made an outcast of me, and the pious company of Ilaria gives me the same sense of separation. We ride on in silence, under the vast arch of trees, a great green basilica, the track its aisle, its god: Nature. I try vainly to express this to the girl, who looks at me as if I've blasphemed. We fall to silence. I long for Catarina's company.

Some way further up the track, Olimpio tells us to dismount and tie up the horses, saying he wants to show us something.

He leads us, in single file, down a steep path, which has been set with large, flat stones like steps. A rocky bank runs along one side, covered with mounds of thick damp moss, like fine green velvet, where tiny violet flowers creep out from miniature crevices. On the other side the ground runs steeply down, the dark earth punctuated here and there by clumps of bluebells.

As we reach the bottom a female voice cries out in surprise: 'Olimpio, what are you doing here?'

The woman is crouched in a hollow and stands as our party reaches her. She is large and muscular, with a ruddy face and dark hair, streaked with grey, escaping in fronds from a loose bun. She wears a most peculiar outfit: a rough linen smock, speckled like the breast of a thrush, a pair of sturdy leather boots to the knees with not skirts but breeches. Her sleeves are rolled up to reveal strong forearms and blunt-fingered hands.

Olimpio introduces her as 'Terza, who cooks for us.'

I wonder why she hadn't been present on the previous evening when the staff lined up to greet us.

'Why are your clothes so strange?' asks Bernardo.

Lucrezia hushes him, apologizing to Terza, who laughs it away. 'He's right. My clothes are strange but they're practical and comfortable.'

'I've brought them to see the spring,' says Olimpio.

'Best water in the whole of Rieti.' She stands aside so we can see the water pouring from the mouth of a carved granite gargoyle set into the rock face. A metal tongue serves as a spout, ensuring that it falls in a perfect stream into a pool below. 'Here, taste it.' A metal cup is attached by a chain to the rock. She fills it, holding it out. Lucrezia takes the first sip, solemnly passing on the cup as if it is some kind of heathen initiation.

I am the last to drink. As Olimpio passes me the vessel, his fingers brush mine. I snatch my hand away, spilling some of the chill liquid onto my dress. *Was it deliberate?* His nails are short and neat and surprisingly pale. When I drink, my mouth fills with a delicious, clean, slightly metallic taste. I refill the cup and greedily drink more.

Terza watches me approvingly. 'Look what I found. Almost never see these at this time of year.' She holds up a trug containing an enormous white ball the size of a severed head. 'The conte will be delighted. He adores *vescia*.'

'We might have had wild boar for supper . . .' Olimpio relates briefly our recent encounter '. . . but I suppose your big mushroom will have to do instead.'

'Do instead!' Terza says in mock dudgeon. '*Vescia* is far more of a delicacy than wild boar. We've sausages and sides of boar hanging all over the kitchens, enough to feed an army, but this . . .' She cradles the white sphere like an infant. 'Just you wait and see what I can do with it.'

'Terza is a magician in the kitchen,' explains Olimpio.

'I look forward to tasting it,' says Lucrezia, who seems to be enjoying the familiarity of Terza and Olimpio, so unlike the staff in Rome bound by their strict hierarchies. 'What do you think, Ilaria?'

Ilaria makes a face. 'I'm not fond of mushrooms.'

'Oh, but you haven't tried Terza's.' Olimpio nudges her. She blushes hotly.

'Lots of mushrooms round here if you know where to look. And plenty at the moment from a thunderstorm the night before last.' I remember seeing the night sky lit by the distant storm from the window of the inn we'd stayed at. 'Storms make them spring up like nobody's business. It's the lightning, you see. Draws them up and out of the ground.'

My fascination is ignited by this unusual androgynous

woman with her strange ideas, her easy manner and odd clothes. She seems to belong entirely to this place and know all its secrets. As we climb back up the steep path, she stops every now and again, crouching for a mushroom, inspecting it and telling us what kind it is. Big terracotta-hatted *porcini* appear from between the ground ferns. 'The best of these are found beside chestnut trees,' she tells us, bringing one to her nose to smell. 'And look here, *fungo ostrica*.' She is breaking off pale grey folds that spill from a rent in the bark of a fallen log. 'When you look you find them everywhere. But you have to know where to look. See, more *porcini* over there. Here, come and pick them.'

We squat to pull the strange forms from the dank earth, where the roots of trees emerge from the ground, like the vast searching fingers of some creature buried alive. 'We shall have a feast.' She gives Olimpio a playful shove, so he almost loses his footing. 'Better than your tough old boar.' She laughs in complete abandon, seeming quite mad, and yet to me, who was raised to laugh only occasionally and politely, she is enthralling. But she and Olimpio clearly know one another well, which sets bells of caution ringing through me.

'Look, there.' She points to some leaf debris from which sprouts a trio of tall white mushrooms, delicate and iridescent as Chinese porcelain.

I crouch to pick them but she grabs me, pulling me away. 'Careful with those. Amanita are very poisonous – even when cooked.' She fastens a look on me, black and deep, more animal than human. Silence falls suddenly – even the birds stop singing. My neck hairs rise. 'Some call them fool's angels.' She strokes the forefinger of her free hand horizontally across her throat with a grimace and gives that strange laugh again. 'But useful if you've become tired of your husband.'

Lucrezia lets out a gleeful snort before slapping a palm

over her mouth, as if Father might have overheard. Olimpio notices. I wonder if that, too, will be reported.

'Shouldn't we be getting back?' My voice is high and strange. I reach for Cala's reins.

Olimpio begins to lead the way. I linger, drawn by those pale fungi, so beguilingly beautiful, and more so now I know their deadly power. When no one is looking I take my handkerchief and, without letting its flesh meet my skin, pluck one, wrap it and slip it into my pocket.

As I join the others, Olimpio says quietly, 'What was that you picked up?'

I hesitate. 'Nothing.'

'Nothing?' He tilts his head.

His scrutiny prickles as I scramble for a response. 'Oh, that! I thought it was a pretty feather, but I was mistaken – only a leaf.'

'I thought I saw you put something into your pocket.'

'My handkerchief!' I pull out the square of linen, showing it to him, the deadly cargo secreted in its folds. He surely hasn't the audacity to inspect it more closely. 'What's it to you, anyway?' My eyes narrow. 'You're not my jailer.'

'Of course I'm not.' His smile is lopsided, one cheek knotting into a dimple. 'I was merely curious.'

The air stiffens, like beaten egg whites. I will him to stop smiling – my body and mind are engaged in a battle to the death. I don't want to want him. I mustn't. 'Curiosity killed the cat,' I snap, turning sharply, walking ahead to join Lucrezia.

8

On our return, we pass Father, leaving with Oskar and Jakob to visit a tenant in arrears with his rent. I feel for the tenant. Father is not known for his lenience and with the two German bruisers the poor man will have the frights put up him. Olimpio stops to have a word out of my earshot before following us inside.

In Father's absence, despite the presence of his watchful proxy, we all breathe a little more easily. Lucrezia says she'd like to bathe, that the journey from Rome has left her stiff and she can't shake off her headache.

The ancient wooden trough, which is lugged up to the bedchamber, is a far cry from the Palazzo Cenci's marble bathhouse, the only one in the city. Father, never wanting to be outdone, had had it installed when he heard the Duke of Milan had one. Nevertheless, when the trough has been set in front of the blazing hearth, lined with muslin and filled with heated water it makes a surprisingly good substitute.

The lugging and heating and filling take a very long time, during which Lucrezia and Ilaria lie on the bed while I read stories from Ovid to them. For Ilaria's sake I keep to the more palatable tales. Even so, the girl is shocked and asks if such literature is allowed. Not if His Holiness has his way, I think. She prefers the scriptures, she tells us. But she can't read very well.

Once the bath is filled, I help Lucrezia out of her clothes and unpin the golden ripples of her hair. She has a bad bruise on her forearm. 'How did you get that?'

'I tripped on the stairs this morning. They're so uneven and slippery and I'm so ungainly.'

We both know it is a lie. She can't look at me. I imagine what it might be like to press a pillow over his face, holding him down, until his life gutters away. The thought makes me hot and agitated.

'Would you go down to the kitchens and see if Terza has any ointment?' I say.

Ilaria points to herself. 'Me?'

'Yes, you.' I manage to stop myself adding sharply, 'Who else?' The girl hesitates nervously but she will have to get used to doing things on her own at some point.

She slides towards the door. 'An ointment?' She says it as if she's never before heard the word.

'That's right. Something for bruises.' I assume that Terza will know where such a thing can be procured.

When she's gone Lucrezia lowers herself into the bath with a sigh, lying back, eyes shut. The water laps right up to the rim. She picks up a cube of soap that one of the servants has put into a dish, sniffing it with a grimace. 'Smells of sheep's hide. Glad I thought to bring some of my own.' Lucrezia is a woman who enjoys the small pleasures of life, and lemon-scented soap from Genoa is one of them. 'Was my coffer brought up here?'

'This one?' I indicate a pretty marquetry box beside the pile of linens.

'There should be some good soap in it.'

I find the soap and a bag of sea sponges, packed with pots of unguent and bottles of herbal oil.

But when I pass a sponge to her, I receive an abrupt 'No, not one of those!'

'What's wrong with it?' It seems perfectly good to me.

'I use them for –' She stops.

'Use them for what?'

'Never mind.'

I realize then what they are for – to be doused in vinegar and pushed up inside – and why Lucrezia hasn't had a single pregnancy in the thirteen years since Bernardo was born. 'You never wanted another child?' I had felt sorry for her, while all the women around her birthed infant after infant and none for her.

'No.' She is quite blunt, then drops her voice, 'I had to get rid of one.'

'What do you mean?'

'Went to one of those midwives. Some kind of herbal concoction.'

I knew what it must have taken for her to go to such lengths. Questions clamour at me. How had she reconciled her actions with her faith? Had she confessed it? Did she fear for her immortal soul?

She looks suddenly gaunt with alarm.

'Of course I won't say anything.' I know the consequences. He wants more sons to replace those who are gone.

'You see, I nearly lost my life with Bernardo. He was such a big baby and . . .' She shakes her head, her eyes slamming shut, the memory of it too much to bear. 'I was very young. I was terrified.'

'I understand.' I do. My own mother had died birthing a stillborn.

'You see, your father has insatiable desires.'

'Don't!' I don't want to hear about Father's desires.

She clutches at my hand. 'Thank the Lord we have each other.'

Would I have the heart to abandon her, should the opportunity arise? The likelihood is too small to consider. I take a cloth and lather up the soap, smoothing it over her well-upholstered shoulders, the sharp lemon scent filling the steamy air. Her secret anguish circles my mind. It makes me think about the invisible sufferings of women, how men have no idea.

I take a wrong turn on my way to the kitchens, finding myself in a dank, windowless passage with four cells running along one side, their iron doors hanging open. The walls are cold to the touch, slimy with damp, and a drip, drip, drip echoes in the stale air. Something is scratching urgently, burrowing. I am momentarily frozen until I see, in the gloom, that it is only Virgil, who must have followed me from the bedchamber.

'What is it, boy?' I approach. He whines. He has uncovered a grille in the floor – an oubliette. My heart rattles. Does it contain the bones of a forgotten soul? Something is down there, scurrying. A rat or a demon. 'Come away from there.' I pull at his collar.

'Is everything all right?' A girl, one of the servants, is at the end of the corridor.

'I was looking for the kitchens.' My heart won't settle.

'I'll take you there.'

I follow her gratefully.

'Took me months to get the lie of the place when I first arrived,' she is saying.

'It is rather a labyrinth.' She looks blankly at me. 'A maze.'

'Yes.' She nods, chatting amiably as she walks. 'Nice dog. What's his name?' The light conversation helps settle me and I tell her that he was the runt of the litter and would have been drowned had I not taken pity on him.

The kitchens are warm and cavernous, with convex ceilings of whitewashed brick. A fireplace takes up most of one wall and is hung with pots. The place is abuzz with comings and goings. A lad sweeps up bloody sawdust, while another turns the spit and a bulky man stacks logs to dry.

I place the pot of ointment on the large, scrubbed table where Terza, wrapped in an enormous apron, stands wielding a knife. 'My stepmother wanted me to thank you.'

'That's quite all right.'

'Is that the mushroom?' I point at the white slices covering the table.

'Yes. Here.' She holds out a piece on the tip of her blade. 'Taste it.'

It is pure white, like swan's down, and dense but feather light. I sniff it. It doesn't have much scent, a touch of earthiness perhaps. I think of the fool's angel and her warning, nibbling only a tiny corner. It tastes unpleasantly of soil and yeast.

'I'm not trying to poison you.' She laughs and passes me a knife. 'You may as well help me.'

I don't know what to make of her disarming lack of ceremony. She clearly isn't prone to deference. I've almost never visited the kitchens at the Palazzo Cenci, or not since childhood, and the cook certainly wouldn't have me chopping mushrooms for him. Here, everything is less formal and this place, muggy with the smells of cooking, feels so very welcoming – too welcoming perhaps. I don't want to be inveigled into a false sense of security. I know nothing about this woman and where her loyalties lie.

'Are you finding your way around?' she says.

'More or less.'

'Have you discovered the battlements yet? There's a wonderful view from up there. Your mother used to like walking them at sunset.'

'You knew my mother?'

'It was she who employed me here in the kitchens. A good and kind woman, God rest her soul. Very adept at dealing with your father.'

I want to ask what exactly she means by that, but she continues, 'You look nothing like her. More like him.'

'I know.' I hate it, hate that I see him in me whenever I catch sight of my reflection unawares.

'I knew him as a boy. We were born on the same day, you know. My mother nursed him as an infant along with me. He came unexpectedly and my mother had milk enough for two, or so the story goes.'

'You're milk twins?'

'That's right. Known him all my life.'

'What was he like as a child?' I wonder if she might have some clue as to what made him the way he is. I want to know if malevolence is bred into his bone – and mine. *More than her fair share of original sin.*

'We were playmates until the age of about five. I don't remember so much from those times but my mother always used to say we were inseparable. It's probably hard to imagine, but he looked almost identical to you then, elfin, troubled – I remember that.'

'Do you think I look troubled?' I work hard to give the impression of being unruffled. Clearly Terza has seen through it. It makes me feel laid bare.

'A little. As if you fear what the future might hold.'

'I try not to think of the future.'

'Because it troubles you.'

This is a statement, rather than a question and Terza is right. I struggle to envisage the shape of my future. Even if Father was inclined to let me go, it is impossible to see myself married to Davide Forlani, or some other noble boy, and living a useless life of luxurious indolence, producing infants year upon year until I am spent. *But what else am I for?* The thought frightens me, that I might have no other purpose. Were I a man, I would travel the world seeking stories to write into verse, of that I am certain. It makes me curse my sex. Though, I consider the alternative – had I been born a boy, I might already have had a sword run through me, like my brothers.

'You're right,' I say. 'It does trouble me.' I think of my letter making its way to Giacomo.

'Sometime when I'm not so busy, I shall read the cards for you.'

'Read the cards?'

'*Tarocchi!* Don't you play it?'

I nod. Games of *tarocchi* might be all we have to occupy ourselves on the long empty evenings here.

'Sometimes I glimpse a person's future in the *tarocchi* cards.'

Despite myself, I'm intrigued. 'I don't think Father would approve.'

Terza leans in conspiratorially. 'I'm sure he wouldn't, but he needn't know.'

We are silent for a moment. The knife slides easily through the dry flesh of the mushroom.

'Your father was taken away from us quite without warning. Or so my mother told me. He was inconsolable, she said, and his father made sure he had the tears beaten out of him, poor little mite.'

'Poor little mite.' I echo her, dissembling. It wouldn't do for her to know what I really think. Not a single iota of sympathy is aroused in me. Plenty of small boys are beaten for weeping. They don't all grow into monsters. Perhaps he was the kind of boy who pulled the legs off spiders and gouged out the eyes of mice.

She continues, 'After that, I saw him only on feast days, when the family would come down to the church in the village. I suppose in time he forgot who I was. Me being so much further down in the world to him, he'd have been made to forget. You don't remember much from that age anyway. And the family came here less and less, eventually only used the place for the occasional hunting party. I'm not even sure he knows who I am now.'

Terza glances up over my shoulder towards the door. 'Look what the cat dragged in.'

It is Olimpio. Of course it is Olimpio, always appearing like a counterfeit coin. I wonder how soon before Father will be telling me I shouldn't loiter in the kitchens with the staff, that it is unbecoming.

'Have I interrupted something?' He strides to the table. 'I see you've got a new kitchen maid.' Grinning at me, he picks up a slice of the mushroom and pops it into his mouth.

Somehow his lack of formality grates, where Terza's doesn't.

He wanders about the kitchen, lifting the lid off a pot and sniffing its contents, stirring something in a bowl, breaking off a corner of cheese to eat. 'Got any bread?'

'Get your great hands off!' Terza flicks him playfully with a cloth. 'You're being a nuisance. What do you want?'

'Just came to say that the conte wants to eat at sunset and no later.' He slices himself some bread, cuts a piece of cheese, pours himself a measure of ale and sits on a stool to eat. 'Any gossip, Terza?'

They swap news from the village – someone's stolen goat, a rejected lover, a dispute over a piece of land, a dog that had bitten a neighbour. I can't drag my eyes from those 'great hands', imagining them on me, hot at the thought.

'I found Don Tomassino' – Olimpio lowers his voice – 'fast asleep, on the floor behind the altar in the chapel, dead drunk. Been there all afternoon. Must have had the communion wine.'

I release an unintended snort of laughter.

'I knew you weren't made of stone.' He turns to me. I don't look at him, keep my gaze on the knife and the mushroom. 'Better get back to my work.' He stands, drains his cup and wipes his mouth on the back of his hand, before leaving.

'Don't mind him,' says Terza, when he has gone. She must have read the wariness on my face. 'I've known him all his life. His mother is a friend. I know he seems insolent, but we're all very informal here. You're likely not used to it.'

I long to confide my doubts about Olimpio's trustworthiness, to find out more about him, but hold my tongue. I will not be lulled into this woman's spell of friendship.

9

Easter is early this year and fast approaching, with no mention of a return to the city. The spring sun shines outside but its warmth barely penetrates the deep walls of La Rocca. I have taken up Terza's suggestion and walk the battlements each evening, in my mother's footsteps, seeking communion with her, taking a moment of solace away from the constant prying eyes of Father's men. I gaze into the blurred distance, dreaming of freedom, imagining another life, the life I might have had if she was still with us. The sunsets are dramatic – great swathes of peachy cloud, with ethereal shafts of light spilling through, the world held in stasis while the dazzling crimson coin slowly slides behind the distant mountains.

Each day, I wait for the messenger to arrive with the pouch from Rome. 'I'll take it up,' I say, shuffling through the contents before delivering it to Father, dragging Ilaria with me, so as not to be alone with him. And each day I suffer the disappointment of it containing nothing for me. I can't understand why Giacomo hasn't responded to my letter, not even a scrawled note. My hope weakens.

One such morning I find Father in the stables, taking short sucks on his pipe. I think of the dry straw catching an ember, flaring up. Something is not right. I hover at the door, Ilaria behind me. Enzo is stooped over, inspecting the hoof of Father's favourite horse. 'It's a thorn,' he says. 'It's become infected.' His voice is pitchy and nervous. 'I'll make a poultice – draw it out.'

Father pulls him to his feet, prodding him with the pointed

end of his pipe. 'This is your doing.' Enzo looks as if he might vomit. 'He shouldn't have been left in the pasture overnight. I should have you whipped for negligence.'

I can see Enzo is on the brink of mounting a defence. Father won't like that. I catch his eye with a minute shake of my head and step in, holding out the pouch. 'Your correspondence has arrived, Father.'

He snaps round, high with rage. 'What are you doing here?'

Enzo throws me a grateful look. The horses have picked up on the tension and are shifting nervously in their stalls.

'Just delivering your letters.'

He steps towards me. I back away, into the yard, until my spine meets the trunk of the stone pine. Ilaria shuffles sideways. He looms, drilling into me with his eyes, his palm flat to my sternum, and takes a slow draw on his pipe. The tobacco sizzles. He blows the smoke into my face. 'Always looking out for the messenger, aren't you? What is it you're waiting for? A letter? Who have you been writing to?'

'Only to Catarina.' I make my voice light. 'Wishing her well for her marriage. Nobody else knows I'm here.'

'Are you sure about that?'

What does he know?

'I wouldn't want to jeopardize our safety, Father.'

'You wouldn't be so foolish. You know what the Orestesi would do to us – to you.' He places a hand round the back of my neck, something burns, like the sting of a wasp. I smell singed hair. He has the hot bowl of his pipe pressed to my soft nape. I don't react, just inhale and exhale, slowly, deeply, imagining I am suspended in cooling water, all sensations dampened, the muffled glug in my ears, the in–out push and pull of my watery body. My deadly tentacles tangle round his throat. 'Don't you?'

Ilaria has begun to sob quietly.

'What's the matter with you?' he bellows, letting me go. She shrinks away. 'Frightened?'

She cowers, a pool of wet seeping out from beneath her skirts, making the ground dark. I see his look of pleasure. He turns back, pointing to his eyes and then to me, 'I'm watching you,' before striding away.

I notice Marzio at the orchard gate with a wheelbarrow full of lumber. He is a big, silent local man, who skulks about the place with his box of tools. He does some of the heavier jobs around La Rocca – general forestry, chopping wood and making repairs on the ancient building, mending rotten timbers and repointing crumbling brickwork. He meets my eye with a slow nod. I wonder if it is a gesture of solidarity.

Ilaria is weeping, hard. 'You must learn not to show your fear,' I say.

'I'm mortified.' She is looking in despair at the puddle of urine.

'There's no shame in it,' I say, guiding her inside. 'I won't tell anyone.'

Thankfully, he is kept busy with his tenants for the next few days, eking every last *sou* out of his lands no doubt. We see him rarely outside mealtimes, often tense affairs depending on his moods. In the evenings, Lucrezia and I are expected to play the dutiful wife and daughter, preparing him the tisane he likes to drink before bed, assiduously careful not to say anything to trip his temper. Sometimes I spit in his drink before serving it with a smile, giving myself a thimbleful of satisfaction.

Terza snips the stitches off my wound with the embroidery scissors. Father inspects it with even greater exactitude than usual, holding my head vice-like, tilting my neck uncomfortably to the light. 'My girl. My favourite girl.' My slumbering vengeance opens an eye to watch this display of sinister tenderness.

Out riding Olimpio says, 'Your stitches are out.' His frankness is surprising. Lucrezia and Ilaria haven't mentioned it. I draw my hair over my cheek. 'It's healed well.'

I don't respond but he must read something in my expression for he says, 'It's not what you think.'

'And what do I think?'

'That it makes you less lovely.'

I want to ask why he believes he knows me, knows what I want, what I think. But another part of me registers the compliment.

'When I was fighting the Turks,' he continues, 'a scar on the face was considered a great prize – showed courage. One of my company was bitten by a dog on the chin. He tried to convince us the wound was made by a Turkish sabre. We teased him mercilessly.'

I can't help my laughter.

'We were young and stupid, the lot of us.' We ride on in silence for a moment, until he says, 'I have a scar of my own.'

'Where?' He doesn't know that I have watched him sparring with Bernardo, his shirt off. I have inspected every rift and ripple of his torso and there is no scar on him.

He grins and pats his backside. There is only one place for my mind to go. I blush. He notices and makes a minute smirk.

I gather my composure. 'They must have teased you about that.'

'They did, and how.' He is laughing now. 'It hurt a lot. I wasn't very brave – made a great fuss.'

'I've rarely come across a man who will admit to weakness.'

'What are you laughing about?' Lucrezia has ridden alongside us, and I become suddenly aware of where I am, of who he is. I had forgotten myself completely, forgotten he's not to be trusted. I have heard that prisoners, after a time, grow strangely close to their jailers. Is that what is happening to me?

Father's words echo: *I'm watching you.*

I stick close to my stepmother for the rest of the ride, but he will not leave my mind all day. He is there while I eat my lunch, under Father's beady gaze. He is there while I read aloud to Lucrezia and Ilaria as they embroider an altar cloth for Holy Week. He is still there later, when I am obliged to make my confession before Sunday's mass.

Don Tomassino holds his face close to the grille. I can feel the heat of his breath and smell the wine that hangs on it. I divulge only the pettiest of my sins, bland envies and misdemeanours, while my head is turbulent with lust and my heart houses a monster of hate. I am silent, too, about the small, greying mushroom that lies wrapped in a handkerchief hidden at the very bottom of my coffer. From time to time, on the rare occasions I am alone, I take it out and ponder on the power over life and death it holds in its pale, shrivelled body.

That evening, as has become our habit, we pass the long, dreary hours playing rounds of *tarocchi*, casting wagers with pennies. Ilaria disapproves. 'Gambling is the Devil's work,' she mutters to herself, declining to join in, and sits with her sewing, attempting to discuss the scriptures with Don Tomassino who is incomprehensibly drunk.

Bernardo inevitably wins every round. He has the magician-like gift of being able to remember which cards are in whose hand and smugly amasses a great stack of coins.

We can hear Father and his men playing a raucous game of dice downstairs. Occasionally a great cheer goes up. I listen for Olimpio's voice but can't tell if he is with them or not. They are drinking hard. I make a mental note to keep out of Father's orbit tonight. He is at his cruellest when drunk and I have an uneasy feeling the business of my letters is not yet done with.

'I'm tired of losing,' says Lucrezia. 'Did you know that Terza can read the future in a pack of *tarocchi* cards?'

I recall our conversation in the kitchen. 'She did mention it. I'm sure it's just a trick.'

'Shall we get her up here to read our fortunes?' Lucrezia seems ignited by the idea. 'Just a bit of fun.'

'Why not?' I would do almost anything to alleviate the tedium of the long evening. 'It can't hurt.'

'Yes, let's.' Bernardo is all eagerness.

'I don't think it's a good idea.' Ilaria, though she has cast off some of her shyness, is rarely so direct. She looks towards Don Tomassino for support but he has fallen asleep.

'It's only a game,' says Lucrezia.

'But you might invite the Devil in.' Ilaria crosses herself with great solemnity, shifting a little closer to the priest. Perhaps she thinks he, even in his stupor, can protect her from a demon seeking a virgin soul to possess.

Terza is sent for and arrives asking if there was anything wrong with the meal we'd eaten earlier.

'Goodness, no. It was delicious, as always,' says Lucrezia. 'We simply thought you might –'

'Invite the Devil in,' interrupts Bernardo.

I notice the horror scored through Ilaria's expression so take my brother firmly to one side. 'That's enough, Bernardo!' To Terza, I say, 'We simply wondered if you might tell our fortunes – just for fun.'

'I'll need to use my own cards,' she says, leaving to fetch them.

I think of the card-sharps who ply their tricks in Rome's piazzas, skinning unsuspecting punters. They use their own cards, too – cards that have been marked or tapered or clipped, so they can't lose, or so my brothers told me. Terza returns with her dog-eared pack, bound in a worn length of crimson silk, which she makes much of unwrapping.

Terza chooses Bernardo to go first, instructing him to shuffle the pack. 'And while you do so, think hard about what you want the future to bring.'

Taking her instructions with great seriousness he does as she says, cutting the pack three times and handing it back.

'Now pick one.' She fans the deck towards him.

He draws one out. She lays it face down on the table, placing a card on either side of it, before turning up the one Bernardo had first chosen. It is the Page of Swords.

Terza points to it. 'This is what you hope for, what you want to be – agile, vigilant, discerning, a good swordsman. And this one' – she flips over the right-hand card: the two of swords – 'tells me that it is possible to become what you wish.' Bernardo seems pleased with her interpretation, sitting a little straighter.

The third card is the Devil and is upside down.

'There he is!' Bernardo jumps from his chair, gleefully. 'We let the Devil in and there he is!'

I notice Terza's expression slide slightly and wonder why. Has she seen ill-fortune? The Devil card cannot mean anything good. A sudden gust from nowhere makes the candles gutter. The room falls momentarily silent. *It's only a game. It's only a game.* Terza must have blown on them when we were distracted. She is more than likely creating a little drama to amuse us, as someone might tell a chilling story on a dark night.

Terza waits for my brother to calm. 'The Devil is a strong card and I'm glad it's upside down, it means that you may well achieve your aspirations. The right way up and it would be very bad indeed. The meaning is not usually literal.' Bernardo's attention has begun to wander. He has seen what he chose to see and is delighted with that. Terza returns the cards to the deck. 'Who's next?'

Lucrezia picks Hope, which leads to a long explanation

of what this means according to the neighbouring cards. I'm only half paying attention. Lucrezia is enthralled, saying how extraordinary it is that it all seems to depict, exactly, mysteriously, her own inner world. 'Things I've never revealed to a soul.' She seems blithely unaware that Terza's interpretation is so featureless and general, it might apply to anyone.

'Your turn, now, Bea,' says my stepmother, all eagerness.

'No need.' I try to make myself sound indifferent. But Terza has me in the grip of her gaze and an irrational apprehension is spreading through me at the very notion of being rendered transparent, of all my secrets exposed.

Terza shrugs and begins to put the cards away.

'Come on, Bea,' says Lucrezia. 'What have you got to hide?'

'Yes, what are you hiding?' joins Bernardo.

'Nothing.' I sound defensive. 'I'm not hiding anything.'

The three of them are looking at me expectantly.

'For goodness' sake.' I force a laugh, take the pack from Terza, give it a rudimentary shuffle and snap down the top three cards.

She flicks the first face up. I might have known it would be the Lovers.

'Well, that doesn't need any explanation,' teases Lucrezia.

Terza remains silent.

I shrivel inwardly.

'Who is it?' says Bernardo.

They are waiting for a response.

I scrabble for something plausible.

'If you must know, I had hoped for a proposal from Davide Forlani. But . . .' My fingers go to my scar. Lucrezia looks chastened.

Meanwhile, I notice Terza half turn the next card. Her expression clouds and she gathers all three cards back into the pack.

The atmosphere distils, as when there was once a partial eclipse of the sun. All of Rome's birds stopped singing and a midday dusk descended, shadows lengthening, bringing the whole of the city to a deathly silence. Our bellies knotted with dread. It felt as if the world was on the brink of ending. Yet moments later daylight began to return, the song of a lone blackbird sounded, bringing with it a febrile atmosphere of relief. It had upset Bernardo greatly, and Lucrezia said it was a bad omen, that ill-fortune was afoot.

'What is it?' says Lucrezia. 'What were the other cards?'

'I couldn't read them.' Terza's face bears a facsimile of a smile. 'Sometimes the gift deserts me quite suddenly.'

'I need some air,' I say, standing. 'Would you like to join me for a walk on the battlements before the sun goes down, Ilaria?'

'Do you regret it?' Ilaria asks, as we leave the room. 'The fortune-telling? Your brother's outburst was . . .' She can't seem to bring herself to say it.

'They are nothing more than ordinary playing cards,' I reply firmly. 'My brother is unpredictable. You must know that by now.' She shrugs. 'I don't believe for a moment that it is possible to read the future.'

'The Lord has mapped out our lives.' She turns her gaze upward. Her indefatigable religious integrity is the one topic for which she seems to have the confidence to speak her mind. In some ways I envy her. How much easier life would be with an incontrovertible moral map to follow such as hers, rather than the slippery philosophies I have discovered in the library that all contradict one another. 'Shall we go to the chapel and say a prayer? That might make you feel better.' This, I am learning, is her answer to any small trouble.

'I feel perfectly all right.' I temper my blunt tone. 'Maybe later. What I really want is some fresh air.' I lead the way, taking the steps that spiral up through the high tower and out through the heavy door at the top.

'So, this is where you disappear to at twilight,' she says.

Do you watch me too?

This evening is different. A brume has risen from the valley, half enveloping the tower, stifling the sun's brightness into a diffuse and spectral glow. The scene has its own beauty, the surrounding trees muffled into vague shapes, the view into the valley obscured in a great cauldron of fog. We amble without speaking along the narrow walkway that circles the battlements. I imagine raiding armies of times long past, rendered invisible, only emerging from the mist when it is too late to secure the fortress doors. Bowmen hail them with futile arrows; boiling oil spills blindly into the abyss.

We stop to admire the scene. Ilaria, with the sun's vague glow behind, catching her outline, is rendered with a strange, angelic luminosity. But without warning the girl's expression collapses, her eyes enormous, her gaze fixed in terror on something beyond my shoulder.

She expels a petrified scream.

I turn, gasping, my body thrumming with fear, for I am confronted by an unearthly figure suspended in the air beyond the walkway. It is a vast, dark, winged thing – something unearthly, a harpy, a fury, enormous, seeming made of shadow and haloed in fire, as if Lucifer has been sent to us from Hell.

Ilaria clutches me. 'What is it?'

The thing moves, transforming its shape, its great wings scooping the air.

An ungodly chill surges through my veins. 'I don't know.'

'It's the cards.' Ilaria's voice is thin with panic. 'The Devil.'

In that moment, I wonder if it might be true, that we have opened the door, welcomed in some terrible demonic visitation. My brother's cry shivers through my head: *We let the Devil in.* The thing shifts again. 'Run,' I scream.

We hurtle back to the battlements door, me half tripping on the mat, Ilaria fumbling with the latch, unable to open it. I dare a glance behind. The figure has disappeared. 'Look,' I pluck at Ilaria's shoulder, 'it's gone. We must have imagined it.' My heart is thumping hard and fast.

Ilaria crosses herself, muttering a breathless prayer.

With all my strength I force the latch up and the door falls open. We slam it behind us, plunging down the steps, round and round, onto the halfway landing, colliding with Olimpio.

'Steady.' His eyes dart between us. 'Whatever's the matter? You look as if you've seen a ghost.'

'Nothing. Nothing's wrong.' My heart is still thudding. 'We couldn't open the door, thought we'd be locked out there all night.'

He takes a step towards me, too close, so close I fear he can see the pulse throbbing in my throat.

Ilaria is still praying silently, worrying at that rosary of hers.

'The latch can be temperamental.' He is looking at me oddly, as if he thinks I've been up to no good. 'I would have found you on my rounds anyway.' He begins to mount the steps away from us but turns. 'Sure you didn't see anything untoward out there?'

'Of course not. Why do you ask?' My tone betrays me.

'It's my job to ensure everything's as it should be before we lock up for the night.' His gaze strikes mine sharply. 'That's all.'

I cast my eyes to the floor. 'I see.' I should turn and leave, firmly, but find I am rooted to the spot. 'You'd better . . .' It is all I can do not to reach out and touch him, run my hands over his face, feel the heat of his skin.

'I'd better . . .' He makes to go but stops again, hooking me with his eyes. 'Mind out for the loose stone on the next flight down. Third from the bottom. Could make for a nasty fall.'

We pick our way down, carefully. When he is out of earshot, I say, 'I think we should keep this to ourselves.' I don't want Father getting wind of it.

I remember, with horrible clarity, when Father had got it into his head that Giacomo was possessed. Someone had told him of his attachment to a painter – Domizio. He was subjected to monstrous indignities by the bishop. He'd been submerged in holy water until he thought he would drown and was strapped down to have the devil beaten out of him. 'And I find,' he'd said, with bitter irony, 'that I'm still in love with Domizio.'

No – I don't want Father deciding I might be possessed. I wouldn't put it past him. He might set Don Tomassino on me. He would relish the task. I grimace inwardly.

Ilaria scrunches her brow, as if carefully contemplating something. 'But won't we have to tell Don Tomassino when we next confess?'

'No need for that. We haven't sinned. We merely witnessed something.' I pause. Ilaria looks at me expectantly. 'We might simply have imagined it.'

'But how could we both have imagined the same thing?'

She is not as gullible as I'd hoped. 'I don't really know. The imagination can work in inexplicable ways.'

Ilaria seems to half accept this explanation. 'But you will have to confess *your* lie.'

'What lie?' The girl is like a tricky hand of cards, always coming up with a new problem.

'You told Olimpio we didn't see anything untoward out there. That was a lie. And when you confess to that you will have to explain what you saw.'

'Well, that is on my head. But *you* didn't lie, so you have no need to say anything about it.' I form as reassuring a smile as I can manage to mask my exasperation.

'Why don't you want anyone to know? Surely if –'

'I don't want them worried,' I say, adding, before she can come up with a response, 'when it is probably nothing more sinister than a figment of fancy.'

We wind our way back through the labyrinthine corridors in silence. The strange sighting has rattled me. It feels like a warning.

10

Time limps forward, and still there is no mention of a return to Rome. My wound knits into a raised pink scar and Lucrezia's headaches wane but she continues to dose herself with the tincture. Nobody mentions it.

The deprivations of Lent give way to the celebrations of Resurrection Sunday. The townspeople of La Petrella process with their simple plaster effigies and the wooden crucifix that normally hangs above the altar. It couldn't be more different from the magnificent solemn pageants of Rome, in which the faithful parade through the streets with the skull of Sant'Andrea Apostolo, the sacred strut from the True Cross and a carved Christ, crowned with thorns, the phial of His blood suspended from his wooden neck, and all the other marvellous relics of the Vatican. There, the whole city gathers, a vast crowd, to hear the Holy Father's sermon.

The Easter Mass is held in the square brick church of Santa Maria. We take the family pew beside the altar, under the intense scrutiny of the hundred or so locals seated in the body of the church. I recognize several faces in the congregation, the girl who does the laundry and the maid-of-all-work, a couple of the kitchen lads, a gardener and, of course, Terza.

Olimpio is far to the rear. His eyes brand my back, distracting me from the service. The choir, a sparse row of boys, sing simple harmonies and the swinging thurible fills the air with a sweet fog. Long gone Cencis lie beneath our feet, their names and epitaphs rendered illegible by age and the bended knees of a hundred thousand worshippers. Inevitably, my dead brothers squat in my mind.

Don Tomassino helps officiate. He is sulking and doesn't seek to hide it. He'd offered to give the sermon and the local priest, elderly and avuncular, had turned him down, so politely, so subtly he hadn't realized for a few moments that he was being refused. He complained about it for days, believed that being attached to a Roman diocese gave him precedence over the rural churchman. Father had declined to intervene on his behalf, which annoyed him further.

After the mass, when we are mounting our horses to return to La Rocca, a man breaks away from the stream of people exiting the church and marches right up to Father. His fists are bunched, body stiff, face simmering with anger. Everyone stops to watch. A woman, perhaps his wife, tugs at his sleeve: 'Please, Mario, no.'

Ignoring her desperate pleas, he presses his forehead almost up to Father's saying, 'You piece of worm-ridden filth . . .' The rest is inaudible.

We all wait for Father's response, as if for a detonation. He exhales like a bull. Someone pushes through the crowd. It is Olimpio, who drags the man away. Father calmly steps up onto the mounting block and onto his horse, kicking it into a trot. We all follow, up the steep path, nobody speaking.

That afternoon we feast on one of the pigs and the incident isn't mentioned. Later I slip away to the kitchens to ask Terza about it. I find her stripping the leftover meat from the pig's carcass, wrist deep in grease. 'He's one of your father's tenants – or was. Evicted last week,' she says. 'Your father doubled the rent. He couldn't pay, begged to have more time. He grew up on that farm.'

I am reminded of that preacher's rant on the day of Rocco's funeral. *While the ordinary man works the shirt off his back to put bread on his table, the nobles sup with Satan.* How I had begrudged his infringement on my grief. Shame makes me rush to my room and fetch a purse of coin, pressing it onto Terza, asking that she pass it to the man's family.

'Don't tell him.' I am suddenly fearful that this will be reported back.

'I wouldn't dream of it,' she says.

I want to believe her.

That evening Ilaria, who is unused to wine, drinks too much and trips on the balcony, crashing into the balustrade with a shriek. Before the rest of us quite understand what is happening, Olimpio catches hold of her, lifting her into his arms and carrying her inside. It is only when I see some of the ancient timbers of the balustrade have broken and fallen into the scrub far below that I realize how nearly she might have plunged to her death. The Easter merriment is instantly doused.

Ilaria is badly shaken. Olimpio lays her on a couch in the yellow chamber and finds her a tot of *acquavite* to calm her nerves. 'You saved my life,' she says, more than once, gazing up at him with her cherubic face, eyes swimming a little from the drink and the shock. He sits with her for a while, distracting her with some story about the orphaned duckling that had adopted him as its mother, when he was a boy, telling her how she followed him everywhere he went, even slept beside him. He named her Topolina.

'But that means mouse,' she says, ever literal.

'I was young,' he replies, with a smile and a shrug.

'What became of Topolina?'

I fear he will say that she ended up on their Christmas table, but he spins a tactful yarn about her laying a clutch of eggs, saying that motherhood cured her of her attachment to him. 'She had her own little troupe of ducklings to follow her everywhere.'

The result of the incident is that Ilaria becomes gooey-eyed whenever Olimpio enters the room and manages to turn any conversation to something about him: an injured fawn he rescued once, his kindness to Bernardo, his excellent horsemanship, his attentiveness. I wonder if she has confessed her longing for Olimpio to Don Tomassino, imagining the priest titivated by her impure thoughts. The very notion makes my flesh crawl.

'Should I ask your father if we can arrange a match between them?' Lucrezia says, when we see Ilaria running after him with the tobacco pouch he has dropped.

'She's far too young.'

'Young, yes. But not *too* young. She'll be sixteen next month.'

'You've seen what she's like. So immature. Like a twelve-year-old.' I look over at the two of them together, she bristling with admiration. 'He treats her like a pet puppy.'

Lucrezia shrugs. 'He's eminently suitable for her – the right class. She's only a lawyer's daughter and not of the first rank, either. She's got no dowry to speak of but your father might provide something. Imagine the offspring – how beautiful they'd be.'

'Father doesn't like her. He wouldn't want to see his *special favourite*' – I invest the words with disdain – 'wed to an insipid little thing like her.' Lucrezia is nonplussed by my vehemence. 'Anyway, I thought she intended to take the veil.'

'I expect she's changed her mind about that. Young girls do, you know. They grow out of it when they feel the first sparks of desire.' She scrutinizes me closely, thinks she's picked up the scent of something. 'If I didn't know you better, I'd think you were jealous.'

'Jealous? That man reports every little thing I do back to Father. Everything *you* do too, probably.' She looks worried now. 'If you think it's a good idea then suggest it. I don't care one way or the other.'

'You're probably right. The girl's too immature for marriage.'
I shrug as if it means nothing. But it does mean something.

The date of Catarina's wedding is almost upon us and I have still had no response to my letters, leaving me with the desperate feeling that I have become nothing but a vague and distant memory to those I hold most dear. I am almost sure, now, that Father has intercepted them and wonder why he hasn't yet punished me. He will. I wait, watching him as he watches me.

I gird myself to ask him about our plans and drag Ilaria out to where he and the two Lorenzos have spread themselves to take in the last of the day's sun, beside the ornamental pool, where the ugly stone fish regurgitates its stream of water. They have removed their jackets and boots, and lounge, drinking wine, stalked by their long dark shadows.

'Ah, Bea! Come and join us.' He pats the bench beside him. Ilaria perches warily on the lip of the pool. 'Could do with some female company, couldn't we?' He is in a convivial mood. The Lorenzos are careful not to look at me, in case their attention is misconstrued.

Ilaria refuses the drink she is offered.

'So dull, this one,' Father exclaims. 'Dull, dull, dull.'

Ilaria reddens and looks at her shoes.

I take tiny sips of the acid wine. Virgil leans his head on my lap, while I stroke him absently. Father watches in silence. An unpleasantly strong smell of sweat and horse emanates from him.

'I was wondering,' I pick a sprig of rosemary from a nearby bush, crushing it between my fingers to breathe its scent, 'if it might be safe to return home soon.'

'Don't you like it here with me?' His tone is clipped. 'Most daughters would be grateful to have so much un-divided attention from their beloved fathers.'

It should be so easy to say it: *Of course, Father, I know how fortunate I am.* But I can't bring myself to tell the easy lie. 'I'm thinking of Catarina's wedding.' I am wondering why I believed he might tell me what I wanted to hear. *Fool!*

'We'll stay here until I say we return.' He gives me a hard blue stare. 'You fuss over that dog too much.' He pushes Virgil's nose from my lap, rolls up his sleeve and presents his left arm to me, laying it heavily over my thigh palm up, as if to be bled. 'How about some daughterly attention for your father?'

I know what is required. I run the tips of my fingers feather-light, up and down his pale, unfreckled inner arm. Veins bulge, blue in the hook of his elbow. He makes sickening, satisfied noises. Ilaria and the Lorenzos don't know where to put their eyes.

My monster wakes, flexing its claws, huge and sharp as the claws on the spotted cat. They slice cleanly through his skin, into those bulging veins, until his blood runs thin and bright. There is a place beneath the ear, Rocco told me once, where an artery runs. A puncture deep enough there will lead to haemorrhage and death within minutes. I sprout feline fangs to sink into the soft flesh, through the sinews and tendons, to split the wall of that artery as I have seen the kitchen mousers do to their prey.

'That's more like it,' he murmurs and begins to talk with his men. They are discussing the Orestesi.

I realize that the older of the two Lorenzos is not the ordinary henchman I'd assumed him to be but is in possession of a fine mind for strategy. '. . . Since yours was the last blow' – I suppose he means the 'reprisals', a dead Orestesi boy – 'it might be opportune to try to negotiate a truce via the younger brother. I have a connection there.'

My ears prick, my hand momentarily stilling.

'Maybe,' Father says, nudging at me to continue. 'It'd get us back to Rome sooner, I suppose.' He looks at me. 'Hear that?'

I don't reply, afraid my voice will come out as the growl of a beast.

He turns back to the Lorenzos. 'See how she manipulates me to get what she wants?'

The older man laughs but the younger, Renzo, seems uneasy and begins to pet Virgil as a distraction. I mark him down as a potential ally.

A cicada starts up a relentless loud thrum.

Eventually Father tires of my humiliation and leaves me. His men follow him inside and Ilaria slinks off towards the kitchens. I languish awhile alone, watching a stork nest in the chimney pot of the gatehouse below, where three stork chicks have hatched. They are strange writhing creatures, more reptilian than avian. At first, I can't make out what they are doing and it is only when I see a small shape fall, that I realize the runt has been pushed from the nest by its siblings. I am strangely riveted and continue to watch them with grim fascination.

My mind ticks with possibility: taking Aquilino and galloping back to Rome. In my imagination it is easy – I know the way and the road is clear of thieves and brigands. But reality obliterates my thoughts: I don't know the way; alone and unarmed, I wouldn't last a day; and, anyway, Father would have me hunted down.

I wander to the walled garden, where everything is flourishing, a cacophony of brilliant colour, mocking me with its beauty. I linger by the pen where the remaining piglet, now doubled in size, rubs itself against the fence, grunting with pleasure. Marzio appears with the kitchen scrap bucket, tipping it in. The creature sets to scoffing with alarming vigour, devouring rinds of cheese so hard they couldn't be cut with an axe, mouldy crusts of bread, old bones, gristle – everything.

He turns to me and, with a strange gap-toothed smile, says, 'A pig could eat a human corpse almost to nothing.'

I shudder and turn away to see Olimpio leaning on the orchard gate, watching us. He lifts a hand to greet me. My insides crimp. *How long have you been there, spying on me?* The warm evening sun is behind him, so his features are in shadow and the wild edges of his curls seem to burn like a halo.

'Hope you're not frightening her, Marzio.'

A few mornings later, we gather in the stable yard for our ride, as usual, to find it is Renzo who is to accompany us. Olimpio, we learn, has been sent to Rome on a special errand. I should be glad – I am glad. The Lorenzos and the Germans will certainly be charged to keep watch for any small transgressions, but they are far from matching Olimpio in vigilance.

The suddenness of his disappearance tilts Bernardo's finely balanced world off its axis. He has become accustomed to the daily training bouts and this unforeseen change in routine makes him insubordinate and wayward. During a midday meal he refuses to eat. Some horseradish, which he detests, has found its way onto his meat and just as I am about to serve him a fresh helping, Father intervenes.

'Stop indulging him!' He points to the slice of ham dangling from the fork in my hand and then to his youngest son, jabbing a finger. 'You will eat what you're given.'

Bernardo's response is to fling his meal to the floor. The room falls silent, save for the hollow echo of the plate ringing against the flagstones.

Father jumps to his feet, chair scraping loudly, grabbing Bernardo by his collar and booming, 'I will not tolerate such insolence at my table.'

'Dearest,' says Lucrezia, tentatively, half rising from her chair. 'He meant nothing by it.'

Still gripping Bernardo, he turns to her, pushing her brusquely back into her seat with his free hand. 'Don't you go to him. He's not a baby.'

'I only –'

'Shut your mouth' – spittle flies from his lips and his eyes flash with anger – 'you useless bitch.' He strikes her across the cheek.

The place falls silent as a tomb.

Everyone stares downwards, all but me. I rise to my feet, approaching Father, attempting to reason with him, but am roughly shoved aside. I am the only one he might have listened to. 'If it wasn't for you' – he is shouting at Lucrezia again – 'I wouldn't have to deal with this imbecile at all. I curse the blasted day I married you and spawned such a creature . . .'

My hatred surges. I wait for a chink that might allow me to intervene. He continues his tirade at Lucrezia, who is shrinking into her seat. Bernardo, seizing the moment of Father's distraction, wrests himself free, and snatches a knife from the display on the wall.

Ilaria makes a petrified gasp.

From the other side of the table I shout to Don Tomassino, who is closest, 'Stop him!'

The priest grabs at the air uselessly.

I rush towards my brother.

Virgil barks manically.

Time seems to slow as, stunned, we watch Bernardo leap towards Father, swiping the blade an inch from his throat. The two Germans, who must have heard the commotion, rush in, one seizing him from behind, the other disarming him perfunctorily.

I reach Virgil, trying and failing to catch hold of his collar.

'Take him downstairs,' Father orders. 'Lock him up until he's cooled off. And someone shut that bloody dog up.' He flails with a boot towards my wildly barking dog, then swings a fist, punching him hard in the head.

'NO!' I yell, as Virgil flies backwards, emitting a blood-curdling yelp as he lands hard on the floor.

He is only half conscious, whimpering. I sink down beside him, gathering him to me, gently stroking his back and whispering soothing nothings, as my vengeful monster swells and protests in my chest.

The Lorenzos arrive, weapons at the ready, to find the silent aftermath of the chaos. 'Take that wretched animal out to the stables,' Father orders them. 'It doesn't belong inside.' He turns to me. 'Does that again, I'll have him shot.'

Renzo scoops Virgil into his arms, with reassuring tenderness. He is a dog-lover. I'd noticed his way with the wolfhounds. 'Make sure he's comfortable,' I tell him under my breath, knowing that to go with him would further rouse Father's anger.

Bernardo meekly allows Oskar and Jakob, one either side of him, to lead him away. He is a child once more, now his rage has abated, and casts a forlorn look back towards me. There is nothing I can do in this moment.

Father returns to his seat, straightening his sleeves. I can see he is more perturbed than he is letting on. 'What are you all staring at?' he says, adding, with a wild laugh, 'Have I got spinach between my teeth?'

Don Tomassino joins in the laughter enthusiastically.

'Are you laughing at me?' booms Father.

'N-n-no, Conte.' The priest shrinks in trepidation.

Lucrezia is still and silent, staring blankly straight ahead. Ilaria is white-faced, breaking off a small piece of bread that never reaches her mouth.

Jakob returns shortly, handing Father a key, which he pockets.

'Don't know why you all look so miserable,' he says. 'Look at the wonderful spread Terza has laid on for us.' He begins to shovel food into his mouth. 'Mmm, delicious!'

I wonder if this would have happened had Olimpio been here. He is the only one of the men who seems able to deal with Father's volatility. Maybe he's gone for good, been sent on a whim of Father's to oversee another Cenci property – a promotion. I find myself hoping not. His absence has upset the fragile balance of this place.

I surreptitiously wrap a cut of meat in my napkin for Virgil.

Once the table is cleared, I slip out to the stables, where I find him sleeping soundly and leave the meat beside him. Renzo has filled a bowl of water and put it nearby. I would sit with him until he wakes but I must see to my brother.

I find Bernardo in the cells behind the kitchen. Someone has left a torch burning in a bracket, which lights the place with a hellish flicker. I can hear moaning, like the lowing of a cow – Bernardo. My heart opens stiffly.

The door is fastened with a large, locked bolt and there is an opening at eye level, through which I can see him tightly hunched, arms around his bent knees, rocking back and forth. He has a bloody bruise on his forehead, which might well have been self-inflicted. I know that when he is distraught he has a habit of hitting his head against the wall repeatedly. I had asked him about this once, why he did it. 'If I make the pain outside my head bad enough, I forget about the pain inside,' he had told me. It is agonizing to witness, knowing that, and knowing there is nothing I can do to assuage his distress.

I try to talk to him, but he is too far wrapped in his rocking and moaning to notice me. I sit for a while leaning my back against the door and sing one of the songs he likes to hear before bed.

Lucrezia comes quietly. She looks haggard. 'How is he?'

I shrug. 'Can't get through to him.'

She has brought some comforts: a blanket and pillow, bread and cheese and a leather canteen of fresh water, which she stuffs through the slot in the door. Pressing her face to the small opening, she whispers desperate words of love and support.

After a while she gives up and comes to sit beside me.

'What will become of him in life?' This question has never pressed at me so urgently, as he approaches manhood far too quickly.

'I don't know.' There is no answer to that. What *does* become of those who are the wrong shape for the world? 'I think of it a good deal. What if something happened to me?'

'I would take care of him.' I don't want to articulate my worry that some misfortune might befall us both and send her to despair.

Our silent qualms spool through the gloom. I am horribly aware of the oubliette in the corner, keeping as far from it as I can, fearing it will suck me into oblivion. I begin to shiver. 'You go, dear,' she says. 'Warm yourself up in the kitchen.'

The kitchens are quiet, just Terza rolling pastry and Marzio skinning rabbits with brutal efficiency. Virgil is on a blanket by the hearth.

'I heard what happened,' says Terza, by way of an explanation. 'Don't worry, he never sets foot in here. This kitchen's *my* domain.' She is shaking her head. 'Bloody tyrant.'

Marzio looks towards her before returning to his work, throwing the rabbit skins to the side, intestines into one dish, flesh and bones into another.

'He ate a little meat,' she says, as I gently stroke Virgil, 'and drank some water. I won't stand for cruelty.'

She picks a sprig of mint from a bunch, which she places in a cup, ladling hot water into it, passing it to me. Her kindness is making me feel tearful as our eyes meet. *Can I trust you, or does your support run only to my dog?*

'I heard what happened.' I suppose news of the incident has reached as far as the village already. 'Your stepmother all right? I gave her some comforts for the boy.'

I nod. 'She's sitting with him.'

'It's cold in there. Marzio, would you take the contessa a blanket and a hot drink?'

Marzio lumbers from the room.

'She's nothing like your mother was. He'd never have dared speak to *her* like that. She was a very strong woman.'

'Lucrezia's so cowed by him.'

'It's hardly surprising.' Terza scoops a spoonful of gravy from a large pie dish and holds it out to me. 'Here, taste this.'

It is rich with meat and mushrooms. 'Mmm. What is it?'

'Rabbit. The warren's overrun with them at this time of year. Marzio traps them by the dozen.'

I have heard talk of the warren in the scrubland some fifty feet below the balcony and can't help but think of how nearly Ilaria fell to her death there.

'It was well managed in your mother's day, when this place was more lived in.'

'What was she like, my mother?'

'She was very like you in character. Strong and independent. Never tolerated any nonsense, particularly from your father.'

I am thinking that Terza's description doesn't sound anything like me and am about to say as much when she adds, 'She couldn't have been much older than you when I first met her. How she loved her food – used to spend hours down here with me planning menus.' She carefully drapes her rolled pastry over the pie dish, pinching the edges to seal it. 'Your father wasn't keen on the idea of a woman in charge of the kitchen. "Over my dead body," he said of it, I gather.'

'That sounds like Father.'

'But she persuaded him. She was a very good musician too, played the lute and sang beautifully. We servants would be invited up to listen on feast days.'

'I remember her singing to me.' I have an enduring memory of a particular song that brings comfort to me in times of difficulty. The tune plays out in my head.

We are silent for a time. I want to ask if she knows where Olimpio has been sent. But though I have evidence, now, that I can trust her – her defiance in bringing Virgil inside and that she never mentioned the purse of money for the unfortunate tenant – something makes me hold back.

'Why don't you take some of these for your brother?' She is indicating a plate of biscuits. 'He'll like them.' His sweet tooth hasn't gone unnoticed. She passes me a cloth to wrap them in.

'I'm worried about him, Terza. God knows what might have happened if Oskar and Jakob hadn't intervened.' A sudden image brushes my mind – Bernardo gleefully pronouncing: *We let the Devil in and there he is.* I sweep it away. It was only a game.

'I'm sure your father can look after himself.'

'But Bernardo . . .' I don't know how to articulate my concerns for my youngest brother, so brimful of anger and yet so fragile.

'I know he's a bit of a special case but all boys of his age rage against their fathers. It'll pass.'

I feel sure I catch a fleeting look of doubt, or something like it, pass over her face. 'Sooner rather than later, I hope.' It is hard to imagine it all being healed by the simple passing of time – that one of them won't end up killing the other.

I take the biscuits and post them through the door of

Bernardo's cell, relieved to find him sound asleep. I watch him for a while, holding my despondency at bay. He looks so young, his skin smooth and unmarked, only the faintest shadow on his upper lip to suggest that manhood, with all its complications, is waiting in the wings.

Before I get into bed, I take extra care to be sure our door is locked. I am glad of it, for lying in the darkness I hear the creep of footfall in the corridor outside and then the quiet metallic slide of the latch being carefully lifted. I lie, still as a stone, listening to the faint rasp of breath beyond the door. Eventually I hear the footsteps leave and can breathe again.

When I drop off, I dream of Olimpio. First, he comes all charm with that dimpled smile, but soon the dream transforms us into beasts of desire, his fingers burrowing urgently, searching out the wet parts of me, his mouth on mine, his salt skin under my tongue, writhing, pulsating – the pleasure of it, the utter abandon. I give myself up to it entirely. But then I become that voracious piglet and he a scaled demon hissing, waving a forked tail, leathery wings beating on his back. I wake with a terrified cry and lie sleepless, unable to cast him from my thoughts. It is like a possession.

I do my best to put him from my mind but images return without warning, sending heat shooting through my body, up to my face, burning, burning with all that lustful abandon. *Shame on you*, some small inner judge says.

As I wait for the arrival of dawn, I consider how I might find relief in unburdening myself. But I can't contemplate confessing such debauched thoughts to Don Tomassino. I can't encumber Lucrezia, who is still walking a knife-edge between her husband and her son. Ilaria would be horrified. I consider confiding in Terza, who seems unshockable, but I barely know her. If only Catarina were here.

I will remain silent. To talk of it might make it somehow real. So, I tell myself that it is just an animal response. After all, Olimpio is, from a purely objective point of view, a physically attractive man – very attractive. Disturbing though it is, it means nothing – absolutely nothing.

11

As dawn begins to break, I rise and creep to the kitchens, seeking the simple company of my dog. He greets me effusively. I take him outside and sit on the far wall, feeding him morsels by hand, thankful that he is well enough to eat them. I luxuriate in the quiet, gazing out at the pinkish-grey daybreak. The morning is still, as if holding its breath and the light low, casting long milky shadows. A lone bird is singing a salutation to the day. I watch the storks' nest for a while, the two chicks, bigger now, a parent standing over them on long pink legs. The other adult glides back to the nest on vast angel wings and the chicks flap and screech and seize upon its regurgitated offerings. It seems impossible that they will grow to be as elegant as their parents.

I can see down to the gatehouse. Jakob is there, slumped, snoring, on the bench outside, dead to the world.

Impulse gains the better of me and, grabbing my chance with both hands, I steal to the stables. In the absence of Olimpio, and Jakob fast asleep, who will know if I sneak to the forest alone before the household wakes? Not caring that I'm wearing only my slippers, my shift and a flimsy wrap, I bridle Aquilino, leading him out, keeping on the soft verges to muffle the ring of his shoes, Virgil padding beside us. We move silently through the vegetable garden and past the pig pen, to the back gate.

The large key lives on the lintel. Revelling in my subterfuge, I turn the lock and we are out. My heart is tight with the thrill of it, as I climb on a fallen log to mount my horse bareback.

The risk makes it all the sweeter. If the household awakes and my absence is noted there will be a price to pay but it will be worth it for a half-hour of longed-for liberty. And I will return before that, anyway.

Virgil skims through the long grass, ears pert, while Aquilino teeters, surefooted, down the steep path. We slip into the forest – I know the way well now – and once on the wide track between the pines, responding to me instinctively, he moves into an agile canter, hoofs thrumming on the hard ground. My unbound hair streams out behind me, the wind making wings of my wrap and I yell with joy, like a hound catching a scent, laughing for the glorious sensation of freedom.

Reaching the narrow way leading to the spring, I vault to the ground and tie Aquilino to a tree, stroking his long nose and velvet muzzle. 'You stay here.' He immediately drops his head to graze contentedly on a clump of vegetation, while Virgil and I take the stepped path downwards.

Dappled light dances on the surface of the pool. The water calls to me. I fling off my clothes and wade in, breath catching with the shock of the cold, mud sucking at my feet. Spreading my arms out I lie back, serenaded by birdsong, floating in the pool's watery hold feeling my deadly tentacles oscillating around me. I am Medusa, striking terror into men. I shape-shift, the fine membrane of my boundaries undulating, transforming, bursting so I am liquid, flowing free, unbounded.

It is a baptism to Nature. My eyes are drawn up the soaring trunks of the surrounding trees. Some are old and gnarled, half suffocated by ivy, others young and fresh and vigorous. Up in the canopy, balls of mistletoe clutch the tangle of woody limbs, and crows' nests snuggle into the crooks of branches, their occupants carking and flapping back and forth. The tops of the trees, I notice, hesitate to touch each other as if in respect of their neighbours, making jagged shapes of the sky beyond. Everything here exists in perfect harmony, all life serving life in its mysterious cycle.

I revel in the wonder that each of these great towers sprouted from a single small nut containing everything that would be a tree: trunk, branches, bark, needles, leaves, and more seeds to make a whole new forest, an infinity of trees. And in my freedom, I am part of Nature's spectacular conjury.

I hear a noise. The crack of a twig. Virgil's head snaps round towards the path. He emits a low growl, a warning. Remembering the boar careering across our way on that first day out, I am suddenly engulfed in fear, feeling foolish for having come so recklessly into the forest unprotected. Scrambling for the bank, I pull my shift over my body, cold now, feet encased in mud, skin puckering. Something is approaching, hidden from view. Virgil springs up with a yelp, to meet it.

I see its boots first.

I recognize them – scuffed toes, worn heels.

Virgil is jigging around them.

It can't be.

He is not here.

I grab my wrap, winding it about my shoulders. It is as inadequate as a cobweb. I could better do with a suit of armour.

'Signorina Beatrice, what on earth –' He rushes towards me. 'What happened? You're soaked to the skin.'

I can see then, from the concern etched over his features, that he thinks some accident has befallen me. Seeing myself through his eyes, bedraggled and mud-clad, shivering, I understand why.

I feel completely exposed, my modesty defiled, my peace broken. Fragments of last night's dream push into my mind, that naked writhing flesh. *Do not think of that.*

'Did you see me?' The swell of my rage is apparent in my blunt tone. Why is it I can't even have an hour to myself uninterrupted? I imagine him laughing about it with the Lorenzos and the Germans and the kitchen lads and that man Marzio, their unhinged hilarity at my expense, as he describes my fear, how I grabbed desperately to cover myself with my inadequate wrap, and the various attributes of my body – my breasts, my private parts – their tongues hanging. He will tell Father and then ... *Do not think of that.* 'What did you see?'

'You'll catch your death.' He has ripped off his coat and placed it very carefully around my shoulders. I sense a thousand questions on his lips. 'I didn't see anything I shouldn't have, if that's what you mean.'

I'm not sure I believe him but am glad he doesn't ask what I'm doing here. Only now do I begin to understand fully the trouble I will be in when he conveys this to Father. I am frozen, my teeth chattering, fingers blue with cold.

Without a word he takes my hands between both of his and rubs, blowing warm air on them as if I am a child who's been throwing snowballs. I want to pull away but instead I passively submit to his touch.

It sounds in the pit of me – my wayward desire.

I temper it with mundane conversation. 'Aren't you meant to be somewhere else?'

He tells me he got back last night and stayed with his grandparents in the village. 'I rose early and wanted to ride up through the woods at daybreak. It's the best time of day. That was when I saw Aquilino tethered at the top.' He nods in the general direction of the path. 'Didn't expect to find *you* here.'

I take my hands back and fold my arms tightly inside his coat, which is lined with rabbit fur and falls almost to my ankles. It has a reassuring smell of musk and tobacco smoke and hay – his smell. He has squatted and is scooping water over my feet to clean them, then dries them on his shirt tails before helping me into my slippers. I would kick him off, insist I can manage, but I haven't the strength.

'I presume you'll go running to Father the minute we cross the threshold.' I sound haughty – the conte's daughter chiming in my tone – while a twist of dread winds down to my guts.

'If we make haste, I think we can slip in unseen. And if anyone's about I shall say I returned last night and took the two horses out early for exercise. If we go in by the orchard gate you can get inside through the back way.'

What is he saying? I don't understand.

'You'd lie for me?' He is behind me so I can't read his expression. We have started to climb the path, and I am warming up with the effort.

'I would, yes. If I felt it would save you from harm.'

I turn then and meet his gaze head-on – those disconcerting eyes. 'Who are you? You speak as if you have some kind of obligation of loyalty to me. I barely know you.'

He flinches as if I've slapped him.

'I know you're his spy.' I turn back to the path. 'You told him I'd been wandering at night.'

'You've got it all –'

I shut him down. 'I don't want your excuses. You can't be trusted.' My dream spools through my mind, making a furnace burn inside me.

We have arrived at the forest track where the horses are waiting. He cups his hands for my foot. In a cold silence I step up and onto Aqualino's broad back.

'You're braver than I, to ride him bareback,' he says.

'It's a question of trust. I know he wouldn't try to throw me.' My tone is pointed.

We make our way back at a gallop, me ahead of him, pressing Aquilino faster as if I can escape.

Where the track narrows, we slow and dismount at the back gate. He presses a finger over his lips as we lead the horses through the little orchard and the walled garden.

When he takes Aquilino's reins from me he hands me a fold of paper from his breast-pocket. A letter.

'What's this?'

'Not here. Read it in private.' He casts his eye over the courtyard. 'There's no one about. Go.'

'But this.' I shrug off his coat and sling it over his horse.

The courtyard is bathed in the warm yellow morning. I sit in a pool of sun to dry out my shift, the last shred of evidence that I have been anywhere other than here since I rose. A few minutes later he comes round the front, wearing his coat, mounted and leading Aquilino, not so much as glancing my way as he goes into the stables. I can hear him talking to Enzo but can't make out what they are saying.

Why is he protecting me?

I take the letter out from where I have concealed it in my sleeve, assuming it will offer some explanation for his behaviour, immediately seeing that it is written in Greek. 'Giacomo,' – my heart leaps – 'at last.'

It is hastily scrawled and full of mistakes, with the occasional phrase in Italian or Latin, where he must have forgotten the Greek.

Most beloved sister,

Olimpio gave me your letter. He told me that Father had intercepted it and that he'd rescued it from the fire. It was half destroyed but I got the gist that you want my help to come back to Rome. You know I would do all in my power to help you, my darling Bea, and I understand that life is intolerable at La Rocca – I've been there, I know what it's like, what he's like. But you know as well as I that if we did manage to get you away he'd only come and take you back, and God only knows what he would do to punish you. I'm not prepared yet to get us both away for good. When I am I will be sure to send word. I'm sorry, my dearest. I wish I could do more. And, besides, it's really not safe here. Someone set upon Domizio and me the other night. I assume one of the Orestesi. He was armed. We managed to get away unscathed. We are leaving for the coast, where we will be safer. Olimpio knows how to reach us if need be.

In haste, your devoted brother, Giaco

I sit in disbelief, trying to make sense of it. What made Olimpio take the risk of fishing my letter from the grate? *Is he setting a trap for me?*

Ilaria is approaching.

I shove the letter back into my sleeve and greet her.

'Where were you? I've been looking for you.'

I am on my guard. 'I came out here early. Been wandering the gardens with Virgil. Watching the storks. Have you seen them?' I lean over the wall to point out the nest. 'See how big the chicks are.' I hope that she is sufficiently distracted not to notice my still damp dress.

From the side of my eye, I see Olimpio leave the stables and mount the side steps leading to the kitchens. I am in a tangle. *Is he friend or foe? How did he know where to find Giacomo?* It comes back to me now that he and Giacomo had done their martial training together. An image casts itself in my mind from years before, of them on the river field at the Palazzo Cenci, fencing with Rocco and Cristofero and a few others of the young men in our household. It was a daily event. Catarina and I had got into the habit of casually walking by to watch them practise. I'd almost forgotten that Catarina had held a torch for Giacomo until she discovered his preferences lay elsewhere. I only dreamed of being noticed by Olimpio. That irony is not lost on me now.

'They're so ugly.' Ilaria jolts me from my thoughts.

'They'll grow into the most beautiful birds.' I force a laugh. The girl is so lacking in imagination. 'Let's go in and find something to eat. I'm starving.'

On entering, the smell of fresh-baked bread assails us. Terza has just taken a loaf from the oven. Olimpio is at the table slicing it. He butters a piece, handing it to me without a word, without even a glance my way.

I take a bite. Hot butter runs down my wrist. I lick it off. My mouth is dry and I want to look at him but don't dare.

Ilaria refuses a slice, saying, as she looks at him longingly, she will save herself for breakfast. From her dreamy tone, she might as well be saying she is saving herself for marriage.

Virgil settles onto his blanket by the hearth, as if he belongs here.

Marzio arrives, grinning, a brace of rabbits hanging from his fist. 'Want them skinned and gutted?'

'One of the boys can do that.' Terza hangs the rabbits from a hook and turns back to Marzio. 'Would you mind taking a look at the spit? It's not turning properly.'

The rabbits, their big dead eyes, upset me, make me sad for the brutality of life. I've seen rabbits killed countless times, am not usually so given to sentimentality. A sharp crack with a cosh and that is it. Rabbit stew.

'What's the matter?' Terza is looking at me.

'Nothing. I was just thinking.' I admonish myself inwardly for letting my guard down. I have become soft and unwary.

'I wouldn't do too much of that.' Terza laughs. 'Get you into all sorts of trouble, thinking will.' I notice tension in her tone. Even she seems to harbour a certain caution this morning.

'Wouldn't you like to get properly dressed?' asks Ilaria. It sounds more like a command, as if still being in my night-clothes at eight in the morning might offend the Lord. The girl is certainly discovering her confidence. I wonder if that might not be such a good thing.

As I leave the room, I cast my eyes for the briefest moment towards Olimpio. He is looking at me. I turn away before anyone can see my cheeks burn hot. 'Are you coming, Ilaria?'

In the afternoon, I watch him surreptitiously in the courtyard with Bernardo. They are fighting – or, rather, Olimpio is teaching him to skip and duck so as to avoid his punches. They are not using their usual weapons, only bare fists. All the swords and daggers on display in the great hall have been removed.

Bernardo is laughing, clearly happy at his mentor's return. Olimpio calls a halt so he can take a drink from his canteen and remove his jacket. They return to their sparring. His shirt still bears the smudges from drying my feet. Its fabric is dark with sweat and sticks to his body so I can see the lean musculature of his back and shoulders and the way it undulates as he parries and skips and thrusts. Desire makes itself known, unfurling deep in my belly.

'What are you looking at?'

Father has crept up without me knowing.

'It's good to see Bernardo back in line.' Can he read the longing in my flushed face? 'Hot today, isn't it?'

He looks at me carefully through narrowed eyes. My heart pulsates. 'You'll ruin your complexion standing in the sun.'

I back into the shadowy interior and pick up my book. He drags his rough gaze over me once more, then turns to leave, heels tapping on the hard floor. I wait to hear his study door close before stealing a last look.

Once alone in my bedchamber, I read and re-read Giacomo's letter. I'm on tenterhooks, unable to settle, too many questions prodding at me.

*

Olimpio corners me later in the chapel stairwell when no one is about, whispering, 'Meet me on the battlements. Half an hour.'

He is gone before I can ask what for. He knows I will meet him. His audacity rankles. But he is right – I *will* go.

I haven't ventured up there since I'd seen that thing – the apparition. I've worked hard to convince myself that it was just my imagination playing tricks, but I know what I saw. What it was, or what it meant, I don't know. If Don Tomassino had been a different kind of person, I might have suggested he perform some ritual, say some prayers, get rid of it, whatever it is. But that is out of the question. Besides, I have a feeling it will take more than prayers from a drunken priest to evict an entity such as we had seen.

I open the heavy door with trepidation. There is no looming demon awaiting me, only Olimpio, glowing against the vivid sunset sky. One cheek curls itself into that dimple as he smiles. 'You came!'

'I suppose I did.'

'I feared you wouldn't.'

Liar. You knew I would. 'I needed to know . . .' For a moment I lose the thread of what I want to say. 'I want to know why you're helping me.' The door swings shut behind me with a thud.

'You don't trust my motives. I see that.'

'How could I when I know you report my every move back to Father?'

'Not your every move. Just the one time. What you wouldn't let me explain earlier was that I did it – that first time – to gain his trust.'

'Really?' Doubt pecks at me. *Don't be a fool, don't be a fool.* I scarcely know what to think. His presence, his smell, the ticking vein in his temple, his clean fingernails, his dimple, his muscular arms are confusing me, drawing me in, pulling me under, like the mud that had sucked at my feet in the pool.

'Yes, really! I thought reporting something innocuous would achieve that, with little harm for you. And I was right, wasn't I?'

If I'd expected an apology, there was nothing indicating regret in his tone. *Do I believe him? I don't know.* 'I suppose so.'

'I don't regret it.' It is as if he can read my thoughts. It makes me uncomfortable, exposed and transparent, makes me imagine he can see my desire for him, those terrible depraved dreams, everything. My skin is burning. 'I want to help you, want you to trust me.'

'Why?' I can barely make the word sound out loud.

He simply meets me with his feline gaze and says nothing.

I am burning hotter and hotter until I fear I might burst into flames. Some of the girls in the convent had talked of spontaneous immolation – a direct path to Heaven. Not in this case. This burning will lead me to Hell.

Eventually he responds. 'Why do you think?'

All I can manage is a small shrug.

'You must realize by now how I feel about you – how I always felt about you, long before I came here . . .' His hands gesticulate gracefully as he speaks. 'You were young, but I admired your spirit even then. Your courage.' He begins to launch into some story about Father's spotted cat and how I'd rescued a puppy that had somehow become caught in its cage, when all the grown men were too afraid to open the door and let it out.

'Oh, that.' I remember the incident. 'That wasn't courage. I was the only one who knew the cat had just been fed.' I laugh. He is looking at me with an intensity that makes the hairs on my neck stiffen.

'Is that how you got this?' Light as a feather, his finger

traces the scar that runs down the right side of my face. 'The spotted cat?'

I step away, out of his reach. 'No. Nothing like that. It was an accident. I told you before.' His question feels intrusive. I have no intention of telling him what really happened, don't even want to give it space to breathe in my mind.

'It's what some people have said.'

'Which people?' I hadn't known my private business was so talked about, and the horrible skinless, transparent feeling returns.

'The Lorenzos. They must have been speculating.'

'They don't know anything. The spotted cat died months ago.' I don't like the idea of those men I barely know discussing me. 'I suppose they said it would damage my marriage prospects.'

'They did.' His honesty is disarming.

'When you've a father as rich as mine, someone will always want you.' I sound bitter and regret it. 'So, you admired me back then? I was barely out of childhood.'

'I wasn't so old myself. You won't remember but I was friendly with Giacomo.'

'I *do* remember. I thought I liked you too.' I realize I have revealed too much of myself. 'But it didn't mean anything.'

He looks as if I've punched him in the gut.

'I mean, I was too young for it to be more than . . .'

We are staring wordlessly at each other. I continue to burn. He breaks the silence.

'For six years I have dreamed of you, waiting, hoping for our paths to cross once more.' His gaze is searching the private pockets of my being. 'And then you arrive here, like a gift from the heavens.' His voice falters slightly. 'Surely you've noticed how I can't keep my eyes from you.'

I don't know what to say, can't untangle anything that

makes sense from the turmoil inside me, can't stop thinking that it is his job to watch me and report back. I remember how he'd appeared at the spring, imagine him hiding in the bushes watching me. Watching. Watching. Always watching with Father's eyes.

'You're paid to keep your eye on me.' I am blunt.

'That's as may be. But every word I've just said is the truth. I know I haven't the right to hope it is reciprocated – you are my employer's daughter.' His tone is fervent. 'But I *know* you feel it too. I've never been more sure of anything.' He begins to recite very quietly, almost as if to himself: '"And, respectfully, he fed that burning heart to her, who shook with dread."'

The familiar lines pull me up abruptly. 'You know Dante?'

'I may be a coarse, low-bred nobody but I can still appreciate poetry.' He is half smiling.

'I didn't mean . . . I only meant . . .'

'I know what you meant.'

'I love Dante.'

'I know that too.'

We stand opposite each other, he holding me with his gaze. I feel seen, not in the familiar way of being watched, but as if he has peeled away my thick outer layer, woven with suspicion, and glimpsed the real me beneath it. I cling desperately to the shredded vestiges of my caution, while all I want is to merge with him, meld into him.

'I've fallen in love with you. It's always been you, Bea.' He reaches a hand into the gulf that separates us. 'You *can* trust me.'

Can I?

A force beyond my control draws me across the void. My hand is in his, his other cups my face, warm, and smoothes over my neck. His lips meet my scar, so careful. Our mouths meet and my boundaries are breached, my heart exploding in a constellation of stars, all my suppressed desire given vent, surging up through me, an unstoppable force, no thought of consequences to mar the exquisite pleasure of being in his arms, of feeling his lips on mine, our tongues twined together in a wet writhe.

Our bodies are pressed tightly as if we are a single being, no border separating us. I feel the strength of his hold, his erection against my belly and myself opening for him. I sense the ending of me as I know myself, as if I've taken a bite of the apple from the Tree of Knowledge and the shape of the world will be for ever altered.

He breaks away momentarily, holding me at arms' length. 'I want to look at you. To believe it's really you.' Gaze heavy as a drunk's, he murmurs my name repeatedly. 'Bea, Bea, Bea . . . my Bea. "To her perfection all of beauty tends."' More Dante.

But doubt slithers into the space between us, a clench of fear gripping my guts. My portcullis drops with a rattle. He wouldn't be the first to learn a few lines of poetry to undo a woman. Had Father told him to test my resistance? I know Father too well, know of what he is capable.

He must read my misgivings as his expression changes. 'What is it? Bea? What?'

Fear drains me. I can't look at him. 'We can't do this.' But I know it is too late. 'I don't know if I can trust you.'

'I gave your letter to your brother, brought his back to you. Does that not show you?' He is good at feigning desperation.

'Did you really snatch that letter from the grate, or did my father give it to you? He's testing me, isn't he? Testing my loyalty.'

He captures my hand. I try to pull it away but he only holds it more tightly. 'What has he done to you to make you so full of wariness?'

'You think you know him. You don't.'

'I will prove my loyalty to you.'

'You can't.' I meet the eyes I have been avoiding, feel their pull and, unable to resist, give myself up to my longing. 'I can't.' I abandon myself to his arms again, having no means to fight my want. I am touching him, pushing him down, pulling at his laces, releasing him, tugging my skirts up and he is inside me. For a blessed moment I forget myself.

When we are done, he turns away to lace himself back together, while I wipe myself on my shift, straightening my skirts, smoothing my hair. I smell of lust. I can hear Ilaria calling for me far down in the yard.

I look at his broad back. *Can I trust you?* I will soon find out, I suppose.

'We can't do that again,' I say.

He doesn't believe me. And I know with every fibre of my being that I am powerless to prevent it.

12

I thought I would understand true passion when it struck me. But this is not something I have encountered in the pages of books or in covert chaste kisses with young men. Songs and poems speak of it as if it is sweet and beautiful and transcendent. But they fail to describe the compulsive, treacherous force that consumes me like madness, no regard for my safety, not a thought for the consequences. I have become devious, seeking out secret moments of contact, the meeting of besotted eyes – *oh, those eyes* – the feather brush of fingers, a stolen kiss in a dark corner. I smoulder with it, with him, with the thought of him, night and day. My desire has its own mind, its own propulsion and I am utterly in its thrall.

We remain alert, assiduously keeping our eyes away from one another if anyone else is present, knowing the slightest look will undo us. We take every opportunity for the kind of touching that doesn't raise suspicion, a guiding palm pressed to the small of my back as I take my place at the table, a hand on mine to help me negotiate a steep set of steps, an arm braced as I mount and dismount from my horse. The clandestine whisper of his breath on my neck, or cheek, or hand is torture, and the more of it I have, the more I must have. On the very rare occasions when it is safe, we snatch a few minutes on the battlements, where no one ever goes. Or we sneak out into the forest before dawn and couple furiously like beasts in the moss and leaf mould, leaving me to pick pine needles from my underthings for the rest of the day. I may have discarded my good sense, but I am not a complete fool, so after that first time I am always careful to use a vinegared sponge filched from my stepmother's hoard.

If we talk at all, we talk only of now, as if there is nothing behind and nothing in front. So, for the weeks of late spring and early summer, we exist in an endless glorious present. Yet we cannot escape Father's long shadow. We both know the consequences. No one dishonours Father and keeps their life. The poor dead girl of our journey here, Lucia, still wanders through my nightmares – her bloodless countenance, pale as parchment, eyes staring into the unknown. I smother all thought of her with the intense fervour of my desire. If I allow Olimpio to inhabit every corner of me, there will be no room left for fear.

One early morning we find ourselves in a new place, an undiscovered corner of the forest. It is a glade, an almost perfect circle where the early-morning light filters and flickers through the thick vegetation onto a carpet of flowers. Someone appears once to have made a secret garden here that has been subsumed into the undergrowth. An ancient stone bench, clad in lichen, nestles beneath a tree, overhung by fragrant woodbine. Violets are scattered over the ground among egg-yolky buttercups and brilliant cornflowers. Clusters of sky-blue forget-me-nots look up at us with their yellow eyes, while here and there are wild orchids, their arrow heads the magenta of bishop's cassocks. An elderly oak, knotted with great woody warts, half throttled by ivy, surveys the scene, whispering gently in the breeze.

'I thought I knew every inch of this forest,' he says. 'But I've never been here before.'

Virgil lolls in a puddle of sun. We spread ourselves on the ground, intoxicated by the sweet scent of the woodbine. I reach to pull at his shirt but he stills my hands, gripping them tightly in one of his. He looks sad or disapproving or concerned, I can't read which, and touching my scar lightly with a finger, says, 'This wasn't an accident, was it?'

'What do you mean?' Discomfort needles at me. I reach again for his shirt, pushing my hand inside to feel his torso, warm and firm.

'No!' He pulls slightly away from my touch. I feel a small sting of rejection. 'Talk to me. *He* did it to you, didn't he?'

The knotted old tree watches me. It whispers with Father's voice: *Whore ... filthy little bitch ... now no one else will want you.* Olimpio has seen the full extent of my damage, so unbeautiful, so shameful.

He touches my scar again.

I recoil. 'You must have a low opinion of yourself to go with spoiled goods like me.' My tone is sour. Scrambling to my feet, I search for the path out of the glade, but I have lost my bearings in the sea of flowers, mocking me with their brightness. I see now the banks of nettles and the thorny tangles of the blackberry thickets blocking my way.

'Oh, Bea,' he stands too, following me, binding his arms around me, 'that's not what I meant at all.'

'What did you mean, then?' I can't look at him, can't allow myself to be drawn back, and struggle to escape.

'You don't need to hide anything from me. There is nothing you could tell me that would stop me loving you.' He lets me go. 'But I won't try to keep you against your will.'

Suddenly exhausted, I slump onto the stone bench, the scent of the woodbine now unpleasantly cloying.

He squats in front of me, not too close, holding his hands open, as if I'm a nervous dog afraid of a beating. 'I have an idea of the terrible things he's done to you. But he can't break your spirit. Your spirit is the thing I love most about you.'

A cataract of bewildering feelings spills through me.

'Have you ever been truly happy?'

Have I ever been happy? 'I don't know. I've never considered it.' He sits and my resistance falls as we draw together, I resting into his embrace. 'I suppose when my mother was alive. It's a long time ago. I don't remember much. But I do have vague memories of summers at the Villa Paradiso.' I find myself telling him about the bathing pool where my brothers would swim in summer, diving from a high platform of rock, where Giacomo taught me to swim. In my mind's eye I see us there together.

'I want to bring you happiness – not just for a moment, but real and sustained. I want you to be content and safe. You need to feel safe.' He winds his fingers through mine. 'It's my calling. Loving you is my calling, Bea.'

I feel choked, can scarcely respond. 'You know him. He'll never let me go.'

He doesn't speak for some time and I assume he is, like me, riven with doubt. But he says, 'There will be a way. We just have to find it. We need to be patient.'

I want to believe him. 'Father will never sanction a match between us.'

'I know that.' He smoothes his hand over my hair. 'We will have our future together without his sanction.'

'Elope?'

'If that's what it takes.' It's not as if I've never before considered escaping but always with such uncertainty. It is Olimpio's conviction that makes it seem possible. 'We must wait for an opportunity to arise.'

We are silent. A bird bats out of the tree above us, skimming up into the sky. Dragonflies waver over the wildflowers. A bee hovers over a clump of forget-me-nots, visiting each bloom, one by one. Olimpio picks a sprig, tucking it behind my ear.

'I have savings,' he says. 'I have family in Naples. We could go there.'

'Father will find us in Naples.' I know his web of connections spreads all the way from Milan to Sicily. An image of Lucia's inert white face in her open coffin drops, heavy as a stone, into my mind. My hope begins to seep away.

'If we can get to Ancona, we can take a boat across the Adriatic to Trieste. I've travelled that route. From there we can go anywhere we want. Make a life somewhere – an ordinary life, together.' He speaks fast without looking at me, thoughts pouring from him.

An ordinary life. It seems so little to want, yet . . .

Virgil springs to his feet, hackles up, teeth bared.

My gut shrinks. His hand tightens on mine.

Something crashes through the bushes. It comes into view, at the lip of the glade, grey, wiry, huge – one of Father's wolfhounds.

'Hide,' he says. 'I'll say I'm on an errand.'

I crouch behind a bank of nettles, stings up my arms.

He strides forward.

Virgil approaches the hound. They eye each other. I can hear Oskar and Jakob shouting in German. My breath is loud – my heart louder. I wait for the rest of the pack. Wolfhounds are bred to sniff out their prey. I sink further into the undergrowth.

How will Olimpio explain the two horses grazing nearby, both saddled, and Virgil? There is no reason for him to be out with my dog. Panic whirs about my head.

I peer through the vegetation and see him marching undaunted towards the two dogs, now circling in a ritual of sniffs. I imagine a fight but see Virgil's long tail waving and the great hound, twice his size, stooping in a show of passivity.

Olimpio ties Virgil's lead on.

I wait for the rest of the pack and the Germans to crash into the clearing.

A distant whistle sounds, high and thin. The wolfhound stands alert a moment, ears pricked. I hold my breath and the animal careers away into the trees, leaving me in a flood of relief.

He comes to me. 'I've been too reckless ... put you in danger.' He takes my hands, seeing the nettle welts up my arms – 'You've been stung' – and picks a dock leaf, rubbing it carefully over the swellings.

After that our times together are few and far between, the briefest, stolen moments here and there – in the grain store, on the battlements, even in the dungeon, the black hole of the oubliette lying in the corner of my eye.

Like magic, forget-me-nots appear, in my pockets, in my shoes, under my pillow. He denies any knowledge, his cat eyes gleaming. Each one brings a thrill of delight, and I feel myself opening, as if he is prising apart my brittle pages, those of a book left unread for a thousand years.

We lay plans. I write to Giacomo for help. We need men we can trust. When we journey back to Rome, they will create a distraction, spirit me away. I thrum with the thought of our ordinary life ahead, keeping faith in the possibility of that future.

'Are you sure?' he asks. 'The risk is great. I need to know you are sure.'

'I would rather die trying than accept this life I have,' I mean it, 'for a life with you.'

We cling to each other in a silent embrace and for a moment we are not here but in another place, untouchable.

We wait and wait, as summer slides by, sustained by the beacon of our ordinary future and our love. There has been no further mention of the truce with the Orestesi, making our return to Rome like a mirage, always distant.

At long last, a letter arrives from Catarina. Father has read it, made no attempt to hide the broken seal. She describes her wedding – *I missed you there, dearest Bea . . . I believe I am already with child and only hope you will be with me for the birth. Despite your absence, and my misgivings, I am relatively content. I seem to have married a decent man – he is kind, at least. I long for your return . . .*

But I will not be returning. I will never see Catarina again. I try to imagine a way in which she can join us in our ordinary life. There is no way. I think back to all the conversations she and I used to have under cover of darkness about our childish passions and whom we would marry. We'd always told each other everything, or almost everything. I ask myself what my friend would think of me now, of my plans. Always more cautious than I, she would try to talk me out of them. 'It's too dangerous,' she would say. I know this. It is not a choice. It is as if the new path of my life has been revealed and I haven't the power to veer from it, even if I wanted to. I don't want to. My whole heart is compelled, by a force greater than me, to follow it. Giacomo's words come to me from far in the past: *You can't choose who you fall for.* Now I understand. When you love – when you are loved – the world is transformed and everything in it.

Catarina and I start a correspondence, letters which tell nothing of what is really going on, letters I know will be read by Father and are designed to mislead him. I long to confide in her, to make it somehow real. But it isn't real – not yet. It is held in suspension in a place outside my life.

'You seem happier, these days,' Terza remarks. We are in the gardens crouched over the herb bed, gathering sorrel for a dish she intends to make. 'You've accepted life here. There's contentment in acceptance.'

'You're very observant.' I register a small inner flicker of worry – *does she know something?* 'I've stopped resisting.'

'It's good to resist a little, though. Your father's very strict and you have spirit.' She looks at me straight. 'Don't let him knock that out of you.' It is said with the intensity of a warning.

I want to ask what she means, what she knows, but can't quite find a way to phrase it. She stands, pushing both hands into the base of her spine and arching backwards with a groan. 'Not as young as I used to be.' The topic is closed.

Half-audible fragments of conversation waft down to us from the high wooden balcony above, where Lucrezia, Ilaria and Bernardo are seated. I hear mention of Olimpio but can't make out the gist. Probably Ilaria waxing on about him. I try to avoid thinking of what the girl might do if she learns the truth about the object of her idolatry.

'Your stepmother seems very nervous and distracted. And those dark rings under her eyes.' She is shaking her head. 'I don't know. She seems unwell to me.'

I feel a stab of guilt for being so wrapped up in my own affairs that I'd barely noticed Lucrezia's deterioration. We had always looked out for one another. I can't let myself think about abandoning her – what he will do to her. 'I don't think she sleeps well. She worries about Bernardo and what will become of him.' I don't mention the tincture – she doses herself with increasing regularity, going about half dazed much of the time.

'With your father as a husband, it's hardly surprising.' She picks up her trug full of sorrel leaves, and we walk back up the steps into the shade of the kitchen.

'Do you have a husband?' I realize I know almost nothing of Terza's private life, had assumed, given the long hours she spends at La Rocca, that she must have been widowed.

'Managed to escape marriage.' She makes a kind of knowing sideways smile but doesn't offer further explanation. 'Surprised your father's not matched you off by now. You're what? More than twenty?'

'Twenty-one. He doesn't want to lose me yet – that's what he says.' The thought of Father arranging a marriage for me sends my panic pulsing, when such a short while ago I wanted nothing more than to be matched with someone, anyone. Now I have a future, almost within reach. *An ordinary life.* I am different – everything is different.

She raises her eyebrows, saying nothing.

Olimpio wanders in. 'Any of that soft cheese left?' He rifles through the pantry, lifting cloths from dishes, tasting morsels of what they contain.

I itch to touch him, stroke his cheek, kiss his lips, press my body to his. I might erupt with wanting. I loosen my collar.

'Top shelf,' says Terza.

He lifts down a plate, uncovering it, bringing it to his nose with a sound of approval. 'Stinks wonderfully.'

'It's a miracle you're not the size of a horse given the amount you eat.'

They bat light-hearted comments back and forth.

My senses are on full alert. The smell of the cheese is so strong it might burn the hairs right out of my nose. My fingertips tingle. My heart patters.

'Don't finish it. I need it for something,' Terza says.

'I think all of that would be too much even for me.' Olimpio points to the pumpkin-sized cheese.

I love you with all my soul, I am thinking, ingesting the sight of him.

'We were talking about marriage, before you rudely interrupted us,' says Terza. 'Weren't we?'

'We were.' I fix my eyes firmly on the sorrel, grinding it into a green mulch in the mortar. I add a clove of garlic, its pungent scent asserting itself.

'I saw your intended the other day,' Terza says. 'I didn't know she was back.'

The pestle slips from my grip, falling with a crash on the stone floor. I stand staring at it and the mess splashed over the flagstones while blood roars through my ears.

'Butter fingers,' says Terza.

My knees give way. Gripping the table edge to stop myself falling, I mumble an apology.

Beyond the roaring, I hear him say, 'Yes, she's back. She was taking care of her grandmother in Borbona.'

Green mulch is spattered all over my dress. He stoops to pick up the pestle, casting a brief indecipherable look my way as he hands it to me. My heart slams shut. It is all I can do to keep myself from crying out: *What intended?*

They continue talking, but all I can hear is the rush in my ears.

'I've remembered I'm supposed to . . .' My words are left hanging as I grapple my way to the door, pulling, pulling, pulling at it. It refuses to budge. I push. It flies open. I half stumble out, palms colliding with the rough walls of the corridor. The door bangs behind me.

I run up the stairs and through the great hall and up the few steps into the yellow chamber, out onto the balcony, stopping to catch stuttering gulps of breath. Distress has rammed itself into my throat. I hold on to the balustrade for fear I might pass out, trying to regulate my breathing.

I notice where Marzio had temporarily repaired the wooden struts after Ilaria's accident, batons nailed across the raw edges of broken wood to hold them together. *He belongs to someone else?* All our moments of intimacy unravel. *He's promised to someone else. What a fool I have been.* He has changed me for ever, softened me up with a lie – our ordinary life – and left me unprotected. *Why? Why would he do so cruel a thing?*

My head swims. I feel sick. How easy it would be to throw myself over. I will hardly know what's happening. It will be a moment of flight and then nothing – a blessed nothing. But the force of rage now boiling up in me, sudden as a pan of milk, won't allow defeat.

I stare into the tangle of vegetation far below, remembering that lamp falling into the darkness, extinguishing itself. I will not be extinguished. Steel threads through my veins, clarifying my thoughts. Not me – I will not be the sacrifice to men's cruelty. Father has made me hard and resilient. I step away from the edge.

'Bea . . . Bea!' Lucrezia's call draws me back to the here and now. 'Are you going to join us?' In my tumult I hadn't noticed her still there at the far end of the balcony with Ilaria and Bernardo, playing *tarocchi*.

'No.' I am too blunt, so I add, 'It's too hot out here.'

'Is something the matter?' she asks. 'You seem distracted.'

I notice then what Terza had pointed out, that my stepmother looks exhausted and drawn, those bright eyes of hers flat. I will not be reduced to that.

'Nothing at all.' I paint on a smile.

I enter the cool interior, mounting the stairs to my bedchamber. As I pass I can hear Father rustling papers in his study. Hate fizzes through my body. Upstairs, I seek solace in the pages of Dante, pulling it from the shelf. It falls open and there is a forget-me-not, fragile and papery, pressed between the leaves. I fling the book across the room. It smacks against the wall, spine broken, and I give way to tears. I have never been someone who cries easily, pride myself on it, have always been able to force away the burning urge behind the eyes, but now I can't stop. I don't recognize myself. Love has made me soft. It has moulded me into a new and unfamiliar shape. *Who am I now?*

Even though every fragment of my being is drawn to him by an inexorable force, my mind a thicket of impressions – the rough evening touch of his chin, the hay and musk smell of his hair, the charge of a stolen look – I manage to avoid him for several days. My shell closes, welded like an oyster that must be forced open with a sharp tool, the tender parts of me hidden again. Father's regime has made me expert at obdurate and stony resistance – and resist I do. When he tries to meet my eye, I do not look at him. When he enters a room, I leave it. When he speaks, I pretend I haven't heard. I make him not exist – but he does exist, as does the malleable inner me who aches for his love.

Seeking to make sense of this new, misshapen self, hidden within, I turn to my books. The poets tell me that love only leads to loss or violence or endless heartbreak, or joy so fleeting as to be barely perceptible – Orpheus and Eurydice, Paris and Helen, Dante and Beatrice. I think of Dante, his lifetime of yearning for the girl he saw only once, waiting to be reunited in the afterlife.

I request that another of Father's men escorts us out riding. I say that Ilaria is 'getting ideas' about Olimpio and it would be wise to nip them in the bud.

Father is amused by this: 'So the little saint turns out to harbour whorish wants. All the same, the fairer sex.'

He seems pleased with me – perhaps he believes I have stopped resisting his will.

Soon enough, though, Olimpio appears in the stables saddling one of the mares. Before I can call Enzo over to help me mount, he steps in. I avoid his gaze stonily, and he makes no attempt at intimacy but presses a shred of paper into my hand and walks back inside without a word. I hang back from the others to read it once they are out of the yard.

I beg of you, Bea. Let me explain. I will wait on the battlements at sunset.

I am determined not to go, but my resolve, it turns out, is not the barnacled shell of an oyster, but thin and friable, an eggshell at best.

What harm could a single conversation, an explanation, do?

I stand away from him, out of his reach, leaning against the door. The gloaming gives his eyes a honey sheen. He looks desperately sad, and it is all I can do to resist submitting to his embrace. I force myself to stand firm, but my guard could be blown asunder by a single sigh.

'So?' I sound half-hearted at best.

'I'm so sorry you had to find out like that. I'd wanted to tell you, had meant to. But . . .'

He, too, is lost for words and we hang in a painful silence for some time while the light takes on an apricot glow that makes him unbearably beautiful. I look away.

'I so feared losing you.' He expels a little sound, half cough, half sigh, his eyes wavering from side to side, resting anywhere but on me. 'And through my own foolishness I have brought that end on myself.'

I find a question: 'When will you marry?' I don't really want the answer. I want to return to the blissful limbo we had once had, yet knowing it is gone for ever.

'It's not like that. We never made proper plans. Our parents arranged it when we were still children. Plautilla loathes me and I don't particularly like her either.'

'Plautilla?' I roll the name round my mouth, spit out: 'She detests you and you dislike her. Sounds like most marriages!' I hate the old familiar bitterness in my voice, hate the knowledge that one day, when Father has tired of me, he will find some man, rich as the Pope, to give me to, in exchange for God only knows what. I had once seen marriage as my escape. I am not that girl any more. I am something else.

'She's been in Borbona for almost a year. I was waiting for

her to return, wanted to free her from any obligation to me. Felt I should do it in person.' His hands reach hopelessly towards me. I step away. He drops his arms, fists balled at his sides.

'You haven't been honest with me.' I feel the stab of tears. He offers me his handkerchief, which is clean white linen, folded into squares. How unlike him, I think, always rumpled, as if he's slept in his clothes. I long to run my hands through that hair, to feel his skin against mine, to breathe him in, to consume him. Denying my love is like trying to force a tree back into the nut it grew out of. It would take a miracle.

I push the handkerchief away and stem the tears before they rise. 'I don't know what made you think I was crying.' My voice is tight with disdain.

He draws a hand over his forehead with a heavy breath. 'I'm sorry, so very sorry. I've been a fool and I can't bear that I've hurt you.'

'Hurt me?' I snort. 'You are just like my father.'

'NO!' He punches one hand into the palm of the other. 'You're wrong. I am not like *him*.'

'Why, then, can you be so cruel as to make promises you have no intention of keeping?'

'I *will* keep those promises. I spoke to Plautilla this morning – freed her from obligation. I'm all yours now.' His tone is freighted with hope.

'How can you expect me to believe that?' I want to believe, so very much, want to allow myself to be drawn back to him, but I am so brittle – dry, rotten, fragmenting.

'I'll show you.' He is undaunted by my resistance and steps towards me. 'I know this isn't the end. We're meant to be together – each, one half of a whole.'

He opens his arms. I am rooted to the spot.

'I made a mistake – a terrible mistake. But I am still the same person who loves you, still your Olimpio.'

His regret seems so genuine.

'It's *me*.' His beautiful face is engraved with wretchedness and love. 'I *know* you – know you want this . . . you want us.'

I feel myself caving.

I am new to love, had no sense of its full power. It has taken me hostage, has eroded my frontiers, rendered me unfamiliar.

I move towards him, pulled by some invisible force.

I feel myself melting into him.

He sighs. 'My love.'

We are in the refuge of each other's arms once more and my brittleness is transformed: new green shoots sprouting, firm and robust.

The tears come now, great racking sobs, every shred of sorrow I have ever known rising to my surface, making way for hope. My love is transmuted once more, to something deeper, the merging of our immortal souls, containing all the joy and despair of human frailty.

The following morning, before dawn, with the household still asleep, we steal to the grain store, making love in the dark, making plans, lingering longer than is sensible. But what is sensible about any of this?

Olimpio has received a letter from Giacomo:

I doubt my father will be returning to Rome just yet. The Orestesi are still on the rampage – or so my contacts tell me. I've heard nothing of the truce you mention. Domizio and I remain here at the coast for our safety. When the return is planned, I will enlist help, if you are sure that is the best plan of action. He will hunt you down, unless you know how to disappear completely.

He seems so doubtful but Olimpio reassures me, reminding

me how risk-averse Giacomo is by nature. 'Not like you,' he says, 'the most courageous of the Cenci.'

The beacon of our future is lit once more and will not be extinguished.

We are about to make our way when the door bursts open.

There is nowhere to hide.

I freeze.

Olimpio stands in front of me. 'Who is it?'

'What are you doing in here?' It is Marzio, the man who unjams the stuck windows and mends the rotten beams, who nailed the broken balustrade back together, who slaughtered the Easter pig, who sees to the mouse traps and bludgeons the rabbits for the pot.

Has Father sent him to search for us?

Is this it? Is this how it ends?

But Olimpio is saying, 'Marzio, thank God it's only you.' I don't understand his easy tone.

Marzio catches sight of me in the gloom. 'Oh, I see!'

I can't breathe, want the floor to swallow me.

'No need to worry about Marzio,' says Olimpio. 'I've known him all my life.'

Knowing someone all one's life doesn't necessarily prove them trustworthy.

'We served together, fighting the Turks, didn't we, Marzio?' He pulls me out beside him.

'If it weren't for this man here,' Marzio claps a hand to Olimpio's shoulder, 'I'd have died in a Turkish dungeon. He saved my life.'

My qualms still simmer.

Marzio removes his cap, offering me a greeting and a brown-toothed smile. He has something suspended from his other hand, some kind of wicker cage containing a creature, a bird, flapping about.

'What's that?' I say, curiosity getting the better of me.

'Seeing to the magpies.' He holds the cage up for me to see its black and white inmate, agitated and afraid.

I turn to him angrily. 'Either kill it or set it free. You can't leave it trapped there like that. It's cruel.'

'It may seem so to you, Signorina.' Marzio squats to test the knots that fasten the cage. 'There is a good reason for this, though.'

'What possible purpose could there be to imprison a terrified creature?'

'The forest fills with magpies come this time of year. They're clever birds. Eat all the eggs and the little fledglings. They wipe out the songbirds altogether, upsets the balance of the place. See, you need the songbirds to spread the seeds for new growth, to control the insects.'

'I don't see how this can help.' I point at the black and white prisoner.

'As I said, they're clever birds. I'll put this one in the forest and when the others find one of their own in the trap, they make themselves scarce. Locals have been doing this for hundreds of years.'

'So, one magpie is sacrificed for the good of all the little birds,' I say. It begins to make a kind of sense but still my heart goes out to the caged creature with its beautiful iridescent feathers languishing alone, waiting for Death to fetch it. I think suddenly, I don't know why, of Iphigenia, the girl sacrificed by her father for a favourable wind. When I read that story, it broke my heart. The girl was promised marriage, and her own father sprang death on her, spilling her blood over her wedding gown.

'Not just the little birds, but for the sake of the whole forest. I should be going.' He makes to leave. 'You'd better take care.'

And he is gone.

'What's the matter?' Olimpio says. 'Marzio won't say a word.'

I cannot describe the feeling I have, like sand pouring through my belly. *Is it misgiving? Is it fear? Is it premonition? What is it?* 'Nothing,' I say, slipping my hand into his, needing, desperately, to feel the warm, dry touch of his skin, wishing I could shrink myself so he could slip me into his pocket.

Summer continues. We wait on. Then, from the blue, we learn that Father has sent the two Lorenzos to Rome to lay out his proposals for a truce.

'I feared he would send me,' says Olimpio. We have snatched a minute in the dungeons. 'He said, "Let those two reprobates risk their lives. I need you here."'

'People are things to him,' I say.

His expression knots. 'I'd like to . . .'

'That makes two of us.' I imagine shoving Father into the oubliette, leaving him to the rats.

'If they arrive at a peace deal, you'll be returning.'

Our future moves a minute step nearer.

Anticipation begins to buzz through me. I feel in the grip of life, every sense alert, everything brighter, clearer, hopeful.

Lucrezia starts to talk of our possible departure. 'Things will be better in Rome.'

'Yes.' I smile, while my conscience chimes. Things will not be better in Rome. I will not be in Rome. I will never return to Rome.

'Oh, to escape this Godforsaken place at last!' She waxes forth: 'Do you think we'll be back by mid-September – the Holy Virgin's birthday? Think of the processions, the gatherings, the pageants.' She seems to forget that Father will be there too.

September is two months away.

On the day we learn that the Lorenzos are dead, the truce in ribbons – our plans thwarted – I discover I am pregnant.

PART TWO

The Tower

13

When I missed my May bleeding, I thought little of it. It wasn't the first time. Unlike Lucrezia, who is as regular as the moon, my menses follow their own path, sometimes surprising me early, sometimes late, occasionally not at all. I'd had no sickness, only the occasional mild nausea, which struck me with hindsight as a symptom of my condition. It was when July arrived and, counting back, I realized I hadn't bled since early April that a new badgering apprehension set in.

'Are you sure?' Olimpio says. His face is half in shadow, but still I am aware of the darkness moving over it.

I nod. 'Absolutely sure.' My hands go to my belly. Its normally concave shape is changed, tighter, not noticeable to anyone but me – for now.

We fall into our own separate thoughts.

'If we can't get away,' he says, 'he'll kill me.'

This is no hyperbole. Father *will* kill him – I have no doubt of that. I will probably, at best, end up back with the nuns. The 'at worst' eventuality doesn't bear scrutiny – and the baby . . . *What will become of our baby?* I pull up my thoughts abruptly. I can't allow myself to think of it as a real baby, as something tangible, as a life.

'We'll be away from this place before then.' I sound confident but I am far from it.

'I wish it were that easily done.'

'He doesn't need to know it's yours.'

He looks aghast, a question forming. I watch as he heads it off. 'Once it's born there'll be no mistaking it's mine.'

It hasn't even occurred to me that our child will surely carry something of its father's Moorish looks.

Dread trickles into me. Drip, drip, drip.

We talk over the possibility of making our escape from here. Insurmountable difficulties arise at each turn. 'It's too great a risk,' he says eventually. 'It is one thing sneaking out at dawn but if we don't return, the Germans will be sent after us with weapons and the wolfhounds.'

'He'll send out word. He's got spies everywhere.' I take his hand. It is cold. 'We won't make it without help and even then . . .'

I am that poor caged magpie, awaiting its inevitable fate. 'I'll be showing before long.'

We are on the battlements. A hawk is circling overhead, wheeling and watching, wheeling and watching, awaiting its moment.

'I wonder if' – an idea is forming – 'if we could make Father unwell. Make him take to his bed. Give ourselves an opportunity to get away.' I dare myself to catch a glimpse of that ordinary life together, holding it tight in my mind's eye, fearing that if I look away it might disappear like a magic trick.

'How?' He is shot through with doubt.

'A mushroom.'

'It's dry as bone, there won't be any mushrooms for months.'

'I have one. A fool's angel.' I remember Terza swiping her finger over her throat and her gleeful laugh: *Useful if you've become tired of your husband.* He looks confused. I continue, 'I picked it and kept it in a handkerchief. Thought I might have need of it one day.' I shake his forearm, looking into his uncertain eyes. A bitter laugh escapes my lips. 'And we do have need of it. Now.'

'Out of the question.' He is firm, drilling into my gaze. 'If the dose is wrong, we'll both hang for it.' He makes the sign of the cross, forcing the stark reality of what I have suggested upon me.

'There is another way.' I am thinking of Lucrezia's confession. *Went to one of those midwives. Some kind of herbal concoction.* Sorrow envelops me as the quicksilver mirage of our ordinary life together disappears, gone to nothing.

'What other way? Do you mean . . .' He stares into my eyes as if he doesn't know me at all.

'There must be a woman, somewhere near . . . a wise woman.'

'Terza,' he says. 'It's Terza women go to when . . . Oh, God.' He covers his face with his palms. 'Our child.'

'It's your life or this one's.' I touch my stomach. 'That's the choice. I choose you.' I weave my pale fingers through his dark ones, desperately wanting him to say something – anything, like, *We will make other infants,* or even some small expression of his love for me, something to indicate he isn't horrified by my proposition.

He appears on the brink of an utterance but changes his mind.

An agonizing prolonged silence falls between us, my thoughts circulating like the great bird above, stretched out in the air, hanging, waiting to spot the slightest movement of its prey, some unwitting animal going about its business below. I wonder where I will find the resolve to go through with it.

'Can we trust Terza?'

'Yes.' He drags his fingers through his curls. 'I'd hoped . . .'

'I know.'

'You are so strong. How are you so strong?'

'I have to be.'

He kisses me then, a desperate, hard, breathtaking kiss, as if it might be our last.

*

'I wondered when you'd come to me,' says Terza. We are talking quietly in a corner of the kitchen.

'What do you mean?' Olimpio echoes my worry. I can hear the lads outside on the step, laughing and ribbing the maid.

'You had an unmistakable bloom on you.' She is looking directly my way. My worry turns to the beginning of panic. If Terza has seen it so easily then maybe someone else has too.

'I have a nose for these things,' continues Terza.

Remembering the Lovers, I expect her to say, *I saw it in the cards*. I had thought it just a game. But I also remember the other cards in my spread that Terza had done her best to conceal. She hadn't been able quite to mask the disquiet that swept over her face.

But she doesn't say that, she says, 'I'm a midwife, after all. I see the signs others don't.' My panic subsides slightly.

'A midwife?' I have always associated the term with birth and joy but of course a midwife oversees death just as often.

'You think I've spent my life in this kitchen when the place has been empty for years? I have to earn my keep.

'Off you go,' Terza says to Olimpio. 'This is women's business.'

He leaves the room, looking back at me briefly, piteously.

Virgil is lolling on his side in the corner. He has become used to life in the kitchens and is quite content.

I follow Terza into the pantry, where bunches of dried herbs are suspended upside down from the ceiling. She reaches for a large bunch of pennyroyal. I have used it occasionally to bring on my menses when I am late. She takes down several other bunches of herbs, breaking off leaves and flower heads and putting them into a spouted pot, with some seeds that she grinds in a small mortar, adding a few drops of an oily substance.

The lads enter the kitchen, joking around, and Terza must read my anxiety, for she says quietly, 'Nothing untoward in brewing a tisane if you have a headache or some small ailment. Doesn't your father like to drink one each evening to promote sleep?'

She is right, it is a commonplace activity, brewing a tisane, but I feel as if our secret intentions hang like a storm cloud over the larder for all to see. 'How do you know it will do the job?' *Do the job.* I sound so brutally plain.

'I've done this enough times before. It's all about the quantities and the mix.' She meets my eyes. 'You should remember that it doesn't work every time. And it can't be taken more than once. Too dangerous.'

We return to the kitchen and Terza ladles hot water from the big pan on the hearth into the mixture. She scolds the lads. 'Keep the noise down. Signorina Beatrice is feeling unwell. Last thing she needs is your racket. There are birds to pluck in the larder.'

They skulk off to their work.

'Listen, it won't be comfortable, and you'll bleed, so prepare yourself.' Terza hands me a cup of the steeped liquid. 'Go straight to bed. I'll say you're ailing.' She reaches out a hand and strokes my cheek fondly. 'Don't worry, love. And don't think too much about it. You'd be surprised how many choose to do this.'

I carry the hot cup up to my chamber, careful not to spill it.

Ilaria is there, folding linens. She stops to peer into the vessel. 'I smell pennyroyal.' She crinkles her nose. 'Got a toothache? My ma used to give it to me for that. Worked wonders.'

I long for a return of the timid Ilaria, who wouldn't have quizzed me in such a way, but for better or worse, the girl has found her confidence.

'Headache,' I say, hoping she hasn't noticed how strong the brew is. 'I'll drink it and go straight to bed. Don't think I feel well enough for supper.'

'You know what it's used for, too?' Ilaria has dropped her voice.

'Pennyroyal has plenty of uses.' I close the topic firmly and sit on the bed, cradling the drink.

'Do you want me to rub some mint balm on your temples?' She is hovering and it takes all my self-control not to snap at her to leave me be.

'No, thank you,' I say. She makes a small, slighted huff, so I add, 'You're a sweetheart, but I need to be quiet for a while,' investing my tone with all the warmth I can muster. I run a hand over my forehead, then round the back of my neck, giving it a roll, feigning the headache.

She shrugs theatrically and goes back to her folding.

I gaze into the amber liquid, gently blowing on it. Its surface ripples. Steam heats my face. It smells strong and earthy. Doubts peck. I wonder if I can go through with it, hesitating with my mouth at the lip of the cup. Which circle of Hell, I wonder, is reserved for women who get rid of their babies? I am on the brink of committing a sin from which I cannot return. It is our baby, the manifestation of our love, a baby I want with all my being, yet don't want equally. I see Olimpio in my mind's eye, the passion in his gaze, his smile and the sudden single dimple that appears with it, giving him that innocent, childish air. Yet he is far from childish. I feel the firmness of his grip, his self-assurance, his kindness and, yes, his undeniable beauty, but most of all, his love. I murmur, 'I choose you.'

'What was that?' Ilaria flicks a glance my way.

'Oh, nothing. Talking to myself.'

'First sign of madness.'

'What?'

'It's what they say. Talking to yourself is the first sign of madness. It was meant in jest.'

'Oh.' Since when did Ilaria make jokes?

I close my eyes, leaning against the bedpost, putting the cup down. I pick it up. Put it down again. 'It's too hot,' I say, to explain my vacillation. *I can't do it.* My mind ploughs through the consequences over and over. It is him or the baby. I *can't* lose him, and the baby is a mere abstraction, barely even the size of a beetle. I am unable to conjure an image of it in the same way I can Olimpio. It doesn't exist yet, except as an idea, and there's no knowing what will become of it anyway. *It's a sin – one of the worst. You are the worst kind of sinner – one who believes she is good. Bad. Bad. Bad. Full of sin. More than my fair share of it. Wicked, that's what you are.*

I take a quivering breath to gird myself. My hand is shaking. Some spills on my dress as I drink. It burns my tongue. A few drops slide down my chin. I wipe them away on my sleeve, where it leaves a yellow stain, hiding my face from Ilaria.

As I lie down on the bed, I am struck by an image of the monstrous floating spectre we saw on the battlements. How hard I had denied it. I find myself clutching my head tight, my face screwed up.

'Are you all right?' I barely hear Ilaria's whisper. 'Shall I fetch your stepmother?'

The girl's concern seems genuine. I force myself to smile and croak, 'No, no. No need. Just need to shut my eyes for a bit.'

'Let me help you out of your clothes. You'll be more comfortable in your nightgown.'

I let Ilaria undress me, then remember I will need some kind of cloth. There will be blood and mess, and I panic that this will give me away. What I truly want is Olimpio, to hold me and feed me soothing platitudes, tell me everything will be fine. I have the grim feeling that I have broken something irreparably, something inside me that will stain our love, wither it, destroy it before it has a chance to be.

'Shall I bring you up something to eat? Some broth?' Ilaria is trying her best.

I reach out for her small hand. 'Maybe later.'

Finally, she leaves and I am able to fetch some of the cloths I use for my monthlies. *What will it be like?* Like a normal heavy bleeding, I hope. *What will it look like? Will it be recognizable or just a blob of matter?* I desperately want Terza to answer the multitude of questions bubbling up in me – things I can't bear to think of. Forcing my mind back to the practicalities, I take one of the big absorbent cloths and fold it over several times, just in case, before tying it into place. If Ilaria notices, I can say I have started my bleeding.

My head spins, making me disoriented and queasy. I imagine shadowy shapes at the sides of my eyes, hear disembodied voices, strange thoughts crashing in and out of my skull. *It's only the effects of the brew.* I slip my body between the cool sheets, and at last allow myself to drift off. I am barely aware of the others coming in at some point – 'Hush, she's sleeping.' My stepmother's quiet singing to Bernardo wafts through to me and the covers agitate gently as Ilaria climbs into the bed.

Nightmares visit me. A demon sits heavily on my back. However hard I try, I can't move it, can scarcely breathe while spectral figures dance around the chamber like flames. My dead brothers are laughing at me. Lucia is with them, laughing the hardest, reaching out to me with girlish fingers – *Come with us, we are the sinners. You belong to the Devil now.*

I am catapulted awake, racked by the most agonizing cramps.

Rocking back and forth in the dark, clutching my belly, I withstand wave after wave of relentless pain, on and on, rocking and rocking, lowing like a desperate animal, incanting silently, *What have I done? What have I done?* I must eventually fall into an exhausted dreamless sleep, for when I next open my eyes it is light, I am alone, and the pain has gone.

Lying still as a corpse, I am overcome with terror of what I will find beneath my nightdress. Eventually I brace myself to look. There is nothing, not even the smallest pinprick of blood. Nothing. Nothing. *Am I still asleep and dreaming?* After all that agony, how can there be nothing?

From nowhere I am hit by a violent nausea and scramble for the pot beneath the bed, retching a few drops of mustard yellow bile into it. I am not still dreaming. I am wide awake and I am still pregnant.

A flicker of something like relief battles my consuming fear. My infant is alive. *Has the Lord intervened? Am I shriven?* A shred of hope beats its way to me, immediately quashed by the reality of my predicament. The sin was in the intention and that can never be erased. It wasn't me but Him who had saved my innocent child. *You belong to the Devil now.*

14

As the days drag by, dread hangs heavily over us. We rarely dare to meet alone. Father has become more watchful, more paranoid, since the murder of his two henchmen. I think of Renzo, how sweet he'd been with Virgil – how casually Father had let those two men be sacrificed. The atmosphere at La Rocca thickens, like the air before a storm.

Father sends me to brew his tisane. He likes me to perform acts of service, says it is proof of my love. I would laugh in his face at that, but slip obediently to the kitchen. The full force of summer has arrived and the place, with its vast hearth permanently lit, is almost unbearably hot. I remove my wrap. Virgil greets me lazily. Terza and the two kitchen lads are clearing up, seemingly unperturbed by the heat, clattering and sharing bursts of laughter.

The larder, with its thick walls and minuscule window, is several degrees cooler and smells strongly of the herbs hanging from the ceiling. I suppress thoughts of that other tisane as I pick a few heads of camomile and return to the kitchen.

'For your father?' Terza asks.

I nod. The lads have gone outside, and the place is quiet, just the murmur of something simmering in a pot on the fire.

'Sit a moment. He can wait.'

I drop onto a stool with a desolate sigh. 'I don't know what to do.'

'I know you don't set much store by the cards,' she says, 'but we could see what they show us.'

'It can't do any harm.' As I say this, I wonder if it is true, remembering Bernardo's gleeful call to the Devil.

'You might find reassurance.' She takes her pack from the niche above the hearth, unfolding the shabby silk scarf they are wrapped in and handing them to me. 'Give them a good shuffle and ask your question.'

I do as she says, cutting them three times, before returning them to her. She asks me to pick one, which she places face down, laying down two more, one on either side. As she is about to turn up the centre card, the back door bangs open and Olimpio comes in.

He looks stricken, coming straight over to me, slipping me a fold of paper, saying quietly, 'From your brother – to me. Read it and then we need to talk about it. Your father has demanded I make up a four for his dice game. I'll do my rounds after. Try and meet me on the back stairs then.' He disappears into the shadows, leaving only the echo of his footsteps.

I scan the text.

In haste.

There has been another attempt on our lives. We had to venture into Rome for Domizio to deliver a painting. Three men ambushed us under cover of darkness. Domizio was badly injured, stabbed in the side. I unmasked one in the scuffle and knew him. He's in Father's pay. I beg of you, my friend, take care of my sister. Tell her this: that the true danger doesn't lie on the outside but at the heart of our family. Oh, God, ours is like the House of Atreus. I fear for us all. It will come to a blood bath – a καταστροφή.

Only the single word in Greek: catastrophe.

It takes a moment for me to register the meaning of Giacomo's words. I know Father is capable of terrible things, but this – to order the killing of his own son. For what?

For the so-called dishonour of loving the man he loves. Questions churn in my head. What other reason could he have? Has he learned of our plans – Giacomo's correspondence with Olimpio? *Oh, God, no! Will we be next?*

Terza registers my distress, saying, 'What is it? What does it say?'

'He sent masked thugs to murder my brother Giacomo.'

'Heavens above!' She claps a hand over her mouth. 'Giacomo – I remember him as a child, a dear boy. Can he be sure your father sent them?'

'He recognized one.'

'That man! I don't know.' She shakes her head. 'How does he live with himself?'

How do we live with him?

I screw up the scrap of paper and throw it into the fire.

The three cards on the table are waiting to be turned up and reveal my fate.

'Let's see what they say.' Terza's fingers hover over them.

'He'll be wanting his tisane.' I rise to leave.

'Let him wait.' There is something about Terza's conviction that makes me stay.

The hearth behind me is throwing heat into the already suffocating room. I loosen the ties of my collar. Sweat gathers on my forehead.

She turns up the central card. It depicts a woman holding open the jaws of a lion. 'There you are,' she says. 'Strength. You will need all your strength for these coming months and this card tells me you have it.'

More questions pick at me.

Terza reveals the card to the right. 'King of Swords reversed. That's your father. A confrontation, maybe.' She seems doubtful. 'This card will tell us.' She flips the final card up, bringing her hands to her face with a sharp intake of breath.

The picture is of a tower struck by a bolt of lightning, the force toppling its turret, flames bursting forth, bricks tumbling, two figures falling.

A catastrophe.

'I'm sorry,' Terza is saying. 'I'd hoped to find something to reassure you but this – the Tower . . .' She seems unsure of what to say. 'A confrontation, certainly.' She puts the cards back into the pack.

'You're not telling me. Tell me what it means.' I grab her hand. 'I'd rather know.'

We look intently at one another for a time before she speaks. 'I see a confrontation with your father. I won't lie to you. It will not end well.'

'For me or for him?' I am surprised at my own question, as if the words are someone else's. Father always comes off best.

'I don't know.' Terza looks down at our clasped hands. 'But know this.' She meets my eye directly. 'You can count on me if you need me.'

'I'd better take him his drink.' A hard conglomeration of dread has lodged itself deep in my gut.

Terza ladles hot water into the tisane pot, placing it and a cup on a small tray, which I take up to the hall.

Father's dice game is in full swing. The table is strewn with coins. He is drunk, his face sweaty. Oskar and Jakob look the worse for wear at either side of Olimpio. Lucrezia, Bernardo, Ilaria and Don Tomassino are across the room, away from the rowdy game.

I approach with the drink, pouring it and placing it beside him, when he grabs me by the waist and pulls me into him. 'You took your time. Gossiping with that witch in the kitchen?' He is in a good mood, teasing me jovially. It makes me wonder if he hasn't heard yet that Giacomo is still alive. I take care not to look towards Olimpio. 'But you're a good girl in the main.' He still has his great paw round my waist. 'She's lovely, isn't she, my girl? She'd be perfect if it weren't for this.' He runs his finger slowly down the length of my scar and looks to the men. 'Don't you think?'

Oskar and Jakob sit in silent embarrassment, but Olimpio says quite casually, 'She's not as beautiful as your wife.'

'How dare you insult my blood?' Father half stands, leaning over the table, pushing his face into Olimpio's. 'You like my wife so much, you can have her. But don't insult my daughter.'

Olimpio doesn't so much as flinch.

Oskar and Jakob draw back aghast. They don't know what is coming next but I do. I've seen him play these games before.

After several moments, he expels a loud blast of laughter. 'You've nerves of steel, man.' He gives Olimpio a playful punch on the shoulder. 'My wife *is* a beauty,' he goes on. 'Should have seen her ten years ago. Her looks are on the wane now. She's getting fat. Greedy bitch.' Across the chamber Lucrezia looks over with narrowed eyes. 'But this one's ripe.' He squeezes me. I suck in my belly, fearing he will notice its thickening but know not to try to escape his grip as he'll only hold me tighter. 'Don't you think?'

'If you say so.' Olimpio plays nonchalant, a cool smile directed at Father.

'And as for you two – lily-livered, the pair of you. I should get rid of you both. Can't even take a joke. They say the Germans have no sense of humour, don't they?' He laughs again. The men, not knowing how to respond or where to look, make nervous laughter with him.

'It's my roll,' says Olimpio, shaking the dice.

Father, bored with torturing Oskar and Jakob, turns to me. 'Go on, Bea. Aren't you going to blow on his dice for good luck?' He gives me a little shove. I hide my discomfort, know he'd enjoy it. I hide my hatred too.

Olimpio holds out his cupped hand for me. I blow. He rolls and loses.

'You can't afford to lose that much. I know. I pay your wages.' Father is thoroughly enjoying himself.

'Then you'd better let me win it back, but I don't want *her* rotten luck this time.' He waves derisively towards me.

Father has my waist again, in both hands. 'What's this?' I hold my breath as he feels my belly. 'You want to watch what you eat, young lady. You don't want to end up fat like your stepmother.' I breathe once more. He pats my behind. 'Off you go – keep her company. She must be dying of boredom with those three.'

Lucrezia is by the window with her embroidery. A shaft of golden evening light spills over her, catching the ripples of her hair and for a moment she is the beautiful Lucrezia of before. Bernardo is next to her, every shred of his focus on solving a wooden puzzle. I sit beside them and, for want of something to do, begin to tidy the sewing box. Ilaria is nearby with Don Tomassino, talking quietly and intensely. Parts of their conversation waft over. 'If someone asks you to keep a secret and you tell your confessor, is that a break of trust?'

'Always agonizing over what is and isn't a sin, what should and shouldn't be confessed,' says Lucrezia. 'Such an odd girl.'

'I've warmed to her,' I say. 'She means well.'

'I'm not sure she does.' Lucrezia looks up from her stitching.

'What makes you think that?'

'If she's so good, why is she tormented about morality?'

'She's only trying to make sense of things that don't make much sense.'

Father roars with laughter once more, the sound of it filling the room, echoing unbearably through my head. I think again of Giacomo, feeling my hatred expand until there is no room for anything else, only that and the great lump of dread. A life is growing inside me. I can't hide it for ever.

I picture that card, the lightning, the falling figures, imagining what it would be like to fall, to jump, air whistling, the ground rushing up. *Would you fall so fast you didn't know anything, or would you regret it and panic before crashing in terror?* I shudder.

Olimpio gets up from the dice game, announcing he must do his evening rounds. After some time, I say I am going to fetch my book.

'You read far too much.' Father is slurring. 'Ruin your eyes.'

I find him on the back stairs. He folds me into his arms and we stand in the gloom holding each other for the few moments we dare.

'What will we do?'

'I don't know.' I can't get those falling figures out of my mind and the despairing expression on Terza's face as she turned the card over.

His voice is quaking. 'He's a fucking beast, your father.'

'Do you think he's learned of our plan? Is that why he did it?'

'I don't see how. We've taken such great care.'

'I should tell you this.' I explain what Terza had seen in the cards.

'You mustn't believe all that, my love. You've got enough to worry about without Terza's *ideas*.' He says the final word as if he'd really meant to say *nonsense*.

I am relieved to be reminded of it. 'I've let it all get to me.'

His hand follows the curve of my belly and his expression hardens. 'I'm working on getting you out of here.'

'How?'

'I can't say yet.' He is steely with determination. 'You have to trust me. And ready yourself.'

'I just wish . . .' *What do I just wish? That I'd never met him? Never fallen pregnant?* No. He has brought so much joy to me, so much wonder, and the baby seals our union. I can't wish him away. I can't expel Terza's words from my head, *a confrontation*, and the dread, huge and unresisting: *a catastrophe.* 'I'm ready.'

'That's the spirit, my love.' He kisses me tenderly on the mouth.

We hear Father's voice booming from the hall below, still ribbing Oskar and Jakob. He begins to climb the stairs, heavy drunken treads mounting ominously towards us.

'I'll distract him,' mouths Olimpio. 'Give you time to get to your room.'

He marches down. I hear their voices as I creep away, Father belligerent, insulting the German brothers, Olimpio stalwart. 'Let me help you, Conte.'

My night is lacerated by terrors and, come the morning, I am in a frightful state of agitation. Ilaria and Bernardo are up already. I drag myself out of bed and into my clothes, clipping on my pearls. They are something of value that could be sold *in extremis*, should the sudden opportunity to flee arise. The coffers in Rome house my rare and beautiful jewels, worth fortunes. But even these everyday pearls are worth an astonishing sum. Before going down, I fasten my collar so they can't be seen, imagining Father – *Who are you getting all dressed up for out here?*

It is hot already in the yard, the sun burning through the dew. I sit on a shaded bench, trying to keep my mind on the birdsong and the beauty of the wildflowers, watching Virgil sniff each of the trees one by one, then roll in the grass. I envy him his simple life.

Ilaria comes down the kitchen steps. 'There you are. I've

been looking for you.' She sits beside me on the bench, offering me a biscuit. 'Warm from the oven.'

She means well, so why does my heart always sink when she appears? I take the biscuit and try to make incidental conversation but I am distracted, my mind churning on our escape and how we will get away safely.

'Don't you want that?' The girl points at my uneaten biscuit.

'I'm not very hungry.' The sweet, cloying smell is causing nausea to roil in my stomach. 'You have it.'

'I need to tell you something.'

Her voice falters and I notice that her big eyes are brimming with tears. 'What is it?'

'It's . . . it's . . .' She is unable to articulate it and takes the handkerchief I offer, blowing her nose loudly.

'Is it Father?'

Ilaria looks appalled. 'No – no! Nothing to do with him. It's Don Tomassino. He . . .' she is mumbling into her lap '. . . he tried to touch me.'

'Oh, God!' I had known there was something off about the priest. 'He tried to, or he did?'

'He tried. One of the maids interrupted us.'

'That's something, at least.'

'I must have led him on, sitting with him and talking to him. But I wanted so much to understand what the Lord expects of us and he's so knowledgeable.' She sniffs loudly, wiping her nose again.

'Let's make one thing clear.' I look straight at her. 'Nothing you did made that happen.'

'But he's a man of God. How can it not be my fault if he's taken vows?'

'Believe me, Ilaria, a man of God is still a man.'

She sniffs again, cocking her head, as if such a notion has never occurred to her. 'Now I'm afraid to make my confession.'

I try to see it from her perspective – her reliance on being shriven of every small transgression. 'I'll make sure you're never left alone with him.'

'Thank you.' She seems slightly reassured, takes a bite of the biscuit.

'Would you like me to tell Father? Don Tomassino will be dismissed then.'

'Goodness, no!' The appalled look returns.

Olimpio arrives, looming over us. Ilaria perks up instantly, like a tulip watered. 'Your father wants to see you.' He looks grave.

'Come with me.' I take Ilaria's hand.

The girl remains rooted to the bench. 'I'd really rather not.'

I am about to try to persuade her, when Olimpio says, 'He wants you alone.' He sounds stilted, formal. I release the girl's hand. Her arm drops back into her lap and she expels a relieved hiss of air.

When I near him, Olimpio murmurs, 'Tread carefully, he's in a terrible mood.'

I follow him inside as if being led to the gallows. I derive some small reassurance from the certain straightness of my lover's posture, his strong, square shoulders and steady, long-legged strides. His curls form into two whorls at his nape, peeping from his collar. I've never noticed them before. There is so much I don't know about him, yet I have the illusion of knowing every minute part of his being.

Arriving on the landing we stop, making a synchronized inhalation, breathing in a measure of courage. I have mustered my grit so many times in this way, after a summons to his study, but this time feels different. 'I'll be out here if you need me.' He knocks.

'Come!'

Olimpio opens the door and stands erect, clicking his heels

together like a soldier, saying, 'Signorina Beatrice is here for you, Conte.'

Forcing my dread into abeyance, I step in, saying brightly, 'You wanted to see me, Father.'

He looks like thunder. I feel unsteady on my feet.

I don't turn to look but sense Olimpio still at my back, as I keep my gaze on Father who is on his feet and coming out from behind the desk.

'You can go now,' he barks.

The door shuts.

'What is it, Father?'

He puts an arm round me, then pats my belly with his free hand and I know he knows. *How?* Fear creeps up my spine as my mind spins through all the possibilities. Had one of the servants seen me throwing up my breakfast in the orchard the other day? Had someone overheard Terza and me when we made the brew? Had the laundry maid been counting the linens? But I'd been sure I was alone in the orchard, Terza and I had been so careful, and the linens are collected from all the bedchambers in one basket, so that can't be it. I can feel his breath on my neck. Nausea grips me. I desperately want to sit but am determined not to show him even a trace of frailty. *Is this the confrontation?* I focus on the image of that woman holding open the jaws of a lion. I am that woman – strong.

'Is it mine?'

I am on the brink of making a horrified denial but stop myself. A chink of opportunity is opening up. There had only been the single plausible occasion, four months ago, on the night before I found Rocco's corpse on the steps – I had been trying to scrub the encounter from my body in the bathhouse, the terrible crawling beneath my skin.

I can make the lie convincing.

'Who else's could it be?' I know not to let relief cause me to drop my guard. As long as he believes it is his, then Olimpio is safe.

He begins to laugh, a deep belly laugh. 'His little joke on us!' He flicks his eyes upwards.

It has nothing to do with God and everything to do with the Devil. 'It's less amusing for me.'

My words are drowned by his. 'There's life in this old boy yet.' He is cupping his crotch, leering.

I can't bring myself to look. Hate seeps from my every pore. I allow myself the fantasy of taking his sword, which is propped against the wall, unsheathing it and running it through him. I feel the punch of my hand meeting his muscle, his thick hot blood pouring over my fist. It will be arterial blood, alarmingly bright. He will look at it, then at me, and back at it, pumping out of him, realizing in that instant that he has only moments of life left. Terror will strike his face, in the knowledge that he is destined to burn in Hell for eternity.

I will dig his heart out of his breast and send it to his enemies. I will slice out his liver and feed it to his wolfhounds. I will cut off his head and display it on a pike above the gates of the Palazzo Cenci. I will send his bloodied jacket to Giacomo and we will dance together on his grave. I will slash the leer from his face, gouge his laugh from his throat. I will cut off his miserable cock and feed it to the pig. That for blighting my youth, for stealing my innocence, for making me his favourite.

'Sit, Bea.' His voice surprises me for an instant. My fantasy had been so vivid I'd momentarily believed him actually dead and disarticulated, the pieces of him scattered. He is indicating two upholstered chairs beside the empty hearth.

I am relieved to sit at last, and stare into the gaping maw of the fireplace waiting for him to speak.

'I assume you've tried to get rid of it?' His gaze is cold and opaque.

I nod, assaulted by memories of that dreadful night.

'I understand Davide Forlani's recently promised, and it's too late now to try to find you another suitor stupid enough not to realize you've been –' He throws me a blunt look, slapping his hand to his stomach. 'Has it been three months?' His fingers twitch as he calculates the passing of time. 'No, four.' He lets out a grim burst of laughter. 'No dislodging the little bastard, then.'

'Marry me to one of your men. I don't care if they're well-born or not.' The moment I say it, I regret it. Pleading is the wrong strategy. He would rather chop off his own fingers than give me something if he knows it is what I want, or even if he knows I might tolerate it. If only I'd begged him *not* to make me marry one of his men, he might have taken a heartless pleasure in forcing such a fate on me.

'My daughter with one of the foreigners or half-breeds that I employ? Over my dead body.'

Your dead body – if only. I am wielding that sword once more.

'No – this is what will happen. You will birth the creature here' – his distaste registers in a shudder – 'away from prying eyes.'

The creature! I will cut out his tongue for that.

'Once it's arrived, I'll deal with it.'

'Deal with it?' My voice cracks. 'What do you mean?' My heart shrivels – I know what he meant. 'We're not heathens, who get rid of infants by exposing them on the mountainside.'

'Don't be so dramatic.' He lets out a long breath and steeples his fingers. 'The most important thing is that no one outside the immediate family learns of your condition. We must preserve your reputation.'

'My reputation or yours?'

He ignores me. 'You will be confined to the upstairs rooms. No one else need know of this. Does your stepmother know?'

I shrug, not wanting to commit to an answer, not knowing if it's better she does or doesn't.

'Lucrezia would *never* dare defy me. We can tell the household you are ailing and if necessary Don what's-his-name can come and say prayers, waft a bit of incense over you, hear your confession. But don't, for pity's sake, get it into your head that you need to confess to this. You haven't, have you?' Sudden alarm shoots through his features.

'I'm not a fool.' But I am a fool and what a fool I have been to believe I had even the remotest chance of ordinary happiness, an ordinary life, an ordinary love.

He hisses his relief. 'We can hide your shape with a loose gown – the priest's not likely to notice anything. He's so drunk he barely knows his own name half the time. That stupid girl can serve you. We can trust her.'

'Ilaria? How do you know *she* can be trusted?'

'I'd have thought you'd know by now that I have a nose for treachery.'

'So, I'm to be held prisoner?' As I say it out loud all hope of escape spirals away into a vortex of despair.

'Don't be so gloomy, poppet.' He sounds as if he is talking to a child. 'It's for your own good. If word gets out about this, you'll be ruined. We've got the Cenci name to think of.'

'What of Bernardo?'

'Your brother can go in with Olimpio. He's much too old to be bunking down with you women anyway.' I resist articulating my approval for this arrangement, or he might change his mind. 'He's a good man, Olimpio. I trust him.'

I laugh inwardly, bitterly, at his misguided confidence. He is so wrapped up in self-belief he can't even see that the man he trusts most is betraying him under his nose.

'And if I need air?'

'You can take the air daily out on the battlements with your stepmother or that girl. I'll post one of the men at your door. Wouldn't want anyone wandering in.' He leans forward and, with his thumbs, presses the corners of my mouth upwards into the shape of a smile. 'Come, don't be downhearted. It'll be for a few short months. Then we can all go back to Rome and no one will be any the wiser. Life will be exactly as it was before.'

I feel a great surge of the inexorable drive for vengeance, furies roosting in my bones, feeding off my marrow. *Giacomo is right. Ours is no different from the House of Atreus, a cursed lineage.*

15

'He knows,' I say, under my breath, as Olimpio escorts me to my rooms. 'But not that it's yours.'

'Small mercies.' He keeps his eyes forward.

I am grateful to him for respecting my privacy and not asking any questions I can't, or won't, answer. 'He thinks *you* can do no wrong.'

'Let's hope it stays that way. I've spent a long time cultivating that trust.' He pauses as the maid-of-all-work clatters past with a bucket and mop. 'When it's born, there'll be no hiding its parentage.' The back of his hand brushes against my forearm, causing desire to unfold through me. 'We must prepare for that.'

'We have time, at least.' It feels like a stay of execution. I imagine the infant growing inside me, the size and colour of a wren.

'And hope,' he says. 'We have hope.'

Falling to silence we both cling to that cobweb-fine thread of hope, unable to see what form it might take.

Ilaria is approaching with a basket of laundry from the other end of the long corridor. As she passes, she drags her eyes over Olimpio in wretched, unrequited longing.

'Meet me in our rooms, when you're done with that.' I indicate the laundry basket. 'I have to talk to you.'

The girl bobs her head, her eyes avoiding me, and bustles off towards the stairs. A certain shiftiness in her demeanour makes me wary.

'If you need to contact me,' I whisper when we are alone

once more, 'leave a note under the mat by the battlements door. I'll do the same. I'm to be allowed to take the air up there each day.'

'I'll send word to Giacomo.'

I nod.

We have arrived at my room and hover a moment at the entrance, both horribly aware that this might be our last sight of one another alone for months. 'Oh, God. I don't think I can –'

'You're stronger than you think.' He runs his hand through his hair, a gesture I've noticed he makes when he is anxious. I have a new vision of our infant, its small head haloed with Olimpio's curls, and I feel my love proliferate, enmeshing me. I am unable to believe that, so recently, I had been prepared to sacrifice it, when now I want it as much as I want its father.

I lean into him, breathing in his smell, committing it to memory before crossing the threshold. The rawness of separation feels like a flaying. He shuts the door behind me and turns the key. Pressing myself against the hard wood, I listen to his departing footfall.

I sit by the small window. Like a suspicious eye, watching me, it is set deeply in the wall thick as the length of my arm. Its glass is thick too, pulling everything beyond it out of shape. The sill is scattered with the small carcasses of flies. This gloomy room will be my whole world for months.

Ilaria enters. The door is shut and locked behind her.

'Who's out there?' I ask.

'Jakob.'

'Stationed?'

'It seems so.'

'Listen, Ilaria. I need to explain what's happening.'

'I know.'

There it is, the shiftiness. I hadn't imagined it. 'What do you know?'

'I know you're pregnant and it's to be kept a secret.'

'Has Father spoken to you?'

She tilts her head and crushes her lips together making a half-nod.

It comes to me then. 'It was you. *You* told him.' My fists curl instinctively, and it takes all my self-control not to set upon her.

A fat tear drools down her cheek. 'He made me.' She sniffs, rummaging in her sleeve for her handkerchief.

I am not swayed to sympathy by this display. 'How did you find out?'

'You've missed your bleeding for months. It's me who sorts the laundry to go down.'

'Whatever motivated you to discuss my private business with my father?' Anger clips my words.

'He asked me to tell him things about you. He said you'd had a dalliance with someone in Rome, that it was another reason he wanted you out here, away from the city. He said it was to protect you.' She begins to sob. 'I was afraid to defy him.'

I am about to tell her it is a lie, that there had been no dalliance in Rome, but stop myself. It will at least serve to explain my condition and prevent her from alighting on the truth. 'Did he threaten you?' I soften, remembering her urine spreading over the courtyard cobbles, how terrifying Father can be.

Ilaria shakes her head, yet answers, 'Yes.'

'How – how did he threaten you?'

'It wasn't a threat exactly, but it made me *feel* threatened. It's hard to explain.' She is sobbing again.

'That sounds like Father.' I am familiar with that feeling. Father is the master of disguising his menace as something benign. It is the girl's inability to explain it that makes me believe her.

'You haven't told any of this to anyone? Confessed it to Don Tomassino?'

'Him.' She screws her face in disgust. I remember now the conversation we had earlier about the priest. 'No. It wasn't *my* sin to confess.'

I can hear the judgement chime in her tone. 'That's right. It is mine.' I'm not about to start explaining how the idea of sin becomes increasingly complicated with age.

She blows her nose. 'If we're to stay until' – she seems to search for a way to say it – 'until the . . . the baby arrives, how will I make my confession? I won't go back to *him*.' Stressing the final word, she screws up her mouth.

'You'll have to ask Father if you can go to the village priest. Olimpio could take you.'

She brightens at that – it had been my intention – and I find a mote of sympathy for her. Being thrown into the Cenci family can't have been easy – and she so young.

The lock scrapes and Lucrezia appears. Her eyes are sunken. She drops onto the bed. 'I'm to stay locked in here with you.' She sighs deeply as if relieved. I understand this to mean she is glad to get out of her husband's bed even if it means incarceration in this miserable chamber.

I turn to Ilaria. 'Would you go and see if Terza's prepared us something to eat?'

Ilaria knocks on the door to be let out.

'Oh, Bea!' Lucrezia worries at the crucifix she wears round her neck. 'I'm so sorry. I tried to stop him, but –'

'I know.' I sit beside her. 'Why you too?'

'Locked up?' She raises her palms upwards. 'Your father doesn't need a reason. Said he couldn't trust me with my "loose mouth". He's likely bored of taking his frustration out on me. Would you help me with this?' She takes a small pot of salve from her pocket, hands it to me – 'I got it from

Terza. She's a wonder, that woman' – and begins to untie her dress, stepping out of it and lifting her shift carefully over her head.

Her back is covered with deep welts and burns, the skin around them raised and pink.

'Good Lord! He did this?'

I don't need to ask, she doesn't need to answer: my back too bears the silvery scars of his punishments. She rummages in her things for her bottle of tincture, dropping a measure into her mouth before sitting in silence while I carefully dab on the salve.

'Why didn't you tell me it was this bad? I could have tried –'

'Keep your voice down.' She indicates the door and the invisible guard in the corridor. 'I don't want them all discussing it. Our private lives. And you know well enough, Bea, that there's no reasoning with him.' Her tone is replete with exhausted despair. 'If it hadn't been me, it would have been you – again.'

I feel a pang of desperate guilt for having shored myself up so firmly, with Bernardo and Ilaria sleeping here in my room, making sure I was never alone, that the door was always locked. It was all at the expense of my stepmother. I remember the terrible sounds I heard so often emanating from the bedchamber below. I should have known. I should have done something. *What could I have done?* I try not to think that there is nothing stopping Father entering this room at night now I no longer have the key and resolve to push one of the heavy chests across the door when we go to bed.

'I curse the day I ever agreed to become his wife.' I detect a new resilience in her. 'I'm worried for Bernardo with neither of us around. After that business with the knife.'

'Olimpio will keep an eye on him.' I try to keep my voice neutral, afraid that even mentioning my lover's name might reveal my secret. Though I trust Lucrezia completely, I don't want to burden her with the truth.

'Thank Heaven for Olimpio.' She winces as I carefully smooth the salve on one of her deeper wounds. The strong scent of mint conjures the outdoors, making me feel all the more entrapped. 'You know your father promised Ilaria she could wed him if she keeps her mouth shut about all this.'

'Wed Olimpio?' I am trying my very best to keep the shock from my voice. Even so, something must register in my tone as she turns to me with an enquiring sideways look. So, this is why Father feels so sure of Ilaria's loyalty. 'So much for her vocation.' What was it she'd said when asked if Father had threatened her? *It wasn't a threat exactly*. I suppose that wasn't a lie exactly, either, but it skimmed close to one. She will *have* to lie. Father will make her tell everyone I am unwell to explain my imprisonment. I suppose the allure of Olimpio is sufficient to make her ready to stain herself with deceit. I wonder how she reconciles *that* with her God. All the fuss and tears she'd made about her confession – the little hypocrite. 'I thought he was betrothed to a woman in the village.'

'It's unlikely your father would see a village betrothal as an obstacle.'

'Has he consulted Olimpio about this arrangement?' I replace the lid on the salve.

'I doubt it. Doubt he even means it.' She tips her head, eyes questioning, pulling herself up to sit. 'Why do you care so much?'

'No reason.' I affect my best indifference, busying myself in search of something to cover her wounds.

'I don't think it'd be a bad thing. Quite like to see the back of that girl.'

'She's harmless,' I say, wondering if this is really so, finding a length of muslin, ripping it into strips.

'Is she?' Lucrezia's tone is pointed but then she adds, 'Perhaps I'm being unfair.' She shifts, stretching herself. Her eyes are beginning to droop – the effect of the tincture.

I dress her wounds with gauze and bandages. 'You know Don Tomassino tried to get beneath her skirts.'

'He *didn't*! The filthy worm.' Lucrezia grimaces. 'He's a cousin of your father, isn't he? Must run in the family.' She gives a scornful little laugh.

'I suppose we should have seen it coming.' I help her into a clean shift and then a loose robe. 'Are you more comfortable now?'

'Much better, thank you.' She takes out her embroidery and sits in a daze, not sewing but staring into space while I read aloud until Ilaria returns with a tray of food.

She places it on the table and removes its cloth covering to reveal a jug of ale, a platter of hams, sausage and cheeses, with bread still warm from the oven and a bowl of oranges. We won't go hungry, at least, as long as Terza's in the kitchen. I seek out advantages of my imprisonment, one being that I won't have to sit at the table with Father. I try to avoid pondering on the stretch of months ahead, my body expanding while my situation tightens about me, my chances of escape diminishing. I have to keep faith that Olimpio and Giacomo will come up with a plan.

Lucrezia asks Ilaria to fetch the *tarocchi* cards, and while she is gone, I take the opportunity to explain the contents of Giacomo's latest letter.

'Tried to have him killed?' She is aghast. 'His own son? Are you sure? How did it reach you, the letter?'

'It was addressed to Olimpio. He brought it to me.'

'Oh, yes. They're friends, aren't they? I'd forgotten.'

'I don't remember. Didn't ask,' I lie. 'I was just glad to hear from Giacomo.'

'Well!' She raises her eyebrows. 'He's a dark horse, that Olimpio. I thought he was your father's faithful pet.'

Thankfully Ilaria returns with the cards, putting an end to the conversation. I will have to confide in Lucrezia at some point. But not yet. Only when a plan begins to form. Whenever I think about how such a plan might take shape, I am headed off at every path. My conscience pricks at the thought of leaving Lucrezia now I've witnessed the results of Father's most recent assaults.

Ilaria tips out the bag of buttons, sorting them into colours for us to bet with and distributing them. I stoke the fire and light a candle while Lucrezia shuffles the cards, dealing one to each of us. 'To see who starts.'

We all throw our cards into the centre face up. There it is again, the toppling edifice, those small, tumbling figures. Momentarily, in some trick of the imagination, I see Father there, dropping like a stone.

'All right?' Lucrezia locks her gaze on me. 'You look as if someone walked over your grave.'

'No – it's nothing.'

Something crashes into the fireplace, startling us, dousing the flames.

Ilaria makes a small cry. 'What was that?'

We sit suspended in a thick silence, listening to a hissing from the direction of the hearth. Lucrezia's breath is unsteady.

I take the candle, crossing the room, to find a cascade of black ash has fallen into the grate, the fine remnants still trickling down, like sand running through some hellish hourglass.

We are all on edge.

16

Time presses, harder and harder. Ascension Day passes and August crawls towards its blistering end, while we swelter incarcerated under the watching eye of the small window. I yearn for Olimpio, aching for the slightest glimpse of him, relishing the rare occasions when Father hasn't need of him elsewhere and he is assigned to accompany me to the battlements. We wait for Giacomo to write with news that he has mustered men to help us get away. Escape becomes increasingly difficult to imagine, so my mind turns on other outcomes.

Mercifully there have been no night visits from Father, though I have heard footfall outside the door several times – probably one of the Germans, but maybe not. I wonder which of the servants is receiving his unwanted attentions. I try to count the small mercies dropped like crumbs into our miserable situation: Lucrezia's burns have healed and she seems in better health, though still I see her dosing herself surreptitiously with tincture when she thinks my back is turned. I say nothing. We all do what is necessary to maintain our sanity.

The baby grows. My belly is distended, but not noticeably so when I am dressed. I feel it quickening, like the popping of a bubble, or the minute flutter of a sea-creature. I think of the medusa. Lucrezia says, 'Now it has a soul.'

She never mentions the infant's genesis, or what she believes its genesis to be, and simply seems delighted at the idea of the child. 'Oh, a baby is a blessing, indeed.' Father must not have told her about dealing with it. I don't say anything.

It is early September when I find a letter under the mat on the battlements. I am no longer closely guarded up here. The only route out is off the crenellated wall into the abyss and the heat is brutal, so whichever of the Germans is with me tends to stay in the shaded stairwell, while I pace back and forth in the blazing sun. Lucrezia rarely joins me, and Ilaria never does.

It is barely a letter, just a few lines from Giacomo, in Greek: *You know the only way out of this, Bea. Make it seem accidental. I can send a poison that leaves no trace. I can come if you need. Just send word.*

I know he is right. That thought has been percolating beneath my surface for weeks. I doubt myself capable of such an act. I have agonized over it warily, as if the idea alone might thrust me to the depths of the underworld. Patricide – even Dante hadn't imagined a circle of Hell for those who kill their fathers. I don't want Giacomo to come. Why involve him if it isn't essential?

Later in the day Ilaria bursts into our chamber, distraught, her white apron spotted with blood. 'Bernardo and the conte came to blows again.' She is shaking and stuttering. 'It was terrible, truly terrible. He upturned the table. I thought he would kill him.'

'Who was hurt?' I have a vision of Father bleeding out on the flagstones.

'Bernardo's nose is broken.' She indicates her apron, to explain the blood.

'And Father?' I find I am holding my breath.

'In his study. He lost a tooth.' Ilaria is calming down. 'He's in a terrible rage and Bernardo's back in the cells.'

'Is he all right? Has he been tended?' Lucrezia is fraught.

'Terza's looking after him.'

'Where was Olimpio? Couldn't he stop it?'

Ilaria looks at me. 'He can't watch Bernardo day and night.' She has a certain possessive petulance in her voice, reminding me she is under the misapprehension that Olimpio will one day be hers.

The news of Bernardo galvanizes me to confide in Lucrezia.

'I had a letter from Giacomo,' I tell her when we are alone.

'What did it say? Show me.'

'You wouldn't be able to read it. It's in Greek.'

'So, tell me.'

As I translate aloud, Lucrezia's expression falls to disbelief. She sits for an infernal moment shaking her head wordlessly. I am waiting for her to say, *We can't do that*, or *We'd be damned*, or, at the very least, *I don't know*.

But what she says is, 'He's right.' She wears a ghoulish face, staring eyes, pupils hugely enlarged, which I've come to learn is one of the effects of the tincture. 'I know I can't cope with any more.' She covers her face with her hands for a long moment. 'It'll be a while before we can get word to Giacomo and for him to get here from the coast. Too long, do you think? He'll kill Bernardo, first, and you'll be birthing come November. We need to take that into consideration.' I wonder if she hasn't also been thinking of this eventuality for some time.

'December, actually, perhaps even January.' It is time to tell her the truth.

'I don't see how . . . Here? I'd thought . . .' She is counting back the months on her fingers.

'Olimpio's the father.'

'Oh, Lord!' She scrutinizes me.

'Don't,' I snap. 'Don't say what you're thinking. That I am shameless.'

'I wasn't . . .' We look at each other without speaking for quite some time. 'Who am I to judge? If any of us is shameless it's your father. I thought you were small. Was worried the baby wasn't growing. Been considering all sorts of . . . you know.'

I *do* know.

'It'll be a beautiful child, if it's his.' It is such an oddly frivolous thing for her to say, but she seems still to be trying to understand how this could have happened.

'It means he'll help us do it.' *It* – a small word for a vast deed.

'But we're not really going to, are we? We're just talking, aren't we?' She is cupping her throat with her palm, as if she'd felt the slice of a knife through it.

'I'm not just talking.' I'm surprised at how steady I sound, how sure. 'This is what we'll do.' I take the mushroom from my coffer, carefully unwrapping its linen shroud and holding it out.

'What is it?' Her bewilderment is almost palpable.

I explain that I'd picked it months ago, on that first day out in the forest, and kept it. I wonder if I'd been responding to some unexpressed murderous impulse even back then. 'I'll ask Ilaria to bring up a charcoal burner from the kitchens and some herbs, tell her we want to brew our own tisanes. I'll disguise the taste with verbena and mint.' The idea emerges from me fully formed. 'Olimpio can take charge of administering it.' I think about them rolling dice in the evening, Father, half drunk, sipping his bedtime tisane oblivious that it will be his last. 'And it will be done.'

'Bea.' Her expression of admiration collapses into one of horror.

I hold firm. 'If we're to do it, we must do it and not think too much about it.'

Now I have made the decision that Father must die, my apprehension and my sentiment fall away. It makes sense to me, the notion of one life being lost to save several – it holds an essential moral logic.

We might have silently cogitated on it, or talked of it for

months without acting, until it was too late. But time is running out. My baby will be born, come what may. I had seen the diagram, long ago, in a book in Father's library. A woman butchered through the middle, all her insides exposed, her intestines coiled, an infant folded into her open womb. At the side was a column of pictures – creatures, each corresponding to the size the child would be at any given month. My baby, who had been the size of a beetle, then a bumblebee a few short weeks ago, a shrew, a dormouse, followed by a wren, a blackbird, now a pigeon, next month a squirrel, then a hare and eventually a fox, will be born and it will be real and human – and I will have to protect it. I will not have my child live even a moment under Father's tyranny, as I have, as have all my siblings, as have all who come within his orbit.

'Why did you keep it?' Lucrezia points at the mushroom in its bed of linen, a thing once so alluring, pure white, luminous, deadly, reduced to a withered scrap of matter with the appearance of an old fragment of rag – still equally deadly. Her hand is shaking, her mouth tight and misarranged.

'I don't know.' I feel the scrutiny of the window's eye. It comes to me that somewhere deep down, so deep I am barely aware, I have always known – known I would have to do this – that Fate is driving me to bring an end to the curse of my family. It is I who is destined to take revenge, who is possessed by that fury.

Him or me. Him or my child. Him or my love.

The vengeful creature inside me is licking its chops. I have not been made strong-willed for no purpose. Strength is in my nature. I am the woman holding the lion's jaws open, driven by some higher power, some ancient goddess of natural order, to right all the wrongs stitched into the weft of my family. I had picked the mushroom for exactly this purpose.

My intention is heroic. Even if it is a crime in the law, even if it is deemed a sin – the worst sin – I know it is for a higher good. I consider men like Don Tomassino and his ilk, casting shame on others but not themselves, men like the crooked bishops and cardinals, who drape their lives in gold yet preach humility and poverty as the path to Heaven. If they are the lawmakers, then the law is as corrupt as they.

'But we can't.' My stepmother's beautiful eyes, those eyes the painters begged to depict, brim with dread.

'One day he'll go too far. You've said it yourself – he'll kill Bernardo or you. Both of you, perhaps. He's tried to have Giacomo killed. The moment this infant is birthed, Olimpio will be a dead man, our child too. I'd rather not think of what will become of me.'

'Oh, God.' She inhales a trembling breath, cradling her head in her hands. 'It's the only way out, isn't it? We have no choice.'

The key scrapes in the lock. I hide the mushroom in my sleeve. It is Ilaria with our evening meal. The girl is fidgety, smiling to herself. I feel a little sorry for her, oblivious of what is about to happen. We try to converse normally about the food, about the weather, about what book we will read this evening, what card game we will play, an almost impossible task when the world has been turned inside out, its guts on view.

'You seem happy,' I say to Ilaria.

'I'm to be married.' She claps a hand over her mouth. 'I wasn't supposed to tell.'

'Don't worry, we won't say anything. Will we?' I look at Lucrezia.

'Who could we tell, imprisoned in here?' Lucrezia sweeps an arm theatrically around the space. 'Who's the lucky man?'

'I can't say – might get into trouble. It won't be just yet anyway.' She is making small, smug, twisting movements with her torso. 'But I'm promised.'

'Promised? I wish you very well.' I make myself smile. 'Would you mind running an errand for me?'

'Of course,' she says.

'Could you please bring some things from the kitchens?' I explain about wanting to brew tisanes, all the while forming my plan. I will alert Olimpio with an explanatory note, find out when he will next be stationed at our door.

In the event, Providence appears to be on our side, as Olimpio is assigned to accompany me to the battlements the following morning. The German brothers have taken the wolfhounds out.

We snatch an embrace, leaning against the door in case we are disturbed, and I rest my head on his chest, enveloped in his scent. The beat of his heart thrums into me. It is comforting, in a base, instinctive way, as a bitch's heartbeat comforts her whelps. He reaches to me with his feline gaze. We are drawn together, slowly, longingly, our mouths hovering, almost touching, until we sink into a kiss so deep it obliterates everything. It is just him and me, the taste of him, the smell, my arousal writhing, his hardness pressed against my hip. I push into him. He groans. We are suspended in time. Even the impossible seems possible.

He is the first to pull away, urgent, business-like. 'What did your brother's letter say?'

'He said what we already know.' I find I can't form the actual words: *we must kill him*.

'What do we already know?'

I want to return to that kiss, to feel him inside me, flesh enveloping flesh.

'That there's only one way out of this.'

'He's right.' A tight little knot forms between his brows and he drags his fingers through his hair, looking out into the blue distance. He understands.

The hawk is wheeling.

'Remember the fool's angel?' I explain the plan. 'I'm relying on you to make sure he drinks it. Are you up to that?'

A little tic starts in his jaw. He doesn't say anything. The air is almost completely still, and the heat creates a shimmering haze over the valley. A deer barks in the forest.

'Yes,' he says eventually. He seems invested with new impenetrable steel. It frightens me a little. 'Any misgivings?'

'Strangely, no,' I reply. 'I feel as if some force is driving me – as if I'm meant to do this.'

He looks at me as if I am an imposter in the skin of his beloved Beatrice.

'You?' I say.

'Misgivings – no.' His look pierces. I feel it in my groin. 'It would be simpler if *I* were to make the tisane.'

'I'd prefer it this way.' I want to be the one to do this, to take the responsibility on my own shoulders, the darkest part of the sin on my conscience. If I am the one to concoct the brew, I tell myself, the others will be free of the guilt. But guilt can seep into even the smallest of fissures, through the pinhole of a broken promise, through the crack of a white lie, through the small rupture of a minor transgression or a bad thought or a wicked intention. Guilt is not only reserved for the worst of the sinners.

'I'll make it,' I continue, 'and you can come and get it from me. You can tell him I wanted to prepare his drink, as I used to. That I miss doing it for him.' I imagine him swelling with pleasure at the idea of his fallen favourite daughter desperate to please him. I know him so very well, almost as well as I know myself. 'He'll enjoy that.'

'You are wicked.' He kisses me on the mouth, so hard it takes my breath.

You are wicked – a memory of that terrible apparition assails me.

'I saw something up here, back in the spring.' I catch a frisson of the fear I'd felt then – a lifetime ago – as if the bottom is dropping out of me.

'What kind of something?'

I don't know how to explain it. 'It was like a visitation, a vast ghoulish demon hovering in a ring of fire. Some kind of fury.' I can't bring myself to express the way I'd felt possessed by it, that it had invested me with the lust for vengeance.

'Was it misty?'

'What do you mean?' I don't understand his question. 'It *was* misty, as it happens.'

He lets out an unexpected laugh. 'You weren't visited by a demon, my love. It was a trick of the light. When the sun's low behind you, it casts your shadow onto the mist. I've seen it a few times up here at sunset when the fog rolls in from the valley. I must confess, the first time I took fright, until I realized it was mimicking my own movements.' He laughs again. 'That wasn't a fury, it was you. A shadow cast on the mist.' He is smiling. 'That's all it was.'

'A trick of the light.' I am thinking how easy it is to believe in a fallacy; spill out a small laugh. 'Ilaria was even more frightened than me.'

'Didn't I see you then? The pair of you looked petrified, I remember, Ilaria particularly.'

We are both laughing now, forgetting for a moment the thing we are going to do, the predicament we are in. But my laughter dies with the thought that now I can't tell myself I am being driven to this by some outside force, that terrible spectre, that it *must* come from me, from within, from the pitch-black place deep inside.

I am my father's daughter. If I weren't, this wouldn't be happening.

'That girl would be scared of a butterfly if it flew too close.'

He is still talking of Ilaria, not noticing that my humour has deserted me.

I can't let him see – not even he, to whom I have bared my soul – into that dark place. I force a look of levity. 'Wouldn't say boo to a goose.' I recall, suddenly now, Ilaria's hoped-for marriage. 'Did Father tell you he promised you to her? That that was how he bought her silence?'

'Heavens above! That poor girl. Your father's a truly wicked man.' His eyes spit rage. 'By tomorrow we'll be free of him.'

'Tomorrow.' If I had doubted it before, I know now that he will be able to do what is needed. 'The baby's moving. Here, feel.' I pull aside my dress, guiding his hand to the place.

His expression opens in wonderment. 'A fluttering – is that it?' He bends forward to kiss it. 'Our baby.' He scatters kisses over my taut skin. 'Oh, my love. This makes it real . . . makes our future real.'

I close my eyes, try to picture our ordinary life together with our child. If only I could put it in my mind and hold it there – but his words bleed through the image: *you are wicked*.

'Tomorrow,' I say again, forcing my thoughts on to the immediate future. It is all I can be sure of.

We descend the spiral tower steps. *Tomorrow. Tomorrow. Tomorrow.* When we arrive at the door to my prison, I ask, 'How's Bernardo?'

'He's calmed a little. But he was in a terrible state. Kept saying he'd kill your father with his bare hands. To be honest, I'm glad he's locked up for fear of what might happen.'

He opens the door.

'Later,' I whisper.

'Later.'

17

'What's the matter with him?' Ilaria is uneasy.

A terrible moaning is coming from the room below – Father's bedchamber. It is a grim echo of my own night of agony after Terza's brew and I cannot pull my thoughts away from how much greater my burden of sin has become since then.

'I can't imagine,' says Lucrezia. 'What did he have for supper?'

'We had rabbit stew,' says Ilaria. 'We all ate it. But he did eat a lot of mortadella and cheese.'

'I expect the mortadella had turned.' Lucrezia nudges me in the dark. 'You can never be sure in this weather.' She sounds as horrified as I at what we have made happen. We haven't talked of it, dare not bring into the light of our own scrutiny the consequences of having crossed a line so deep.

The three of us are sharing the big bed. Bernardo is back on the couch in the corner, sleeping through the noise. I'd asked Olimpio to release him from the cell once Father had retired to his chamber. I couldn't bear the thought of him spending even one more night in that damp, airless place with the oubliette, hungry for souls, in the corner. We have had to pretend to Ilaria it was Father's command that he be locked up with us.

The poor boy has two black eyes and his nose is swollen completely out of shape with a visible break on its bridge. Bruising, like storm clouds of purple and bilious yellow, covers his torso. I wanted to ask him what had happened, whether he'd done any damage to Father in return, but he is caught in a sullen black gloom that is best left alone.

The moaning from below worsens to a roaring and cursing. *My blasted gut.* We hear him staggering about, banging into things. Something shatters.

'Don't you think we'd better make sure he's all right?' Ilaria says.

'*We* are not allowed to leave this room,' says Lucrezia. 'But *you* could go and see to him.'

Ilaria shrinks back. 'I don't know . . .' She is terrified, and no wonder.

'I'm sure one of his men will go to him soon,' I say.

It is his turn to suffer. I press my ears into the pillow remembering the noises I heard rising through the floor as he burned and beat and tortured his wife and her explanations for the injuries: *I fell, silly me, the steps were so slippery, I'm so clumsy.* And I did nothing. I also hid my scars – years and years of damage visible and invisible.

Well, I have done something now.

I had expected to feel dread, had shored myself up for it. But the thought of what I have set in motion, instead of making me fearful, makes me feel enormously, inhumanly powerful, as if nothing can touch me any more or ever again.

That wasn't a fury. It was you.

I am on the brink of release – we all are. I dare not look too far beyond that abstracted idea to a possible reality.

At some point we hear the Germans trying to settle him. There seems to be a struggle, a thump, and then a loud thud that sounds like someone falling heavily. We hear him retching and puking and gagging and discharging his rage: *Don't just stand there, you imbecile, help me up . . . Water! I need water. Can't you see I've a thirst? Get out, the pair of you . . . Piss off back to Germany, you useless wretches . . . For the Devil's sake, fetch Olimpio.*

Eventually the ranting dies down, leaving only a persistent loud rumbling snore. When eventually it ceases, Lucrezia's hand finds mine in the bed.

'Are you awake?' It is almost inaudible, barely more than a breath.

I squeeze her fingers and turn to face her. Dawn is beginning to gather, spilling a thin shaft of grey light through the small window. All I can see of her is a vague shadowy outline, her eyes dark pits, like those in a skull.

'You're shaking,' she breathes.

I realize only then, it is not fear but elation that is making me tremble.

My baby shifts, as if responding to my rapture.

We are on the cusp of freedom.

18

The cock crows, a vague finger of morning filters into the room and early birdsong begins to permeate the quiet. I must have slept a few moments, for I was jolted from a dream of catching sight of myself in a mirror. The face looking back at me was not mine but Father's. He said, 'You and I, we are the same.'

I lie awake, waiting and waiting, trying to ignore my conscience that sounds through me like a pulse. A fly vibrates about the bed canopy, around and around. I swipe at it with my hand but still it circulates. Lucrezia, Bernardo and Ilaria are sprawled like corpses.

I tiptoe from the bed and try the door. It opens. Olimpio had assured me he'd leave it unlocked the night before. 'In case something should go wrong,' he'd said. Neither Jakob nor Oskar is anywhere to be seen and the place is quiet as a morgue.

I take the back stairs to the kitchens. Why can't I hear the lads ribbing each other as they clatter about? Where is the smell of fresh bread? Where is the maid-of-all-work with her buckets and brushes? The sun is up, so why is the place dead? Something feels wrong. Is guilt making everything seem off kilter?

I tentatively push at the kitchen door.

Through the crack I see the hulking shape of Father slumped at the table. Panic gouges at my throat. I lose my breath. *Has he returned in death to haunt me?* But, no, he is real. He looks terrible, jaundiced, his face beaded with sweat and very much alive.

He sees me.

'Father!' *Why are you not dead? How is this possible?*

'What are you doing here? How did you get out?' His tone seems surprisingly flat rather than angry and accusatory.

I am struck by the grim realization that I tried to kill my child and now my father and failed both times. The furies' laughter rings round my skull.

I rack my mind for some kind of response, for some kind of expression to paint on my face. Steadying my voice, I say, 'I found the door unlocked and no one was posted outside. I thought there must be something wrong. I came to see where everyone is.' I move warily into the room. 'Where *is* everyone?'

'I sent those two German clowns away.'

'Why?'

'Useless hunks of meat.'

'Where's Terza?' I try to sound curious, rather than afraid.

'I dismissed her, and the others. The bitch served me rotten food. Been suffering all night. Nearly brought my guts up.'

'Oh, Father, that's terrible.' I half reach out to stroke his shoulder but can't quite bring myself to touch him. 'Let me fetch you something to settle your stomach.' I am desperate to ask where Olimpio is but don't, for fear of being betrayed by some inflection in my voice.

I enter the larder, seeking a remedy for him, or at least something to give that impression. The small, cool room is in a state of chaos. Food has been stuffed into an old sack, some spilled onto the floor. I can see cured sausages, wheels of cheese, a pigeon pie, the remains of last night's rabbit stew all flung in together. It must have been Father's doing. Or he'd made the lads do it before he sent them packing. I fish out some of the pie and put it in a dish for Virgil. He will feast like a king today. The idea of being reunited with my dog drips a tiny measure of optimism through the silt of disquiet that clogs my whole being.

I find a jar of powdered ginger and some dried mint, tipping a measure of both into a pot. That will have to do. In the kitchen, one eye on Father, I stir the embers in the hearth, adding a fistful of kindling and a couple of logs, waiting until ribbons of flame leap upwards, before suspending a pan of water over them. I scorch my forearm and have to plunge it into the ewer. Father doesn't appear to notice, sitting silently, staring at nothing.

The water takes an interminable time to heat. I can't remain in the room with him, so I return to the larder, searching for something to eat that hasn't been cast into the stinking mess in the sack. I find a half-loaf that is only slightly stale and some scrapings of dripping at the bottom of a bowl. Tearing a piece of bread, wiping it over the fat, I stuff it into my mouth. I am ravenous. I can't remember the last time I ate properly.

By the time the drink is ready, Father is fast asleep, head cradled in his arms on the table, snoring. I take Virgil's rescued pie outside, searching for my dog, finding him in the stables. He is beside himself with excitement to see me, writhing round my legs, licking me with his pink tongue in a prolonged and heart-warming greeting. All those weeks of separation are collapsed to nothing. It is a blessed moment of respite from my unease.

He gobbles the pie with keen efficiency and follows me out to the garden. Desperate for some means to occupy myself, I take the pig bucket from the back step, tipping it into the orchard pen. The pig has grown huge and falls upon the leftovers, grunting and scoffing rapaciously, making short work of the rabbit carcasses from last night's stew, crunching the bones until every last scrap is gone. *A pig could eat a human corpse almost to nothing.*

Remembering Terza's routine of morning chores, I let the hens out, throwing down some grain for them, and collect the eggs, warm, smooth and reassuring in my hands, before seeking tranquillity in the orchard. I pick a low-hanging apple, biting into it, only to find it is horribly sour. It makes me think of Eve and the Tree of Knowledge. *Beatrice has been given more than her fair share of original sin.* Mother Superior had seen something in me that makes sense only now.

Hoofs echo from the courtyard, the jangle of a bridle, the sound of someone dismounting. Running to the gate, I see Olimpio handing his horse to Enzo. The sight of him makes my heart stutter with relief that he has not been banished like the others, a fear I'd not had the courage to consider. He spies me. I wave and slip out of sight behind the garden wall to wait for him.

The vines cling thick, hung with bunches of grapes, abundant but still unripe, tight dusted green orbs framed by curlicue fronds and delicate pointed leaves. The insects are ticking and flitting in the morning air and the light gilds everything beautifully. But to me the garden's beauty is corrupted, the grapes sour, the insects vicious, the sun scalding. When he comes, I can see the exhaustion in his posture and in the strain blighting his beautiful eyes.

'He's in the kitchen,' I whisper.

'I've seen him. He was on the rampage. Dismissed everyone in a rage. He sent me to shoo Terza and the servants back to the village. Just as well. Better Terza's not wrapped up in all this. He thought she'd served him bad meat. He cleared every scrap of food from the larder. Said it was all contaminated.'

'I know. He told me.'

'He wanted me to replace the servants but no one's prepared to come here.'

'He sent the Germans away as well.'

'They were angry. Said they weren't paid enough to be treated so badly.'

'Who's still here, then?'

'Enzo and the stable lad – but they never set foot inside. There's your stepmother, Bernardo, Ilaria. Oh, and Don Tomassino. Has he appeared yet?'

'I'd forgotten about him – haven't seen him.'

'I asked Marzio to come up later and bring food or we'll have nothing to eat.'

I picture the big, lumbering man, going about the place with his mallet in his belt loop and a packet of nails in his pocket, making sure La Rocca doesn't fall apart around us, remembering the poor caged magpie. 'And he'll come?' I can imagine what they're saying in the village: *I wouldn't want to be stuck up there with that man raging, not for all the Pope's gold.*

'He'll come.'

Our baby kicks. A huge, furred bee blunders through the morning. A lizard scuttles over the path – it has lost its tail. A thrush is singing somewhere. The wolfhounds yelp in the kennels, scratching at the doors. One of the horses whinnies. It seems wrong that the world simply continues about its ordinary business. I absently run my fingers over my string of pearls, the pearls that are worth more than Olimpio earns in a year. We look at each other, both having the same thought. *We could go. Right now, we could get away, find that other future waiting somewhere for us.*

'What are we going to do, Bea?'

'We're going to finish what we've started.' *How? How will we finish what we've started? Set fire to his bed, while he sleeps? Push him from the balcony?* I see that playing card, the figures falling from the blasted tower, seeing, in that instant, what I had not seen before, that a fall can be figurative as well as literal – Olimpio and I are those falling figures. We are the fallen.

Olimpio rifles in the pocket of his jacket and produces a small fold of paper – a sachet. 'From Giacomo. It was waiting for me in the village. He'd hidden it in a box of sugared plums, of all things.'

His eyes widen and he looks, for a moment, unfamiliar, like someone you think you've met before, then realize you haven't, and that they are nothing like the person you thought they were. It disturbs me and I understand, in this moment, that when it is all over, we will have to live in the shadow of what we have done, each knowing what the other is capable of, suspicion burrowing into our love like a canker, rotting it from the inside.

'I'll slip it into his drink,' he says.

'Won't it taste bitter? Better to put it in his food – something with a strong flavour.'

I reach for the sachet. He holds it tight. 'Sure?'

I nod, taking it and secreting it by my heart, as if it is a love token.

'At least when we go to Hell, we'll be together,' he says.

We hear someone arriving, dismounting in the yard. It is Marzio on his stocky roan, saddlebags full of provisions. Olimpio goes to meet him, while I return inside, stomach in my mouth, afraid of what I will find. But Father is still sleeping and the place is silent as a tomb, the only sound the crack of the fire. I consider what it might be like to take one of the spit skewers and ram it into his temple, shocked by the violence of my thought. That is who I have become. It starts with a brew of pennyroyal and rue, then a fool's angel, simple things that can be picked in the forest, and then it is poison that has been processed for the subtle initiation of death. Before you know it, you are contemplating hammering a spit skewer into your father's brain.

He stirs, eyes half opening. 'Is that you, Bea?' He pushes himself upright, seeming half drunk with sleep. 'You're the only one.' He is slurring. 'The only one of my blasted offspring I can trust.'

I have heard *that* before. I want to cut out his tongue.

'Marzio's here. He's brought bread. I'll ask him to draw fresh water from the well.' Going to the door with the pail, I call to him. I am desperate to keep busy, to keep myself from thinking, yet I know I must think – think and plan.

'Did you make this for me?' He is sniffing at the cup of mint and ginger.

'It should settle your stomach. Is it still warm? I can heat it for you if you like.' The sachet is burning a hole beside my heart.

'No need.' He sips at the drink. His stomach growls loudly and he grimaces with a moan. 'I'm still not right.' He seems childlike, as if he needs tending, until he spits, 'A curse on that witch,' and slams a fist onto the table. I jump back a little. He sees. He likes my fear. I suppose he meant Terza – lovely warm Terza, his milk twin. Terza, for whom he cried desperately, and had his tears beaten out of him, his memory of her beaten out of him, his innocence beaten out of him. 'Heedless bitch.' There is nothing left of that boy. *Don't become sentimental now.* I remind myself of the burns on Lucrezia's back, of Bernardo's bruises, his broken nose, of Domizio fighting for his life in some infirmary, of my slashed face: the list is endless. I consider the baby taking shape inside me. *It will not take his shape – no, no, no, not my child . . . It will not.*

I tiptoe around him, stacking the pots that have been left to drain and arrange them on the shelf. I drag the sack of rejected food outside – it will keep the pig going for a week – then start to sweep the floor. These ordinary tasks settle me slightly.

Olimpio comes in and begins to unpack the provisions, followed by Marzio with a bucket of well-water, which he pours into the big ewer. I don't look at my lover. I am used to not looking at him. He places two fresh loaves on the table.

Their scent spills into the room – gloriously simple, the scent of warm bread, redolent of benign domesticity, something of which I have no knowledge yet I crave. Father shoves them away from him. He looks green. The smell is making him nauseous.

'Would you like me to help you to your bedchamber, Conte?' Olimpio says. Father allows himself to be pulled to his feet and slowly manoeuvred from the kitchen. I hear the splat of his vomit on the stairs. He'd only drunk half the cup of mint and ginger. The only thing on my mind is how to administer the powder if he can't keep anything down.

I eat – bread dipped in egg, browned in a pan and drizzled with honey – food I enjoyed in childhood. It is almost the only dish I know how to make. I only know it because the cook had shown me once as a little girl, something to occupy me when my nurse was unwell. Lucrezia arrives with Bernardo and Ilaria. I make the same for them too, explaining that Father is unwell and that he has sent the staff away. Lucrezia has a question scrawled over her face. 'Later,' I mouth.

Eventually Don Tomassino joins us and Olimpio returns. 'He's resting.'

'I'll say a prayer for his swift recovery,' says the priest, through a mouthful.

We eat in silence.

Bernardo's eyes have turned a ghoulish purple, his uncombed hair sticking up in spikes. He looks like one of the damned.

I continue dipping the bread in the viscous egg and placing it in the pan of spitting butter. Ilaria takes a plate out to the stables for Enzo and the under-groom. Don Tomassino goes to the chapel for morning prayers. None of us has the inclination to join him.

'I wish he was dead,' says Bernardo.

Lucrezia takes his hand, bringing it to her lips to kiss it. She has tears in her eyes.

I take the dirty dishes outside and scrub them clean, drying them and stacking them, searching for more chores, anything to keep me from my thoughts. The cherry tree, I notice, is dripping with fruit. We could make a *crostata*, Father's favourite. Between us, Lucrezia and I can surely work out how to make a simple sour cherry tart. I fill a basket with the fruit, enlisting Ilaria's help, and return to the kitchen.

'Do you know a recipe for cherry *crostata*?' I ask Lucrezia.

She looks at me strangely. 'No. Of course I don't.'

'I do,' pipes up Ilaria. 'We need to make jam first.'

The girl takes charge, showing us what to do, making me see how unrealistic my fantasy of an ordinary life has been. I may be able to read Greek and Latin but I don't know how to make bread or pastry. I can't milk a cow, churn butter, make cheese, chop wood, build a fire, plant a crop or turn grapes into wine – I don't even know how to wash the clothes on my back. In my world clean laundry conjures itself to my rooms, dust disappears as if by magic and food is manifested on the table. It is not a real world. I will have to learn to live in the real world.

We start by stoning the sour cherries.

19

Father rises later, saying he feels much better.

'Do you think you might manage a little broth?' I ask him. Ilaria has been boiling bones all afternoon. We'd discovered, much to our surprise, that she is a capable cook. Taught by her mother, she said.

Under her instruction we have made the *crostate*. Small tarts, one for each of us, decorated with our initials. That was my idea. I had been the one to decorate Father's, carefully cutting the pastry strips, weaving them into a lattice, and placing the F C for Francesco Cenci, large and unmistakable, on the top, brushing milk over it and putting it on the tray with the others for baking. Only Olimpio and I know of its secret ingredient.

Those tarts lie now in the larder under a net to stop the flies. I have buried my conscience. It thrums deep in my bowels, like some live thing imprisoned, rattling its bars. I can't allow it out for the sake of my body's other resident, growing, forming, quickening in my womb. My body, with its ripening occupant, is a ticking clock.

Father sips the broth and keeps it down, the colour beginning to return to his cheeks.

We all creep round him with great caution – *can I bring you a drink, your book, shall I read to you, strum you a song?* – in much the same way we had all crept around the vicious spotted cat of my childhood. Bernardo is kept away from him. Olimpio is helping him build a miniature of the mechanical catapults the ancient Romans used in war. The task occupies him completely.

The day is balmy, warm with a gentle breeze – a perfect day. *And yet.*

When I find a moment, in the quiet end of the afternoon, I pull Lucrezia outside. We sit on the wall at the far end of the courtyard, where we won't be overheard. My intention is to tell her about the sachet from Giacomo and the tart destined for Father, but it is she who insists on speaking first.

'We've been saved, Bea. The Lord has intervened, brought us back from the brink of damnation.' Her forehead is creased and she clutches tightly at my hand as if starving and begging for alms. I notice she has attached her rosary to her belt, which she rarely does unless it is a feast day. 'I saw Hell last night.'

The air is clear and the view reaches far into the valley, each tree vibrantly green against the parched yellow of the pastures, the distant river gleaming, making its endless way. I can see Olimpio with Bernardo outside the stables, sawing lengths of wood for the catapult. Virgil sits beside me. Everything seems as it should be. But it is not.

'We've lived in Hell for a long time,' I say. 'If we've been saved, why are we still creeping about like shadows, terrified?'

Her fingers wander over her beads. 'We have to accept the fate our Lord has laid out for us.'

'You sound like Ilaria.' I didn't mean to be so scathing. She is now in tears. I remember her weeping when she was newly married and me being too young to comfort her, a grown woman, not knowing what to do. But she had toughened up, hadn't cried for a long time, or not in front of anyone. She takes out her delicately embroidered handkerchief, too fine and ornamental to be of any real use, and dabs at her eyes. Their rims are ruddy. Virgil nudges me with his muzzle, ever sensitive to my need for comfort.

'It's just . . . I'm just . . . I know what we must do but . . . but . . .' She gives in to her sobs and I pull her into an embrace, feeling the heave of her distress. 'I'm frightened, Bea. I'm not strong enough. I'm not like you.'

'We can't stop now.' I don't need to remind her of the reasons. I stroke her hair. It has the texture of straw.

'I know. I know.' Her voice is muffled in the folds of my gown. 'I don't have the fortitude for it. You're going to have to do it. I don't want to know how it's done. I can't bear the knowing.'

'I understand.' For me not knowing is worse. 'Let's go in. We've those *crostate* to eat.'

Father takes a bite of the tart, the one decorated with the pastry F C. 'My favourite,' he says. 'Was this your doing, Bea?'

'It was my idea but it was Ilaria who knew the recipe.'

'Not as stupid as you look.' He ruffles Ilaria's hair. She flinches. 'Scared of me?' He tugs at a lock.

'This is most delicious,' says Don Tomassino. His tart is almost gone, pastry scattered over his lips and down his front.

'They really are very good,' says Lucrezia. 'I can scarcely believe we made them ourselves.'

Virgil is sniffing around the crumbs on the floor. I take him to the door and shut him out, for fear a contaminated morsel might find its way to him.

I try not to look too closely as Father eats. Something isn't quite right. He is eating so slowly, looks sweaty and bilious, casting the tart away half eaten. I had tipped the entire sachet of Giacomo's powder into it. I feel sure just half will be sufficient to finish the job. Or will it? Doubt starts to prod at me. Should we have waited until we were certain the effects of the mushroom had passed? It is too late for that now.

The arrival of a messenger with the pouch of correspondence from Rome interrupts us. Father takes it, saying, 'Bea, help me to my study.'

As he rises, both Lucrezia and Don Tomassino reach for his discarded half of tart. I whip the plate away. 'He might want the rest later,' before announcing to Father, 'I just have to see to something in the kitchen and then I'll be with you.'

He grumbles vaguely, slumping back into his chair, but lacks the energy for impatience. I rush down the kitchen steps, almost tripping over my feet in my haste and tip the remains of the tart into the scraps bucket, shoving it safely beneath the putrid contents. Scurrying back up to the hall I say brightly, 'Let's go up to your study, Father.' I pick up the correspondence pouch and take his arm, helping him to his feet.

He leans heavily on me, and we make slow progress, mounting the stairs one excruciating step at a time. He smells rancid, repulsive.

On the landing he says, 'I don't feel quite right. You'd better take me to my bedchamber instead. Need to lie down.'

We shuffle along the passage. Once in the room I leave the door open and he half collapses onto the bed, which is still in disarray from the previous night. The stink of faeces and vomit hang in the air. I arrange the pillows to prop him up and give him his pouch of letters. I open the window and cover the chamber pot with a heavy cloth, blanching at its foul contents, far, far worse than the reek of the scraps bucket.

'Pass me that,' he says, pointing to an empty washbasin. His skin has taken on a corpse-like tinge. 'Quick.'

I get the basin to him just as, with a terrible retching sound, he spews into it. He wipes his face on the corner of the sheet, before heaving once more, and again, and again, until there is nothing more to throw up. Lying back against the pillows for a minute, he pants laboriously, eyes shut, then draws a deep breath, exhaling wheezily, and says, 'That's better.'

Scrabbling around for his correspondence, he complains that it is too dark. I have barely noticed the fading of the day.

A few embers are still alive under the ash in the grate, and I manage to tease a flame onto a wax taper to light the lamp. It is bronze, an ugly object in the shape of a mermaid, the sort of thing he might throw at someone in anger. As I place it beside him, he puts his great paw on my belly. 'I thought you'd be bigger by now. If I didn't know, I wouldn't even think there was anything in there.'

I shrink back, nerves jangling. 'Probably because it's my first.'

He makes a harrumphing sound, which might mean anything.

'I'd better get rid of this.' I pick up the basin. It is a vile toxic mass of gluey pastry and sour cherry jam, so undigested it doesn't even stink. My resolve is draining. Even the Devil doesn't want him.

'Stay with me in case I need anything. Where's Olimpio?'

'I won't be long.' I try my best to sound normal but it comes out falsely spry. 'I'll fetch him for you. Really need to get this out of here. And I'll bring up some herbs to burn – clear the air. You're looking a little better.' This is true. The deathly colouring has gone from his cheeks. I leave the room with the basin and the chamber pot.

As I negotiate the stairs, careful not to spill the revolting cargo, I try to keep my panic from flaring, forcing my thoughts away from the full horror of what I have set in train.

Ilaria and Lucrezia are in the kitchen sitting blankly at the table. Virgil stands as I enter, stretching his body with a yawn and waving his long tail. Lucrezia wears a terrible, haunted expression and looks briefly, questioningly at me.

'He's been sick again. Seems to be feeling a bit better now.' I thrust the chamber pot into Ilaria's hands. 'Could you take this out to the cess pit.'

Her face crumples in disgust. 'I'm not doing *that*!'

'Here, give them both to me.' It is Marzio, who has appeared from nowhere. I remember him arriving with supplies this morning, thought he'd gone back to La Petrella. He must have been here all day. He takes the pot and the basin, saying, 'I'll get rid of that too,' indicating the scraps bucket.

'Thank you, Marzio.' I am doing my best to maintain some semblance of normality, while beneath my surface all hell has been let loose and I barely know if I am coming or going. 'When you've done that, could you bring some fresh linens up to Father's room and help me change the bed? Ilaria will find them for you, won't you?' The girl returns my firm look with a sullen nod. 'Where's Olimpio? He's wanted upstairs.'

'I'll tell him, Signorina. And I'll bring up the linens as soon as I've done this.'

I find a bunch of burning-sage in the larder and some strewing herbs and scented oil for the lamp, which I shove into a basket to take up.

Lucrezia rises, saying, 'Hurry and fetch the linens, Ilaria. Then we can go to chapel. I'd like to say my prayers.' I notice her rosary is gripped in her fist. 'Won't you join us, Bea?' There is a plea in her tone.

'Father wants me.'

I find him sitting up, his correspondence scattered over the bed. The thought flits across my mind that if the lamp, which he has balanced perilously close to all that paper, tips over, the whole bed will go up and him with it. My mind's eye conjures a scene in which he is staggering about the room in flames, screaming.

'Come over here.' My stomach turns over. I know that tone, light yet concealing a full measure of menace.

'Let me just light this sage, freshen the air in here.'

'I said come here.'

I do as asked, hovering out of his reach. Something is wrong. 'What is it?'

'Look at this.' He is holding out an opened letter. 'Read it to me.'

Relief washes through me. He wants me to decipher someone's bad script. That is all that has irritated him.

I look at the letter. This can't be right. How did he get this?

Alarm sounds through me.

It is my own handwriting.

No. NO. I am shaking.

I must not shake.

'Read it to me,' he repeats.

'You know what it says.' It sounds like someone else's voice, someone trying to contain their terror. 'You don't need me to read it.'

'I want to hear it from your mouth – what you wrote to the authorities when I was in prison.' His voice is tight with venom. 'Just the middle paragraph.'

The paper quivers in my hand. He'll be enjoying the visible indication of my panic. I do not need to read it. I remember well enough. Swallowing my fear, I recite the plea I made months ago: 'I beg of you, good sir, not to release my father.' My voice shrinks. 'He has subjected me and others in our family to unspeakable acts –'

All at once he rises up and grabs me hard by the throat. 'You filthy little traitor. Do you know what happens to traitors?' I attempt to mount a defence, try to convince him I'd meant something else, but words fail me. 'They have their heads hacked from their bodies.' Spit flies from his mouth, landing on my face.

I struggle, flailing my arms, scratching at his eyes. I am so small, too small, useless, like a doll, and he a giant. I can't catch my breath. Terrible guttural sounds fill the air. They are coming from me. I waver in and out of blackness. My life flickers – a guttering candle.

I am half aware of Virgil leaping to my defence, lips drawn back, teeth bared. He must have followed me up. Father curses, kicking out at him. He yelps as he falls.

Suddenly, mercifully, Olimpio bursts into the room, Marzio too, dropping the pile of linens, rushing to my aid.

Only moments behind them is Bernardo.

Through my dwindling consciousness I find a thread of clarity. *Get Bernardo out of here.*

Father's grip slackens slightly. Air floods my lungs. 'Take the dog, Bernardo,' I croak. 'Take him away.'

Everything happens so fast.

The two men seize Father by the shoulders, flinging him violently onto the bed.

I lurch backwards, landing winded against the wall.

Virgil barks frantically, incessantly. Bernardo has ignored my request or didn't hear me. Had I even said it aloud? I don't know any more.

The lamp tumbles to the floor with a thud and fizzles out, throwing the room into darkness, the only light the grey dusk from the window, casting strange shadows that flap around the room.

Father writhes, legs thrashing manically.

I force myself to my feet, staggering, managing to grab Virgil's scruff before he pounces again.

Father roars. The men grunt with the effort of holding him down.

Then, from nowhere, comes a dull metallic flash in the gloom.

I can't make sense of it.

Then I see.

Bernardo has Marzio's hammer in his fist, high above his head.

Time slows.

Father lets out a petrified bellow as Bernardo's arm thrusts downwards.

The hammer meets his skull with a bone-splitting crack.

That is the first sound.

The next is a terrible moist thud.

Again and again and again – thud, thud, thud.

Soft matter flies up, spattering the bed hangings – blood and brains.

It is Olimpio who eventually manages to disarm my brother and pull him off. He slides to the floor, back against the wall, knees up in a hunch, eyes screwed, fingers in his ears and starts to rock.

The rest of us stand in stunned silence, staring at the bed where my mutilated father lies snarled in the bloody sheets, his head half buried in a saturated pillow.

The blood looks black in the dim light.

My heart bangs in my breast, my throat constricts, but beneath the shock something emerges: a tiny spark of relief.

It is over.

As if to remind me of why this had had to happen, my baby moves. I bring my hands to my stomach and expel a glut of breath. This small life is saved.

My mind cranks into action. Giacomo's words come to me: *Make it look like an accident.* But how? The letter that caused this, my letter, is still in my hand. I put it in the fire, watching it disappear in a gust of blue and orange flame. I fling fistfuls of strewing herbs on top, dousing the stench of death in a perfumed blaze.

Olimpio is watching. 'We should set fire to the bed.'

Marzio is shaking his head. 'The whole place'll go up and take the forest with it. We'd be lucky to escape with our lives. Dry as a tinderbox.'

My mind runs wild, seeing the whole place burn down with us inside, catching the hillside, terrified creatures running out of the blazing forest.

What, then?

'Feed him to the pig,' says Marzio.

I find my voice. 'What if some recognizable piece of bone or gristle remains and is found?' Can we really be talking of Father's body? 'The oubliette!'

'That grille is welded down, hasn't been opened in a hundred years,' says Marzio.

We fall quiet.

Olimpio speaks first. 'Like your brother said, we need to make it look like an accident.'

I am back in the kitchens, Terza across the table from me, flicking up that card – the Tower.

Clarity comes to me. 'Take him down to the balcony. Throw him over.' I see his body plummeting, a dead weight, hitting the ground below with a thump.

The room smells of a summer meadow, lavender and rosemary – my mother's scent – making my heart lurch.

'Break the balustrade. The story will go that he was unwell, had eaten bad meat, was not in his right mind, and must have fallen into the rotten timbers in the night. Maybe he went out there for air. He had been sick, you see, and he'd sent everyone away, wanted to be alone. The balustrade hadn't been properly mended after Ilaria nearly fell.' The pieces of story come together so easily.

'It's a good plan,' says Marzio.

I can see the splats of blood over his face and shirt, Olimpio's too. Bernardo is drenched in it.

'Then we must flee,' I say.

'And advertise our guilt?' Olimpio is firm. 'They will come after us. Do you want a life looking perpetually over your shoulder?' He shakes his head, despair emanating from him. His dreams are dying – our dreams. 'We must hold firm, here.' He reaches for my hand, whispering, 'See this through. Then we will be free, my love.' Our eyes meet. I know he is right.

He sets to work, wrapping the bloody head in a blanket.

'Don't forget to remove that before you throw him over and, for God's sake, burn it after.' My mind turns on details. 'Burn your shirts too.' Of the four of us, only I am free of gore. 'I'll take care of Bernardo.' My brother is still rocking, ears blocked. 'I'll lock the door. We can see to this tomorrow morning' – I point to the bed, its blood-drenched mattress and pillows, the dark clots on the hangings – 'when we've worked out how best to get rid of it all. Then we can raise the alarm.'

The two men bundle the body into a blanket. Marzio heaves it over his broad shoulder. Olimpio picks up the hammer, gives it a cursory wipe on the bed hangings and shoves it into his belt. 'This can go down the well.'

'For God's sake, make sure no one sees you.' I have the vague memory, from what seems like a lifetime ago, yet must only be a few minutes, of Lucrezia saying she wanted to pray. 'I think the others are in chapel.' I hope they are, at the far end of the building, and Don Tomassino with them.

Olimpio nods grimly as he leaves.

'Be careful,' I say to his departing figure.

I light the lamp from the fading fire and coax Bernardo up to the bedchamber under the eaves he'd shared with Olimpio in recent months. He says nothing, seems struck dumb with shock. Thankfully, the bedroom ewer is full. I pour water into the basin and undress him, washing him, teasing the clots out of his hair, cleaning the crevices of his ears and the caverns of his throat. Rinsing and wiping, rinsing and wiping, until the water turns scarlet. I tip it from the window into the ravine and refill the basin, repeating the process until the water runs clear. I find him a clean shirt and breeches. Like a child he raises his arms for me to pull the shirt over his head and I hold the breeches for him to step into, securing the waist for him.

He sinks onto the edge of the bed, watching in silence, as I light the fire with the flame from the lamp, rip apart his soiled clothes and feed them into it piece by piece. Grey billows of smoke curl into the room, making my eyes smart. I open the window and fan vigorously with a book to coax it up the chimney until all evidence is gone.

The two of us are sitting at the kitchen table by the time Lucrezia and Ilaria return from their prayers.

'Look at this.' Lucrezia means the food that I have laid out for us, sliced sausage and cheese, a meat pie, bread and butter, fruits, all of which came up from the village that morning in Marzio's saddlebags.

'Sit. Eat,' I say, trying to inject some normality into the evening.

'How is he?' Lucrezia tilts her head upwards in the vague direction of the stairs.

'Dead to the world.' I place my palms together and tilt my head against them to mimic sleep.

'Good. Have you finished building your catapult?' she asks Bernardo.

He shrugs. He still hasn't uttered a word since it happened.

'Where's Don Tomassino?' I ask.

'Haven't seen him for hours,' says Ilaria. 'Thank goodness.'

'He wasn't in chapel with you?'

'No.'

A new splinter of worry burrows down with my other dreads.

Olimpio and Marzio arrive then, in clean shirts, hair slicked. I imagine them sluicing themselves down at the well. I scrutinize their faces for signs that something has gone wrong, that they had been seen, but find nothing.

'You look spick and span,' says Lucrezia.

'Thank you.' Olimpio gives her a little bow. 'We've to keep standards up, even if it is just for a kitchen supper.'

'Been doing heavy work, Contessa,' adds Marzio. 'Chopping wood for the fires.'

'You'll be hungry then, I expect.' I make my voice light, as I pile food onto a tray, saying, 'Olimpio, would you take this out to the stables for Enzo and the boy?'

'Let me.' Marzio picks up the tray. 'I'll eat with them.'

I smile, understanding that even in this household turned upside down, he feels out of place sharing a table with me and my stepmother.

We drink wine. It makes my head swim pleasantly, pushes the horrors of the last hour to a distance. After we have eaten, we pad off to bed. No one is in the mood for cards or stories.

Bernardo has become strangely docile, still hasn't said a thing and seems to have enclosed himself in an invisible caul.

'Thank goodness the conte's not making all that noise like last night,' says Ilaria, pointing to the floor, as she climbs between the covers.

'Indeed.' Lucrezia sounds sombre.

My mind flies to the room below and the blood-soaked bed.

When Lucrezia and Ilaria are fast asleep, I steal from the bedchamber, slink through the dark corridors and up the narrow stairs to Olimpio's room. We copulate silently, furiously, like animals, trying to erase the events of the day, to feel nothing except the urgent response of each other's body, and fall asleep in an exhausted tangle.

I dream of the trapped magpie and other disturbing visions, the spectre on the battlements wearing my face, Father dripping with gore, songbirds plucking out his eyes.

20

A terrible sound jolts me awake, clamorous piercing screams that echo around the building, loud enough to wake the dead in the graveyard.

I rush down to find Lucrezia on the balcony beside the broken struts, still screaming, pointing into the warren below. Her cries are tumbling down the valley all the way to the village.

Dawn is spread over the sky, red and glorious.

It is too soon.

I picture the bloody chaos still behind the locked doors of Father's bedchamber.

I take her inside, calm her and call for Ilaria to sit with her in the yellow chamber while I go in search of Olimpio and Marzio. I find them behind the orchard, near the pig pen. The pig is lying on its side, dead. I remember then, in my panicked haste, the uneaten half of the cherry tart I had tipped into the scraps bucket.

Don't think of that now.

They have lit a bonfire.

'Where's the key?' says Olimpio. 'We'll fetch down the mattress and hangings. Bring it all round the back.'

The key is still in my pocket. He takes it and they disappear inside. I run back in through the kitchens, up the stairs, into the yellow chamber, where I find Lucrezia, silent now. Ilaria is with her.

'Your father' – the girl is white as bone – 'he must have fallen.' She points to the broken balustrade, visible beyond the doors.

I step out but can't bring myself to look into the abyss. I see people from the village climbing the path. Some are already at the gates. Enzo is on his way down to let them in.

'Stay here,' I say. 'I just have to . . .' I run from the room, up to Father's bedchamber.

The men are tearing down the hangings. It is far worse than I remember. Droplets of it are sprayed all over the walls, pools of it soaked into the floorboards. It smells like a knacker's yard. 'There's no time,' I say. 'People are here.'

Olimpio shoves the rolled-up curtains into Marzio's arms.

'Wait.' I pile the soiled pillows on top of his load, wiping the worst of the mess from the floor with a sheet. He takes it all away to burn.

'Help me turn the mattress,' says Olimpio.

It is a dead weight, cumbersome and awkward. I am sweating with the effort. Finally, it relents, revealing its underside. The blood has penetrated all the way through the layers of wool and straw. I rummage in the linen chest, finding a thick, quilted blanket, flinging it over and tucking it firmly in all the way round, then covering it with a clean white sheet.

He finds a pair of unsoiled pillows, and a rabbit-fur coverlet that he throws over the bed, rumpling it artfully and punching a dent in one of the pillows, as if the bed has been slept in.

'That'll have to do.' The spatters on the walls are the colour of rust.

'We should have burned the bedroom down,' he says.

'But Marzio said . . .'

'Marzio wasn't thinking straight. This place is made of stone. We could have controlled it.'

It is too late for regret.

'We just need to hold firm,' I remind him. 'And we'll be free.'

He draws me to him. I don't want to let go.

'Where's Bernardo?' he says.

'I don't know.'

We find him sitting on his bed, his face hidden in his hands. Virgil is sprawled beside him. Olimpio sits beside Bernardo, saying firmly, 'If anyone asks, you don't know anything. Is that clear?' He doesn't respond. 'You didn't see your father at all after he took to his bed in the afternoon. Understood?' Bernardo still says nothing. The shock must have stolen his voice.

I look from the small window to see what is happening. The glass is dimpled, making it hard to see properly. I open it, peering out and down. A smattering of locals has gathered in the yard. The village priest is among them and with him a man in a hat with a feather, who seems to be some kind of local *consigliere*. Their voices rise up to me in fragments, a word here and there. I hear them say my stepmother's name and one points a finger to his ear, circling it to indicate her hysteria.

From what I can hear, they begin to discuss that Father sent all the staff away. It must have been the talk of the village yesterday. I can see the smoke from the bonfire behind the orchard, the shape of the dead pig, Aquilino and Cala out in the meadow. A group of men have dropped a ladder into the warren and are bringing Father's body up on ropes.

They lay him out in the yard, by the pool. Its pale green surface is ruffled by a sudden breeze. The gust catches the priest's robes and, for a moment, he seems to sprout wings. He approaches the corpse, sprinkling holy water over it and muttering prayers. Several men are bent over the body. A cluster of women are huddled together by the steps. One in a red headscarf stands alone to one side and looks up, catching my eye, holding me with an unsettling blunt stare. I shrink back from the window. When I look again the woman has gone and I wonder if my conscience had conjured her.

One of the men calls to the *consigliere*, pointing at Father's caved-in skull.

I hear bits of their discussion: '. . . hit something when he fell . . .'

The *consigliere* is shaking his head and walks back to speak to the priest. Don Tomassino appears then, moving swiftly towards them. He speaks, gesticulating.

I remember Ilaria saying he hadn't been in the chapel with them yesterday evening.

Where had he been?

Had he seen something?

What is he telling those officials with such animation?

My guts contract.

The only word I hear of their discussion is the *consigliere* saying, 'Coroner.'

He calls over a man, saying something to him. The man mounts his horse and makes for the gates.

'They're fetching a coroner, Olimpio.' My voice is broken but my thoughts are crystal clear.

'It means they doubt it was an accident.' He looks at me.

'They'll assume it was you. You must go. Find Marzio, take Aquilino and Cala – they're in the meadow. You can get into the tack room for their saddles through the side door without being seen. Go out through the back gate and away through the forest.'

'I won't leave you to deal with this alone.' His gaze stutters. 'I'm ready to –'

I don't let him finish. 'No! Go . . . please.'

His jaw is tight and he shakes his head minutely.

'They won't think a woman capable of . . .' I look at my brother's hunched figure, so diminished, nothing of the crazed creature of last night. 'Or a boy.'

Understanding alights in him, his eyes flashing with inner

turmoil. 'I can't leave you unprotected – and our child.'

'They will arrest you. They will . . .' I can't say it. 'Please. You know it's for the best.'

He wavers, a few seconds seeming to stretch into hours, eventually saying, 'You're right. I'll go.' He looks wretched.

'Thank God.' My urgency returns. 'Wait here a moment.'

I rush to Father's study where I know he kept a stock of coin, pulling out drawers and rummaging in boxes, searching for the key to his lockbox. I find it in a jar on the mantel. The box contains three full purses. I grab them and return to Olimpio, thrusting them into his hands.

We embrace, our bodies pressed tightly together, eyes shut, desperately wanting to hold on to the feeling of each other, both knowing it may be months before we are together again. When we break apart, I unclasp my pearls and press them into his hand. 'Go. Now.' I push him towards the door, and he is gone.

My heart shuts down.

'Will you be all right here alone?' I ask Bernardo. He looks at me vaguely, as if through a fog and makes a half-nod. I stroke his hair, kissing his forehead. 'Virgil will keep you company.'

I steel myself, exiting through the main doors and descending the steps, making my way to the huddle around the priest. When they see me approaching, they fall silent and turn towards me, as if I am a bride walking down a church aisle to a waiting husband. Their faces, though, are not lit with the joy of witnesses to nuptials but set in grave sympathy.

I make a solemn greeting. Someone takes my arm. My first thought is that I am to be carted away but I quickly realize it is because they believe I might collapse with grief.

'Please come inside.' My voice sounds feeble, like that of a daughter who has lost her father in appalling circumstances.

We make a solemn little procession – me, the priest, the *consigliere* and Don Tomassino – up the steps and into the hall.

'Wait here, if you please, and I will fetch refreshments. I'm afraid we have no servants. My father sent them all away yesterday. He wasn't in his right mind, you see.'

'Dear child,' the priest is avuncular and kindly, taking both my hands in his, 'you have had a terrible shock. I'm sure Don Tomassino, here, would oblige.'

Don Tomassino reluctantly does as bade and disappears down the kitchen steps.

'My stepmother – the contessa – is through here. I'm afraid she is quite beside herself with distress.' I lead the way into the yellow chamber, where Lucrezia and Ilaria sit arm in arm, still in a listless daze of disbelief.

The priest squats before them, offering prayers for their loss, and the *consigliere*, removing his hat, explains that the coroner has been called for but will likely be several hours.

'The coroner?' Lucrezia tips her beautiful, red-rimmed eyes up to the man. 'But my husband fell. He had been unwell and was unsteady on his feet. Look,' she points to the balcony where the broken timbers are visible, 'the balustrade was rotten.'

'I nearly fell from there, a few weeks ago.' Ilaria is distraught. 'Marzio had mended it temporarily. If it hadn't been for Olimpio, I'd have fallen to my death, like . . . like . . .' She succumbs to tears.

'Ah, yes, Marzio Catalano and Olimpio Calvetti, are they here?' asks the *consigliere*, wandering to the balcony doors, inspecting the damage. His boots tap loudly on the oak boards.

'I haven't seen them.' I think of the two men, somewhere away in the forest, and wonder if we should all have fled yesterday, when we could. At least we would have been together. *If. If. If. If we had burned the bedroom, what then? Too many ifs.*

I picture Olimpio on Aquilino, remembering what Lucrezia had said of him once: like a Moorish prince. My want for him is raw, as if I've been flayed. *How far will they have got? Not far enough. Not yet.* All I can do is try to buy them time. I turn to Lucrezia. 'Have you seen either of them?'

'I expect Olimpio's with Bernardo. Bernardo is my son,' Lucrezia says, by way of explanation.

'Olimpio is very good with him,' I explain. 'He needs special care, you see. He's not quite right. Younger than his years. Shall I see if I can find them?' Anything to remove myself from the hollow atmosphere of the room and the damaged balustrade. I can see that the gap where the struts have broken is narrow – quite possibly too narrow for a big man like Father to have fallen through. The *consigliere* seems to have come to a similar thought, measuring it with his beady eyes, doubt and puzzlement on his face.

My heart flaps.

As I leave the room, Don Tomassino enters with a flagon and some cups. He gives me a pitying look. 'Have you seen Olimpio or Marzio?' I make myself sound matter-of-fact.

'Not today.'

Once out of the door, I stop, back against the wall, close my eyes and take a breath. I can hear the murmur of their voices. *Not today. Did I detect something in the way he said it? Not today. Did he see them yesterday? What did he see?* I draw the scattered parts of myself back together with the thought that had he seen them disposing of Father's body yesterday he would have raised the alarm immediately. But as I mount the stairs it dawns on me that he might have seen them, but not quite known what he was seeing until this morning, when Father's body was found in the warren.

Bernardo is still in the bedchamber, sitting face to the wall. Virgil has stayed by his side, as if he knows. I join them in silence for a while, eventually reiterating what Olimpio said yesterday. 'There are people coming, who will want to ask you questions about what happened to . . . to Father. You don't know anything about it. As far as you know, Father was sick and took to his bed in the afternoon. That's all. Do you understand?' He doesn't respond, as if he hasn't heard a word I've said. I place a tentative hand on his arm. He pushes me off. I notice with a rush of panic that he still has dried blood under his nails. *All that blood.* If I have overlooked that, then what else have I overlooked? 'Tell me you understand.'

He meets my gaze then and nods. His eyes are flat and empty but seem not to harbour any distress.

'We need to clean your nails. Will you let me?'

Another nod.

Finding my small hard-bristled brush and a fragrant sliver of Lucrezia's lemon-scented soap, I lead him to the basin. One by one I scrub his fingernails, until all visible trace of what happened has gone.

He returns to his perch facing the wall. I wonder what thoughts run through that impenetrable head of his. It is impossible to know. He doesn't seem afraid or rueful. Indeed, he is unusually calm. *Is he glad?*

I can see Father's body, laid out in the yard, awaiting the coroner. Someone has placed flowers on his chest. He wouldn't have liked that. Flowers are for women. The crowd has grown, more locals to gawp at the rich people in their castle and their misfortune.

'Do you want to stay up here?' He doesn't respond. 'Are you hungry? I'll bring you something to eat in a while.' Still nothing.

I take Virgil down to the kitchen, find some scraps to feed him and fill his water bowl. Performing those ordinary tasks calms me, allows me to believe in my innocence. But respite from my state of high alert is short-lived as I hear footfall mounting the back steps. It is Terza with a basket of provisions.

'I heard what happened,' she says. 'Thought you might need me.' She pulls me into her arms. 'You poor, poor girl.'

As I allow myself to be enveloped, I find I am fighting the sharp prick of tears. I can't succumb to weakness, not now, not ever. Over Terza's shoulder I can see the pack of *tarocchi* cards in the niche above the hearth, reminding myself of the woman holding open the lion's jaws. That is the strength I need to maintain.

'I'm glad you came.' Reluctantly, I break out of her hold.

'Where's Olimpio?' she asks.

'I don't know.'

She gives me a long, quizzical look. 'Listen, I've no idea what happened up here when I was gone. Better that way. But all I can say, between you and me' – she shifts in close and lowers her voice – 'and the Lord strike me down for my wickedness, is that however it came about, I am glad that monster is dead.' She steps back and takes her apron off the peg. 'Now, what can I do to help?'

'The priest and the *consigliere* are in the yellow chamber with my stepmother and Ilaria. And I think Don Tomassino is with them.' I notice Terza's slight roll of the eyes at his name. 'We should probably offer our guests something to eat while they wait for the coroner to arrive.'

'And your brother? Where's Bernardo?'

'He's upstairs – in shock but not in distress.'

Terza drops her voice again. 'Should think he's relieved like the rest of us.'

'I need to go upstairs and see to something.'

'I'll prepare a meal.'

'Have you any lye and a scrubbing brush?' I ask.

Without asking any questions, Terza produces the items, puts them in a bucket and hands them to me, only saying, 'Be careful.' She also finds a pair of thick hide gloves. 'You'll need these, if you don't want your skin to blister with the lye.'

I half fill the bucket with water and take everything up the back stairs to Father's chamber. The bed itself looks pristine, a bed that has been got out of and not returned to. There is nothing I can do about the blood-stained mattress beneath. The plastered walls are discoloured and mildewed with age, so the spatters are invisible to eyes that don't know they are there.

I get on my hands and knees, pull on the leather gloves and scrub the floor with lye. When I am done, I open the window, hoping the floor will dry before the coroner and his men arrive to search the place. I return the cleaning things to the kitchens, where Terza spirits them away.

She has prepared some toasted bread with meat paste, 'to be going on with', that I take up to the yellow chamber. Plastering my face with the kind of wan expression appropriate for a grieving daughter, I offer the food, playing hostess to the visitors.

'Terza is preparing a proper meal for you.'

'Terza is here?' The *consigliere* speaks through a mouthful.

'She arrived not long ago. I was very glad to see her.'

'And remind me why it was she was absent.' He regards me intently. Food is stuck between his teeth. My stomach rolls over. Surely he knows the answer already.

'My father' – I press my palm to my heart – 'sent her away. He was unwell and believed she'd served him bad meat. Apparently, he was very upset by this and sent all the servants away, including his two men, Oskar and Jakob. You must understand that my father sometimes, if he is upset, has a tendency to overreact – *had* a tendency – and I can only imagine that this was the case yesterday morning.'

'I see.' He makes a thin kind of smile. 'And is it your opinion that Terza *did* serve him bad meat?'

Don Tomassino's hard gaze from across the room makes the hairs on my neck stiffen.

'I think it most unlikely. I have only known her to be fastidious in her food preparation. No one else fell ill from her food but, having said that, we didn't all eat the same things. Habitually, my stepmother and I supped upstairs. Not with the men.'

'But mistakes can be made.'

'Of course, but as I said, Terza is a fastidious cook. I'm sure if you didn't agree, you wouldn't have eaten her delicious meat paste with such gusto.'

I wonder if I've gone too far but he emits a small cough of laughter, saying, 'Indeed. And very good it was, too.'

As if on cue, Terza appears to say that a meal awaits them in the hall.

'Will your son be joining us?' the priest asks Lucrezia.

'I very much doubt he's in a fit state. When things are too much for him, he needs to be alone. I'll take something up for him.' She slices some meat and bread, arranges it on a plate and leaves for the stairs.

I wish I, too, could absent myself from the heavy atmosphere and the waiting, waiting, waiting for the coroner and his questions.

21

It is mid-afternoon when the coroner finally arrives, with three men. I watch from the window as they inspect every inch of the corpse thoroughly with measuring instruments, magnifiers and other appurtenances of their trade. They look inside his mouth and his ears. They roll him over and lift his shirt to look at his back, which has turned purple where the blood has pooled, I suppose. One of the men records everything meticulously in a ledger.

Once they are satisfied each detail has been covered, the priest is called. He arranges for my father's remains to be taken to the church in La Petrella. The body is heaved onto a stretcher to be carried down the hill. We are called out to say prayers before he is taken away. I cannot put my mind to prayer, not while the coroner and his men are in a huddle discussing their findings, pointing up to the broken balcony, gesturing, pondering, formulating their theories. I am too far away to be able to hear.

We are all questioned separately in Father's study about the events of the previous two days. First Lucrezia, who returns weeping, then Ilaria, then Don Tomassino, who informs me, his thin mouth tight, eyes narrow, that I am next.

The coroner is a ferrety-looking man, slender and tall, with eyes like currants and a small, pointed white beard that contrasts starkly with his skin, burned russet by the sun. He is apologetic, even deferent, as he asks me to sit. But he is sharp and I suspect he is deliberately putting me at my ease so my guard will drop.

He is opposite me at Father's desk and two of his men are in the upholstered chairs by the hearth, where Father and I had sat on the day he confronted me about my condition. *Don't think about that.* The third is at a side table with his ledger and pen.

The study is in disarray from my search for the key, making it seem that Father was messy and careless with his papers, which he wasn't.

'I understand that your father fell ill the night before last.'

'Yes.'

'Can you please tell me what you know of that?' He picks up a paperweight, made of Venetian glass, appraising it, weighing it in his palm.

I tell him about finding Father unwell in the kitchen, with all the staff dismissed. 'He believed he'd been served bad meat.'

'And what do you think?'

'It seems a plausible explanation. The weather has been very hot and Father is' – I allow my voice to crack – 'was fond of meat and offal. But I wasn't there, you see, so I don't know what it was.'

'He kept you locked up, I understand.' Those eyes are boring into me. *Who told him that?*

'He did. He was very strict with me.'

'Why is that?'

'I don't know.'

'Was he worried about your reputation?' A shower of spit escapes his mouth.

'I don't know.'

He shifts in his seat. 'Now, tell me about Olimpio Calvetti.'

'He's the *castellano*, here at La Rocca.'

'I know that. What I mean is . . .' he pauses, appraising me '. . . where is he?'

'I don't know.'

'It seems to me, with all respect, Signorina Cenci, you don't know very much.'

'I suppose not. Is Signore Calvetti not at La Petrella?'

'He is not. Nor Marzio Catalano. We have spoken to a number of locals already and your stable staff. Neither man has been seen since yesterday.'

'I can't explain that.' I am curious as to what the locals say of the Cencis – are we hated or pitied or both? I think of the tenant Father evicted at Easter, his distress. He can't be the only one. They must loathe us all.

'Perhaps, then, you can explain why the coin your father kept locked up here' – he is pointing to Father's lockbox – 'is missing?'

My breath shallows, and my nerves are ticking. 'I'm afraid I can't explain that either. I didn't know where he kept his coin.'

'I see.' His eyebrows are raised as if he thinks I am lying. 'Are you aware, Signorina,' he passes the paperweight from palm to palm, 'that the wounds on your father's head are not commensurate with a fall?'

I slip my hands beneath my thighs to stop them shaking. 'Not a fall?' I feign surprise under his burrowing gaze. 'No.'

The man with the ledger looks up, meeting the coroner's eye, before returning to his recording.

'Why do you think that is?'

I look into my lap and mumble, 'It is too distressing for me to think of Father's injuries and know how he must have suffered.'

After several more questions, the coroner's interest in me seems to wane. Relief unfolds within, until he says: 'I'd like to talk to your brother now.'

'You must understand that the shock of losing his father so suddenly seems to have rendered him mute. He might become distressed,' I warn. 'He is not quite . . .'

'I know what he is – an imbecile. I wouldn't be doing my job if I didn't find out if he has any light to shed on the situation.' He seems to be smirking slightly.

I hate him for using that vile word to describe my brother. I make for the door. 'One more thing, Signorina Cenci...'

I stop.

'I understand there was some kind of altercation between your brother and your father recently.'

'Yes.' I turn to look towards him, heart thumping. 'I didn't witness it but I gather it was nothing. Just a silly argument.'

'A silly argument?'

'Yes.' Then I remember Bernardo's bruised face. *What have the others said of it?* 'And my brother must have managed to bang his nose. A mistake, as far as I'm aware.'

'A mistake?' I nod. 'He bruised himself.' He exchanges another look with the man who is writing it all down. 'And you were locked up at this time?'

'Yes.'

'So, you don't *really* know what happened?'

'I suppose not.'

He dispatches me to fetch Bernardo.

Bernardo seems pathetically forlorn and blank and young – certainly not like a boy capable of bludgeoning his father to death. Or so I hope. His bruises have faded a little and the small cut on his nose has scabbed over. At least they don't have the appearance of injuries sustained yesterday. That might really get the coroner thinking.

At the door, I say, 'If you can't speak, you can simply answer with a nod or a shake of the head.' I squeeze his hand, whispering, 'You didn't see anything, remember.'

He nods minutely, pulling his hand out of mine. It does not reassure me.

I lead him in and fear he might protest when I am instructed to leave the room, but he is passive as a stone.

I wait outside. Bernardo doesn't lie easily. This worries me. I lean into the door but can't hear anything other than the coroner's rumbling tone through the thick wood. I hang on tenterhooks until he emerges. He seems unscathed. It is impossible to read, in the coroner's expression, what might or might not have been divulged.

Once the questioning is done with, they announce they will make a search of the premises and that we are to remain in the yellow chamber. The coroner asks Lucrezia to show them her husband's bedchamber, but she says she is too upset and 'Would you mind if Signorina Beatrice took you up instead?' She casts a pleading look my way.

I lead them upstairs, heart in mouth, waiting outside while they search the room. The door is left open. I hear them opening chests, rummaging through Father's things. 'There's nothing here,' says one of the men.

'What are we looking for, anyway?' asks another.

'Strip that bed,' says the coroner.

Oh, God, no!

The next utterance I hear is 'Good grief,' and the order: 'Turn over the mattress.'

I picture all the blood, soaked into its weft, pooled around its buttons, caked in its seams.

And then the coroner: 'Well, I think we have established the scene of the crime.'

Soon after, they rush past me, along the passage and down the stairs, as if they've forgotten I am here. Enzo is in the hall, telling them that two of the best horses are missing from the meadow and that two saddles have gone from the tack room.

A pair of the coroner's men is sent to muster a search party from the town.

'We want reliable armed men, as many as can be found, dogs too.'

The other two are enlisted to make another, more thorough, search of the building.

While this is being carried out, we are questioned once more, together this time. The focus seems to have shifted away from us. I hope I am not imagining this. Did any of us hear any unusual or loud sounds yesterday evening? Did we see anything that seemed strange or out of place?

Bernardo stands a little way from the rest of us, brooding and silent. Still no words have escaped his lips since it happened.

'I've told you what I saw,' says Don Tomassino.

'What did you see?' Lucrezia asks him. She is emerging from her torpor.

'I saw Signor Calvetti with Signor Catalano, on the middle landing,' says Don Tomassino. 'Signor Catalano was carrying a large object over his shoulder. At the time I thought it was some kind of bolster. Now I'm not so sure.'

'The bolsters on the beds here *are* very large. Never seen anything like them before.' It is Ilaria who says this. She is ignored.

'Is there anything else?' continues the coroner. 'Some small detail you might think insignificant. Something unexpected or out of place, something not quite right.'

'*Nothing* at all was quite right yesterday,' I say. 'Everything had been turned upside down with Father being so unwell.' My voice wobbles involuntarily. 'He . . . We were very worried about him.'

'Did no one think to summon a doctor?'

'We *all* thought about it, but my husband was firm that he didn't want that.' The coroner is staring at Lucrezia, seems beguiled by her faded beauty and demure manner – he wouldn't be the first. 'His word was final. He was not in the best of moods and he only trusts his physician in Rome. He'd sent all the staff away. He could be . . . he could be, well, rather intimidating when he was like that.'

Rays of sympathy for the bereaved widow emanate from the coroner.

'And he'd seemed so much better,' I add. 'Said he wanted to sleep it off.' I can hear the men upstairs searching, the doors of cupboards slamming, the lids of trunks banging, the scrape of furniture being moved.

'But he hadn't sent Olimpio Calvetti or Marzio Catalano away, had he? Why do you think that was?' He appears to direct his question at me.

My resolve stutters. 'I can't speak for Marzio. As far as I know he lives in La Petrella and comes up by the day. He does repairs, chops firewood and suchlike, manages the woodland, rarely comes inside. But Olimpio, I know, was implicitly trusted by Father. He's worked for our family for many years. He was in Rome with us when I was a girl.'

'That may be so, but it seems abundantly clear to me that these two men murdered the conte. Their absence alone indicates their guilt.'

Ilaria makes a loud sobbing sound.

'Why?' says Lucrezia. 'I don't understand why they would do such a thing. What possible motive could they have had? He has so many enemies, but not them!'

'Your husband was a very wealthy man. There are valuables missing. It appears that theft was the motive.'

The reality of what I have done in giving Olimpio Father's coin thuds into me. I have made him a marked man. 'As the contessa said, Father had many enemies.' I am hoping to send him off the scent. 'We left Rome for this place to escape those who wished him harm. Do you think –'

'Ah!' he says, before I can suggest that someone might have gained access to La Rocca under cover of darkness. I am clutching at the most friable of straws. 'It seems more than likely, then, that these two men were in the pay of Conte Cenci's enemies. They won't be the first to have been turned. I will have to report to the authorities in Rome. They will doubtless take charge of the investigation.'

I am wondering if I should offer them something, a bribe. That is what Father always did. I think of all the dead: my brothers; the nameless 'reprisals'; the two Lorenzos and so many more. Their deaths were not looked into – like deaths in a war. Perhaps it is considered different when a nobleman is murdered in his own bed, not a youth or a henchman stabbed in a street brawl. But I have nothing to offer – even my pearls are gone. Lucrezia left all her valuables in Rome, as did I.

Of course – I pull myself up – to offer a bribe identifies me as a guilty party.

My knees are like water. My baby uncoils and recoils inside me.

We can hear riders gathering outside in the yard, horses scuffing in the grit, bridles chinking, dogs barking, men shouting to each other.

'Our search party has arrived.' The coroner makes for the door. 'I will remain here for the night to write up my report. Two of my men will stay. I assume you will want to return to Rome as soon as possible.' He directs this to Lucrezia.

'So, we are free to go?'

'Yes, Contessa,' he says, with respectful deference. 'The Roman authorities may require you to make witness statements, but we have our culprits. All we need do now is find them.'

'And the body. Will you release his body, so I can give him a proper burial?'

I am glad she thought to ask this. It is the correct response of a grieving widow. It hadn't even occurred to me.

'Of course. I will ensure that arrangements are made, Contessa, and you will be kept informed.'

'We cannot travel alone to Rome,' says Lucrezia. 'I would send for the German brothers – the guards my husband dismissed – if I knew where they were.'

'In which case, my men and I will accompany you.'

The prospect of a journey with those men is unbearable. 'We don't want to bother you while you are so busy with all this. I'm sure we can find someone in La Petrella to –'

He interrupts me. 'On the contrary, it would be my pleasure.' His smile is broad, but I have no idea if it is genuine. I don't know anything any more. 'And I will need to travel to Rome anyway to hand over the case.'

The search party is at least thirty strong. Lucrezia and I watch from the door as they divide up into smaller groups, each to go in different directions.

One of the coroner's men has taken charge. 'We want them alive but not at the expense of your safety. They may be armed and dangerous.'

I am in a tightening vice.

Lucrezia squeezes my hand. I turn, intending to whisper that I wonder how far they've got, but she says, 'Don't tell me anything. I don't want to know.' She pauses for a long moment. Then, 'I'm glad it is done.'

Don Tomassino performs the vespers service as if it is any ordinary day. Lucrezia and Ilaria are on their knees deep in prayer for its duration. I beg silently for Olimpio's safe escape. The chapel is cold, the chill penetrating into my knees, and I have no sense that my prayers are heard.

I seek sanctuary in the kitchen afterwards. The place has

been ransacked by the search, pots scattered, some broken. The contents of the larder are piled on the kitchen table. Even the hearth has been doused and scraped out.

Terza is on her knees gathering her *tarocchi* cards, which are scattered over the floor. I brew a tisane of mint, which we take outside to drink on the bench in the orchard. The jasmine that clings to the wall emits its pungent evening scent; the kitchen cat prowls; Virgil rolls in the grass; the sky blushes beautifully. Everything is normal.

Nothing is normal.

'We'll be returning to Rome tomorrow.' It occurs to me that I may never see Terza again. I have grown fond of her and wonder what my life might have been had I been born into an ordinary village family such as Terza's and not been the favourite daughter of one of the richest men in Rome, with a noble title, like a ball and chain.

'I thought you would be.' We are silent for a moment before Terza nods towards my belly. 'Shame I won't be with you for the arrival.'

I feel suddenly mired in sadness.

'Better make sure the chickens are in.' Terza bends to pick up a feathered straggler pecking at the base of the cherry tree. At the coop, she shoos in a few loiterers and bolts the door. We walk back past the pig pen, aware of the vast shape of the dead animal, pale against the dark ground. It smells rank.

'They asked me about that,' says Terza. 'I said it most likely died of a twisted gut.'

'Better burn it, in case it was diseased.' I hope Terza will understand my implication. I don't want to be responsible for any more deaths if the meat is poisoned.

Terza doesn't ask what really happened during the day she'd been banished from La Rocca, to the pig or anything else.

She is like Olimpio in that respect – doesn't probe. I am very glad of it.

'I'll miss you,' I say.

'And I you.'

As we return towards the kitchen steps, I smell a faint trace of tobacco smoke and see the indefinite dark shape of a tall curly-haired man leaning against the orchard gate.

My heart lists.

It is only one of the coroner's men having an evening smoke.

I run back over the conversation we've just had, hoping there was nothing in it for him to report back to his superior. Even Terza's comment about my pregnancy had been vague and might have applied to anything. So much searching and I am still hiding *that* evidence beneath my dress.

Inside, I bid goodbye to Terza, and as we embrace, I notice a stray card lying beneath the table. I stoop to recover it, handing it to her. It has a picture of a man suspended upside down, tied by one ankle. 'What does it mean?'

'Depends where it sits in conjunction to the other cards in the spread. Sacrifice, change, life in suspension, surrender.'

I scrutinize Terza's expression for clues as to whether this means something about my own future, about Olimpio's escape, about whether we will ever be reunited, but can find no outward sign.

'You love him very much, don't you?'

'I do.' I am struck with the awful realization that I never told him so, and maybe now, I never will. He was always so easy with his words: *I've fallen in love with you*; *loving you is my calling*. I am hounded by regret that I didn't send him on his way with a declaration of love that he can remember when he is alone.

'Couldn't you come to Rome with us?' I feel the relentless pull of imminent separation.

'No, dear. My life is here. I'd be lost in a big city like Rome.'

'Of course. I'm being selfish. I'll come back and visit you, once the dust has settled.'

We both know that no one will ever go back to La Rocca, that it will be boarded up, and fall to ruin, that vegetation will creep in through its windows and rats will reign in its cellars, that the roof timbers will rot and cave in, its ancient stones will crumble and the oubliette, with all its secrets, will fill with rubble. Little by little the forest will take it back.

Early the following morning, someone arrives with news from the search. I stop unseen at the turn in the stairs to listen to him delivering it to the coroner, who is breakfasting in the hall. 'They found one of the men, tried to arrest him peacefully but he resisted.'

'Which of the two was it?' asks the coroner.

'We don't know yet. News is coming in dribs and drabs.'

'Was he taken alive?'

'Afraid not.'

The air cracks.

I grab the banister to prevent myself from falling. Surely I would know if Olimpio was dead. I would feel it in my gut, in my heart, in my being. I would have dreamed it. I try to picture him but can't form the image in my mind.

Later that day, Aquilino comes galloping into the yard, wild-eyed and striated with foam. He is riderless.

PART THREE
The Hanged Man

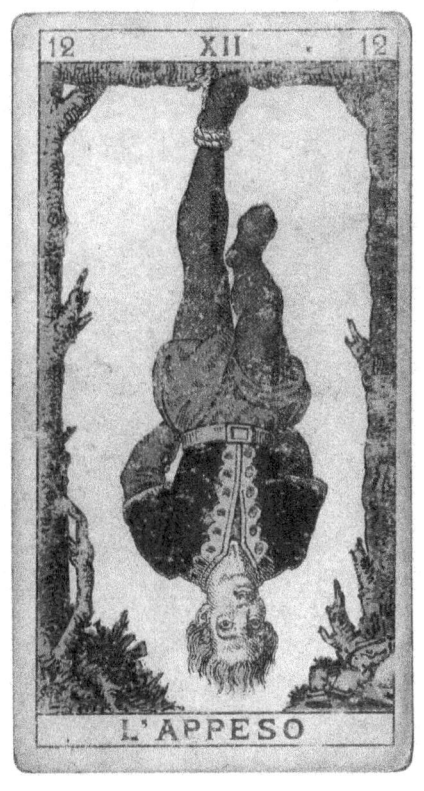

22

We teeter down the steep path away from La Rocca, the forest dark on either side. When we reach La Petrella the villagers are standing in their doorways to watch in silence as we go by. Some make the sign of the cross. I wonder what they could be thinking. I am on Aquilino. Lucrezia had done her best to convince me it was a bad idea to ride, that I should travel in the carriage 'in my condition', but I can do as I please now. Olimpio, I feel horribly certain, was the last person to ride him. My whole being is numb with grief and longing.

We stop briefly at the church, where Father's coffin awaits. I am thankful it is nailed down – thankful it will travel to Rome separately. The others mumble out a few prayers. It is a plain pine box. He would have hated that.

As we pass out of the village, I feel a compulsion to look back at the towering edifice to see if it is really there and I have not been living in some strange and terrible fever-dream or in some Stygian underworld. Thinking of Orpheus, I resist the temptation, hoping against hope that in doing so I will somehow be reunited with my beloved, bring him back to the land of the living.

We make our slow, lumbering return towards Rome through the parched September countryside. Fields are stripped to their stubble and rivers dried to a trickle. The road has compacted into deep furrows, mud scorched granite hard, making the going very slow. It is the grape harvest, the vineyards full of pickers. Carts piled high with fruit move with the excruciating sluggishness of funeral biers along the rutted roads, holding us up further. In the small towns on our route there is an atmosphere of carnival, people dressed in costumes and masks, the air high with the sulphur smell of fermentation.

As we near the city, it is as if we are travelling forwards in time, leaving behind the past – the curious roadside shrines, the staring locals, the village gibbets and stocks. The roads widen, the vineyards becoming grander: large estates, symmetrical villas with shapely trees standing sentry along their driveways. We pass other carriages and riders on thoroughbreds, wearing gleaming brocade coats and hats decorated with ostrich feathers.

The coroner and two of his men accompany us. They will hand over the case formally in Rome. Letters go back and forth between our party and the authorities there, who seem strangely disinterested in questioning us. As far as the coroner is concerned, or so it would appear, he has decided upon the culprits and their motive – one is dead, the other remains at large – and I suppose he has made this clear to the Roman authorities.

We have been informed that once their preliminary investigations are made, if they need further help from us, they will be in touch. All they ask is that we make our whereabouts known to them and remain in the environs of Rome. It is impossible to say if we are entirely free of suspicion – the coroner holds his cards tightly to his chest – but I begin to feel cautiously like someone who has got away with murder. It seems too easy, and I assume Giacomo must have paid someone off.

The coroner rides alongside me. It's hard to believe he is the same man who interrogated me in such an intimidating manner only days before. He chats, talking with ill-disguised excitement about Rome, telling me he has never been, and quizzes me about the great basilica of San Pietro, still under construction. Do I think he will be able to visit it? Is it larger than the great Duomo in Florence, which had impressed him as a young man? Might he even get a glimpse of His Holiness?

I gently attempt to prise information out of him. 'Which of the "fugitive murderers"' – this is his term – 'remains at large?' I ask casually.

'I'm not at liberty to discuss the case,' he replies. He is the kind of country coroner who likes all his *i*s dotted and *t*s crossed. The Roman officials will likely find him very amusing.

I hold tight to a mote of hope against hope, the forlorn belief that it is Olimpio who is still alive. I construct a story, more a fantasy, that he has made it to Trieste and imagine our reunion there, the tears and the joy.

It is that thought, a wavering flame burning in an indistinct future, that keeps me going – that and our infant who, whenever I stop to rest, makes gleeful somersaults inside me. By my calculations I am a little more than five months gone, and feel colossal, but still the coroner and his men seem to think me a fleshy woman like my stepmother.

We stop for the night at an inn, Ilaria, Lucrezia and I crammed together in a narrow bed. He comes to me in my sleep, where we cling together, our naked bodies pulsating with love as we rub and grind against each other. *You are here*, I whisper into his hot ear. *You are here, my love.* And then I wake to find myself in a vortex of emptiness. I touch myself, trying to regain the feeling of him, of him on me, in me, a moment of that exquisite pleasure. My breath is heavy. I scarcely dare move for fear I will wake my bed-fellows. But I cannot regain even the smallest scintilla of him.

My mind churns on things that can't be changed: should we have escaped together while we could? Should we have set fire to those gore-spattered bed hangings? Should I have left Father's coin in the lockbox? I don't know. I am left to wonder what lies ahead.

Bernardo remains silent, has turned in on himself, mired in his own interior desolation. He travels with Ilaria and Lucrezia in the carriage and Don Tomassino, who leaves our party at a monastery in Sabina, where he says he will spend a little time in contemplation. He makes an effusive, disingenuous farewell to us, and particularly Lucrezia: 'I sincerely hope, my dear Contessa,' he kisses the back of her hand and bows so deeply his nose is almost in the earth, 'that we shall be reunited before long.'

Ilaria refuses to leave the carriage to wave goodbye.

'Good riddance to him,' says Lucrezia, once he is out of earshot.

When we reach Parioli, on the outskirts of the city, Giacomo is there to meet us. We'd made arrangements for him to escort me and Ilaria to the Villa Paradiso – near enough to Rome to satisfy the authorities – where I will wait out the rest of my pregnancy. Lucrezia will go on to the Palazzo Cenci, with Bernardo.

He is waiting in front of the old church, his dear, dear face like the sun after a storm. He helps me dismount and we fall into each other's arms. I cannot count the years since we have been able to hold each other in this way and I am the little sister once more.

'How is Domizio?' I ask. 'Is he out of danger?'

'The surgeon said an inch one way or another and he'd have been dead. As it was, his lung collapsed. But he's on the mend, thank the Lord.' He crosses himself. 'We'd better get going. Don't want to be on the road after dark. And there is a surprise waiting for you at the villa.'

'What is it?'

He refuses to be drawn.

We tear ourselves apart. Our luggage is loaded onto his cart, where Virgil curls up, exhausted, on a rug, and we make our goodbyes.

Ilaria chooses to sit up front with the carter, rather than ride pillion with me – she makes no attempt to hide her fear of Aquilino – and we journey mostly in silence. As we near, I can smell the sea, nearer and I can hear it, and once we have made the last climb we see it, stopping a moment to take in the setting sun, which casts its flush across the distant water. Giacomo reaches over to take my hand. He looks older, new lines gathering in the corners of his eyes and between his brows.

I am dead tired by the time we arrive and have forgotten about the surprise, until Catarina opens the door to usher us in.

As we hug, I feel her belly, distended like mine. 'You too?'

'Me too.'

'Where's your husband? Away?'

She dips her head and I notice the memento-mori ring on her little finger.

'Oh, Catarina, I'm so very sorry.'

'He fell ill. It was quick.' She pauses for a long moment. 'And I am here.'

'You are here.'

She takes my hand to lead me inside.

The place is shabby and neglected. It is a long time since it was lived in. But a fire is lit, and I have never been gladder to be anywhere. We eat and talk, and it feels like home.

'Your children will grow up together,' says Giacomo, as he bids us goodnight. It is a future I'd never imagined, a real future I can hold on to – I hope.

I take him to one side and ask if he has paid off any officials. 'They seem to have so little interest in us.'

'Father had several stipends set up. I've kept them running, so we should be left alone.' He almost smiles, then adds, suddenly serious, 'Unless something unforeseen arises.'

*

The weeks pass, winter draws in as Catarina and I become huge and ungainly.

Giacomo, on one of his frequent visits, has news from the authorities. My heart tightens. *Have they found him?*

'There was a hearing.'

'And what did you learn?' My splinter of hope sharpens. *Is he alive?* I gird myself to discover the worst truth.

'It was confirmed that Marzio Catalano died resisting arrest.'

'Marzio?' I can't help my elation. 'Only him?'

'Olimpio is still abroad.'

Giacomo meets my gaze with a slow blink. 'Their search continues.'

A sound escapes me, like the low bellow of an animal in pain. It is relief. *He is alive.* That knowledge overflows with possibility. Now I can picture him in Trieste. I can imagine our reunion. My heart billows, then sinks at the impossibility of it.

Catarina catches my eye. She knows everything – or almost everything. She doesn't know what happened on that night, and best she never does.

'I was always scared of Marzio,' says Ilaria. 'And I was right to be.'

I don't say anything but think of Marzio, who must have been riding Aquilino on that fateful day. So like Olimpio to give his friend the better horse to ride. Poor Marzio, who had had nothing really to do with Father's death, who had simply been bringing linens up to the bedchamber at *my* request. It all runs back to me, the decisions I made. Olimpio had always said Marzio would do anything for him, that he'd saved the man's life once. I'd never learned the story behind that.

Our baby stretches inside me and I want so much to hold Olimpio's hand to my belly. *Where are you, my love?* Yearning uproots me. I miss his smell, his touch, the pulse, the throb and thrust of him. I put myself back in his arms. He is talking so easily of his love. *Why didn't I tell him of mine?* My heart was too tightly bound. *Did you know?* I hollow suddenly. A stab of reality, emptying me, reminding me that he is a fugitive, and if he were to contact me, he would endanger himself. *There is so much I don't know about you.* My hope drains as the thought arises that I must learn to be stoic, like Dante, who loved his absent Beatrice for a lifetime. *Your words return to me: we will be together in Hell.*

On the first day of Advent Catarina's labour begins and we call for the midwife, who delivers a daughter. Despite my protests, I am kept from the birthing room. The midwife said, given my condition, it would be best I stayed away, that it might frighten me. I still heard Catarina's chilling cries and watched as Ilaria was dispatched for hot water and more towels and carried away the blood-drenched sheets. I was frightened anyway, for her and for me.

But all is well, and mother and baby Vittoria thrive. That is birth, messy and bloody and painful. It is the fate of most women. Though Ilaria tells us she will not have children, 'not ever'.

'Do you still hope to take the veil?' I ask her.

'It is my greatest wish,' she says, looking, for all the world, like an angel. 'What I always wanted.' I have a memory of the timorous devout girl who arrived with us at La Rocca, her dream of a religious life blown off course by her situation, her convent dowry spent by her father. What a grim turn of Fate it was for her, when Father offered her a place in our household.

'I'd like to help you,' I say. 'I could sponsor you to go to the convent at Montecitorio, where I went as a girl.'

'You would truly do such a thing for me?' Her delight is

tempered with disbelief, making me realize that she has rarely ever had her own wishes taken into consideration.

How reassuring to have a vocation. I remember, as a child, praying fervently that I would be blessed with one, wishing I was the kind of girl who could live a life of contemplation. But my only reason for wanting that was to get away from Father and, however I looked at it, I was unsuitable for such a life.

'I'll make arrangements in the new year, once this one's arrived and we are settled.' It is such a small gesture on my part and yet the way she lights up makes me see that I am making her dream come true. She will relish spending her time on her knees before that plaster Madonna with her resin tears.

For the last two weeks of Advent, it rains torrentially. The horses have to be brought in from the paddock and kick at the stable doors, complaining of their loss of freedom, and the hens are so disturbed they stop laying. The ancient roof leaks, and buckets are scattered about the house to catch the drips, which must be emptied regularly. We are reminded constantly of our good fortune that the house is on a hill. On Christmas Eve the river below breaks its banks and we receive word that the village is flooded. There will be no Nativity Mass, as the church is knee deep in water.

The weather disturbs Ilaria.

'It's the Lord's way of telling us there is too much wickedness in the world.' She talks of Noah and the flood in the Bible.

'I swear she would start building an ark if she could,' I whisper to Catarina, and we stifle our laughter. Despite myself, there are moments when I wonder if Ilaria might not have a point.

The tempest reaches a pitch in the night, lashing rain onto the leaky windows. The shutters rattle as the wind buffets and whistles round the roof. I lie awake, plagued as ever by my conscience. A sudden bang echoes through the house, shooting terror through me. Catarina rushes in, responding to my screams. 'Wake up, Bea!' She shakes me gently. 'Wake up. It's only one of your bad dreams.'

But it is not a bad dream. It is the sound, reverberating through me, of that hammer – *thud, thud, thud* – from which I will never be free.

Water is pouring into the hearth, pooling in the room.

'A chimney pot must have blown from the roof,' says Ilaria, standing like a pale spectre behind her.

'I'll call for the roofer in the morning.' Catarina's tone is brisk. 'Put a bucket there in the meantime. Nothing to worry about.'

I can't explain that there will never again be nothing to worry about.

I pull myself to my feet, huge and graceless and uncomfortable, no space in me left for breath. Something seems to burst deep inside me, sloshing over my bare feet. Everything is wet.

'Your waters!' says Ilaria.

For a moment, I don't quite understand what she means, until I am racked by an agonizing bolt of pain that moves round my belly and into my back. An unearthly sound, half moan, half roar, bursts from me.

'We'll never get the midwife out in this.' The storm shows no sign of abating.

Ilaria is suddenly practical, moving me to one of the other rooms so we are not wading through water, lighting a fire, and setting a pot to boil, gathering clean linens. I remember how she took charge of the cooking on that day at La Rocca. *Don't think of that, not now!* But the memory has got beneath my skin and is burrowing deeper.

'Breathe! Breathe through it,' Catarina is saying.

The pain has me in its claws and is making me wish I would die.

Catarina, smiling radiantly, places my infant in my arms. 'A baby boy.'

I gaze at the scrunched purple face and the grim hours of agony begin to fade. His hands waver as if underwater, his mouth is a shell, his eyelids pulsate minutely. A wave of fear crashes into me: he is so tiny and frail and I must keep him alive.

Ilaria is shoving dirty linens into a basket. 'What will you call him?' She and Catarina stand over me with my infant, gazing like magi at the holy crib.

'Pio.' I want to name my child for his father but only dare take a part of his name. I scrutinize Ilaria for signs that she has put two and two together, finding nothing. People see what they want to see.

'Pio.' The girl seems to try the name. 'Pious – I like it.' Of course she does. Her beautiful face breaks into a smile.

She would be horrified to know the truth. All her unrequited love had drained the instant she decided what Olimpio was, what everyone thought he was – thinks he is. She never spoke of him again. How I long to set the story straight but I must live with the lie. So many lies. I don't allow myself to ponder on the possibility that building my son's life on so many lies may blight him. Nothing could blight him more than the truth.

'Pio Cenci,' she says. 'Yes, I like it.'

'No!' The slight roll of Catarina's eyes betrays her impatience. 'He'll not be a Cenci. He's an orphan Bea has adopted.' Her tone is pointed. 'Have you forgotten already? It's Pio Poverelli.'

Ilaria's hand jumps to cover her mouth. 'Of course.'

We had discussed how we would hide my baby's parentage. It was to protect my reputation. I'd not thought it necessary but Catarina, always so pragmatic, had been insistent. Poverelli had been her choice – it is a name often given to foundlings.

'No one will know *unless someone tells them.*' I look sharply at Ilaria, who drags her fingers across her lips to indicate they are sealed. I don't like asking her to lie, but she can reassure herself with the knowledge that it is my lie, not hers. I wonder what she will think when Pio starts to resemble his father, when his eyes open and they are dark, when the down on his head springs into inky curls. I see Olimpio in him already – something about the proportions of his face, his long limbs, his colouring. The familiar, wretched tug of longing pulls through me and with it a wave of despair that Pio may never know his father, that this small creature is here and Olimpio is not.

'Look at him,' says Catarina, cutting through my sadness. 'He's simply perfect.' She holds out a finger towards the tiny hand, which finds and grips it, tight as a marmoset to a branch.

I want to feel the wash of love and joy that people talk of. But all I can feel is fear – fear that I, being Father's daughter, his favourite, his thing, may contaminate him. He is so pure, untouched. *And what am I? More than her fair share of original sin.*

'I'm so happy our children will grow up together,' Catarina is saying.

I grab my friend's hand suddenly, feeling the force of an unknown future bearing down on me.

'What is it?'

'Promise, if anything happens to me, you'll take care of him?'

Catarina strokes my hair with the gentlest of smiles. 'You don't need to ask. You're more than family to me. You know that, Bea. I promise. Nothing will happen. We will be old maids together.' She lifts the atmosphere with a playful nudge. I produce something akin to a smile but cannot shake off the pessimism that is holding me hostage. I thank God for Catarina's friendship. We two women, so close anyway, are cleaved closer by our misfortunes.

'He's hungry, look!' Catarina shows me how to help my blindly searching infant to latch on so he can feed. 'There you are. It all comes naturally.' She watches us a moment. As he begins to suck, I feel a searing pain in my breast, like the needle of tears at the back of the eye, only more so, much, much more so. It robs me of my breath. 'There. You see.' She is smiling her beatific smile. 'Will you be all right alone for a few minutes?' She leaves with the creaking basket of laundry. His little cheeks hollow rhythmically, tiny bellows and I'm gripped by the thought that I am poisoning him.

He falls asleep, lolling softly in my arms. I wrap him tightly against the cold, settle him onto a soft pillow, and crawl from the bed. My body feels battered, as if assaulted. I get down the stairs and to the hall. I can hear Ilaria and Catarina talking in the kitchen. I open the front door. Rain still falls in lashing rods. I walk out into it. It engulfs me, running through my hair, soaking through my nightgown, down my legs. I slosh across the sodden garden, drawn to the swollen stream at its far end. I wade in. Now knee deep. Now hip deep. Now waist deep in the blessed, purifying cold, where I belong. I float, weightless, as the water transforms me. My flesh quivers, thin, transparent snakes of hair tangling. Hair of snakes. You are calling to me. *In Hell we'll be together*. I can hear the yelps and howls of Cerberus at the gates.

I am not afraid.

23

'Bea. Bea.' Catarina's whisper wafts into my awareness.

My eyelids unfold slowly, to brightness, my vision swimming, finding her, a vague shape, nearby. Slowly she comes into focus suckling two babies. *Milk twins.* The term chimes deep in me and I can't remember why.

'You're awake! She's awake, look.'

Faces loom over me: Ilaria, Giacomo and someone else, a man I don't recognize. A cool hand passes over my forehead.

I am alive.

'Thank you, Lord . . .' Ilaria is praying.

'You had us worried,' Giacomo, the master of understatement, is saying. 'Been in delirium for days. We thought you wouldn't make it.'

Virgil jumps onto the bed, licking my face.

'This dog saved your life,' says Catarina. 'If it hadn't been for his howling . . .'

'Don't excite her.' The man shoos Virgil from the bed. I would ask him not to but I can't find my voice. 'She needs calm.' He tips some drops of something into a spoon and slips it into my mouth. It tastes bitter. He must be a physician. I waft into the distance.

I recover slowly, with Catarina at my side, suckling our two babies. Even the physician, who calls each morning, has no inkling that one of them is mine. Giacomo tells me of the floods in Rome. Hundreds of dead, all the grand palazzi underwater, the Pantheon too, the barge that ended up in the

Piazza di Spagna, the riverbank slums that were swept clean away.

'Did many survive from the riverbanks?' I ask, the horror of it sinking in.

'Some, yes.' He is solemn. 'We've taken in several families above the stables. Lucrezia's camped on the upper floors with Bernardo. I tried to get them to come with me here, and Domizio, but they're busy helping the displaced souls. The force of the water was so strong it broke our statue of Neptune into pieces.'

Father had had that Neptune sculpted in his image.

Unable to take in the extent of the disaster, all the loss of life, while I was here birthing my baby, I drift in and out of sleep. Neptune appears in my dreams, crumbling, broken, defeated by water, Medusa's revenge for his rape of her. There is a strange and unnerving logic to those dreams.

My strength returns, slowly and stiffly, like an unused muscle prickling back to life. But with my strength comes the return of my longing, a hunger that will never be sated. Pio has his father's dimple, the finest halo of black curls and blacker eyes. There's nothing of his Cenci side, not a fleck of russet in his hair, not a freckle on his skin, the colour of oak. I begin to fall in love with my infant.

'He looks just like his father,' says Giacomo, when we are alone.

Ilaria still doesn't seem to have noticed the resemblance. Or if she has, she has said nothing. It makes me wonder whether Father might not have seen it either – the thing we were so afraid of. But scrutiny and suspicion were embedded deep in Father's nature.

We reminisce awhile about contented long-ago summers spent here at the Villa Paradiso, when Mother was still alive. The memories are mostly his, stitching mine, so fragmented and partial, into coherence. I had looked up to him, the eldest of my siblings, and followed him about adoringly, like a gosling. He would lift me onto his shoulders so I could pick the late-summer walnuts from the tree in the garden. He showed me how to force them from their leathery casings with his paring knife, staining our fingers dark, excavating the shell inside, so hard to break, and in that was the nut, like a treasure. One year, squirrels took the whole crop. 'How they managed to get through the layers of protection with their tiny paws, I'll never know,' he says.

'I love this house,' I say.

'It needs some work, if you want to settle here. The place is half falling down.'

'Do you remember how incensed Antonina was when Mother left it to me?'

'How could I forget?'

In childhood Antonina, as siblings can be, was freighted with envy of me. She craved to be the only daughter, wanted to be Father's favourite. She didn't know what it entailed. 'She refused to believe that the jewellery Mother left her was worth far more than this place.'

'Does she know about this one?' He touches Pio's head lightly.

I shake my head. 'The fewer who know, the better.'

So many lies. So many lies.

We take Pio to the small stone church in the village to be baptized. The priest is furious I left it so late. I endangered my child's soul, he tells me. I blame the floods. All that's left of the inundation is a watermark at knee height running round the walls. Giacomo and Catarina stand as godparents. Ilaria attends the service with us. She would also have been a godmother were it not that in a week she will leave to take her place with the nuns at Montecitorio.

We gather around the font to denounce the Devil while the priest douses little Pio with holy water. He cries his lungs out. The priest seems pleased. Says later it's a sign that the Devil has been properly ousted.

When the weather improves, and the early blossom begins to appear on the fruit trees, a family who lost their home in the floods arrive. A builder by trade, he will make the repairs, and she will be our housekeeper.

Catarina and I leave the babies with her, a large, warm, motherly woman, who clucks around them contentedly. We saddle the horses and ride out. Aqualino, like me, is frisky, pulling at the bit, eager to stretch his legs after a winter in the stables with only the dreary home paddock in which to kick his heels.

We take the path down beside the river where vast willows hang their green fronds into the water. Virgil runs ahead, after rabbits. I remember this route from childhood. It takes us to the bathing pool.

As we ride past it, I look up at the high ledge and see myself as a child, holding Rocco's hand as we throw ourselves into the air. I feel the glorious sensation of freedom. I was the air. I was the water. I was full of endless possibility.

Catarina has cantered ahead. I catch her up and we climb the steep path to the common where we let the horses fly. All thought is blown from our heads, leaving just the rush of wind and the thunder of galloping hoofs. We stop on the brink of the plateau from which we can see the sea, gazing silently into the grey distance for some time.

We loop back along the other side of the river where we stop and dismount to let the horses drink.

'We'll be back in Rome in a month,' I say. 'Seems a shame we'll miss spring here.'

'Do we *have* to go? I could happily live out my days here, watching the babies grow up.'

'Once the repairs are done, we'll come back. Bernardo could come with us. I think he might find a measure of happiness here. The babies would bring him some joy.'

'It's a good place to raise children.'

'And only a morning's ride from the city.'

We plot a future together. I can almost reach out and touch the possibility of simple happiness lying ahead, but Olimpio's absence is a relentless shadow in the side of my eye, cluttering me with doubt. I can't snuff out the flame of hope that burns for Trieste. 'If anything happens to me, you will promise to take care of Pio?' I ask once more.

I can see the torment in her eyes when I talk like this. 'Nothing will happen to you.' She touches my hand.

'Don't worry. I won't do that again.'

'You're free of all that, now.'

I know I will never truly be free. 'But promise me.'

'I swear. I'll raise him with Vittoria.' Catarina is solemn. 'But you must return the promise, if Fate comes for me instead of you.'

'You have my word.'

We walk the horses back in silence.

We invited in the Devil and here he is.

24

Palazzo Cenci, Rome

We arrive in Rome for Easter. Evidence of the deluge is everywhere. In the outskirts we pass makeshift graveyards, mounds of earth with simple wooden crosses, some bearing sad bouquets of dead flowers and the tattered remains of messages. The watermarks on the walls are unimaginably high, in some almost up to the second-floor windows. Most heartbreaking are the displaced and homeless, whole families squatting in corners, their forlorn children begging for scraps. We stop often on the way to distribute coins and they crowd about us pushing and shoving, driven by desperation.

Despite this we find the city centre abuzz with preparations for the Easter-week processions. Hawkers shout their wares and the markets are bursting with colour. Stalls are set out with meats and cheeses and all manner of delicacies in anticipation of the feasting to mark the end of Lent. Platforms are being built in the piazzas to stage the various pageants. It is as if the floods never happened.

In the Piazza del Popolo I hear the rantings of a preacher: *The Lord sent the deluge to punish the nobles* . . . I peer from the carriage window to see the same man who was preaching his tirade against the corrupt aristocracy as we arrived at Rocco's funeral, as if he never left. His voice is swallowed by the sound of hammering and sawing. Thankful, for once, to be in the carriage and not riding, I press my hands to my ears to prevent the banging from penetrating my skull. *Thud, thud, thud.*

The city gets under my skin. After a whole year away, I'd forgotten how much I once loved the thrill of the place, something happening on every corner, so much life, so much excitement. The vast domes of the basilicas rise like great bubbles towards the sky – the ringing of their bells carving the day into slices, and across the river San Pietro sits in all its splendour, its great new dome the largest of them all. But now I find it loud and oppressive.

We clatter into the cobbled court through the gates of my childhood home. Giacomo and Lucrezia are there to greet us, each delightedly taking one of the babies. The place feels at once familiar and unfamiliar, its towering ceilings and acres of marble seeming too vast for comfort after the modest proportions of the Villa Paradiso. I find evidence of the inundation here, some staining on the walls, a little mildew here and there, a musty smell in the air, and the long-unused wing of the building housing families who once lived on the riverbanks.

I walk from room to room, memories surprising me beyond each door. Father's apartments are shuttered, their furniture removed, so they are echoing and empty, like a mausoleum. On the pale floor there is a vague stain, the indelible remainder of my own blood that even the floods couldn't erase.

'We don't use his rooms any more,' says Lucrezia.

I insist upon going to the library. The shelves are empty, books everywhere laid out to dry, pages crimped, text smudged, spots of mould obliterating their words, many beyond repair. I find a copy of Aeschylus' plays. Opening its creaking pages, I find its words washed away, unreadable, and the red dye of the cover has seeped into the paper, making it appear blood-drenched. It falls to the floor and I don't pick it up.

'What's the matter?' Lucrezia asks.

'How can you ask that?'

'No need to snap. I only . . .'

I look at her. Something has released in her demeanour – she has a new calmness. But she didn't see the blood, didn't hear the glutinous thud of that hammer, didn't smell the gore, or feel the slip of it under her fingers. For her the misery has gone. She has her life back.

'I'm sorry.'

'I know.'

Taking my arm she leads me through to the light-filled spaces around the inner court. There we find Domizio at his easel working on a portrait of someone I don't recognize and Bernardo nearby at a table, drawing the intricate plan for an imaginary war machine. He stands and seems to think about approaching me, taking a step forwards but changes his mind, giving me a small smile instead.

'This is lovely, Domizio,' says Catarina, of the painting, out of politeness. Really the perspective is slightly off and the colours don't quite ring true.

It is the sort of comment Bernardo might have refuted. I imagine him saying, *No, it's not*, and pointing out the painting's weaknesses. But he is mute as ever, though I see his disapproval in his expression. I laugh inwardly, remembering all those insulted by his inability to tell a lie, even out of politeness, all the women whose outfits he picked apart and all the priests whose sermons he found fault with.

'I've put you in Cristofero's old rooms,' Lucrezia says. 'They are larger and airier. Plenty of space for both of you and a nursery for the babies.' She knows I won't want to return to my old bedchamber. It is too full of ghosts.

Pio and Vittoria are absorbed into the household; the maids dote on them. Nobody questions what we have told them, that Pio is an orphan, the child of a couple from Monte

Caminetto who drowned in the floods, and that I, out of the kindness of my heart, have taken him in.

The older staff look on me with pity. I see it in the way they scrunch their faces, lips pressed together, heads angled in sympathy, brows gathered. *Poor Signorina Beatrice*, I imagine them saying gravely in the kitchens and in the stables and in the wine cellars. *How she suffered at the hands of that beast.* I can see they believe it a good thing he is gone. I loathe that they know, that they remember, that for years they were the silent witnesses to Father's brutality – and sometimes were also its recipients. Their compassion flays me, makes me feel exposed and vulnerable.

I notice that same regard of pity on the faces at the Easter service and hear the whispers as we file out of the basilica and into the piazza. Two women don't realize I am within earshot when they discuss my situation in loud whispers.

'She wrote a letter begging for him not to be released. He did terrible things. Unnatural things.' They tut and nod, heads together, and when one looks round to find me behind her, she blushes hotly and changes the subject, stuttering, 'Wh-wh-which tailor made your dress? It really is lovely and fits so well.' I push past them. I hate it. I hate them for knowing my most private business, for thinking they have the right to an opinion on it. But I hate myself even more for my shame.

To avoid exposure to all the compassion-cloaked gossip, under the guise of mourning, I stay increasingly in the confines of the palazzo planning our return to the blessed obscurity of the Villa Paradiso. The renovations are progressing but, still, it will be several months.

Pio, an infant of a gloriously sunny disposition, brings an infectious joy to the Palazzo Cenci. The place, mired in fear for so long, is transformed – even Father's enemies have melted away or made truces. I watch my son grow to resemble his father increasingly. It is bitter-sweet for me, who feels his loss so deeply. I miss him in the pit of my body, miss the wet suck of our sex, the mulch smell of his seed, the tenderness of his love, of my love for him.

Giacomo has engaged the services of a lawyer, Prospero Farinacci, the best money can buy. Money is one thing we do not lack. Farinacci, who I am told has important contacts, is keeping an eye on the investigation the authorities are conducting. Giacomo reports back to us that his lawyer is sanguine, says that unless the fugitive is unearthed, nothing more will be done, meaning the case, if not quite closed, is suspended indefinitely.

I can't help fantasizing about Olimpio's return as an unrecognized stranger. We have performed a conjuring trick over Pio's parentage, why not over his father too? Yet I know well enough that his return would not bring the joy of my imaginings, only more heartbreak, for he would be tried and executed. I consider the grim question of whether it would be right, if it came to it, to save him by incriminating Bernardo. It is a terrible thought that snares itself in my conscience, impossible to untangle. Should I do so, the likelihood is that both would be found guilty. Besides, the point is moot – Olimpio will never resurface, and I come eventually to an inner resolution: it is better that he is alive and safe somewhere in the world, even if it means I never set eyes on him again.

June arrives with an unremitting, sultry heat that keeps us all inside with the shutters closed. Catarina and I cool ourselves by bathing in the courtyard fountain, from which the broken and headless Neptune has been removed, showering ourselves beneath the sea creatures that spout water from their mouths. We do it because there is no one to tell us not to. Afterwards we lie flat on the marble floor in our saturated shifts, wet hair splayed like seaweed, to gain a few minutes of blessed coolness. There we share memories, neither of us touching on the recent past that we want to forget. *Do you remember when you rescued that puppy from the spotted cat? Do you remember when we used to get dressed up to walk across the parade ground when the boys were doing their drills? Do you remember, do you remember, do you remember?* Each memory contains a splinter of Olimpio.

He is everywhere and nowhere.

I press my cheek against the cold floor, having a sudden image of myself in a marble tomb.

'What is it?' asks Catarina.

'Nothing.' I know I will never escape the dark thoughts that creep up on me when I least expect it.

The infants are rolling between us, laughing and laughing at the silliness of us being wet and on the floor. Catarina pulls herself to her feet, picking Vittoria up, swinging her high, making her giggle uncontrollably. 'Let's dunk you in the fountain.'

A knock at the door interrupts us. It is one of the pages. 'Someone is here for you, Signorina.' He addresses me.

'Who?'

'I don't know' – the page seems unsettled, can't quite look at me straight on – 'but he said it was a matter of vital importance.'

I dress hurriedly, while distress attempts to capture my attention like a pebble thrown on a window at night. What could be of such vital importance that it necessitates an unannounced visit during the hottest part of the day, when everyone sensible is resting?

The man waiting in the hall has his back to me when I enter. He is gazing at the ceiling, a magnificent *trompe l'œil* of gilded balconies scaling ever upwards to an impossibly blue sky decorated with lambskin clouds. Painted figures lean over balustrades calling to one another, while *putti* flutter prettily between them. It is the work of a great painter and, like the towering marble pillars and the walls hung with canvases, is designed to impress.

I bid him good day and he turns, seeming surprised. He hadn't heard me enter. I don't know him but by his livery I deduce that he is a papal vassal of one kind or another.

He removes his cap, a velvet feathered affair, and clears his throat, casting his eyes once over me, his puzzlement apparent, a thread pulling at his brow. He seems unable to reconcile the plainness of my clothes with the elaborate chamber, disappointed, as if at the very least I might have attempted to match the palazzo in splendour.

I hold out a hand. 'You asked for me.'

He approaches to kiss it, not quite touching my skin. Perhaps he fears contamination. His cheeks are sallow and pitted and he has a small shaving cut below his lip that is slightly swollen and crusted with dried blood. 'Furiere Romano.'

Furiere: so, he *is* a papal orderly. I give him a cool smile while distress continues quietly to tap at me. 'What can I do for you?'

'It would seem' – he runs the pheasant feather adorning his cap through his fingers – 'that new evidence has emerged with regard to your father's death.'

My heart raps hard at my breast. I maintain the smile. 'New evidence?'

'Yes.' His eyes are shifting one way and another. 'And we are hoping you might help us with a few details.'

'What kind of details? I told everything I knew to the officials at the time. They gave the impression of being very thorough.' I make a noncommittal shrug.

'I'm sure they were. But we are hoping you might shed

some more light, given the emergence of this new evidence.'

'Ask me. I will try my very best to help you.' I offer him a seat, but he refuses, which sets me on edge.

'With all respect, Signorina' – he makes much of a little bow – 'I would like you to accompany me to a place of greater privacy.'

'What's all this?' Lucrezia has arrived, floating in like a galleon. The *furiere* drops to his knee. Her black brocade and triple strand of pearls big as grapes that falls to her waist have clearly made a deeper impression than my plain dress.

I turn to her. 'Furiere Romano wants me to go with him. It's to do with Father's death – new evidence.'

She thumbs at her rosary, raising herself to her full height. 'Shame on you, Furiere! You would seek to tear open the barely healed scars of my stepdaughter's grief for her father, lost in such violent and perplexing circumstances?'

He shifts his weight from one foot to the other. 'I understand your concerns, Contessa. But this matter is of the most vital importance. I have orders from the highest level.'

'And where is it you are planning to take her?'

He looks uncomfortable and speaks into his collar. 'The Castel Sant'Angelo.'

'You can't – not there!' Lucrezia's composure snaps and she is scattering in fragments across the marble floor.

'Why that place?' I hold myself together, despite the pit of fear that has opened in me.

'We are holding a suspect there.'

Olimpio! It is all I can do to prevent myself from saying it aloud.

'If you insist upon this, then I will come with her.' Lucrezia is doing her best to regain her poise, but she is pale as ash.

'There's no need.' I know my stepmother is liable to fall apart at the slightest sign of difficulty.

'You can't go alone. Catarina can accompany you.'

'No. The children need Catarina.' I lower my voice. The *furiere* is looking away, sunk in embarrassment. 'Tell her to keep them safe, to get them away if things take a turn for the worse.'

'Giacomo, then. He will go with you.'

'And' – the *furiere* seems to regain a little of his confidence – 'with the greatest respect. I have orders that you, Contessa' – he dips his head again – 'your stepson, Giacomo, and your son, Bernardo, do not leave the Palazzo Cenci until further notice.'

'Are we under house arrest?' she says, panic jittering over her. She twists her pearls making small chinking sounds like coins being counted.

I take her arm to steady her, remembering the frenetic screaming that had brought everyone up from the village that morning. 'I'm sure it's simply a formality.' I fear this is not the case. 'Nevertheless, you'd better tell Giacomo to call for his lawyer.' I know that the authorities fear Farinacci, who has a thousand tricks up his sleeve – or so Giacomo has put it.

25

The carriage rattles over the cobbles. In the end it was decided that Domizio would accompany me. He and I sit in silence, Furiere Romano opposite, looking mainly at his gloves. Guards had already been posted at the palazzo gates when we left. It is a beautiful day, a bright, baking June day, the sky brilliant, all the colours of Rome softened by the heat haze – a day for joy and blithe pursuits and lolling about. Yet I am trundling towards the Castel Sant'Angelo where something terrible awaits.

I gaze from the small window as we cross the bridge. The vast squat drum of the *castel* looms ahead and before it lies the open, paved expanse where the public executions take place. The old dread gathers in my gut. This is where they will hang Olimpio. It is surely he they are taking me to now.

I tell myself that it may be someone else: one of the German brothers, from whom they have taken a witness statement; one of the villagers; one of the kitchen lads; anyone but he. But in the deepest part of me I know it is him, for my heart bristles as we near, like iron filings drawn to a magnet – my apprehension, the fear of what might be done to me, obliterated by the thought of seeing him again. Is it possible I may be able to save him? I cling to that finest of threads and picture myself as that woman holding open the lion's jaws.

We jerk to a halt halfway across the bridge and wait for a drover to herd his geese in the other direction – a huge honking racket of a flock. It is market day. The world, life, continues as it always has, while I feel like one of those geese destined for the pot. Faces peer in, eager to see who is behind the barred window, who is being taken to the Castel Sant'Angelo, a place where many who enter don't leave. Someone shouts, 'It's a woman.' I shrink back. Domizio puts himself between me and them. The carriage makes a sudden lurch as we move forward. I want to shout to the driver to stop, tell him there has been a mistake, but I can feel Olimpio calling me – it is no mistake: Fate is bringing us together.

All at once, the bright day is snatched from us as the carriage is swallowed into the tunnel entrance, great gates crashing shut in our wake. I feel for Domizio's hand in the dark. We come to a halt in a central courtyard and are hustled up steps and inside, up more steps, across a large, high-windowed hall, along a corridor and up a wide staircase, another corridor and into a chamber, where the *furiere* says we are to wait, before leaving us.

To my relief, it is not a cell but an airy space with a table and chairs, hangings on the walls and gleaming floors that smell of beeswax polish.

'What do you think they want?' Apprehension shoots through Domizio's voice. I wonder how much he knows – how much Giacomo has told him.

'I can't imagine.' But I can. *If they have Olimpio* . . . I don't want to imagine and douse the terrible scenes that are igniting in my head, small fires spreading, catching. I pace, thinking about what I will say. I don't know.

Eventually we hear footsteps approaching. It is not the *furiere* this time, but another man like him, only this one is altogether bigger and more stern, his face rigid, seeming incapable of even the smallest smile. I had assumed they would bring Olimpio here. I was wrong: the man leads me brusquely out of the room. Domizio makes to join us but is told, plainly, he is to wait where he is. He tries to insist to no avail.

I am marched, like a prisoner, down several flights of steps, different from those we had mounted. They narrow as we descend into the bowels of the building where there are no windows, only torches in sconces at intervals along the walls. We arrive at a barred interior gate, which swings open for us and closes with an ominous metallic clang. It gives onto another dark corridor, arched and tight, so tight my skirts brush up against the guards posted on either side, fists clutching halberds, eyes following me. At the corridor's end is a door. My escort raps at it with the hilt of his sword.

The first person I see on entering is a priest, round-faced with protruding eyes and almost no hair. He wears a plain cassock with a wooden cross suspended over his chest. Nothing indicates his rank. He isn't wearing a ring, but as my eyes adjust to the low light, I am able to see that the cross is intricately carved in ebony, his garment is of heavy silk and his undershirt, just visible at his throat, is the finest linen, beautifully embroidered. He is not just any priest but must be some kind of papal enforcer. He doesn't give me his name, merely says, 'Ah! Signorina Cenci,' baring a set of tombstone teeth in an insincere smile. 'We have been waiting for you.'

I manage to muster a polite greeting, adding, 'I don't know how I will be able to help you, Reverendo, but I will do my best.'

I search the room for Olimpio, without finding him. I can make out several figures in the gloom. One looms forward. 'We have a friend of yours in here.' I hadn't noticed the further door, studded and strapped with steel. 'Would you like to see him?'

My heart springs into my mouth.

I am propelled through the door into a chamber high as a church with a vast beam running across its vaulted ceiling. Suspended from this beam, like a side of meat, upside down, tied by one ankle to what appears to be a system of pulleys, bleeding from his nose and mouth, is Olimpio.

All the months spent longing for him and here he is.

What have they done to you?

Scenes from our time together run through my head. I am back on the battlements in his arms, that great bird wheeling above. He is laughing – *That wasn't a fury, it was you*. And there is his sweet, crooked smile, and the dimple, the facsimile of which is written miraculously into my son's – our son's – round, soft cheek. We are in the woods, on velvety moss, he on me, in me, his breath warm, my body melting. He is holding Father's gaze saying, *She's not as beautiful as your wife*. We are on that stone bench fringed with woodbine, its syrupy smell, his fingers laced through mine. I hear him: *Loving you is my calling*.

Why didn't I tell you then? Why couldn't I?

I can see the marvel in his eyes when I tell him I am carrying his child, then the dread. Together we are turning the blood-soaked mattress. I can feel its great, unwieldy weight, the effort it takes. I am pressing those purses into his hand, telling him to flee, to save himself, can feel the urgent wrench of our parting. There is that card on the kitchen flagstones – the Hanged Man: *Sacrifice, change, life in suspension, surrender*.

I prevent myself from calling out to him, from wresting myself out of my escort's grip to rush forward, to cut him down, to take him in my arms, to press my lips to his precious mouth. Instinct tells me that to say his name, or reveal anything of our relationship, might betray him. If I learned anything under Father's regime, it is to be hard and shrewd, and cautious.

My head is light.

I draw in a deep breath.

He is blinking. Blood has dripped from his nose and mouth

into his eyes. I doubt he can see me. *Do you know I am here? Can you smell me? Can you sense me?*

The priest's interrogating gaze is like sand beneath my skin. 'Do you know this man?'

'I don't know why you have brought me to this place.'

'You haven't answered my question.'

'Do I know him? It's hard to say. The poor wretch is covered with blood.'

'Clean him up,' he says to one of the guards, who picks up a rag and wipes some of the blood from Olimpio's face.

Oh, God, your dear, dear face.

His eyes are rolling, lids at half-mast.

The priest clears his throat. 'Let me make this easier for you. He has told us his name – Olimpio Calvetti. Is this correct?'

'Yes,' I say, then realize they may have lied. They may be teasing answers from me. A knot in my gut tightens.

'How do you know him?'

'He was in my father's service for many years.' I make it sound noncommittal. He must know all this already. I become aware of another man at a table to one side, some sort of recording scribe, scratching a pen on paper. Taking it all down.

'And what is he to you?'

'As I said, he was my father's vassal.'

A pulse throbs in my temple. Can he see it?

'And more specifically?'

'More specifically, *castellano* of La Rocca, the Cenci property in Rieti where my father died.'

'Where your father died?' His mouth quivers at its corner.

Why did I say it? My breath comes fast and shallow. I battle to temper it.

The priest sighs wheezily, irritated. 'Since you insist on disingenuity, I'll be more direct. Was this man your lover?'

I say nothing.

A bead of sweat slides down my back.

He repeats himself.

I notice a minute movement in Olimpio's hanging hand.

Adopting as imperious a tone as I can find, I say, 'Take him down and I'll answer your question.'

The priest orders two of the men to release him. I'd expected more resistance from my interrogator. They lower the rope. Groaning, he slumps slowly to the floor head first, where he lies inert. My instinct is to rush to his aid, but I am held back firmly by the muscular grasp of my escort.

'So?' The priest awaits my answer with a dull stare. His face is meaty and ruddy, his breath rancid.

I can see now the vague movement of Olimpio's chest. His lips are moving. He makes a croak. I could swear he says, 'My love.'

My heart swells painfully.

'I am waiting for your answer.' His eyes are empty – no compassion, nothing, just a chilling flatness.

I gather my fortitude. 'You seem to know already that we are lovers.' I can't bring myself to say it in the past tense.

Scratch, scratch, scratch goes the scribe's pen.

'Indeed.' He looks pleased with himself now. 'Someone saw you together on a number of occasions. Said you were most indiscreet.'

Who said? Who knew? My mind is racing. We thought we had been so careful. It wouldn't have been Terza. She would never have spoken. One of the maids, the kitchen lads? Surely not Ilaria. She didn't know anything, did she? But now I am remembering how easily the girl was persuaded to reveal my secrets before, how she had carefully counted the linens and reported back to Father. She had played the fool to perfection. Ilaria *had* wanted Olimpio for herself once. Perhaps this is her revenge. I cannot reconcile this with the girl at the Villa

Paradiso, so happy for the opportunity to embrace her calling, so grateful for my sponsorship. *I hope she is begging forgiveness in that convent of hers.* I can taste bitterness on my tongue. *Or was she threatened?*

'And what of it? It is not a crime.' Though it skims dangerously close to suspicion, to be in love with the man they all believe caved my father's head in with a hammer. And a betrothed man at that. I say it again, loud and firm, so Olimpio will surely hear: 'It is not a crime to be in love.' Now, at last, it is said. Is it my imagination, or do I see something flicker over his battered face?

'We are merely establishing a full picture of the situation.' The *reverendo* smiles his vile tombstone smile. 'The morality of your behaviour is not of concern to me. That is between you and your confessor. But it does cast you in a certain kind of light.'

'A certain kind of light?' My anger surges but I tame it.

'You are not being very forthcoming, Signorina. I'd have thought you'd want the matter of your father's murder properly resolved. Tell us what you remember of that day.'

'All I know is in the statement I gave to the coroner.' My voice is small and unsteady.

'I want to hear it from you – for the sake of accuracy. It's what we all want, isn't it?'

I feel my throat choke up. I can't remember what I said – the detail of it. It was months ago. I stand in silence. I am shaking. I can't stop.

'Do we need to jog your memory?'

I can't meet that blank gaze.

'Continue,' he says to the guards, as if talking of a meal or a game of dice.

Continue what? There is only one kind of continuation in this place. I brace myself.

They heave him upright. He staggers, groaning, almost falling, unable to support his own weight, having to be held up. I wonder how long he has been suspended upside down like that, whether his hip is pulled out of joint and what other terrible trials they have submitted him to. I can see black bruises flowering over his chest and shoulders and face. Four guards work together with terrifying efficiency, one propping him beneath the arms, one adjusting the pulley system, another tying his wrists together behind his back. The last binds his ankles and attaches a large metal hook to the ropes.

I feel my knees cave and have to put a hand to the wall to stay upright.

He has fallen unconscious, his head lolling. One of the men throws a bucket of water over him. He starts, sputtering, coughing, shaking off the water.

'Hoist him up.' The priest is folding and unfolding his hands like a money-lender, as he approaches his prisoner.

Olimpio's arms lift back and up slowly. His teeth are gritted. He looks at me and I hold him with my eyes.

'Since the signorina is so tight-lipped, I hope you are going finally to tell us what happened, Calvetti. You have been frustratingly stubborn . . .'

The scribe dips his pen.

I wonder how long they have been trying to screw a confession from him.

Olimpio says nothing.

'. . . which leaves me with little choice.'

The pulley winches him higher until only the tips of his toes are skimming the floor.

He grimaces but keeps his silence.

Would I be so strong?

He spits at the priest's feet.

One of the men kicks his ankle. 'Have some respect.'

Pushing his face right up to Olimpio's he breathes, 'Black bastard.'

When the guard steps away, Olimpio spits again. I want to cheer. The priest skips back, lifting his vestment to inspect the damage, revealing yellow-stockinged ankles and a trail of drool spoiling one of his velvet slippers.

'I counsel you not to continue this belligerence.' The priest remains horribly calm. 'You will only make it worse. Make your confession and all this will stop.'

He is met with defiant silence.

The hoist squeals as Olimpio is lifted a foot off the ground. He is panting, his face twisted in agony. The winch lifts him further so his head is almost level with the beam. I can see the soles of his feet, black with dirt. He swings slightly. I imagine the terrible pain of each small movement, feeling the shadow of it in my own shoulders.

The priest turns to me. 'Perhaps *you* can enlighten us.'

Olimpio speaks at last. 'Leave her out of it.' His voice is low and rasping but quite clear.

The scribe continues: scratch, scratch, scratch.

The priest indicates something to one of the guards who climbs onto a stool to suspend a weight from the hook at Olimpio's ankles. Then the winch releases suddenly, dropping him fast.

He judders to a stop with a scream.

The gristly pop of his shoulders dislocating sounds through the room.

He howls.

It is unbearable to watch but I must keep holding him with my eyes as he hangs there six feet from the floor. It is all I can do.

'You must know *something*,' the priest says to me, his impatience brewing. 'You were his mistress. Was it your lover here who battered your father to death?'

I am about to say it, the only thing that can save him, and even that might not be believed: *My brother did it. He bludgeoned our father to death with a hammer. I saw it with my own eyes.*

The winch lurches, dropping further.

'Stop!' I shriek. 'No!'

He screams again.

The sound reverberates through the marrow of my bones.

'You've got it all wrong,' I cry, but Olimpio interrupts me.

'The crime is mine.' His voice is clear. 'Leave her be.'

'Take him down,' I demand, hatred echoing through my voice. 'You have what you want.'

I realize the guards are lowering him anyway, one of them barking urgently and someone has thrown water on him again. The priest is agitated, those hands covering his mouth now.

Something is happening. What is happening?

The men are untying him, all four crouched over him on the floor. One of them slaps his face, shouting at him to wake up, another presses his fingertips to his neck, shaking his head. 'It's no good.'

'You've killed him!' The words leap out of me. 'Murderers! I hope you rot in Hell.'

The priest directs that terrible gaze on me once more. 'He's the man who slaughtered your father. I'd have thought you'd be glad that justice has been meted out.'

'Justice?' I find some unearthly force and break out of my escort's grip to leap at the priest, grabbing his ebony cross, tugging it hard. 'Call yourself a man of God?' The string snaps and wooden beads clatter over the floor, leaving the cross in my fist.

Someone tries to hold me from behind but I shake them off and drop to the ground where Olimpio is lying beyond pain, beyond life. I take his hand and press it to my heart, kissing his face. Behind the metallic stench of blood, I catch a whiff of his scent, hay and musk and love, the very faintest dregs of it and whisper into the empty shell of his ear, 'My love, my own dear love.'

The lawyer, Farinacci, comes to take me home. I am barely aware of him. Two of the guards unpick my fingers from Olimpio's blood-caked shirt. Someone is keening and wailing. I realize it is me. Once in the carriage, where Domizio is waiting to scoop me in, Farinacci makes his anger clear.

'They have some gall to subject you to that. They have broken every single code of correct treatment of prisoners, for one. And to make you witness . . . It's an outrage.'

In a daze, I listen to the rhythm of the horses' hoofs on the cobbles, the whir of the wheels, as terrible scenes from the last hours play through my head.

'Can you recount exactly how it happened in there?' he asks. 'I want your version of events.'

'She's in no fit state,' says Domizio. 'Your questions will have to wait.'

We pull to a halt at the steps, where Domizio and Giacomo half carry me into the Palazzo Cenci. I am led to a couch where I flop like a corpse, not caring whether I live or die. Lucrezia makes a great fuss over me and, thankfully, Catarina leads her away, saying, 'She's probably best left alone for the moment.'

Farinacci falls into deep discussion with Giacomo. 'That's likely the end of it now,' I hear him say. 'I counsel you not to pursue a complaint over Signorina Beatrice's treatment. It may only churn up unwanted matter.'

Through my morbid torpor I understand that for Farinacci, Olimpio's death and his last-minute confession is the best outcome for us all. From a purely pragmatic point of view, he is right. But human emotion is not pragmatic.

For days I am torn apart by my grief, inconsolable, wishing myself into the grave with my love. Catarina tries to coax me into drinking small measures of broth but it feels a herculean task. It is only my son, with his oblivious delight in all the small pleasures of the world, who can tease a grain of muted joy from me.

Come June's end we begin to prepare to return to the Villa Paradiso. The repairs are almost done and our quiet future awaits.

'It'll do you good to get away from this place,' says Catarina, who is packing our things, when Giacomo arrives.

'I'm so, so sorry.' His face is grim.

My heart buckles. I don't think I can take more bad news.

'We're forbidden to leave Rome – just for the moment,' he adds, with false brightness. 'Farinacci assures me it won't be long before all the loose ends are tied.'

So, we wait.

The passing of time and the love of my family help, eventually, to transform the intensity of my anguish into stultification, then to a great clog of anger that sits in my breast, and eventually to a subdued acceptance. Catarina and I spend long afternoons in the vast sanctuary of the Palazzo Cenci library, our infants sleeping in their cradles. We sort the books, separating those beyond hope from those that can be restored, and secreting some in case they are put on the Pope's index. It is a seemingly endless and reassuringly monotonous task. I slowly come to understand that death gives love a potency I had never anticipated. So, I return to Dante's poems, to his dead beloved, with new eyes.

On one such afternoon I happen upon an illustrated volume, only a little watermarked, describing the various properties of the fungi of Latium and find myself searching for the fool's angel. I locate it listed among the Aminata, of which there are a number. I would recognize it anywhere. The crude engraving brings back instantly the allure of its delicate stem and perfect domed head, the almost transparent flesh and its otherworldly whiteness. Beneath the image is a description in Latin, when and where it can be found, and a warning that it is deadly poisonous. *If consumed the victim will have symptoms of grave illness, nausea, vomiting and acute pains of the stomach, all of which will subside for up to two days. After this death will inevitably occur.* I don't know what to think as I spool through the chaotic events of Father's last day on earth. All we needed to do was nothing. The mushroom would have done its work.

I ask myself if, had we known this, the outcome would have been different but, still, Father would have received notice of my treacherous letter. No, I cannot wind the story back and find another outcome.

The engraving doesn't convey anything of the translucent and ethereal flesh of a real fool's angel. I am struck, as I remember plucking it from the leaf debris, by its similarity to the medusa of that long-ago sea voyage. That was the attraction – deep and intrinsic and mysterious, akin to the incomprehensible allure of death.

26

Prospero Farinacci is standing before us twisting his white moustache. He had requested an urgent meeting with Giacomo, Lucrezia and myself. We are all a little unsettled by his stipulation of urgency but hopeful he has come to announce that the case is fully closed, leaving us free to depart from Rome.

The last time I had encountered Farinacci I hadn't been in a fit state to take him in, and on previous visits I had seen him only in passing. But this time he makes an impression. He is a tall man with a patrician nose, an immobile Venetian glass eye, expressive hands and an air of authority. He, like me, has a facial scar. Where mine is neat and set to the side, partially hidden by my hair, his is more prominent, a jagged line running diagonally from the inner corner of the glass eye to the middle of his cheek – stabbed in a street fight, they say. It lends him, despite his refined manner and dress, a brutish air. He is clearly a man who has seen both sides of the law.

'I'm not supposed to know this,' he is saying, 'but I make it my business to find out what's going on. It's what you pay me so handsomely for, isn't it?' He raises his eyebrows. 'More new evidence has come to light. The case has been reopened and things look a little . . .' he seems to search for the correct word '. . . complicated for you.'

My throat tightens. 'Meaning?'

He makes a kind of smile. 'It's nothing we can't deal with.'

'When you say "you",' Giacomo says, agitating at the fringe on his jacket, 'do you mean all three of us?'

'You and your sister, primarily.' He looks gravely at us, his gaze moving from Giacomo to me and back. My old adversary Dread returns to peck at me. I must hold myself together. I fear I've forgotten how. We'd believed it was over, that we could begin to piece our lives back together but now Signor Farinacci is here with his news.

'What is this new evidence?' I say.

'It's a letter, found at La Rocca.'

'But the place was thoroughly searched. Every scrap of paper was gone through.' Lucrezia pulls her rosary from her pocket. It has almost become a reflex with her.

'It would seem,' Farinacci says, 'that because this letter wasn't in Italian it hadn't been read at the time.'

'I don't see why Latin would pose a problem, even in La Petrella.' Lucrezia looks confused.

'It was in Greek.'

My heart plummets, panic sending heat radiating into the pits of my arms and across my breast.

I catch my brother's eye. The colour has dropped from his face. 'Have you seen this letter?' he asks.

'I've seen a translation.'

'What does it say?' Lucrezia is still confused.

'It is from you, Giacomo, to Beatrice. In it you say –'

I talk over him. 'We all know what it says.' I can see it now: *Make it seem like an accident. I can send a poison that leaves no trace.* It is an irony, I think, that the written word, so long my succour, my place of safety, might end up as my undoing.

'*I* don't know what it says.' Lucrezia's eyes waver between me and my brother.

'You do. I told you at the time.' As the words leave my mouth, I realize I shouldn't have said it. It incriminates Lucrezia, who is otherwise untouched by suspicion. Thank heavens Farinacci is on our side. I berate myself. *Be more careful.*

All my mistakes crowd back. Like a fool, in my distress I had neglected so much. *Make it seem like an accident.* All the small errors, each one an intrinsic part that comes together to make an entire picture. I am riven with regrets. It had seemed so clear to me at the time. *Make it seem like an accident.* All it would have taken was to touch the flame of that ugly bronze mermaid lamp to the bedclothes, make sure every one of our letters had been thrown on the fire, and all evidence would have been obliterated. I hear Marzio warning us against it. We should have challenged him. Olimpio would be alive; he would know his son; we would have each other. But we were none of us in our right minds. *I can send a poison that leaves no trace.* There in black and white, the indelible stain over us all that no scrubbing will ever remove.

'Best you don't know, Contessa.' Farinacci is firm. 'They want to question you all. The less you know the better.'

'They want to question *me*?' Lucrezia takes the handkerchief I offer to wipe away the single tear that has spilled down her cheek.

'I'm afraid so.' Farinacci looks grave. 'Also, the boy, your son Bernardo.'

I jump immediately to my brother's defence. 'What could anyone possibly think *he* had to do with any of this? He was only thirteen at the time, and in sensibility far younger. You've seen him, haven't you, Farinacci? You've seen how he isn't of sound mind. He's still not recovered from the shock, still hasn't uttered a word since . . .' I have in mind that terrible priest with his torture machines and his velvet slippers, his tombstone teeth and his bile-yellow stockings. An image of Olimpio's corpse appears, his torso deformed, his face twisted in pain even in death. 'They'll break him . . .'

Giacomo puts a hand on my sleeve.

I stop.

'I'll do what I can to protect your brother.' Farinacci then turns to Lucrezia, who is clutching the handkerchief with a shaking hand. 'I shouldn't worry. You simply have to say what you've said all along. You were the first to find him, the broken balcony, his body below. The last time you'd seen him was in the afternoon when he was ailing and went to bed, and so on. I've seen a transcript of your testimony. It's nothing whatsoever to worry about.'

I am wishing I hadn't, in my distress, told my stepmother what they'd done to Olimpio, as that must be on her mind now too. My description had been imprecise, but torture is torture, and the bald fact is that it killed him. It certainly seems that fear is getting the better of her.

'When?' she asks, in a quaking voice.

'They will be here shortly.'

Lucrezia's breath comes shallow and fast. 'No. It's too soon. I'm not ready.'

'Better get it out of the way.' I take her arm. It is rigid. 'As Farinacci said, all you need tell them is that the first you knew of it was finding his body in the warren. That's the truth, isn't it?'

She turns her fear-filled eyes on me. 'Is it?'

'It is.' I am firm. 'You know it is.' I take her in my arms, comforting her, our roles reversed, whispering, 'This need not touch you.'

'Will you stay with me?' Lucrezia asks the lawyer.

'I fear not. Indeed, we must take the greatest care to conceal that I have been here at all, or they will know I've given you advance warning and assume I've helped you align your stories.'

Over Lucrezia's shoulder, through the window in the shade of the arcade on the other side of the courtyard, I can see Catarina with Pio on her hip. He must have woken from his sleep early. Virgil is nearby, drinking from the fountain. Catarina moves towards it, holding Pio so he can splash at the water with his small hands. His joyful chuckles ring out, filtering into the solemn atmosphere of the room. We can flee, find a place, go into hiding. But we can't. Not now. The letter I neglected to destroy has changed the course of our fates. I am choking up, can't bear to look at my happy boy. I turn back to face the room and my precarious future.

'Here?' says Giacomo. 'They're going to question us all here, *today*?'

'Just your stepmother and brother.' The lawyer has become business-like. 'I'm afraid you and your sister are to be taken to the Corte Savella.'

Lucrezia lets out a wail.

I acknowledge the small mercy that I won't be taken back to that room in the Castel Sant'Angelo with its terrifying machines. What may await us at the Corte Savella, I don't know. It is a prison, after all, but not one for the worst offenders. That must be a good sign.

Giacomo is pacing the room. 'How do you plan to defend us in the light of that letter?' Alarm has sharpened his tone.

'It's not good.' Farinacci strokes his beard slowly, deep in thought. 'However, it suggests only an intention. It is not proof.' He perches himself on the edge of the desk and seems to be thinking aloud. 'Your father didn't die by poison. The two men who committed the killing are dead – that we do know. And one made a confession.'

My heart collapses at the memory.

'We must convince the judges that the murderers weren't following your orders.' His gaze moves once more between me and my brother.

Does he think we are guilty?

Giacomo claps a hand to his forehead. 'I don't like this.'

The past assaults me suddenly, that chaotic minute in time, the crack of the hammer splitting Father's skull and then the terrible moist thud, over and over and over – *thud, thud, thud.* The sound I will never be able to exorcize.

Farinacci steeples his long fingers. 'It's possible . . .' He pauses. We all wait suspended in that moment, hoping the lawyer who is charging a king's ransom for his services, will concoct a miracle. 'There is a faint possibility that even if they choose to find you guilty' – how well he selects his words: *choose* to find us guilty – 'enough is known of your father's deeds against Signorina Beatrice to warrant a pardon. There's a record of a plea you made at the beginning of last year.' He is now talking directly to me. 'Begging for your father not to be released from prison because you feared a reprisal of his "unspeakable acts". I take it there's no need for me to go into what else you said.'

'For goodness' sake, no.' It is dawning on me that this will all come out at the trial, all the grim details of the abuse Father meted out, all my private matters subjected to the scrutiny of anyone who cares to know. Where people had a vague idea, based in hearsay, they will have the facts. They will judge me, call me terrible things, but I must put that to one side.

'Not just against me,' I say. 'He tried to have Giacomo killed. He recognized one of the men who attacked him. It was one of Father's vassals.' The idea of me being pardoned and not Giacomo, who wasn't even there, feels horribly wrong. 'Surely we can find him and make him testify. Domizio too. He was there. They nearly killed him, didn't they? He can tell the court.'

'Yes, yes.' Farinacci shakes his head minutely. Why does he look so full of doubt? 'But we must take the greatest care that such evidence doesn't simply make the prosecutors see it as a motive.'

'Can't we pay someone off?' Giacomo says. 'It's not as if we haven't plenty of money.' His tone has become acerbic. 'How much would it take?'

'We'll see.' Farinacci is reassuringly calm. 'First things first. Let them question you and then we will mount our defence. If payments might help in certain situations, we can make them discreetly, but not yet. Makes you look guilty. Now, where is Bernardo? You'd better bring him in here. Prepare him.'

The idea of what might happen if Bernardo makes a full confession is unimaginable, but now it has entered my head I'm finding it hard to keep it at bay. This is not the provincial coroner, with his half-hearted queries. If Bernardo says nothing, I realize, with a sickening jolt, the consequences are likely to be just as bad. 'He needs to be protected. He shouldn't be questioned at all.'

'I'm here to protect all of you,' says Farinacci. 'Now I must make myself scarce. I shall leave via the back gate and no one need know I've been with you. Then I will return by the front a little after they arrive. They will assume a servant has tipped me off.' He stands and gives a little bow in the general direction of Lucrezia. She is deathly pale and stares silently into space, holding tight to her crucifix. I have seen her like this before.

A thousand questions surge up in me but there is no time. 'Look after her,' I say to Giacomo, of our stepmother. 'I'll fetch Bernardo.'

I rush from the room. Everything has become alarmingly urgent. Any moment that monstrous priest, or someone like him, will be rolling up in the courtyard, dismounting from his carriage, entering the hall, flanked by lackeys, the scribe with his scratching pen, a pair of burly henchmen, no doubt, there to intimidate. What instruments will they bring with them to help their case – the *sybilla*, to break their fingers, or the knotted rope to be tightened round the temples, or some other apparatus I have not yet heard of? Then it will be too late.

I run through the courtyard. Catarina and Pio are still there. Pio is playing with Virgil. The dog is so gentle with him allowing Catarina to suspend him over his back, pretending to ride. Seeing me, Virgil waves his tail, pricking his ears.

'What's the rush?' says Catarina. Pio holds his arms out for me to take him.

'Not now, Pio poppet.' I kiss the soft skin of his cheek, running my fingers over his tight curls, his father's curls, sensing the running down of time, that these moments are limited.

Speaking quietly, I say, 'I need you to do something for me, Catarina. Take him away from Rome for a bit. Can you do that? Please? Take all the jewellery in my coffer, all the coin, and go to the Villa Paradiso. Take the carriage. We won't need it.'

'What is it, Bea? What's going on?' Apprehension spreads over her face.

'Giacomo and I are being taken to the Corte Savella. I think they might hold us there for a time.'

Her expression crumples. 'Why?' She brings her free hand to cover her mouth.

Pio sensing the atmosphere begins to wail persistently.

'Please don't worry. I'll write to you and explain everything. Just keep him safe for me.'

Catarina is pretending things are fine, jigging Pio up and down, cooing at him – 'Come on, Pio, you'll make Virgil sad if you cry. Let's see if Vittoria is awake, shall we?' – but there is a distinct wobble in her voice and Pio, screaming now, has seen right through her counterfeit gaiety.

'I have to go. I need to find Bernardo. Have you seen him?'

'He's in his chamber.' She nods to an upper window, where

my younger brother is looking out at us. I wave with a forced smile. He doesn't respond. My gut shrinks. He looks so young.

With my son's screams echoing round the courtyard, I take the steps two at a time, running along the corridor, stopping myself bursting through the door. Waiting a moment to catch my breath. He mustn't sense my agitation. I knock quietly – 'It's only me' – and enter slowly.

He remains at the window. On the table there are pens and ink, carefully arranged. A large sheet of paper is spread out, on which he has drawn, in the most intricate detail, his latest war machine. With a lurch I remember the model he built with Olimpio. *Don't look back. You must only look forward.* I approach, speaking softly, calmly, though calm is the last thing I feel.

'Listen, Bernardo, some people are coming soon. They want to ask you about what happened at La Rocca.' He doesn't respond, not even so much as a twitch. 'This is important. Can you look at me?' He half turns my way. His mouth is set in a tight knot, his eyes flat and opaque. I see a flash of Father in him. I reach out a hand not quite touching. 'If you don't speak, they might . . . they might . . .' He is waiting. I can't bring myself to be explicit about what means they use to make people talk. 'They might hurt you.'

He looks right at me as he makes a grim impression of a man hanged by the neck, tilting his head sharply, lifting his fist above it, and letting his tongue loll out to the side.

I don't know what to say.

I can still hear Pio's cries. They cut me to the core, give rise to the visceral need to protect him.

'All you have to say is that you don't know what happened, that Father was unwell one day and that he was found the next in the warren.' He doesn't respond with any kind of gesture but holds a steely gaze on me. 'Don't say what happened in the bedchamber. You were never there.' I grab his shoulders.

He shakes me off. 'You were never there. Do you understand?'
Desperation has crept into my voice. 'Please, Bernardo, show me you understand.'

He produces a small huff.

I hope it is the sound of his agreement yet fear it might have been the opposite. He loathes deceit – cannot make sense of it. It is the reason he came to blows with Father in the first place, watching us all wheeling around him, humouring him, for fear of what he would do to us. It was the insincerity as much as the violence that he hated. As a small boy, he couldn't grasp the idea of even a white lie. I remember when our grandmother insisted that he greet her with a kiss on the cheek. I had urged him on by saying, 'Show Nonna that you love her.' His reply was 'But I don't love her.' He is not a small boy now. He is a boy of fourteen and he can understand the importance of this one lie. Surely he can. If only he would say something.

Silently he shrugs on his jacket, ties the collar of his shirt and slips his feet into his shoes before leading the way to the door.

27

The Corte Savella

Giacomo and I have been separated. I suppose it is to prevent us from aligning our testimonies, when, thanks to Farinacci's advance warning, we have already done so. He will say he didn't mean what he wrote in the letter. It was written in anger and never acted upon. I will say I knew he didn't mean anything by it, that my brother is often prone to outbursts of hyperbole. It has been a few days now and still no one has come to interrogate me. I wonder if this is true for Giacomo too. Farinacci hasn't been allowed to see me, so I know nothing of Lucrezia or Bernardo's questioning, nothing of anything, and I wait in an interminable limbo.

I have been left to stew, to sit with my fears until I am good and soft and my spirit is broken. Then they will come. But I am made of stern stuff. I must keep reminding myself of that. Father made me that way. I have asked for writing materials from the turnip-faced guard at my door but I wait for them too. As I was escorted from the Palazzo Cenci I snatched the nearest book to hand, knowing I would need something with which to occupy myself, to prevent my mind from wandering into the darkness. Alas, it is the Greek plays that tell of the House of Atreus. It seems a cruel coincidence. I shan't read it, don't want to be reminded of how it ends, of how much blood is shed. To distract myself from the waiting and the dread, I read instead the Bible they have provided, finding in its pages only a harsh God and equally bloody stories. I make attempts at prayer but fear only the Devil can hear me. The knowledge that Pio is safe with Catarina gives me a pip of succour.

I have been allotted a chamber of middling size on a high floor, with a modest stone hearth, of which I have no need as Rome remains a furnace. My quarters are sparse: a bed without hangings, two chairs, a table, a wash bowl and ewer and a prayer-stand. A pale square is visible on one wall where a picture must have been and above the bed hangs a carved wooden crucifix, alarmingly lifelike – Christ's body emaciated, the flesh of His wounds swollen, oozing drops of gore, His expression serene, eyes raised to Heaven. He offers little comfort to me.

I prefer to stare out of the window from which I can see a sliver of the Tiber between buildings and the squabbling gulls that come to scavenge on the city's waste. This may not be the grim dungeons of the Castel Sant'Angelo yet the room bears evidence of its previous occupants. I have found scratches hidden behind the bed head, marking off the weeks, a few illegible names etched into the wood and an unidentifiable stain on the floorboards that hints at spilled blood. At night I meet those other inmates' vague mute ghosts. I am one of them now.

A woman comes to see to my needs. She is small yet rotund and seems kind with a sympathetic mien but, I gather, has been instructed not to talk to me, as she is completely silent. Consequently, I don't know even her name. She moves quietly about the room for a half-hour each morning, folding, dusting, sweeping, tidying, though there is little to tidy. I keep the place meticulously neat. I have nothing else to do but sit with my churning thoughts. Meals arrive. I try to make myself eat but my mouth is dry as sawdust, my tongue scattered with ulcers. Sometimes I wonder if I'm not dead already and lingering in Purgatory.

Giacomo is somewhere in the building. Occasionally I hear a tapping sound and imagine he is making contact, reminding me that I am not alone. It is more likely to be the timbers shrinking, or vermin between the walls. When I turn my thoughts to Pio my heart swells with the agony of longing. I wonder if I will ever see him again. The thought is too much to bear. He is safe. I cling to that hopeful scrap and stare from the window, counting the passing of time by the bells that come in a cacophony on the hours of prayer. I take their cue, getting on my knees to recite the angelus. Its words, so familiar, so ingrained in me, have lost their meaning, like a painting looked at too closely, its image nothing but a chaos of brushstrokes and colour. I make my own prayers, each night begging God to send Olimpio into my dreams but my sleep is short, shallow and empty. I'd be better asking it of the Devil. *We invited the Devil in and here he is.*

On the morning of the fourth day the turnip-faced guard informs me they are ready to question me. Who they are, I dread to think. There is not even the slightest hint of warmth in his expression. I hadn't noticed before how young he is, not so much older than Bernardo. Or perhaps he only appears so. He holds my arm, quite tightly, as he conveys me down a flight of stairs and into a chamber that must face south as it is hot and blindingly bright. I shade my eyes with my free hand, becoming aware of the three men sitting at a table with their backs to the sun, dark as a row of shadows. My guard ushers me to sit opposite them. I will myself to maintain my poise, to show nothing of my inner turmoil.

My eyes adjust to the glare. I try to judge what kind of men they are. From their outfits the one seated at the centre appears to be clergy of some prestige. He has a ruffed collar, upon which sits a gaunt face studded with a pair of sharp eyes. I am thankful not to encounter the yellow-stockinged monster from the Castel Sant'Angelo, though I can't be sure this one will be better. On the left side is a priest in a rough cassock with no concession to luxury. To the right sits the recording scribe, if his ink-stained fingers are anything to go by.

Dread ticks in my throat.

Looking around the room I see, to my relief, none of the terrible instruments I had feared, only a couple of large pieces of furniture, a trunk and, above it, a painting of Sant'Agnese, her hair hanging almost to her feet. She looks devotedly at the strangely docile lamb in her arms, while opposite, Santa Lucia is offering us her eyes, jellied orbs on a plate in a small pool of congealed gore.

The man at the centre introduces himself as Monsignore de Luca and his colleague as Don Rinaldi. He is smiling as though it is a social visit. 'Most glad you have come to answer our questions, Signorina Cenci.' He speaks as if I have the choice, as if he isn't aware I've been stewing in an upstairs room for the better part of a week. 'It shouldn't take long, if you choose to cooperate.' He is still smiling, his pointed eye-teeth protruding slightly. I squint, half blinded by the light. 'Is the sun in your eyes? Don Rinaldi, would you please do something about it?' Don Rinaldi draws a curtain. A moth flutters out from its folds with a puff of dust. The drape is fine and filters the glare without making the room dark. 'That's much better.' The *monsignore* is still smiling. 'Now, Don Rinaldi, would you begin?'

Don Rinaldi returns to his seat. He isn't smiling. Everything about him is harsh, from his close-cropped hair, clean-shaven face and mean mouth to his angular hands and sharp fingers. I wonder if he is one of the hooded flagellants, who make such a public spectacle of their mortification. The recording scribe shuffles his papers and dips his pen. My guts pulsate. I force myself to hold my composure. The situation feels horribly familiar, only we are not in a dungeon with my lover hanging from a beam, his dislocated joints distorting his shape beyond recognition, his terrible screams cutting to my core. I shouldn't have brought that to mind. Now it is here it will not go, and trepidation is banging through my head.

'Would you please recount for us what happened on the day before your father was found dead?' Don Rinaldi's voice is surprisingly soft, at odds with his sharp exterior.

I tell myself not to be lulled into a false sense of security.

I must get my story straight. It was months ago and so much has happened since.

My breath shortens.

I clear my throat and find the words to go over the events, telling it as I remember I told it to those who questioned me at La Rocca. I tell how Father had been unwell and how I'd found him in the kitchen early that morning having dismissed all the staff. 'Father would sometimes lose control of his temper,' I reply, when asked why he'd dismissed the staff, 'and he believed he'd been served bad meat.' The *monsignore* makes a half-cough and raises his eyebrows. The whole of Rome knows about Francesco Cenci's bad temper.

I recount how he'd slept and seemed better and how we'd made him his favourite sour-cherry *crostate* to cheer him up. I am surprised at how even I sound when I say this, as if I believe in my own innocence. But soon the events of that day begin to seep up through me like a noxious gas.

My mouth is dry. I ask for a drink. Don Rinaldi tells the guard to send to the kitchens.

We sit, waiting, a grim silence pressing down. Don Rinaldi paces slowly around me scrutinizing my every movement, making me wish I hadn't asked for the drink. The *monsignore* taps absently on the desk. I can hear sounds outside the room, the clang of a door, the clash of keys, hushed voices.

After an interminable time, a jug of lemon-flavoured water is brought. They study me as I offer some to them, which they refuse, pour myself a measure and drink it, as if something in my manner might provide them with a clue to my guilt.

'And who made these *crostate* if the servants were sent away?' The younger priest is probing far deeper than the provincial coroner. Does he know something? I am the only one alive who knows what the tart contained. Is he one of those who teases confessions out of unbelievers? Panic flutters in my breast. I keep my fear from my face, or hope I do.

'It was the girl, Ilaria, who was in our household before she took the veil. She was a good cook and showed my stepmother and me how to make them. It made me quite ashamed' – his face lights minutely – 'to have so few domestic skills.'

'It's hardly surprising. You are a noblewoman.' He is disappointed, I can tell by his sneer. He must have expected, after my admission of shame, a proper confession.

'We are all the same in the Lord's eyes.' I make much of dipping my gaze.

'Indeed.' He comes close with a strange unpleasant smile. 'So, where was Signor Calvetti while this was going on?'

Where was he? I can't remember. What did I tell the coroner?

'I . . . I . . .' *Get a hold of yourself.* He is still close, so close I can see his stubble growing back after this morning's shave. 'I'm not sure.'

He raises his eyebrows. 'You're not sure?'

'It was a very distressing time.'

The *monsignore* is still tapping and the sound is getting inside my head like that terrible thudding. *Don't think of that.*

'I wonder, then, if you might not be sure of other points you have made.'

My throat tightens as if grasped in some great clawed talon. 'You have the testimony I gave to the . . .'

'Yes, yes, yes.' He says nothing more.

I swallow.

Thud, thud, thud.

'So, after your father ate, what happened?'

'He couldn't eat much as he began to feel ill again, so I helped him up to his bedchamber, where he – I'm sorry to be so indelicate but I want to give you the full picture – vomited the contents of his stomach, which made him feel better, or so he said. The correspondence pouch had arrived from Rome and he wanted to see to his business. So, I left him. That is the last time I saw him alive.'

'What correspondence arrived for him on that day?' Don Rinaldo's gaze bores into me.

The *monsignore* shifts in his seat expectantly.

My palms are clammy. I rub them on my skirts. 'I wouldn't know. Father never involved me in his business matters.'

'Is that so?'

'That's correct.' I take a breath and look at my lap.

He doesn't say anything.

Silence rings in my ears.

It is the *monsignore* who eventually breaks it. 'You are not aware, then, that a letter was sent informing your father of a request you made to the Roman authorities?'

My breath stumbles. How do they know of this?

They both, now, have me pinned with their eyes.

'As I said' – my voice is high, brimful of guilt – 'he didn't involve me with his correspondence.'

Don Rinaldi clears his throat. 'Because such a letter would have upset him, surely. You said yourself, he was in ill temper. Might that have been the reason?'

'I wouldn't know.'

'But it might have been so?' He can smell blood.

Heat rises through me.

'He was in ill temper because he believed he'd been served bad meat.'

'Might the letter have contributed to his temper?'

'I don't know. I have no knowledge of such a letter. He was in a better mood when I left him.' I pause, slow myself, take a steady breath. 'He dismissed the staff in a rage early that morning. By then it was late afternoon and his mood was quite different.'

'But if he'd read the letter, learning that his daughter had betrayed him then surely . . .'

'How can you know that he read this letter? Surely if the letter had been delivered it would have been found when the coroner made his search.'

He blinks, inhales, says nothing. He hadn't thought of this. It seems extraordinary to me. I feel a spark of steel.

'Wouldn't you think so?' My voice sounds different, sturdier. I have the wind behind me now.

He juts his chin and narrows his eyes. He doesn't like having the questions turned on him.

He is about to say something when the *monsignore* cuts in. '*Supposing* he had read the letter' – his tone is genial, disingenuous – 'how might it have affected his mood?'

I look from one to the other before saying, 'He'd have killed me.'

'Metaphorically, you mean, of course.' He seems wrong-footed by my directness.

'No. I mean it literally.' The scribe looks up, gaping at me. I pour some more of the lemon water and take a sip, feeling myself invigorated, like a watered plant. 'So, I'd have known if he'd read it.' My lies embed themselves in my conscience, but what are a few lies when I have sought to murder my own father? The *monsignore* touches his fingertips to the cross suspended round his neck. His nails are bitten. The two men look at each other.

'Let's move on, shall we?' Don Rinaldi sits. 'You say that you last saw him alive late on that afternoon. What did you do then?'

'Without servants, I was obliged to clean up, to dispose of the foul matter in the washbasin.' A look of disgust passes over my interlocutor's face. 'So, I took it to the kitchen and gave it to Marzio to dispose of in the cess pit.'

Before I have a chance to continue, he asks, 'You mean Marzio Catalano?'

'I only knew him as Marzio. The man who did the heavier jobs around La Rocca.'

'Marzio Catalano who scarpered with Olimpio Calvetti, the man who confessed to the murder?'

I nod, jaw tight.

'Olimpio Calvetti, your lover.'

It is not a question, so I don't answer it.

'And where was Olimpio Calvetti while you were doing this? Did you see him that afternoon?'

'He must have been about. I don't really remember.'

'And then what did you do?'

'We all supped and went to bed.'

There is another silence.

'Who was it then that cleaned your father's bedchamber?'

'I don't know anything about that.' I am disconcerted by the abrupt turn in the line of questioning. I have lost the upper hand, can feel myself wilting. I manage a noncommittal shrug.

'Someone turned the mattress and mopped the floor, yet there were no servants.'

'Are you suggesting it was me?' My heart thumps so loud it might burst from my chest.

'Was it you?'

'You can see for yourself how small I am. How could I

possibly turn a heavy mattress?' Images of that bloody bed are returning to me. I force them away.

'Hmm.' He tips his head. 'I understand that the pig died suddenly.'

'Y-yes.' I wasn't expecting that and, by his smug expression, he knows it.

'What happened to it?'

I gather my composure. 'The cook said it had twisted its gut.'

'A twisted gut?' He stops, gives me a long look before saying, 'I think that covers everything.' He smoothes his palms together, as if to rub salve into them.

The scribe stoppers his ink pot. I can smell freedom, like sea air. That wasn't so bad.

'Just one more thing before you go, Signorina Cenci.' This is the *monsignore*. 'Tell me about the mushroom tisane you made for your father on the evening before all this happened.'

My moorings snap. An involuntary sound pushes out of me. Their two pairs of eyes clap onto my every gesture. 'Excuse me – my throat.' I force a small cough and take another drink though there is almost nothing left in the cup. *Only three people knew of the tisane – one is dead, one is me and the other . . . Oh, God!* Lucrezia must have broken. What did they do to her? She must have been terrified. Or was it a crisis of conscience? *What did she say?*

'I don't know what you're talking about.'

They don't believe me.

'And tell me about your younger brother, Bernardo. I understand he has a temper like his father.'

'My brother is not of sound mind. If you had met him, you would know that.' My voice betrays me again – pitchy and defensive in tone.

'I have met him.' He makes a long uncomfortable pause. 'You seem keen to jump to his defence.'

'He's my little brother.' My thoughts tangle. They know I am hiding something. I hollow out. 'What did you do to him?'

'If you are asking whether we applied pressure on the boy' – the *monsignore*'s tone is calm – 'it wasn't necessary. We are not monsters, Signorina Cenci. Merely trying to get to the bottom of things.' There is that insincere smile again. 'Both he and your stepmother were most helpful.'

I stop myself accusing him of lying. I know he might be, know I must control myself but beads of sweat are gathering on my brow.

Don Rinaldi, sensing he has me cornered, fires a volley of questions: 'Where was your brother? What kind of mushroom? Who mopped the bedchamber floor? Who turned the mattress? Where were you when . . . where is the . . . why, why why?' On and on.

'I don't know,' I repeat to each of them. 'I can't remember.' My voice is quivering, my hands shaking, my distress now impossible to conceal. 'I've told you all I know.' My shouts reverberate around the walls. 'I've told you all I know,' I say again, this time very quietly, desperately.

'Is that so?' The *monsignore* weaves his fingers together, elbows on the table. 'We shall have to see if we can jog your memory, then. Would you mind, Don Rinaldi?'

I watch Don Rinaldi rise and walk towards the chest beneath the painting of Sant'Agnese. The lamb in her arms, so lovingly cradled, reminds me of Pio. The thought of him now is like a blade slicing out my heart, when only minutes ago it had been a source of succour.

The hinges rasp as the lid opens. He leans into the dark belly of the chest, lifting from its bowels a length of knotted rope and a wooden baton. He holds these items up for the *monsignore* to see. The *monsignore* nods. Don Rinaldi places it on the table in front of me.

'Do you know what this is?'

I am paralysed by fear. I know exactly what it is but find myself incapable of a response.

'It's very simple. This,' he holds up the circle of rope with its knots like knuckles, 'goes around your head, and this,' he taps the baton against the table edge, 'threads into this loop here. And as I twist it, the rope tightens.' His face is cut in half by a grimace of a smile. 'Creates pressure.'

Father used to threaten me with something similar, though never used it. Recalling Father's brutality, the beatings, the burnings, the threats, the humiliations, the rest, reminds me of my strength. I resisted all that, years and years of it, so I can resist this. Don Rinaldi is asking me once more what happened on that evening in Father's bedchamber. I don't respond, rather shut my eyes and grit myself.

He asks again but I have nothing to say.

I feel the rope crowning me, and the baton being threaded into its loop.

'Save yourself,' says the *monsignore*, his tone making it clear that he doesn't want to do this. 'All you need do is tell us what you know, as your relatives did.' I say nothing, just float. 'Don't make me do this, my child.'

My knuckled crown tightens, a strand of hair catching in the twist of the baton, ripping out with searing pain. The knots dig into the soft flesh of my temples. I breathe slowly and deeply as the discomfort sharpens, building to agony, as if the knots have penetrated my skull and are nudging at my grey matter. Olimpio is in my mind. He resisted so much more than this. The ache in my heart for him renders anything these men can do to me as nothing. I feel a warm trickle of blood run down the side of my face. I seal the pain in a caul and set it to one side, all my focus on my breath. I have birthed a child. I know how to make a truce with pain. I drift into the place where I feel safe, underwater, floating, all sound muffled.

Nothing can touch me here, where I am nothing.

I am only vaguely aware of their questions, of brief lulls in which they wait for me to speak. I don't speak, so they continue.

I must lose consciousness because I come round and the rope has been removed, is nowhere to be seen. It must be back in its chest, presided over by the beatific Sant'Agnese, awaiting its next victim. My head throbs terribly. I bring a hand up to find a bandage in the place of my rope-crown. The three men have gone, replaced by the kind, rotund woman who shepherds me back to the upstairs room, where she removes the bandage and gently smoothes salve onto my wounds.

I am reminded of all the times I have done this for Lucrezia, who never wanted the servants to know what happened to her behind closed doors and the countless times Lucrezia has done it for me. Both our bodies, the living maps of Father's destruction. And despite my situation, the awful dead vacuum of my future, I am glad he is dead. I am only sorry that I will not be the only one to pay for it.

28

Farinacci is furious about the torture. 'And you a noblewoman.'

I say, 'It's nothing when compared to what they did to Olimpio.'

Farinacci had never shown a jot of outrage about Olimpio's fate. Indeed, he sees it as a convenience. It makes me like him less.

The pain in my head is relentless. When he arrived, I'd stood up to greet him but found the throbbing intolerable, so I am back on the bed prone, while he sits beside me. 'It's as if you are at my deathbed,' I say. His face moves from horror to relief as he realizes I am attempting a joke. Gallows humour. 'How did you gain entry to see me? I thought –'

'Anything can be achieved if you tip the right people.'

'*Almost* anything.' I fix my eyes on his, which are full of sympathy. Even his blindly staring glass eye seems so.

'You are made of stern stuff. I gather they tried very hard to break you. They were surprised by your resilience. It threw them apparently.'

'I'm my father's daughter.' I shrug, absorbing that grim truth. 'How do you know this, anyway?'

'I have my informers.' He taps the side of his nose.

'Ah, yes, tips to the right people,' I say wryly.

'Shame your brother hasn't your capacity for resistance.'

'Which brother?' The hairs on my neck tingle.

'Your elder brother. He made a full confession.'

'What did they do to him?'

'Not very much, by all accounts.'

'Oh, Giacomo!' He could have saved himself. He wasn't even there. 'So, he told them he sent poison?'

'Yes, and that his intentions in the letter were meant literally.' He is shaking his head.

That letter again. My fault. This is all my fault. 'I don't know why I didn't get rid of that blasted letter.'

'If he'd only held out –'

'I know,' I say. 'They'd have had nothing on him. Why do you think he didn't?'

'It's like a reflex – the need to tell the truth to a clergyman. I've seen it countless times. We're all trained to it in the same way – fear of God, fear of the eternal fires. Very few learn how to resist it.'

I am reminded once again of that comment, *more than her fair share of original sin*. I am drawing nearer to an understanding of what was meant by it. It was in me even then, not just the ability to lie to a priest without compunction but, far, far worse, the capacity not only to wish my father dead but to act on that wish. I like to think I am a better person than him. *But am I?* I am equally mired in sin – wickedness bred into my bones. Panic claws at me. Have I passed this wickedness to my son? Is it something deep in my flesh, in my blood, that is in his flesh and blood too? He is far away at the Villa Paradiso with Catarina, breathing the unpolluted country air. He will forget me. Maybe he already has. Perhaps it is a good thing that I cannot blot his life with my darkness.

'Lucrezia confessed, I assume.' This had been clear to me the moment my interrogators mentioned the mushroom tisane. She will have thought of it as a necessary sacrifice.

He nods. 'I'm afraid so, as did Bernardo.'

I emit a little sound of dismay, not quite a cry, not quite a gasp. 'Bernardo? But he can't speak, was rendered mute after it happened. It was the shock.' I pause for a moment assailed with images of Bernardo strapped into some petrifying contraption. 'They didn't force it from him, did they?'

'As far as I've been able to gather, they asked him questions to which he either nodded or shook his head. They asked if he knew of and consented to the plan to kill your father, to which he responded affirmatively. You might know better than I why he responded in such a way.'

'They didn't ask him if he did it, then?'

'Why would they ask that' – he studies me with a puzzled look – 'when it has already been established that Olimpio Calvetti and Marzio Catalano are the murderers?' A flash of suspicion shows in his eyes. 'They want to know who plotted the killing.'

'Of course... Yes, of course. I am not thinking straight. Yesterday's events have made me muddle-headed.'

I realize only now that Farinacci has never asked or even hinted at whether I am guilty or not. Is it irrelevant to him provided he draws his fee?

'Bernardo had nothing to do with any of it,' I say. 'It is more than likely he was confused by their questioning or afraid they would apply force.'

'Yes – I can see how that could be. It is manifestly clear his mind is not sound. He might have had Olimpio Calvetti's torture in mind. Fear of that might make anyone confess to anything, I should think.'

'I'm not aware of him knowing what happened to Olimpio.'

'I gather Giacomo told him.'

I feel suddenly afraid, not for myself, but for Bernardo fearing a punishment he doesn't fully comprehend. The old anger and hatred boil up in me – towards Father. Since he'd died I had no longer felt it so intensely but here it is again, his spectre that will haunt me to the grave. 'Whatever happens, you must make sure he is spared the –' I can't quite bring myself to say it: *the block*. It seems too final. But that is where this ends, where I end. It is the price of my sins. I hadn't looked so far into the abyss until now. 'Do you promise me? I can pay you well.'

'You already pay me quite enough. You have my word. I'll do everything in my power for Bernardo.'

'Thank you.' I graze the back of his papery hand with my fingers and we exchange muted smiles. I see it now, that we have all behaved according to our own characters. I should have seen it before. Bernardo, who can't lie, Lucrezia, who in the end always turns to God, Giacomo, who grew up in permanent terror of the exposure of his private affairs: they all made their confessions, and I, who learned to resist in the cradle, resisted. I did see it, I suppose, but chose to believe in hope instead, fool that I am.

'I suppose there will be proceedings that I will have to attend.'

'Yes. I don't know when yet.'

Something taps hard at the window startling us both. He jumps back with a gasp. 'What was that?' I wonder what happened to him in the past to be so jolted by a sudden sound.

'Just a bird,' I say. 'They see the sky reflected in the glass and fly into it.' I can't remember who first told me that. A jagged smear is left on the pane, a dusty pattern of wings and feathers. I am struck that I will leave behind so little, less even than that. But there is Pio – bright and new and full of life – to carry some small part of me into the future. That thought is a comfort.

'Before the trial, I'm going to canvass Cardinal Colonna. I understand he is sympathetic to your cause. He saw the wrong side of your father, I'm told, and is horrified by the treatment he meted out to you.'

Nobody ever calls it what it was: rape. It is always *treatment* or *unspeakable acts* or *terrible things*. But I know beside all the other abuses, some so much worse, so much more painful and terrifying, it is that which appals the most. It is the going against nature. God should have struck him down for it, but in the end, He left it to me. 'I don't really see, given all the confessions, how Cardinal Colonna can help.'

'Ultimately, even when –' he corrects himself '– even *if* you are condemned, His Holiness can transmute the punishment. Cardinal Colonna might certainly help me to make a plea.'

'I understand.' I don't want, despite the temptation, to clutch at new strands of hope – not any more – I must face my fate stoically. But it is not just *my* fate that hangs in the scales. 'If you think an appeal to the cardinal will help.'

'I'm going to see if, now the interrogations are done with, you can be held with your brothers and stepmother while you await the trial. There is a suitable room on the floor below. I don't see that such a request should pose a problem.' I suppose he means someone will be paid off for our privilege.

He smiles, his scar creasing. 'I can provide you with pen and paper if you'd like to write to anyone. I can deliver any correspondence discreetly, if you understand what I mean.' He touches a finger to his lips to signify silence. 'And I'll see if I can arrange a visit from Giacomo. He's housed along this very corridor. He'll be glad to see you, I'm sure.'

Giacomo stands by the door. We eye each other warily. 'What did they do to you?'

He looks shocked, and so he should. A glut of anger has lodged in my throat. He steps close. I pummel his chest with my fists but I have no strength left. 'You . . . How could you?'

He takes my wrists gently. 'I'm so sorry. So, so sorry, Bea. Such a bloody coward.' His eyes shine with tears and he drops his head. 'I'm so full of shame. Can you ever forgive me?'

'You could have saved yourself. All you needed to do was keep your mouth shut.'

'I'm not strong like you.'

'I can't be the only one of us to be strong.' I am half shouting.

'I'm sorry. I wish . . .' He is distraught.

I finally allow him to draw me into a hug and my anger steps aside.

'You didn't break, Farinacci said.' The sensation of his warm body against mine, the grip of his arms, makes me feel weak with love for him. 'What did they do to you?'

I touch the bandage round my head. 'It looks worse than it is.' I make myself blithe, not wanting his pity. We break out of each other's arms and I, still unsteady on my feet, sit at the table. I gently massage my throbbing temples, careful to avoid the wounds.

'You must hate me for my cowardice. I'm so full of regret.'

'There's no use in regret now.' Or hate, I think. I am about to ask him why he told Bernardo about Olimpio's torture but stop myself. Knowing why won't change anything. 'How's Domizio? He must be beside himself with worry.'

'He went to the Villa Paradiso with Catarina and the little ones. I told him he'd be safer there. I feared they might try to get to me by threatening him.'

'I'm glad they have each other.' My heart feels a little lighter knowing this. 'Farinacci's going to try to have us all held together while we await the trial – with Lucrezia and Bernardo. It'll be better, won't it?'

He sighs, sounding relieved. 'I didn't know how I was going to cope alone. I can't control my thoughts – they take me to places . . .' He brings up his hands to clasp his head. 'It's unbearable, Bea. I might have taken my own life.'

'I know.' I rub a palm over his back. 'You would destroy

Domizio if you did that.' I realize that Domizio will be destroyed anyway, but somehow suicide seems worse because it derives from despair. 'You should make over a property to him now, set him up. If it comes to the worst the Vatican will likely sequester all the Cenci estates.'

'I hadn't thought of that. Oh, God, Bea, how are you able to be so practical?' His hands are on his head again. 'You're making a will?'

'I'm starting to think about it. I hope to leave what came to me from Mother to Catarina, for Pio.' Mother had included a letter with her bequest, for me to read when I came of age. In it she'd said that an income of my own, separate from Father's or a husband's, might one day come as a Godsend. This is that day.

The kind, round woman, whose name, I have learned, is Dorotea, comes to tell me I am to be moved to different rooms. We gather my few things and a guard escorts us to the floor below where I find Lucrezia and Bernardo. Lucrezia rushes to me, taking me in her arms and weeps, while Bernardo stops rocking back and forth a moment to look at me, white-faced, his brow in a troubled scrunch, before returning to his swaying.

'We shall be comfortable in here,' I say, looking round the well-proportioned chamber with large windows, an ornate fireplace and a large and alarmingly lifelike painting of San Sebastiano. It may be well appointed, but it is still a prison. 'Where's Giacomo?'

Lucrezia nods her head in the direction of a door that I hadn't noticed half concealed in the panelling. 'Sleeping.'

'We've two rooms?' I am wondering how much was paid for this privilege. Whatever sum it was, double would still have been worth it to be together again. A small pile of books sits on a side table. I take out a volume. 'My copy of Ovid.'

'I had some of your things brought here, to make it tolerable.'

I don't know how to express my gratitude. Just to have a few of my books after the deprivation of the last days feels like the most wonderful gift.

'And you can change into some proper clothes.' Lucrezia is armoured in one of her best dresses, a crucifix of emeralds and rubies at her throat.

I have hardly been aware of the plainness of the comfortable dress I was wearing when they came for me. It is now grimy at the cuffs and spotted with rusty drops of dried blood at the collar. It makes me long for the bathhouse at the Palazzo Cenci. I will have to make do with the washbasin in the corner, into which I pour a measure of water and sluice my face. I imagine myself shrinking so I can slide my entire body into its tepid shallows.

'Cardinal Colonna has pulled some strings and is sending a painter to make your likeness.'

'My likeness?' I am confused. 'Whatever for?'

'He thinks it will help our cause. If people see what you look like, how young and fragile you are.' Lucrezia is simmering with a manic kind of effervescence.

'Our cause?'

'So we might be pardoned. So the cardinal can petition the Holy Father.' I remember Farinacci talking of Cardinal Colonna in the wake of my interrogation when my mind was too muddled to take things in.

'I don't see how a picture of me looking young and fragile can help our case. Besides, I'm *not* young or fragile. I'm twenty-two and tough as old leather.'

'It's how you *appear*. People will see the portrait and think of what that brute did to you, and they will take pity.'

'I don't want people's pity.' The idea of people turning me

inside out in their minds makes me feel like a piece of meat on a butcher's block. They will see me in church, out riding on the river fields, at the festivals and they will know I was defiled by my father. But, of course, there will be no church, no riding, no festivals. They will see me in the courtroom.

'Oh, Bea, you do. We all do. People are already beginning to say we have suffered enough. Even your father's old enemies are turning their sympathy towards us.'

Lucrezia is clinging to this, and I begin to see the source of her contrary high spirits. It is hope. She believes her life – all our lives – depends upon it. 'How do you know all this?'

'Farinacci was here. I'm very glad we have him on our side. Goodness knows what might happen to us without him.'

'When's he meant to come, this painter?'

'In a few days. Best these heal first.' She gently touches the skin beside one of the lesions on my forehead.

Though I still can't see what a likeness of me can really do to help our situation, I recognize Lucrezia's belief in the cardinal as our saviour. If only I, too, could believe that salvation was so easy. But Lucrezia wasn't crowned with a knotted rope. Lucrezia didn't see her lover dislocated to death.

'And the cardinal himself will come to hear our confessions.'

I don't say that the last thing I wish for is to make my confession to the cardinal, or anyone for that matter, that I believe I am far beyond redemption.

29

'*You* are the painter?' Lucrezia is perplexed. The woman, who was shown in by the turnip-faced guard, is standing before her, wearing an amused expression, while a young man sets up an easel nearby. Lucrezia looks at him, then back at the woman. 'I'd expected . . . I'd thought . . .' She is tongue-tied.

'You'd expected a man?' The painter has clearly heard this before. 'This' – she indicates the young man – 'is my assistant.'

'Good heavens! Well . . .' Lucrezia looks towards me, aghast.

I say nothing. My stepmother is giving me a moment of much-needed levity.

'. . . in that case, I'd better show you the outfit we've prepared.' She presents the bejewelled dress laid out on the bed.

'I'd prefer something simple,' the painter says, asking me politely if I would please unpin my hair. 'Would you mind if I painted you in your linen shift.'

'Her shift!' Lucrezia's face is a picture of dismay.

'You see, Contessa' – she takes one of Lucrezia's hands in both of hers with an appealing smile – 'I seek to conjure the atmosphere of a virgin martyr. The simplicity of apparel will serve to display your stepdaughter's purity of soul.'

The woman's obvious charm and meticulous manners seem to work on Lucrezia, who says, 'Oh, yes. I see it now,' as she helps to undo one of my long plaits. This painter has clearly had experience with bringing noblewomen of a certain age round to her way of thinking. Even Giacomo, who has been so taciturn and agitated, seems to eke a measure of amusement at the sight of our stepmother eating out of the painter's long and elegant hand. It is not just her hands: everything about her is elegant, from the jaunty velvet cap to her slender, black-stockinged ankles and the tumbling brown curls that frame her sharp eyes.

Her animated presence provides respite from the hours of waiting, holding fear at bay with card games and the stories of Ovid or gazing hopelessly at the gruesome San Sebastiano on the wall.

The assistant, a silent boy with a shock of fiery hair, spreads a large oilcloth over the table and on it carefully lays out an array of jars and brushes. Each jar contains a different pigment. As he opens them and spreads a little colour of each on a palette, the room fills with a pleasing mineral scent.

The painter takes a stool, asking me to sit on it in different parts of the room, assessing the quality of the light in each, discussing it with her assistant: 'See here how it falls over her hair . . . but here it reflects off the wall, making the tone cooler.' She eventually opts to put me against a dark hanging with the light coming from one side, filtered through a length of muslin she has suspended over the window. She sits me faced half away, turning my head back towards her. I think this is to make the most of the scar on my cheek – surely a means to garner sympathy in the viewer. *That monstrous father of hers did that to her*, they will say, *poor child*. I am beginning to see how hearts can be won.

Asking first if she may, she arranges my hair so it hangs in long, loose coppery ripples, covering almost entirely the stark whiteness of my shift, giving me the air of a saint. I wonder if she has been directed to create this impression by the cardinal. Did he say, 'Make her like Sant'Agnese,' the noble Roman girl condemned for her Christian piety, dragged naked through the streets, whose hair miraculously grew to cover her modesty. We have a supposed lock of that hair in the chapel at the

Palazzo Cenci. I am reminded of the Sant'Agnese cradling her lamb that hangs over the chest full of torture instruments, somewhere in this very building. With the recollection comes an echo of pain in my temples.

The painter wraps herself in a large apron and sets to work. The soft scuff of her brushes and her benign, concentrated regard have a lulling effect on me. It is strange, I think, how the human spirit has the capacity to achieve periods of contentment, even when facing a maelstrom of horror; even when having lost those one loves; even when harbouring the deepest of sins. I sit with my thoughts. The pain in my head returns from time to time, sudden and sharp, and my tongue absently explores a developing toothache.

She looks at me with a penetrating thoroughness, occasionally approaching me to adjust minutely a fold in my shift or a wandering strand of hair, sometimes standing back and simply staring at me for several minutes at a time. She has instructed me to look directly at her and I wonder if the painting will be one of those in which the eyes follow the viewer. I have always found them unsettling, as if the painted figure will come to life when my back is turned.

When the light goes each evening, the assistant covers the canvas and cleans the brushes, filling the room with the eye-watering smell of the cleaning spirit. All the jars of pigment are stoppered and stashed in their wooden box. Before the two of them leave, the painter asks us, please, to resist the temptation to look. Her expression is so sincere and serious as to render the covered painting like some mysterious sacrament. We dare not even peep – not even Lucrezia who is the most given to temptation – having the sense that the painter will know when she arrives the following morning and somehow the magic will be broken.

The maid Dorotea is a warm and reassuring presence as she

goes about her twice-daily cleaning and tidying ritual, treating us with kindness. Indeed, she pays such deference to Lucrezia it is almost as if she doesn't believe my stepmother is waiting to be tried for plotting the murder of her husband. It causes me to ponder on what it is about the aristocracy that has such a great allure. Father was heavily gilded with the brush of nobility but there wasn't a noble or dignified or deserving hair on his head. Nobility is nothing more than good fortune. Look at me, who stole a woman's intended and who, in the coldest blood, sought to commit patricide – *what am I?* But I can see how the cardinal and Farinacci might hope to use this force of misapplied goodwill to save us all from the block.

Dorotea doesn't like the painter's materials. She says the smell of the cleaning spirit cannot be healthy in a bedchamber and opens the windows wide, allowing in the street sounds: laughter, the rumble of carriages, the patter of feet, the clop of hoofs. Ordinary life goes on out there. I think of Father's thoroughbred horses languishing in the Palazzo Cenci stables, exercised by the grooms, one ridden, one on either side on halters – such a waste of beauty, of strength.

'What will happen to the horses?' I ask Giacomo. 'If . . .' I don't say it.

'I haven't thought about that.'

I long for a morning of riding, the feeling of the air catching in my hair, the vigour of Aquilino beneath me, gleeful to be out, Virgil at our side, hurtling after hares. Virgil and Aquilino are at the Villa Paradiso with Catarina and the infants. I want to feel my son nuzzling in my arms. I am losing everything I hold dear, one by one. The thought drills fear deep into me. I must keep it at bay.

To distract myself I scatter breadcrumbs on the open windowsill, watching as the little birds come, twitchy and nervous, to feed. Their legs are so fine it seems impossible that they can support their rotund bodies but, then, feathers weigh almost nothing, their bright plumage disguising their minuteness. Still my thoughts trail into the shadows.

The painter's arrival is a welcome distraction.

'I should be finished in an hour or so,' she says, removing the cover to peruse her work. She seems pleased. I can feel Giacomo and Lucrezia's eagerness to see the painting mingle with my own curiosity, creating a heady atmosphere as I sit for the final time, watching the painter's gaze move from me to her picture and back again and again as her brush caresses tiny specks of colour onto the canvas.

She stands back and discusses quietly with her assistant. 'A spot of white to light the eye here?'

The assistant nods with great seriousness. 'And perhaps here, in the shadow, a fine line of umber where the pale shift fades to darkness?'

They continue this for several minutes before the painter says, 'It's done. Would you like to see it?'

Lucrezia and Giacomo can hardly be contained, commenting on its beauty, the fineness of the brushwork, the extraordinary detail, while Bernardo continues to build and destroy card houses. I stand, stretching away the stiffness from sitting in one position for so long, and move to the face of the painting, to be confronted by a stranger.

I see a young woman, very young, barely beyond girlhood, an invented crucifix hanging on a chain from her neck, her hair rippling gloriously around narrow shoulders, small arms, arms incapable of lugging a basket of soiled linens, or heaving an iron kettle from the fire – or turning a heavy mattress. What strikes me most is the sad little plea in her countenance. It is not me. Where is my strength, my stubbornness, my toughness, my wild disposition, my rage? Who is this girl, so sinned against? Where is the woman who did what I did? Where is the steel in my gaze, the abandon I cannot suppress? Where is the imprint of my sins, my shamelessness? I am absent from this portrait.

'It doesn't please you?' says the painter.

'It's not that,' I say. 'I am unaccustomed to seeing myself as others see me.'

She laughs. I hadn't meant to be light-hearted but smile, nonetheless.

The painting is perfection, but it is a lie. 'It is exquisite,' I say.

That afternoon Farinacci brings Cardinal Colonna to see the work. The only things to betray his status are the scarlet piping on his cassock, the red silk *zucchetto* perched on his balding pate, and the numerous rings cluttering his short fingers. He has a flat nose, a ruddy complexion and high arched brows that give him an air of permanent surprise. He greets Giacomo warmly, expressing his dismay at our situation. I wasn't aware they were acquainted but they seem to know one another quite well, and I wonder if this is one of the reasons he has taken up our cause. He is delighted by the painting, deems it 'ideal', and tells his servant to arrange for it to be packed and transported to his house.

'I will have copies printed and distributed as pamphlets,' he says. 'Even the hardest of hearts couldn't fail to be moved to pity on seeing that face.'

'Why are you helping us?' I ask him, ignoring the glare from Lucrezia that says I'm being too direct.

'I knew your father.' He doesn't explain himself further, but the fleeting look of loathing that crosses his face says something. 'I am of the mind that the circumstances of your situation are enough to mitigate any sentence that might be decided at the trial.' Lucrezia expels a small noise of relief.

'Indeed, I expect a full pardon. You have all suffered enough.'

Lucrezia expresses her gratitude effusively. She trusts so eagerly but I am left still questioning his motives.

'Do you not consider what we have done a sin?' I say, registering another disapproving glare from my stepmother, and Farinacci clears his throat.

'That, my child,' he places a benevolent hand over mine, 'is between you and the Lord.'

He offers, then, to hear our confessions and we explain that Bernardo, who has been regarding our visitor from across the room with a level of suspicion, is mute. 'It was a most terrible shock, you see,' explains Lucrezia.

'That, I can imagine. I will confer a blessing on him instead.'

He moves towards Bernardo who shifts in his seat, throwing him a wary look from the tail of his eye. The cardinal hovers a hand above his head, incanting a prayer. Bernardo closes his eyes and seems at peace for a moment. I am suddenly sad that my brother has had so little peace in his short life, always so guarded, always riven with distrust.

Lucrezia is the first to follow the cardinal into the adjoining chamber. Giacomo and I wait in silence under the gaze of the unfamiliar girl in the painting, while Farinacci quietly occupies himself with correspondence. I watch the birds on the sill, the way the sun filters in patterns through the window and the formations of clouds interrupting the sheer clean blueness of the sky. So much beauty in the world. I want to soak it all up, every last fleck of it. 'Do you think he can secure our pardon?' I say to Giacomo.

'We'd better hope so.'

'Are you afraid?'

'Oh, Bea – why must you be so direct? Of course I'm afraid, but I try to keep my mind elsewhere.' He sighs deeply. 'I miss Domizio.'

'You truly love him, don't you?' I am jolted by the memory of Terza once saying the same thing to me.

As he nods in reply, I see that his eyes are glossy with tears. 'Father deserved what he got,' he blurts, seeming to gird himself. 'He was a wicked, wicked monster.'

It is the first time he has spoken so directly of it.

'And you – you truly loved Olimpio. He was one of the good ones.'

'What was he like when you were friends as young men?' My tongue worries at my aching tooth.

'He was the most loyal and big-hearted person I ever knew. I wish . . .' He stops himself. We both know there is no point in wishing.

'We have Pio,' I say, feeling intensely the wrench of separation.

'Dear little Pio.' A tear spills from one of his eyes, trailing down his cheek. I wipe it away with my thumb. 'You must miss him terribly. Can't he be brought here to visit?'

I have thought about this a great deal. 'I feel . . .' it is hard to articulate what I really feel '. . . that it's better he forgets me.' The truth of this battles with my bitterness. 'If things shouldn't go . . .' A defeated sigh bursts from me. 'Oh, you know what I mean.'

'Bea,' he puts his arm around my shoulder, 'you mustn't let yourself think that way. When we are pardoned you can be reunited.'

'Yes, when we know.' My tone is empty of conviction.

When I am called in to make my confession, I tell the cardinal that I am not ready yet to account fully for my sins. He is understanding, tells me I have been through a great deal but that the Lord is a merciful master.

'I – I wonder,' I stammer, 'if I deserve His mercy.'

'My child, it is my opinion that even had you wielded the

weapon that killed your father, in the eyes of the Lord you are still deserving of his forgiveness. Unlike the law of Rome, God's law is compassionate to the repentant.' He places his big, gnarled hand over mine. 'You are safe to speak freely.'

There is something so comforting and kindly about him that lulls me towards trust.

'I don't know if I'm ready to repent. The thing is' – I meet his gaze, which holds me softly – 'I am glad he is dead. I am only sorry for the situation I find myself in, and my family, though I recognize that I deserve everything the law brings to my door.'

'Your father was your tormentor, so your gladness is quite understandable. You are only human, my child, and the Lord will recognize your father's acts against you as unnatural. He will understand your frailty, and when you find the strength to overcome it, you will be shriven.'

'Even though I have doubted Him so often? Can He forgive that? And all the lies. Will He forgive all the lies?'

'All you need do is repent, and if you are not quite ready now, you will be, my child. And remember, as the Lord says in Isaiah, "Though your sins are like scarlet, they shall be white as snow; though they are red like crimson, they shall become like wool."' He then asks me if I read Latin well and recommends a number of Bible verses that he says will help me in my darkest hours.

The desire presses at me to ask him what was meant by Mother Superior all those years ago – *more than her fair share of original sin* – but I dare not. What if the truth of it is something so monstrous as to nullify any possible redemption?

What if?

30

A small but persistent gathering of people has assembled beneath our window at the Corte Savella, the effect of the cardinal's campaign. They remain throughout the day despite the blazing late-August sun beating down, and even at night one or two stand vigil. Sometimes they chant: *Beatrice Cenci è innocente. La famiglia Cenci è innocente.* They stop passers-by to hand them pamphlets, and sometimes one beats a drum when they chant. It started with an enthusiastic pair, but their numbers proliferate as the weeks pass.

Today the entire street is filled with people, pushing and shoving and chanting. Today is the day we will be tried in the courtroom downstairs. With each arrival at the building the crowd shouts and surges. They call for me to come to the window, to show myself to them.

'Go on,' urges Lucrezia, whose hope has burgeoned with this proof of public support. She and Giacomo are buoyant with it. I am more circumspect.

'Better not,' says Farinacci. 'You don't want them to become overwrought. Someone might be crushed.'

'I hadn't thought,' says Lucrezia, backing away from the window.

I am playing cards with Bernardo, trying to distract him, to keep him from becoming fretful. We will only be called to state under oath that our testimonies are truthful. Otherwise we will not be obliged to speak, and concessions have been made for Bernardo's muteness. 'The trial is only a formality,' Farinacci has told us. 'A few witnesses will be called and you,

Beatrice, will be found guilty. The rest of you have already made your guilty pleas, so there will be nothing unexpected. It is the sentencing that can't be planned for.'

Lucrezia can't stay still and fusses over her appearance. She has changed her dress twice already this morning and is considering a third. 'Do you think this one, which gives me a more sober air, or this?' She is holding up a splendid garment, embroidered with black birds on green satin.

'The sober one,' says Farinacci, who is the only one of us Lucrezia will listen to for advice.

My toothache has worsened to a permanent dull ache with the occasional shooting pain that reaches up through my jaw and into my skull. Lucrezia has dosed me with her tincture, which has deadened almost all sensation in my body and muffled my mind, making me less anxious about the trial than I might be. I understand now how she came to crave this befuddlement. The cardinal's voice runs through my head: *Though your sins are like scarlet, they shall be white as snow.* I remain unconvinced about my potential for redemption. My nightmares have returned in force, filled with hordes of demons, the circles of Dante's inferno spiralling down through my sleep.

As we are escorted from our rooms, Bernardo grabs my hand, holding it all the way down the staircase and into the large courtroom, where the public gallery, crammed to the gunwales, falls to a deathly silence, so even the soft scuff of our feet on the stone floor can be heard as we are led to our bench. Despite Farinacci's reassurances, his conviction, I am taut with trepidation.

We are seated with our backs to the gallery. Lucrezia is white and Giacomo is grey. His Adam's apple moves up and down his gullet as he attempts to swallow his fear. Bernardo reaches for my hand again. It is damp in mine and he smells pungently of teenage boy. I see Cardinal Colonna, relieved by his benevolent presence in the ranks of churchmen behind the three bishops who will judge our case. All three are stern-faced in their robes the colour of wine, seated at a table on a dais. I recognize, too, the yellow-stockinged priest who oversaw Olimpio's death. *Murderer!* I wish I had the courage to shout it, to point at him, tell the gallery of his crime and watch them tear him limb from limb. I rein in my thoughts for fear they will undo me.

Bernardo is called first. 'Don't worry,' I whisper, releasing his hand. He looks at me, his eyes wheeling like those of a startled horse. 'Just do as they ask.' He turns and walks the twenty paces to the rostrum before the judges. He looks so young. I am glad of that, as perhaps it will inspire mercy in them. A hairpin is agitating my scalp. Lucrezia had dressed my hair too tightly for comfort. I pull it out, twisting it, pressing its sharp point into the pad of my thumb.

Bernardo nods to affirm the oath and nods in response to the question of whether he stands by his testimony and his plea, before returning to his seat. I feel a measure of relief that he managed to retain his poise. The process is repeated for Lucrezia and Giacomo.

When I am called a hubbub starts up in the chamber, increasing in volume as I walk across the floor. My slippers register no sound on the marble surface, making me feel like a wraith. '*Innocente*,' someone shouts, repeating it over and over until he is removed from the court. Once the place is silent again, a Bible is brought for me to make my oath. My throat constricts and I am asked to speak louder. There is a faint quiver in my voice and I hold tight to the lip of the rostrum for fear of my legs giving way beneath me. My muffled head swims a little, transforming the churchmen in their vivid vestments into a sea of colour. I am asked if I stand by my plea of innocence.

I feel tight, as if my skin has shrunk.

'I do.'

A collective inhalation comes from the gallery behind.

I cannot plead guilty to the charge of ordering the death of my father, as it is not the truth. Had they charged me with wishing death on my father, or attempting and failing to kill my father with poison, or of dosing him with a brew of fool's angel that I didn't know would take two days to snuff out his life, I would have pleaded guilty. But it is not a crime to wish someone dead, not by this law – only by God's. But neither is God's law straightforward. *An eye for an eye.* I have thought about it a great deal. If I'd been born a thousand years ago, I would have been obligated to take revenge for Father's deeds. So, the law is not firm in my mind.

If they want me guilty, they must find me so. I press the point of the hairpin into my flesh so hard it draws a bead of blood.

Farinacci had advised me – well, begged me really – to admit my guilt as the others had done, said it would make things easier for me. But I can't do that. My own self stands in my way – *but why?* Do I fear that if I say more than I already have, the whole story will tumble out of me and Bernardo will be done for?

Parts of my statement are read out and after each I am asked if I stand by them. I do. My tooth throbs. My head aches. My mind spins. The minuscule wound on my thumb stings. I am glad to be led back to my seat and Bernardo's clammy hand. I, too, need reassurance now.

We retire at noon for an interminable hour during which Farinacci attempts, unsuccessfully, to persuade me to change my plea. When we return, witnesses are called. Terza catches my eye briefly as she crosses the floor, barely recognizable in a dress, her hair pinned under a coif. She is run through the events of that fateful day, as are Enzo the groom, the kitchen lads and the maids from La Rocca. Don Tomassino is called and relates how he'd seen Marzio Catalano and Olimpio Calvetti carrying a large object in the direction of the balcony. 'No,' he didn't know where I was at the time, he says when asked. Nothing is teased from any of them that is not already known.

Then comes Ilaria, floating in like an angel in her white habit. I can barely look at her, the girl who spilled my secrets, and wait for her to spill them again, a knot of bitterness tightening in my belly. Lucrezia's elbow presses into my side – she had never trusted Ilaria. I brace myself. But Ilaria recounts only the events of that day. My pregnancy isn't mentioned, Olimpio isn't mentioned, except when she answers their question about whether she had seen him. 'Only in passing.'

'Did he seem suspicious to you?'

'He seemed as he always did.'

My ill-will disperses. Whatever she might have said in the past, and they may well have threatened her into speaking then, she is revealing nothing now. I hope the girl has found peace in the convent.

She meets me with her angelic grey gaze, making a tiny nod as she pads from the chamber.

The announcer then cries, 'The court calls Signorina Gasparini.'

I can't help but stare at the handsome young woman, well turned out in a black dress, who walks slowly in, her head set proudly, expression grim.

Recognition strikes me like a mallet.

I remember with absolute clarity, looking from the window at La Rocca, when Father's body had been found, and seeing this very face, framed by a scarlet headscarf. I cannot forget the force of the woman's blunt stare that made me shrink back into the shadows.

'Who is she?' whispers Lucrezia.

'I don't know.' There is something about the face this woman wears that is making me uneasy. Even from behind, when she is standing at the rostrum, the rigidity of her posture exudes hostility.

She is taken through the oath.

The blood from my thumb has smudged over my cuff and my mind is suddenly full of all that blood and the unholy thudding. My breath shortens. I force the memory away.

Farinacci approaches the bishops, speaking in a low voice, his hands gesticulating, revealing that he, too, is disconcerted by the appearance of this Signorina Gasparini. He is summarily dismissed, reminded that he hasn't the right to register such a complaint.

When the disgruntled Farinacci is back in his seat the woman is asked a few questions, which she answers soberly.

'I was one of the first to arrive at La Rocca. When the screaming was heard, they came to fetch me. I was housekeeper at the castle, you see, well, I had been housekeeper previously, so that's why they came to me first. I had only a few weeks before returned from tending my dying grandmother.' Her voice cracks slightly and she stops to cross herself. 'I hadn't reprised my duties.'

'When you were made aware of the contessa's screams, what did you then do?'

'I rushed up the hill as fast as I could.' She goes on to explain about Father's body in the warren. 'His fall appeared at first to have been broken by a large mulberry tree but when they brought him up and laid him out' – she pauses once more to cross herself – 'it was plain to see that his wounds couldn't have been caused by any fall.'

One of the bishops raises his hand. 'With respect, Signorina Gasparini, we are aware of all this, and we know who the perpetrators were. I understood there was something more you wanted to add?'

Then she seems to lose all her poise. 'We know who the perpetrators were, yes, indeed! And one of them was my husband-to-be, inveigled into murder by that woman' – she whips round and points at me – 'who seduced him for her evil purposes.'

Plautilla!

The gallery gasps.

I stare at my hands and worry at the tiny wound on my thumb, while fear scratches at my skull.

'I saw them,' she spits. 'He came to me to tell me he was releasing me from my obligation to wed him. I knew why that was.' She pauses, seething. 'I'd seen them in the forest together.'

All the time I had blamed Ilaria when it was Plautilla who had exposed us, and now she is doing so in public, crumbling the fragile façade of saintly innocence Cardinal Colonna has so carefully constructed. She doesn't have the air of a woman glad to be rid of the intended she loathed. She is a woman wronged.

'*She* made him do it. She turned a good man into a murderer.' She is thrusting her finger at me again and again. I feel each stab pierce my flesh, lacerate my organs.

The gallery has fallen to a deathly silence.

Farinacci is on his feet. 'This is supposition at best and slander at the very least.'

Plautilla Gasparini is eventually dismissed but the air remains thick with her accusations.

I am asked once more if I stand by my plea.

'I have nothing to add.' I don't recognize my own voice, so pathetic and quivering.

'Is it the case that you seduced your father's vassal, Olimpio Calvetti, into performing the deed on your behalf?'

'It is not.' I want to shout at them: *How dare you make something so perfect, so beautiful, into something so base?*

'Remember you are under oath, Signorina Cenci.'

'I speak the truth.' I trace the cross embossed into the Bible, leaving a tiny blot of blood on the pigskin and hang there under their judging eyes for what seems an age. What do they see in me that makes them wear such grim masks?

Back in my seat again, I must listen to the prosecutor describing what we have done.

'Beatrice Cenci did conspire with her brothers and stepmother to murder her father . . .' The crowd shifts – they don't like it either. *Did conspire.* He makes our fumbled attempts on Father's life sound like a conspiracy, organized and carefully – coldly – planned, not the desperate scramble for survival it was.

Farinacci now mounts his defence, describing the reign of terror our family lived through under Father, explaining how we deserve mercy. 'Frightened, and in fear of their lives . . .' I'm not listening any more.

Eventually the bishops rise and the court is dismissed until the following day, for sentencing.

Farinacci is furious that he hadn't found out in advance of Plautilla's appearance to testify. 'You were good. Very calm,' he says to me. 'She came over as a woman touched by lunacy – quite mad.' He coaxes me to the far end of the room, away from my stepmother and brothers, who seem exhausted, slumped on the chairs near the empty hearth. 'Was there any truth in what she said?' He speaks under his breath. 'You didn't –'

I don't let him finish, saying firmly, 'I did not. It is well known we were lovers, but seduce him as a means to inveigle him to murder – certainly not.' I can see how it might appear to be so but am still swilling with horrified indignation from Plautilla's accusation.

'It is not *so well known* that you were lovers. That lot out there' – he indicates the window, where the crowds can still be heard below – 'weren't aware of it.' He looks worried.

'Well, they are now.' I am losing my patience.

We fall to silence.

My tooth is nagging.

Dorotea brings a tray of victuals. Giacomo pours drinks from a jug, handing them round. He seems to have folded in on himself. Bernardo rocks quietly and Lucrezia obsessively tidies her hair and straightens her dress.

I hear a commotion below the window and a familiar voice: *His Holiness will not let the sinners go free* . . . It is the wretched preacher from the Piazza del Popolo, come to haunt us. We all hear it, looking round at each other. Dread buzzes in the air. Then we hear the chanting start up again, louder and louder: *Beatrice Cenci è innocente.*

'Listen!' Farinacci says, seeming quite triumphant. 'We haven't lost their support. Thank the Lord for that.'

Lucrezia drops to her knees in prayer. Giacomo crosses himself.

It would seem, then, that the girl in the painting has garnered her own momentum: the crowd have simply chosen to overlook Beatrice Cenci as the wicked creature who seduced another woman's intended into murdering her father, in favour of that frail innocent girl, so sinned against.

Between these two poles lies the real me, almost invisible, spectral, an ephemera, like that watery medusa.

We are led down to the courtroom on the following morning after a torrid, sleepless night. The crowds in the gallery are restless, a shout going up, others joining in. They call repeatedly for our pardon. It takes some time to quieten them.

Bernardo has my hand again. He is jigging his leg and

grinding his teeth. I worry he will fall into a fit, right there before the court. Lucrezia is on his other side today. She also holds his hand but doesn't look much calmer than he. Giacomo is breathing loudly to my other side and muttering a prayer to himself. *How do I feel?* Insubstantial, as if I might dissolve into the air, pinned to the earth only by Bernardo's hot quivering grip. I worry at my bad tooth with my tongue.

The bishops file in and the various interminable ceremonies of the court are gone through. The bishops shuffle their papers and straighten their clothes.

Finally, one stands to pronounce the sentence. A torrent of blood rushes through my head.

We have been called in judgement to assess the part the four accused, sitting here before us, he wafts his gaze over us, *played in the death of Conte Francesco Cenci, father to three of the accused and husband to one, and come to an appropriate sentence. We have taken into account the circumstances that led to the count's death and it has been well demonstrated that the conte's behaviour to his family was unnatural in the extreme and it is our unanimous opinion that . . .*

He drones on, finally drawing towards his conclusion.

The sentences are as follows: Lucrezia, Dowager Contessa Cenci, to be executed by the axe. Lucrezia expels a distressed hissing groan and seems to collapse in on herself. My heart taps frantically. *Giacomo, Conte Cenci, to be hanged, drawn and quartered, his entrails to be . . .* I cannot listen. Giacomo brings his hand absently to his throat but holds his gaze firmly ahead, not showing the fear that I know is roiling beneath his surface. *Bernardo Cenci, in recognition that he has not yet reached his majority, is to be executed by the axe . . .*

A sound starts up, thud, thud, thud, rhythmic as a funeral drum, not in my mind but resounding loudly through the hushed space. Bernardo is banging his head against the back of the pew.

The bishop stops his speech, looking about, unable to ascertain the source of the noise. The ranks of churchmen whisper and the gallery agitates, wondering where this ghostly drummer hides. They begin to stamp their feet in time.

I try to coax my brother to stop. 'Listen to me. I won't let it happen.' He stares ahead, continuing, as if I'm not there, thud, thud, thud, echoing back those terrible wet thuds into Father's skull. All the blood. I am saturated in gore. *Don't think of that – not now, not ever.*

Giacomo is strung on his nerves. 'Do something. Stop him.'

Lucrezia on his other side is tearfully reminding Bernardo what Farinacci told them. 'This is just a formality, sweetheart.' Her voice is brittle with tension.

I grip my youngest brother's fisted hand, tight. 'I promise I will make sure you are pardoned if it is the last thing I do on earth.' I wish I could believe my own words. I vow silently to do everything in my power to keep that promise.

Bernardo stops the banging to hang his head, eyes screwed shut, but the gallery continues stamping.

The bishop, now brimming with irritation, clears his throat and cracks something hard against the table.

The place falls to quiet.

The bishop continues.

Beatrice Cenci, despite her plea of innocence, is unanimously found guilty as the principal agent of the crime and will be executed by the axe . . .

I don't want to hear. I want to duck beneath the surface of my life where the only sound is a watery echo.

The gallery explodes into a spontaneous uproar of objection.

I am completely numb.

. . . The sentences will be carried out on the eleventh day of September, in the frontmost court of the Castel Sant'Angelo . . .

He continues speaking but I can't hear over the angry baying of the crowd, now being held back by a phalanx of guards.

I can't tell if they are baying for our blood or our freedom.

Once we are back in the upstairs rooms and have managed to calm Bernardo, we are surprised by a visit from Ilaria. She slips into the room gently as a whisper. 'I was given leave to come and say prayers with you.' She looks scrubbed and fresh and has retained a slight edge of shyness yet inhabits herself more substantially, with more confidence, than she used to. Her presence is a quiet and much-needed distraction.

We sit – she, Lucrezia and I – in a puddle of sun that has spilled in from the window, where the muffled sound of the crowd drifts up from the street. Ilaria glows in her white habit, looking more than ever like a heavenly being. I wish the painter could have seen her. If there is anyone who should be immortalized, it is this girl, in whom vanity is wholly absent.

'You seem happy,' I say, castigating myself inwardly for having mistrusted her. Plautilla slides into my mind with her righteous rage, shedding a shadow of disgrace across me.

'I have found my place in the world.' She takes my hand, something she would have hesitated to do before. 'For that, I am grateful to you.'

'I'm glad for you, dear.' Lucrezia is pallid and twitchy, adjusting her coif, fiddling with her pearls, dosing herself discreetly with a measure of tincture, but she manages a smile.

'Shall we pray?' Ilaria suggests, and we line up on our knees at the prayer-stand while she asks forgiveness for us all, and mercy. The voice of the bishop and his sentence nip at me, making my belly swill with fear, despite Farinacci's conviction that it is nothing more than a legal formality.

The guard arrives to escort Ilaria out, leaving us alone in a hollow silence.

Not much later, Farinacci comes. 'We have two weeks to prepare our plea.'

I wonder why he always makes it sound – *our plea* – as if we are all behind his legal machinations, when it is only he and his assistants building their case. 'I have persuaded them to allow you to stay together for the meantime, but this might change.'

'How much do you need? I'll make the funds available.' Giacomo looks almost dead with exhaustion. 'We can buy our way out of this, I assume.'

'It won't be straightforward, and you might have to hand over a great deal.'

'Meaning?' Giacomo says.

'With the cardinal's help I will endeavour to petition His Holiness directly. He might be persuaded if we offer him the Palazzo Cenci.'

'The whole palazzo?' Lucrezia is outraged.

'For our lives!' snaps Giacomo, his patience gone.

'But it is our home.'

'It's not as if we will be on the streets.'

'I own a third of it.'

'So, *your* third will buy *your* life.'

They argue bitterly for a few moments.

I say nothing. I don't care about the palazzo, a place filled with the ghosts of misery and violence. All I long for is a quiet life at the modest Villa Paradiso, with Pio and Catarina and Vittoria, away from the capital, with the sea in the distance. I sit quietly beside Bernardo, who has disappeared into his own world – I hope it is a peaceful one. Night is beginning to fall and I can still hear the clamour of the crowd in the street below.

31

My toothache becomes intolerable. I imagine I am rotting from the inside and remind myself, bitterly, that I have only a few days left on earth. But even so I call for a barber-surgeon, so a small part of me must by convinced by Farinacci's belief in our imminent pardon. Otherwise, I suppose, I would simply resort to the befuddlement of Lucrezia's drops.

He is a youngish man, large and muscular, who says, after greeting us, 'I can't believe they're keeping you imprisoned like this. The whole of Rome can see that the circumstances are mitigating. Excuse me for saying, but the conte deserved everything he got.' He crosses himself half-heartedly and, as he lays out his implements, the pliers and the pelican hooks, and ties his leather apron over his clothes, goes on to tell of his young relative who was once employed by Father and was badly ill-treated.

I look at his tools as they emerge from his bag, my stomach buckling, and remember the chest downstairs presided over by Sant'Agnese, imagining it contains similar ironmongery along with its knotted ropes and truncheons.

The barber instructs me to sit in a chair near the light from the window, where he inspects the bothersome tooth from different angles. 'Definitely needs to be extracted.'

Giacomo holds me from behind, firm arms around my chest, while the barber places one foot on the seat of my chair for traction. He pulls at the wretched thing with his pelican hook. It comes away with a horrible sucking sound and a great shudder of pain.

'Half rotted away,' he says, holding out the tooth in his palm. 'Full of infection. Big canker in the root. It's no wonder you've been suffering. Should feel much better when it's settled down and the poison's had a chance to drain.'

The tooth is black in parts and almost completely hollow. Like me, I think, imagining that poison pumping through my heart, through my veins, pooling in the cavities of my body. It will take an eternity to drain away. He gives me a measure of opiate tincture before he leaves and I drift into a sleep filled with dreams in which parts of my body are dying and falling away – first my fingers and toes, rotting on the bone, then my arms and legs. Once I am all decomposed, I shall be reborn new, my sleeping self thinks. I search desperately for the parts of myself I have lost, thwarted at every turn. I climb the steep path to La Rocca, standing on the balcony, my hair flying up into the empty sky. A great pair of harpy wings bursts from my spine, opening.

I wake abruptly, confused. I am not in the bed. I am at the window. Fear alights in me with a stuttering inhalation. In my mind's eye I can see my body sprawled below, the shocked supporters gathering round. I feel death's chilled clutch on my shoulder.

It is a long time since I have sleepwalked, and it is as unnerving as ever. I shake the image from my head, closing the window. The supporters have seen me from below. A shadowy figure shouts, 'She's up there,' and waves, his companions gathering, staring up and pointing, as if at an eclipse or a shooting star. I press my hands and my forehead to the glass. The small night crowd flickers in the light of their torches. If only they knew who I really was, how deep my sin runs, they would not be standing vigil. But they think I am the girl in the painting, and now this belief has embedded, it is sprouting with more vigour each day. Nothing, it seems, will uproot it from their hearts.

Retreating into the depths of the room, I sink into a chair in the darkness, thoughts circling like crows about a carcass.

When the guard announces that Farinacci is here, I am still in the chair, stiff-necked, having dropped off sometime before dawn. A blanket has been thrown over me. Mercifully the pain has gone from my jaw. With Lucrezia's help I hurriedly shrug my gown over my nightclothes before he enters.

He is wearing what appears to be his best suit and is in unusually buoyant spirits. 'The cardinal has an audience with His Holiness this afternoon. I have permission to accompany him and make my plea on your behalf, directly.'

Giacomo is ebullient. 'Thank Heaven,' he says, several times. He even finds a smile. 'I must let Domizio know.' He is already at the table scrawling on a sheet of paper.

'Thank the Lord.' Lucrezia has dropped onto her knees at the prayer-stand.

Bernardo is scrunched in a corner, like a discarded ball of paper.

I don't know what to think or who to thank.

I wish I could share in Farinacci's confidence, which seems to have rubbed off on the others so easily.

'I've been working on the plea all night.' Farinacci pulls a sheaf of papers from his satchel. His cheeks are a high colour and he appears ferociously stimulated by the task. He begins to run through what he intends to say. He talks initially of my part in the crime, or what he believes it to be, going on to say how Father imprisoned me and Lucrezia in La Rocca and how he had forced us to live under a terrible regime of fear.

I don't want to be reminded about what life was like under Father's aegis. I was there. I don't need to have it described to me again. So, I only half listen while he speaks as if addressing the Holy Father in person.

'It is clearly established law that the penalty of death affixed to the crime of parricide is not applicable where the crime proceeds from one of the fourteen causes . . .' He goes on, citing several cases of precedence. One is of a son who lay with his own stepmother and was killed by his father. 'The father escaped execution. But to compromise the chastity of a daughter is legally a grave and infamous outrage . . . a crime far greater than a son corrupting the concubine of his father . . .' On and on he goes, listing his citations and his precedents, his pardoned murderers, a litany of the terrible things people are capable of doing to one another.

Eventually he brings up the ancients: Cyane who stabbed her father because he debauched her, and Medullina, who did likewise. His examples seem inexhaustible. Inevitably he arrives at 'Orestes, who killed his mother for her crimes and was first condemned but finally acquitted by Minerva herself.'

As he says it, I am thinking, too, of the reasons Orestes' mother killed her husband, he who put to death their daughter to appease the gods and have his war. Minerva never pardoned the mother, no, she was condemned to the cycle of revenge that blighted the House of Atreus.

I sense that grim inheritance reverberating down the centuries, consuming families in its curse – ending with us. My mind is scrambling to recall what happens to Orestes' sisters in that bleak tale. I know what became of Iphigenia, in her blood-drenched wedding dress. But what of Electra, she who pushed her brother to take vengeance? It seems to me a dreadful parallel, history repeating and repeating: sons killing their mothers, fathers killing their daughters, wives killing their husbands, the furies hounding them all for retribution.

Olimpio is whispering to me: *It's not a fury, it's you.*

I remember now, Electra lives. A thread of hope, fine as a hair, catches in me. But no – it snaps – what have these characters, dragged from myth, in common with us here? Our world and our laws have nothing to do with them. But Farinacci is convinced by his argument, and he is the expert.

It seems his exemplars have no end. 'Virginius was acquitted of the homicide of his daughter, though she was innocent, because he killed her to save her from the brutality of Appius. It follows then that Beatrice Cenci is much more to be dealt with indulgently by the law for seeking to kill her father who was a criminal, and assaulted her chastity . . .' He comes to the question of self-defence as against cold blood: 'It is not immediate fear alone but fear occasioned by future danger, as indeed Beatrice lived with danger constantly hanging over her . . .'

He moves his plea to Bernardo's case making much of his youth and suggesting that his confession should be deemed unreliable as it came about in fear of torture. 'But, most of all,' he continues, 'he is not only a minor but is and was of an unsound mind and fragile disposition . . .'

Bernardo, on hearing his name, looks towards Farinacci, making a strange guttural noise. We all turn to look at him expectantly as he seems on the brink of speech. Fearing a spontaneous confession, I silently will him to keep his words to himself. His mouth opens. I am back in that blood-spattered chamber. I see the gleam of the hammer as it arcs through the gloom. But he says nothing.

Farinacci then comes to the arguments he has constructed for Lucrezia and Giacomo, listing several and stating there are many more that he is compelled by time to omit. 'If Beatrice, whom the court has found to be the principal agent in the commission of the crime, is deserving of indulgence then it follows that her brothers and stepmother, too, deserve clemency.'

He looks up from his papers then. 'After which I will tie it up, ask His Holiness for mitigation of punishment, beg for his compassion, say you await on bended knees and with the most profound submission, for his judgement, et cetera, et cetera.' He stops, folds the sheaf of papers and places it on the table. 'What do you think?'

Lucrezia takes both his hands in hers. 'You have saved our lives with this.' A brightness has returned to her eyes and I notice, too, that Giacomo has shed his haunted look.

'I don't know how to thank you. The work you have put in . . .' My brother is effusive.

'His Holiness would have to have a heart of stone not to take pity on us,' says Lucrezia.

'Not only that,' Giacomo interrupts, slapping Farinacci on the back. 'Your legal reasoning can't fail to convince.'

All three of them, Lucrezia, Giacomo and Farinacci, are smiling. I am not smiling. I don't know what to think, whether to allow myself the luxury of hope. My conscience flaps in my skull, like a trapped bird. I can't help but think of Olimpio and Marzio, who, none of them seem to care, are dead. Indeed, they must all believe it is a convenience. Bernardo is rocking manically. I do not want to know what is going through his mind.

Farinacci leaves, saying he will send word as to how his plea is received the minute his audience is over. 'I feel sure,' he says, 'that the news will be good.'

We watch from the window as he emerges from the building and into the street, where he stops to speak to the crowd of supporters. A cheer goes up. Hats are thrown into the air.

We wait like expectant fathers. Giacomo paces, Lucrezia offers prayers of gratitude, Bernardo builds and breaks down card houses, while I try to read, but my belly is full of moths.

I turn a page and find a pressed forget-me-not, a faded ghost. My heart swells and I am there in that glade with its sweet scent and its carpet of flowers – a place out of time.

He whispers, *That's why I love you.* I catch the faintest whiff of musk and sense him drifting close.

Hope creeps up on me and I begin, for the first time in months, to imagine the shape of my future. I am riding to the Villa Paradiso. Aquilino is frisky, pulling at the bit. I let him have his head and he gallops full-tilt across the pasture. Virgil dashes beside us, fleet as an arrow. The wind rushes through me, cleaning me of the past. We slow along the riverbank, the green water gleaming lazily – it is summer and the wildflowers make the verges a rebellion of colour. We climb to the place where we can see the panorama of the faraway city, its spires and domes like toys – an unreal place, a painted world.

In the other direction, the land rolls flat and hazy to the sea, its liquid blue spreading into the distance, indistinguishable from the sky, a single, eternal, unbounded vastness. For a moment I am back on that boat, that childhood sea voyage, feeling the surge and pitch of the ocean, and that medusa is spilling from a net onto the deck. *Don't touch it. It's deadly poisonous.*

I arrive at the house and they are waiting for me, Pio with his gummy smile and Catarina with her oval Madonna's face, little Vittoria her facsimile. My heart bursts with pent-up love. I have forgotten how it feels – the wonderful whirling, spilling generosity of joy.

'What is it?' asks Giacomo.

I find my eyes have welled with tears.

'Oh, I don't know. Hope, relief . . .'

'Me too,' he says.

The sound of the key turning distracts us. It is Dorotea.

'This came for you.' She is waving a fold of paper.

Lucrezia pounces on it. 'He says it went as well as he'd hoped and we have good reason to anticipate a positive outcome.' She bursts into tears. 'It's over. It's over.'

I read out the letter: . . . *We will have a definitive decision in three days. But I have no doubt about the outcome.*

Three days. The time it took for Christ to be resurrected. It seems a lifetime.

I can hear the supporters below, the drum beating out its rhythm and the chant: *Beatrice Cenci è innocente. La famiglia Cenci è innocente.*

32

Our continued incarceration feels increasingly like a formality. The guards have become quite lax and we have been permitted visitors. Domizio is the first to come. He takes Giacomo in his arms, and they stand in a tight clinch for several minutes, eyes shut, saying nothing, before retreating to the other room for privacy.

Lucrezia's sister comes next. Angelina is a woman I barely know but, judging by the way the sisters fall into an embrace, they are, or once were, very close. She has travelled from Florence. I can see in Angelina, who is a beauty with an open generous mien, how Lucrezia might have been had she not married my father and had every last shred of her joy purloined. Perhaps my stepmother will have the chance now to release herself from the armour of stiff brocades and jewels and the muffle of her tinctures, to become the woman she was supposed to be.

I am on tenterhooks waiting for Catarina and Pio to come. Catarina had said they would arrive at noon, and it is well past that hour now. Worries begin to filter through my shell, images of their carriage overturned, of an assault by thieves on the road, of a sudden fever, Pio's small, swaddled corpse.

When they arrive, my relief is profound.

'One of the horses lost a shoe and we had to wait more than an hour at the blacksmith,' Catarina tells me.

Pio has grown. He has two teeth – pearls in his lower gums. And there is his dimple. My heart is breaking and mending simultaneously. Catarina presses him into my arms. My maternal instinct flares, every fibre of my being wanting to protect him, to nurture him, to love him.

He bawls, desperate to return to Catarina, his body stiff, bending back, struggling desperately to escape my hold.

I return him to her, forlorn. He calms instantly, burbling his baby sounds. He must be able to sense my wickedness.

'He's just become unaccustomed to you. That's all,' she says. 'When you are home, he will adjust. You wait and see.' Instinctively sensing my need for distraction, she goes on to describe the garden at the Villa Paradiso, which flowers are still out, which fruits are ripe. 'The walnut tree has quite a crop.'

The distant past dashes back to me. I am on Giacomo's shoulders picking walnuts, I am in the river pool supported by his arms, I am holding Rocco's hand and we are leaping into the unknown. I will do all those things and more with Pio. I will watch him grow, become a boy and then a man. I long to begin our future. The future that was an impossible dream now rolls out before me like a Turkish carpet awaiting my tread.

Catarina sets Pio on the floor. He sits, straight-backed, playing with a peg doll she has produced from her bag. And then, bored, he throws it down and grabs my knee to heave himself to his feet, where he stands wobbling, gripping my skirts for dear life. I offer him my hand. He takes it, his small fingers curling tightly round mine, and gives me a wide smile. I rejoice.

'See?' says Catarina.

'How is Vittoria?'

'She's well. I left her with the housekeeper. Thought she might be a distraction. But you will see her soon.'

'Tomorrow.' This is the third of our three days and Farinacci has said he anticipates the Holy Father's official statement late this evening. We will be released first thing tomorrow.

'I planned to stay in Rome tonight,' she says, 'so we can all return home together.'

'Home,' I say, flooding with happiness at the thought – the word alone has its own force of elation.

'Careful,' cries Lucrezia to Bernardo.

Pio has crawled over to him, pulled himself up on the edge of a chair and is swiping a chubby fist at the card house he has spent the last hour carefully constructing. Cards fly everywhere. Pio giggles. I jump up, ready to intervene but, to our surprise, Bernardo laughs too, gathering the cards and deliberately scattering them again for Pio's pleasure. It feels like a miracle, as if something has released. I wonder if it is an indication that God has forgiven us.

I catch Lucrezia's eye and see her delight, only truly understanding now the challenges that motherhood has brought her. I think of Pio's small rejection of me, how deeply it cut, and realize what it must have been to raise a child who only rarely tolerated being touched and almost never expressed his love. I lean over and kiss her cheek.

'What was that for?' She is full of smiles.

'I felt like it.'

Giacomo and Domizio join us. They are cheerful. We are all cheerful. Domizio has reams of gossip. He talks of the painters, whose company he keeps, and which of them has achieved the best commissions. 'Merisi and Orazio Gentileschi came to blows over an altarpiece in San Paolo. Gentileschi thought he had the commission in the bag, but Merisi was offered it at the eleventh hour. Now they won't speak. They sit backs turned in the artists' tavern.'

It is good to listen to ordinary gossip. A glorious glimpse of what lies ahead.

'Just two days ago,' continues Domizio, 'Girolamo Santacroce was arrested for the murder of his mother.' There is something gleeful in his tone. 'They say he wanted to get his hands on the family fortune before his time.'

'He'd better call for Farinacci then.' Giacomo can't help his elated guffaw.

'Listen to yourselves,' scolds Lucrezia. 'A woman has been killed.'

Not long after they have gone, Farinacci arrives. 'I'm sorry to be so late.'

Lucrezia rushes to him. 'That's no matter.' She is beaming. Giacomo is shaking his hand enthusiastically.

Can neither of them see that there is something wrong in the lawyer's expression, in the stitch of his brow and the serious set of his mouth? I stand and one of the cups on the table tips, spilling wine over the floor. I can smell it, sharp like vinegar – Father's smell. I crumple inside.

Farinacci is stepping away from them, the tortured look deepening. 'I'm afraid the news isn't good.'

'What do you mean?' Panic scurries over Lucrezia's face.

'His Holiness feels that in the light of the Santacroce murder... Well, he thinks the nobility are becoming ungovernable – fears a spate of familial killings, feels the need to make an example.'

'An example of us?' I say. I am heavy and immobile, as if my body is carved from a lump of granite. I've been fooled by hope.

Lucrezia sinks to the floor with a wail. 'Are we not to be spared, then, after all?' Her face has caved in on itself.

Giacomo is white as Carrara marble. 'Did you offer the Palazzo Cenci?'

'It's no good,' Farinacci says. 'The palazzo will be requisitioned anyway. But I did manage to convince him to mitigate young Bernardo's sentence. He is to be spared.'

I step towards him, taking his hands, thanking him, my heart a shred lighter.

'But I'm afraid the three of you will . . .' He continues, distress playing over his features. 'They will come for you at dawn.'

Lucrezia vomits onto the floorboards. I help her up and onto the bed where I sit with her, trying to keep my mind from the gut-wrenching reality of our situation. 'Send for my physician,' she croaks, when she can find the words.

'You will want to make your peace with God,' says Farinacci. 'I've already called for the cardinal.'

'There must be something more you can do.' Giacomo is insistent, his tone edged with desperation. 'We can offer more. All the estates. The horses. The art. The jewels. Whatever it takes.'

Farinacci is shaking his head slowly. 'His Holiness's word is final. He will have all the chattels, as it is.'

'You said you could save us.' Giacomo is angry now. 'We've paid you a king's ransom and you've failed us.'

Farinacci begins to mount a feeble defence. 'I understand how you –'

'How could you possibly understand?' My brother rants on furiously, attacking the lawyer, until his rage is spent.

Lucrezia wails quietly.

I am doing my best to keep dread at bay.

Bernardo continues banging his head.

Giacomo paces in circles, his skull cupped in his hands.

The fire cracks, spitting a spark onto the floor.

Farinacci stamps it out.

Dorotea arrives with a pan and a bucket of sawdust, which she tips onto Lucrezia's vomit, sweeping it up, opening the window to let out the stench. The crowd is chanting joyfully. They don't know yet. Dorotea throws some lavender and rosemary stems on the fire and the room fills with the sweet scent – my mother's scent. It chokes me. *Will she be there to meet me? Or Olimpio? Or will it be Father? Please not him.*

The cardinal and the physician arrive at the same time.

The cardinal removes his round-brimmed, scarlet hat, to reveal the *zucchetto* beneath. He must have come directly from preaching as he is dressed head to toe in red – the colour of God's wounds. *Your sins are as scarlet.* I suddenly see blood gushing everywhere but staunch the image before it takes hold. 'This is the wrong outcome.' He looks heavy-browed with what seems to be anger. 'Wrong, wrong, wrong. Of course I will continue to petition. Until it is done, there is always a mote of hope.'

A mote, a minuscule speck of matter, is not much to cling to.

The physician has opened his bag on the table and is shuffling through several phials. Chink, chink, chink, they go. Finally, he produces two, tipping one into the other, handing it to Lucrezia. She kisses it, as if it contains the blood of Christ.

The cardinal guides her to the other room to hear her confession. Their murmuring can be heard through the closed door. I hope it provides succour for her. I attempt to reach Bernardo, but he is locked inside his poor bruised head.

Farinacci is deep in conversation with Giacomo, who still believes there is a way out of this. He indicates for me to join them, saying quietly, 'I don't want the boy to hear this, or his mother,' he vaguely nods at the closed door to the other room, 'but Bernardo is required to watch . . . tomorrow.'

'To watch. NO. That can't be right.' I am shaking. 'It's worse. He'll lose his mind altogether.'

'I shall try everything to make them change the ruling on this,' Farinacci says. 'His sentence states that he will be sent to the galleys.'

'The galleys.' I am struggling to tease out some advantage to this miserable fate.

'It's highly unlikely to be followed through,' continues the lawyer. 'When they meet him, it will be abundantly clear to them that he's unsuitable. I'll argue his case. They'll want to hold him for a time. But you have my word' – he presses his palm to his heart – 'that I will do my utmost, once the dust has settled, to ensure he is freed.'

Lucrezia reappears, seeming a little soothed and engages the physician in quiet conversation. He hands her another phial. 'This should be more than enough for the four of you to help you sleep tonight.'

'And for tomorrow? For my boy.' He gives her another small bottle. 'This will keep him calm. Mind, it's powerful stuff. Just a couple of drops. You don't want to –' His unsaid words hang in the room: *you don't want to kill him.*

Perhaps it is more merciful for Bernardo to die than to live without us, alone with his memories. Was I wrong to beg Farinacci to save him? I don't know. I don't know anything any more.

The past is trying to break down my defences, but I hold my poise and walk the physician to the door, thanking him before he leaves. He gives me his assurance that he will return if we call for him.

Lucrezia manages to calm Bernardo sufficiently to give him a measure of the sleeping draught, before taking some herself. Giacomo goes to confess next, on my insistence. I am still not ready.

I hear the crowd's mood shift to outrage, their chants filled with anger now. They must have got wind of our fate.

Farinacci is deep in his paperwork, searching for something that might save us. It is a futile endeavour.

'I hope I can trust you to oversee my will, make sure my

wishes are carried out.' A niggling doubt pecks at me. 'I need to know, though, whether the papal authorities will requisition the property and the monies that came to me from my mother.'

'As far as I'm aware it is only the Cenci estates. Your mother's assets are not listed with them and, anyway, are not of sufficient value to turn heads at the Vatican. I can look into it.'

This is some small succour. 'I shall make a few final adjustments to my will and ask my brother to act as witness.'

'I'll ensure that all is correctly dealt with. You have my word.'

When it is my turn to confess, the cardinal bids me kneel, saying, 'I trust you are ready now, my child.'

I tell him of the years of abuse and injury, of the regime of fear that was normal life to us. And I tell him of the mushroom and the poisoned tart and the vomit, and of the letter and how Father had me by the throat and that just as I felt the life leaving my body we were interrupted by Olimpio and Marzio. It is something of a relief to divulge. His mouth tightens – he can't keep the horror from his eyes.

'It is God's grace that sent those men to you in your moment of need.' He crosses himself. 'God bless their souls, indeed.'

I omit Bernardo's part in it. I omit to tell of Pio. But I confess to stealing a man promised to another woman. 'I am a sinner.'

'We are all sinners, my child. Are you repentant? That is what matters to the Lord.'

'I am.' *Am I?* I do regret how it all unfolded. I don't let myself think on it too deeply, for I do not regret loving Olimpio.

The cardinal tells me he is certain I will receive the Lord's forgiveness – 'abundant mercy', is how he puts it – and gives me my penance prayers. They seem so small, those familiar prayers, when compared to my sins, so vast. It is like trying to contain the oceans in a thimble. I want so much to believe the cardinal is right. After all he is a man steeped for a lifetime in prayer and devout contemplation. But he was certain, too, that we would receive the Holy Father's clemency.

'I am so full of doubt.' I feel Hell's heat creeping up my ankles, Dante's descriptions, so vivid, burning through my mind.

'Faith wavers in all humans, my child.' He places his hands on my head. The warmth of his palms radiates into my skull, where those images continue. 'Truly repent and you will receive God's grace.' He murmurs the prayers in Latin.

When he removes his hands, I stand and kiss his ring, thanking him.

As I am leaving, he says, 'There is something I'm curious about.'

I look at him, at his old man's filmy eyes.

'Why did you not tell the authorities what you just told me? Your father made an attempt on your life. It would have added grist to your defence.'

'I twice served him poison. I wanted him dead. He tyrannized us all and I tried to release us from that. It would have made little difference to the outcome, had I recounted it thus.'

'I see.' He looks somehow stricken. 'But you repent?'

I cannot answer him. I cannot repent of my love, the sinful love that has been the whole meaning of my life. I make a vague nod, which he takes for agreement, and leave the room, my demons prowling after me.

Taking the will I began a month ago from between the pages of my volume of Dante, I sit at the table, the flicker of the candle playing over the paper. My pen whispers. I make my final wishes: an annuity for Ilaria and an endowment for her to distribute to charities for poor widows at her discretion, a request for her to pray for my soul; an endowment to help those who lost all they had in the floods; something for Terza and for Bernardo; an amount each for my childhood nurse and my maid at the Palazzo Cenci. I add a sum for Dorotea, who has been so kind. Everything else, including the Villa Paradiso, goes to Catarina for Pio's care.

I find comfort knowing that my son, our son, the legacy of our love will continue. But the idea of him living on when I am no longer here digs me out with dread. I want to stand and scream and tear at my skin, when I hear your whisper again: *We will meet again in Hell.* Oh, Olimpio, for another glimpse of you, Hell seems an Eden.

I rise, opening the door to the adjacent chamber, hoping Giacomo will bring me some distraction. He pulls me into a desperate embrace. 'Oh, God, Bea!'

The small room is suffocatingly hot. A half-written letter lies on the desk, the ink pot unstoppered, a black drip hanging from the tip of his discarded quill. We sign my will, which I seal and leave, addressed to Farinacci.

'Who are you writing to?' I pick up his letter, scanning it. It is in Greek. That other letter flits into my mind. My own fatal carelessness catches my breath.

I gather that he is planning for Domizio to come with horses and ropes and ladders – *to spring us from this place*. I can't help thinking how Domizio, delightful company he may be, is the last person I would call on in an emergency. There is no one else, though. Giacomo babbles on about our escape, small flames licking in his eyes. Otherwise, his expression is grey and drawn. *We can go to Milan and then on to* . . .

I stroke his dear face. 'Don't waste your precious time imagining the impossible.'

'I can't give up.'

His fear diminishes mine.

'Put your feelings for Domizio on paper, not this.' I point at the letter. 'Tell him you love him. Tell him to squirrel away what valuables he can find at the palazzo to fund his future.'

'There will be a way.'

'It's no use. The place is seething with guards. This is a prison.'

'Such pessimism.'

'Not pessimism, Giaco, realism.'

I find courage creeping up on me.

'I could bribe the guards. They must have their price.'

I don't answer for a few moments, eventually saying, 'If you ask Domizio to help us escape, he will suffer all the more for feeling he has failed us.'

He stares at me a moment, haunted, the flames in his eyes doused, then crumbles into loud snotty heaves of grief and fear.

'Do you regret it?' he says.

'That he died? No.'

'Not even . . .'

'It was us, or him. It was always so. You know that.' My voice is hard and matter-of-fact.

I have a vision of that bronze Minotaur hurtling towards me, of the flash of the knife he slashed my face with – my bewilderment, my fear of him looming over me, always with a threat, never knowing what he would do. I will not be Iphigenia, tricked to my death. I will walk to my fate, knowing, head high like Sant'Agnese – she who presides over the torture instruments in the room below. She was known for her courage.

'It's too late for regret,' I say.

'Where's the sleeping draught?'

I fetch it. He snatches it from me, opening it, sniffing it. 'Blessed oblivion. I'm pathetic, aren't I? A real man wouldn't need this.' The past crashes back. Father's shout: *Call yourself a real man?*

'That's not true. We all do what we must.'

He looks desperate, eyes swollen and red, skin blotched and rimed with sweat, trepidation emanating silently from him, like a poison gas. He holds up the phial. 'How much of it?'

'I'd say half of what's in there.'

He holds a candle to it, trying to assess what quantity it contains. 'Are you sure that's enough?'

'Lucrezia was knocked right out by a few drops.' I gesture to the door, beyond which our stepmother and brother are sleeping like the dead. 'It'll be enough.'

'Will you have some?'

'I don't think so.'

He looks at me, his features clouded with despair. 'You always had nerves of steel – more courage than the rest of us put together.' He swallows some of the liquid, grimacing at its bitterness.

I shrug. 'Just better at hiding it.' If I have only a limited number of hours of life left then, however tainted by fear, I'd rather live them than obliterate them. 'Plenty of time for sleep after.' On seeing his look of horror, I immediately regret my statement. 'I need to think, get things straight in my head. Make sense of it all.'

'You'll find no sense in it, Bea.' He drains the bottle. I wonder if he will even see the morning. Perhaps that is his intention. It makes me think of what the physician said of the other tincture – *Be careful, it's powerful stuff* – and the thought slithers into my mind that perhaps I could ensure that Bernardo will not wake up. A mother cat will kill her kittens if she believes them endangered. Appalled by the idea, I bat it away. *Who am I to play God?* But I have killed once and I am my father's daughter, steeped in cold blood. I try to speak to God, but my prayers don't come easily. *Are you testing me, Lord?*

Once Giacomo is asleep, I stand at the window. The view of the city is sucked into darkness, so all I can see are shadows and looming shapes and the occasional blur of candlelight in a distant window. A throng of supporters is still gathered around a brazier below. My head swims and they transform into figures at the mouth of Hell, misshapen, faces formed in terror. I force that image from my mind and I am perched on the battlements of La Rocca's tower, high as an eyrie, looking far down into the ravine where the forest thrives and the low roofs of La Petrella wind towards the large brick church that dominates the village. Far beyond snakes the river, beaten to iridescence by the sun. And you are there, my love, taking my hand as we leap into the unknown.

33

They come just after dawn to take my brothers away. Giacomo is green with fear, his eyes skating back and forth. I fold him into my arms and can feel him trembling. He doesn't look back as he is led away. Bernardo is barely aware of what's happening. He won't let me touch him and can't meet my eyes. I try to give him words of encouragement, but he is elsewhere. Lucrezia has dosed him up with the physician's drops, until he seems barely to know who we are. I am powerless to protect him now.

My fate looms. I cannot see its form. I must submit to it – to the unknown. *Let go – let it all go*. Lucrezia clutches me. She is shaking uncontrollably.

'Let go,' I whisper to her.

She turns slowly to me, her eyes half shut, threads of terror stitching through her features. 'How?'

I have no answer for that, so pull her to me, holding her tight.

The crowd below fills the street with its roar.

We wait only minutes before four guards arrive and bundle us down the stairs to where the holy men are waiting by the door to escort us to the place where death awaits.

The great doors are opened and the crowd thunders – fists and horrified faces, eyes boiling in anger. A line of guards has to hold them back. They chant my name. They shout I am innocent. They ask, into the air, where is my pardon?

I look down, following my feet.

Our escort numbers at least twenty, who march slowly in

two columns, chanting psalms. At the front is a drummer. It is like a funeral march. Like the Easter parade. I walk in time with the drum, letting its rhythm absorb me entirely, leaving no space in me for thought, just the *douff, douff, douff*, a heartbeat.

Lucrezia stumbles on a loose cobble, staggering. I take her elbow and guide her along, trying not to look at her petrified expression for fear it might be contagious.

We arrive at the river.

Douff, douff, douff.

Seagulls swoop over us as we cross the bridge. Someone once told me that when the seagulls come to Rome it means there is a storm at sea. There is no evidence of stormy weather here. The sky is a beautiful endless September blue. The sky's own blue. We are almost at the piazza under the vast squat edifice of the Castel Sant'Angelo.

Olimpio creeps into my mind between the beats of the drum. *I watch you die again. I draw courage from your courage. You confessed to save me. Defiance from your defiance.*

We enter the chapel on the bridgehead. It is quiet, the outside clamour muffled. Our feet whisper on the flagstones. Sweet incense hangs among the prayers in the air. Sanctuary. The saints look down from the walls as I open my mouth for the Host. It is dry on my tongue.

Will you be there to meet me, my love?

The whole city has come to watch us die. Ranks of benches have been built as if it is a festival. When we enter the piazza, the crowd falls silent. *Douff, douff, douff.* I can hear the gulls carking now.

Lucrezia is taken first. We embrace. The guards have to prise the tight clutch of her fingers from my cuff. They half carry her up the steps. The scaffold is high, so the crowds can see, I suppose – see what happens to those who plot to kill their fathers and husbands. I am glad she won't have to watch me die in the knowledge that her turn is to come. Better me than her, for I am ready – ready to merge with eternity.

Will you be there to meet me, my love?

I keep my eyes down, so I don't have to see my stepmother bend over the block, and on the ground, dusty from being trodden underfoot, is a pamphlet. I stoop to pick it up. It bears my name above a crudely printed version of the cardinal's painting. In it the girl, supposed to be me, seems even younger than she did in the original, saintly, untouched by the world or sin. *Is this how I will be remembered? Will I be remembered? If I am remembered, it will not be as who I am. The pamphlet may bear my name, but it is a lie. Nobody will ever know my true story. They will only know the lie and the lies that will breed from the lie.*

My index finger is still ink-stained. I let the paper float away.

A priest has hold of my hands and is saying prayers for me. More prayers for my blighted soul.

Mea culpa; mea culpa; mea maxima culpa . . .

When I am pushed up the steps, the scaffold is a sea of blood – Lucrezia's blood. *Your sins are as scarlet.* I wade through it. I might drown in it before they have the chance to cut off my head. I see Bernardo. He lolls, his eyes at half-mast. He is propped up by two guards. He is somewhere else altogether – mercifully.

I hand a purse to the hooded man and forgive him for what he is about to do.

The holy men are still singing.

The gulls cry above.

I sink down, my skirts puffing out around me, and I am back on that ship. I smell salt. I taste it on the breeze that winds my hair into coils. The sea surges beneath me. I am not afraid. The medusa spills onto the wet deck. The sun burns down. The blade catches it, reflecting brightly – a sunbeam.

The horizon is blue as the sky, the sky blue as the sea, not even the faintest line to mark one from the other. I am no more than a puddle gathered into the finest of membranes.

The breeze hisses in my hair. The axe whistles. My waters break
    My caul is breached the boundary of my body – gone
    I drift
    I am weightless
    I merge with you my love
    I will evaporate
    we are evaporating
    we are air

Author's Note

Beatrice Cenci, Saint or Sinner?

'Sometimes it takes something other than perfect fidelity to sharpen our senses, to focus our attention sympathetically, in order to give us emotional access to the past.' *Lisa Jardine*

If you search the internet for Beatrice Cenci – the young woman who plotted the murder of her abusive father and was tried and executed in Rome in 1599 – there is a single image that comes up time after time. It is a painting of a girl. Her huge brown heavy-lidded eyes, set in a heart-shaped face, gaze back over one shoulder at the viewer, in much the same engaging attitude as Vermeer's *Girl with a Pearl Earring*. Her mouth is slightly open, her look the epitome of innocence, but the most striking thing about this girl is that she looks so very young – she is barely out of childhood. It is a picture so full of pathos as to rouse pity in even the most callous and indifferent viewer. It was long thought to be the work of Guido Reni, an artist of some renown working in Rome in the early seventeenth century and labelled at some point as a possible likeness of Beatrice. It has been reattributed several times since, most recently to Ginevra Cantofoli, one of a number of female painters working in Bologna in the 1660s and is very likely a self-portrait. Certainly, when compared to another Cantofoli self-portrait the features are strikingly similar. What it is emphatically not is a likeness of

Beatrice Cenci – a fact we have known for almost a century and a half. Yet still this remains the image most closely associated with her.

In his illuminating essay about the Cenci case in the *London Review of Books*, 'Screaming in the Castle' (1998), Charles Nicholl proposes another painting with a tenuous link to Beatrice. He suggests that Caravaggio's *Judith Slaying Holofernes* might have been inspired by her execution, which the painter was said to have witnessed. Those who have read my previous novel *Disobedient*, about the painter Artemisia Gentileschi, will have encountered this notion, and the proposal that the six-year-old Artemisia Gentileschi was also at the execution, accompanied by Caravaggio and her father. An anecdote in Corrado Augias's *The Secrets of Rome* (2005) inspired me to devote my opening chapter to this scene, and it provides a pleasing bridge between *Disobedient* and *Sinners*, the protagonists of which share so much common ground. Tempting though it is, we cannot claim Caravaggio's work as a likeness of Beatrice.

To return to the Cantofoli portrait, the insistence of this beguiling image, as central to the myth surrounding the Cenci patricide, is testimony to the way we tell and retell the stories of tragic women. The heroines of tragedy typically conform to two distinct archetypes: cunning and ruthless like Clytemnestra and Lady Macbeth, or young, innocent and preferably beautiful, like Iphigenia or Cordelia. Beatrice has been emphatically cast as the second type. Yet, if you read some accounts of her story, she might just as well belong in the first. The force of this painted girl urges us to believe in her innocence, even while knowing she was instrumental in the cold-blooded murder of her abusive father. As Oscar Wilde said, 'Sin is a thing that writes itself across a man's face,' and we want this to be the case because we want to be able to identify danger on the surface of people. So, this unblemished girl simply cannot be a sinner, or so we are compelled to believe. In the absence of any other image of her, this picture continues to carry the legend, though we know it is a lie.

I see the imagined figure of Beatrice Cenci as embodying both archetypes simultaneously, similarly to Medusa – the much-misunderstood Gorgon, a victim of rape who is transformed into a snake-headed monster and eventually decapitated, also famously depicted by Caravaggio. If we accept that Francesco Cenci raped his daughter, an assault so heinously against nature and firmly attached to her story as part of the public outcry around her trial, we can then accept the circumstances of the patricide as extenuating. However, evidence for the rape is tenuous.

The strongest source for it comes from the plea of Cenci's lawyer, Prospero Farinacci, in which he makes clear more than once that both Beatrice and her stepmother feared such an assault. This is somewhat backed up by the testimony of one of the household maids, who overheard Cenci threaten his daughter, though with burning rather than rape. There is sufficient documentary evidence that Beatrice was subjected to other sexual abuses, some of which I found too repulsive for inclusion in *The Sinners*. It could be that she was discouraged from testifying about the rape, or rapes, as it would have given her a strong motive for the murder, consequently weakening her primary defence: that she had no motive. What is manifestly clear is that the family lived under a reign of terror, but the more you dig for firm proof, the more the story turns to dust. Like the wrongly attributed painting, however, the rape has become part of the mythology that sees her as, to use Shakespeare's term, 'more sinned against than sinning'.

This version of her story evolved at the time of the Cenci

trial, when there was a great popular uprising in Beatrice's favour, believing the circumstances for the patricide as mitigating and clamouring for her pardon. It came from an amalgam of contemporary accounts, under the general heading of *Relation of the Death of the Cenci Family*, different versions of which were widely circulated in the aftermath of the execution. Given its tragic romantic underpinnings it is unsurprising that this version of Beatrice's story captured the imagination of writers and musicians, primarily male, giving rise to a plethora of retellings – dramas, literature and, most inevitably, operas. Shelley, Dumas, Dickens and Stendhal are four of the many writers who fell under the spell of the girl in the painting, whom Dickens described in *Pictures from Italy* as filled with 'celestial hope, and a beautiful sorrow, and a desolate earthly helplessness' (1846).

It wasn't until the late nineteenth century that eager archival researchers, also all male, began to turn up transcripts from the Cenci court case, and other documentary evidence, which exposed much of the existing literature as fanciful. A number of 'serious' accounts of the patricide and subsequent trial emerged, each purporting to tell the definitive 'truth'. This led to a new compulsion to cast Beatrice in a darker light or, in the words of Richard Davey in the *Antiquary Magazine* (1886), to 'hurl her from her pedestal'. These accounts, based as they are on contemporary records, certainly offer some new facts to help pin the story down a little more firmly. Beatrice's birth date turns out to have been earlier than believed, meaning that at the time of her execution she was twenty-two rather than seventeen. It is clear, too, she had been involved in a sexual relationship with Olimpio Calvetti, one of the two men hired to commit the murder. Often, she is cast as the seducer who inveigles a man to murder by giving herself to him – a Clytemnestra. Morality so often runs to the condemnation of the female as conniver so, for the purposes of my novel, I chose to see this relationship instead as a love story, a great passion that produced a child. The idea of the child came from the discovery of a will Beatrice made leaving an enormous bequest to her friend, Catarina de Santos, for the care of a 'poor boy' (*poveri fanciullo*) leading to further speculation that the boy was born of this affair.

These new pieces of evidence certainly work to change the tone of her story. Problematically, though, much of the material in the different 'true' accounts outlining the archival findings that I have read is contradictory. Bearing in mind, too, that most of the testimonies would have been the result of torture, as was the norm in the Rome of 1599, what we have is a vast amount of new evidence, much of which is unreliable. Moreover, the compunction to 'hurl' Beatrice 'from her pedestal' suggests a bias that corrupts the findings. The only thing we can be sure of, then, is that nothing about the Cenci patricide is clear. Perhaps this is why the figure of Beatrice Cenci became a cipher onto which artists, filmmakers and writers – I being one – have projected their own ideas.

For *Sinners*, it was never my intention to exonerate Beatrice of her crimes, or write a hagiography, or to search for absolute verisimilitude. Rather, given the elusive nature of the source material, I sought to write a fiction that responds to the many threads of story that have embroidered her legend. It is her courage and will to self-determination that stand out as the overwhelming truth behind all the differing accounts, and which sparked my desire to explore her character against the backdrop of the ways in which we mythologize women. If you will, I sought to reveal the tangled and knotted back of the tapestry, which tells all her stories, working with impressions rather than certainty and raising, rather than answering, questions. In my mind she is not simply the innocent victim of her father's brutality, or the cunning instigator of her father's murder: she is complex, she is both, she is innocent *and* guilty, saint *and* sinner. She is human.

Historical Note

As I have described above, *Sinners* is a work of fiction drawn from the bones of a true story. For the sake of more specific clarity on the history, I have outlined instances where firm facts have been knowingly sacrificed for the sake of narrative fluency.

I have condensed the timeline of the novel. Beatrice and Lucrezia were incarcerated at La Rocca – a property that Francesco Cenci leased from the Colonna family, rather than owned – for some three years, not just a few months. There they were locked into a room with the windows boarded up, their meals delivered through a hatch. Lucrezia herself is often depicted, in opposition to Beatrice, negatively. She is the stout virago whose breasts were so big she couldn't comfortably lay her head on the block – a lurid detail that is surely someone's invention. We do know that she had three daughters from her first marriage, a fact that I chose to omit from the novel. I found several mentions of opium in accounts of her, which gave rise to my characterization of her as drug-dependent. Speaking of opium, it is recorded that Francesco Cenci was dosed with it before he was bludgeoned to death or, in some accounts, had a skewer hammered into his head. The poisonous mushroom is my invention, as is Bernardo's part in the killing.

Bernardo is described as an 'imbecile' in Farinacci's plea yet, in other accounts, is described as old enough and competent enough to have been an integral part of the murder plot, and in others barely out of childhood. I have taken Farinacci's comment and embroidered it into what I hope is a humane portrayal of a neuro-divergent teenage boy. Another younger brother is Paolo, who seems to have been involved tangentially in the murder plot. Paolo is a spectral figure, sometimes described as disabled, who barely makes it into many of the accounts, possibly because he died before the trial. It seems likely that the two brothers became confused over the years, explaining the wide range of ages applied to Bernardo.

Giacomo, the eldest of the Cenci siblings, who was estranged from his father, and tried emphatically to push all blame onto Beatrice in his testimony, is often described as an unpleasant and criminal character who married beneath his station. For the purposes of my novel, I imagined a more nuanced portrayal of him. His homosexuality, for which there is no firm evidence, has driven a wedge between him and his father and also provides a motive for his betrayal of Beatrice.

Olimpio Calvetti was married, not simply betrothed, to Plautilla Gasparini and they had three children. He did not die under torture, though in some accounts he was tortured in the presence of Beatrice – a pivotal scene in my novel. It is recorded that he was, gruesomely, beheaded when trying to escape, some say by Cenci sympathizers seeking to silence him. It was Marzio Catalano, also known as Marzio Floriani and Il Catalano, who died under, or just after, torture.

As for the feuding noble houses I created two, the Rietini and the Orestesi, to stand in for the many who had serious quarrels with the Cenci family. Other invented characters with pivotal roles in the novel are Terza, Ilaria and Don Tomassino.

Pio Poverelli is the name I gave to Beatrice and Olimpio's rumoured son, as Poverelli was one of the names commonly given to orphans at the time. I wanted his name to nod to the poor boy (*poveri fanciullo*) of Beatrice's will. The will is interesting as the death sentence also technically included confiscation of all her property, so whether her heirs received their bequests is unknown. I have specifically addressed this issue in the novel, but the solution I came to is my own deduction.

The wording of the interrogations and the procedure of the trial as I have described them in the novel, are mostly fictionalized for dramatic effect, particularly the confrontation with Plautilla. Witnesses were not generally called in person in papal courts and neither would the defendants have had the right to a lawyer in court to plead their case. Farinacci did, though, make his plea to the Pope post-trial in a bid to have the family pardoned. I have largely adhered to his words and ideas from the plea, though have used only short passages from what is a long, and often dull, document.

The story of the young girl subjected to 'honour killing', whom I named Lucia, is taken from a legal record of 1555 (Cohen & Cohen, *Daily Life in Renaissance Italy*, 2001) in which a girl named Bernardina was impregnated by the local judge in a rural community in the Sabine Hills to the east of Rome. An attempt to force the couple to marry resulted in the judge escaping and being cut down by his pursuers. Bernardina was subsequently murdered by her father. This horrific splinter of history serves as a reminder of the demands of absolute chastity placed on young women in sixteenth-century Italy.

The eight men burned at San Giovanni in Laterano for performing same-sex marriage ceremonies is taken from a true account (Fergusson, Gary, *Same Sex Marriage in Renaissance Rome*, 2016). The plight of the families swept away from the riverbanks near the Palazzo Cenci I created out of the fact that in the 1590s there was widespread famine across northern Italy – the result of several years of poor harvests. This caused the migration of people from the countryside to the cities searching for a living. The devastating Christmas floods of 1598 in Rome, in which thousands died, are well documented and flood markers can still be seen on the city's walls.

The Palazzo Cenci and La Rocca are the real sites where Beatrice's life unfolded – the palazzo is now divided into offices and flats and the fortress is a ruin. But the Villa Paradiso is a place I imagined into being to offer the possibility of a happy outcome for Pio and thereby shed a small ray of light into what is a mercilessly dark ending for my protagonist.

Acknowledgements

I owe immense gratitude to Jillian Taylor and the team at Michael Joseph, including Paula Flanagan, Gaby Young and Yasmin Anshoor, as well as the Penguin Rights and Sales teams, with: Lucy Beresford-Knox, Bethany Wood, Agnes Watters, Christina Ellicott, Kelly Mason and Bronwen Davies; not forgetting Beatrix McIntyre, Hazel Orme and Lee Motley. Heartfelt thanks too, to my agent Alice Lutyens and Rakhi Kohli at Curtis Brown, also to Dane Millard and Simona Lascala-Style.

ARTEMISIA GENTILESCHI IS A SURVIVOR.

THIS IS HER STORY.

READ ON FOR AN EXTRACT

NURTURING WRITERS SINCE 1935

The Nightingale

Rome, March 1611.

Two painters, a father and daughter, are deep in concentration. A large canvas holds court in the centre of the studio. It depicts Judith and her maidservant fleeing the Assyrian camp. Judith grips a half-visible sword in one fist. Her servant carries the severed head of Holofernes in a basket beneath her sky-blue arm. Both women look back and away into the night, as if in response to a sound.

Two models at the end of the studio, bathed in light from the window to their left, make a living approximation of the painting. The older of the two stifles a yawn. The other fidgets, eyes flickering. A melon substitutes the severed head.

The daughter, crouched on her haunches, deep in concentration, paints the imagined drips of gore that seep through the wicker. The head, the napkin it is wrapped in, stained with the blood of a slaughtered hen, and the basket, are all her work. Her father is putting the meticulous final details to the gauzy folds of the servant's white shawl.

Peace is shattered with the arrival of a small brown bird flying in through the open door. It ricochets back and forth, striking one wall then another, then a beam, then the underside of the roof. The models cry out as if a demon has entered, one turning to follow the panicked creature with her eyes, the other crouching, head in hands, as if it might peck out her brains.

Artemisia, her gore-tipped paintbrush held aloft, seems to recognize its fear, each collision causing her own body to jolt minutely.

Orazio slams down his palette with an exasperated grunt.

The bird skims the upper edge of the canvas, depositing a chalky white blot, bright against the dark ground of the painting, the painting that is late, the only commission Orazio has had in six months.

The studio assistant emits a guffaw of laughter from the back of the room.

Artemisia suppresses a snort.

A curse bursts from Orazio, loud and sudden as a shot, shocking the place into absolute stillness.

The bird flits up to perch under the roof.

Time is suspended for a moment as they wait for what will happen next, four pairs of wary eyes fixed on Orazio.

Orazio frowns, watching the white stain drool downward over the painstakingly rendered detail in the brooch on Judith's painted shoulder.

The bird takes flight once more. Orazio springs up, arm high, fingers snapping round the small form as if it is a *pallone* ball.

'NO!' Without thinking Artemisia kicks her father hard on the shin, causing his hand to open.

The models shrink back, clasping each other.

The bird escapes, darting towards the light of the closed window. It makes a thud as it meets the glass and drops stunned to the sill. Ignoring her father's order to stop,

Artemisia yanks the gauze shawl from the model's head, wafting it over the oblivious bird to gather it tenderly into her hand.

She glares at him as she stalks towards the door.

'Where do you think you're going?' Orazio rubs his smarting shin. He is battling the urge to grab his disobedient daughter by the scruff and retaliate, curbed only by the presence of witnesses.

She says nothing as she continues on out of the studio, the tiny creature cupped in her palm as if it is the sacrament. 'Fetch her back,' he barks at the assistant, who gives him an insolent look before following her out.

Orazio doesn't like the boy, doesn't like having a mincing *finocchio* about the place, around his sons, particularly since he discovered him locked in an embrace with the youth he sometimes uses as a model if he needs an angel. At least he doesn't pose a threat to his daughter's virtue. Orazio is supposed to be teaching him to paint as a favour to the Stiatessis. Giovanni Stiatessi is his oldest friend and is Piero's uncle, but the boy hasn't a jot of artistic ability. He does have an eye for colour, though, and a particular gift for milling pigments, so he is of some small use.

Orazio surveys the stain on the painting, worrying now about the client, who has already demanded a discount for late delivery. He can envisage the commission given instead to one of the young artists, brimming with talent and enthusiasm, who hang about the Piazza del Popolo touting for business. He knows they will undercut him. They don't have families to support.

Orazio's thoughts swirl. The light is fading. Time is running away. They are moving from this house in a few days to a cheaper district – saving money, always having to save money. He is calculating how long it will take to restore the damage the bird has wreaked, taking up a palette knife to scrape away the stain carefully. It is not as bad as he'd thought. The brooch is relatively unscathed. It is the chalky mark on the dark swathes of curtain behind that will need repairing.

He stands a moment to admire his work on Judith's red dress, the woven pattern in the brocade, the subtle changes of colour where the light catches the undulations and folds, the places where the material is pulled taut across the bodice, so the eye becomes aware of the invisible starched interfacing. Orazio reminds himself that he is known for his gift in painting fabrics.

His eye is drawn down to his daughter's work. She had fought him to allow her to paint the severed head, such an unsuitable subject for a girl. He had reasoned that no one would know. The painting would bear his name, after all. The head nestled in its basket seems, rather than dead, in a tormented sleep. Its skin is colourless as vellum, all its warmth seeping away through the wicker in trails of crimson ooze. He can feel the chill on those blue-grey lips. The napkin, trailing over the basket's edge, is exquisitely rendered. Pinkish smudges seep along the linen's weft where the women appear to have wiped their bloodied hands.

A shiver runs through him. The gruesome bundle seems to contain the very act itself that caused those bloody marks. And all concocted in his daughter's head. Why have none of his three sons shown such ability? She, at seventeen, is more accomplished even – it galls him to admit – than he, who has a lifetime of painting behind him. He fancies he can hear God's laughter.

Orazio comforts himself with the beauty of his brocade, a careful mix of madder lake, with a few grains of vermilion and enough earth-red ochre to dull any hint of garishness. He is pleased with the effect, very pleased. He takes up a fine brush and carefully begins to stipple a blackish green over the residue left by the bird's mess.

The bird is almost weightless in Artemisia's hands. She'd thought it would flap and scramble to escape but its talons are clasped around her thumb and it is absolutely still, except for the staccato tick of its tiny heart. She opens her fingers carefully. Its sharp little grip tightens, eye rotating.

How easily life can be doused – one moment a thing exists and the next it is gone. She feels sick at the thought of how nearly this small creature was crushed in her father's fist as if it were nothing more than a fly. But even a fly is a life. On occasion she has felt a pang of guilt, sent up a prayer for forgiveness, having slapped a mosquito between her palms, then felt silly for it.

All life is sacred – all God's creatures. Sister Ilaria, scourge of her childhood catechism classes, had labelled her overly sentimental for caring about things she herself deemed unimportant. 'God put all the creatures on this earth to labour for us and feed us, just as he created woman to serve man.'

'Why?'

'It is not for you to question, Artemisia, but simply to accept that it is so.'

The red-hot shock of the ferule across her open palm

ensured she never voiced such a query again, though it germinated in a mossy niche at the back of her mind: why is it so?

In the hot gasp of late afternoon Artemisia slips through the gate and into the small public garden behind the house, enjoying the thrill of freedom, no one to watch in case she should carelessly misplace her virtue. The condition of his only daughter's reputation is a constant preoccupation of her father. He seems to think her curious nature imperils it. But it is he who raised her as an artist, and without curiosity there is no art, or so she firmly believes.

She reaches up, lifting the bird high into the blossom-heavy branches of the Judas tree, an embarrassment of pink. It flits up, perching to sing, the audacity of its trills and whistles at odds with its ordinary buff plumage. She imagines its performance is a show of gratitude for her, when in truth she knows it is rejoicing in its liberty.

In the garden Piero watches her unseen as she gazes at the nightingale, entranced, inscrutable. Like the bird, she is not a beauty in the conventional sense, unlike the models who come and go in her father's studio with their coppery curls and painted pillowy flesh. Artemisia's smile is crooked, her hair wayward, her body spare and angular. Piero cannot say whence her magnetism comes but suspects it is generated by the belief she has in her own abilities. And it is no delusion: she could transform a dishcloth into a holy relic with her brush.

He is about to speak but she turns, placing a finger over her mouth, glancing back and up towards the bird, not wanting to disturb its song. He follows her to the shaded stone bench where an ancient dryad gurgles water into a little pond and the air is thick with the scent of spring.

'Your father wants you to go back in. Help him paint over the stain the bird made.'

She laughs, covering her mouth with her hand. 'It shat on his painting, Piero. Clever little bird.' Her once-white apron is smeared with crimson paint. 'He doesn't need my help. Just doesn't want me outside.' Her tone has soured.

'Just as well I'm here to preserve your honour.' He teases another cough of laughter from her.

The bird flies away as the bells ring for compline, a bellowing chorus marking the shift to evening. She scrutinizes Piero, as if working out how she will paint him. 'Why do you look so tired?'

'Out late last night.'

'Where?' She prods him with her elbow.

'Just around.'

Raising her eyebrows towards him briefly, she takes her sketchbook and a nub of chalk from her pocket, beginning to draw. She has no intention of obeying her irascible father and Piero is glad. It is this defiant spirit he so admires.

'Why so secretive?' she asks, after some time.

He shrugs.

'You were at the cardinal's palazzo, weren't you?'

He nods.

He has told her a little of the goings-on there, parties just for men, where youths dress in girls' clothes, so convincing you would never know what hung between their legs, and of the cardinal himself, who likes to watch them when they fall to drunken abandonment. He'd thought she might be shocked but she wasn't. She asked if he'd ever dressed up like that. He'd told her the opportunity hadn't arisen.

She draws in silence.

All at once the garden is invaded by gangs of whistling swifts, fleet as arrows. Piero watches them, dazzled by their agility, swooping and diving overhead.

Had it not been for his friendship with Artemisia, his stay in Rome would have been a great disappointment. His inadequacies as an artist were soon and starkly exposed, his ambition to earn his living as a painter dashed within days of his arrival. But meeting Artemisia had softened the blow.

Some believe that there exists for everyone in the world a perfect match, like a pair of gloves. Piero believes he has found his own lost glove in Artemisia. Uncomplicated by desires of the flesh, their friendship is instinctive – as if they are twins separated and reunited. For her there is nothing but her art, and his corporeal needs are well met elsewhere.

'Tell me about the evening. Did anything happen?' She doesn't look up from her drawing.

He knows what she means. 'As a matter of fact, yes.'

'Go on.' She looks up, now.

'I was shown something secret. I'm not supposed to say.'

'But you can tell *me*.'

'He has a marble statue that he keeps in a locked closet. It's older than the Colosseum.'

'Why? Why locked away?'

'It is of Hermaphroditus . . .'

She tilts her head, not understanding.

'You know . . .' He lowers his voice, though there is no one in earshot. 'The parts of a man *and* a woman.'

'You mean . . . ?' She puts one hand to her breast and the other in the fold of her lap.

He nods. 'Don't you know the story of the nymph who fell for the son of Hermes and Aphrodite? When he cast her off, she prayed to the gods that they never be separated. So she clung to his back and her body fused with his. It's from Ovid.'

'Girls are not told *those* stories. Apparently, they will corrupt us.' She returns to her drawing and they are silent for some time until she looks right at him saying: 'The parts of a man and a woman. I'd like to see that.'

He doesn't have the heart to tell her that the likelihood of her being given the chance to see the *Hermaphroditus* is infinitesimally small. She must already know it. 'The cardinal's looking for a sculptor to carve a couch for it to lie on.'

They both stare wordlessly into the surface of the pond a moment. Patterns of reflected light ripple its surface. 'Do you think one day I shall be commissioned to paint for him – people like him?'

'I do.' Piero hopes this is true.

She changes the subject. 'I'll miss this place. There's not even a balcony at the via della Croce, just a gloomy yard where the drain runs. It is a quarter of the size of this house *and* we will be sharing with Zita Medaglia and her children, whom I have never even met.' She slumps. 'Father says I will benefit from having another woman about the place. But really he wants her to . . .'

'Spy on you!'

'Exactly.' Despondency invades her tone. 'He wants to

keep me cooped up, doesn't trust me. Thinks I will ruin my reputation by "going about".'

'But you need inspiration. And how will you meet other painters, see their work, gain commissions, if you don't "go about"?'

'How indeed? Father wants me preserved, like a pickled egg, for some fat burgher, who counts his money every day and will expect a string of children to spoil.'

'You were not made for some fat burgher. You were made to paint. If I were your husband I would insist upon your freedom.' It is not the first time they have touched on this topic.

Piero has tried not to think about her inevitable marriage because it will certainly sound the death knell for their friendship.

'Imagine if you were to come to Florence. I could be in charge of arranging your multitudes of commissions.'

'It's a nice dream, Piero.' She gets up abruptly, walking back towards the studio.

The garden seems sapped of its colour when she is gone. He picks up her abandoned sketchbook. She has drawn the nightingale – no, not drawn, but embodied, as if there is some invisible conduit travelling from her eye to her heart, to her hand, to the paper. In just a few smudges the bird has sprung into existence, so much so he can almost hear its song once more.

He is reminded of another story from Ovid, can't quite remember how it goes, of a woman who is transformed into a nightingale. The memory leaves a bad feeling trailing in his mind.

Taking up the charcoal he attempts to copy her sketch. It

begins well but soon becomes flat and lifeless, serving to illustrate his friend's superior gifts. All Rome is abuzz with talk of the Bernini boy, who, at twelve years of age, is being touted as a genius for his sculpture. His talents have already caught the attention of the cardinal. His career is made before it has begun, for the cardinal seeks to amass the greatest collection of art in all Rome and, being the Pope's nephew, has the means to do so. All the has-beens in the city are scrambling to gain his attention. An averagely gifted painter like Orazio would kill for a commission. In Piero's opinion, Artemisia is every bit as skilled with a paintbrush as young Bernini is with a chisel, if only she were allowed to prove it so.

He rips his shameful sketch from the book, screwing it into a ball and tossing it away as he returns inside.

Orazio's temper seems to have abated. Artemisia says he wasn't always so disagreeable, but Piero finds that hard to believe. She is sitting at the table with him and the model, Fillide, still in the red dress, drinking wine. The melon, so recently standing in for a severed head, sits on a board, sliced in half, a knife stuck upright in its body.

'May I?' Piero points towards the fruit. Orazio wordlessly shunts it towards him. He slices it, aware of the other man's simmering disdain.

The melon's flesh is the colour of fresh trout. It releases its fragrant aroma and Artemisia takes a slice. A sticky trail runs down her wrist that she brings to her mouth to lick.

'Are you not going to cut some for me?' Fillide is smiling up at Piero from under her lashes, flirting pointlessly.

Artemisia rolls her eyes. Fillide is the kind of woman who must be desired by all, even by a boy who prefers boys. Piero offers her a piece on the point of the knife, which she takes between the tips of her fingers to nibble delicately.

Turning back to Orazio, Fillide says, 'You've flattered me in your painting.' She speaks in a little girl's sing-song voice.

The stain on the painting is all but gone, the only evidence a glossy patch in the dark background. It will be invisible once it has dried, as if it was never there. He remembers Orazio's rage, so out of proportion to the damage.

'You've made me young again.' Fillide slurs slightly. Up close Piero can see the tangle of fine red veins on her cheeks and the lines around her eyes. It's true Orazio has flattered her. She is still undeniably striking but in his opinion her vanity mutes her beauty more than her age.

'Needs must. Judith was a young woman. Younger than you, Fillide.' Orazio's laugh is a kind of porcine grunt. He swigs his wine and refills their cups.

Piero can see his large paint-smudged hand massaging the woman's knee beneath the table. There is nothing of Artemisia in this uncouth man and it makes him wonder what her mother was like. Artemisia was twelve when she died.

When she'd told him of her mother's death she'd said only: 'Don't pity me, for it will make me hate you.'

She, too, has noticed her father's hand kneading Fillide's thigh, and swaps a raised eyebrow with Piero. He imagines for a moment how different her life would have been had she gone, after the death of her mother, into the household of his uncle, Giovanni Stiatessi and his aunt Porzia, here in Rome. The two women had been as close as sisters.

It was discussed at the time but Orazio had changed his mind.

Piero begins to scrape the freshly milled paint into a container, sealing it carefully so the air won't get to it, then wiping the residue from the mixing slab with a cloth soaked in turpentine.

'You'd better pack everything away for the move before you go,' says Orazio.

'It's a shame you are leaving this place.'

Orazio snaps back, something about how Piero has no inkling of what it is to support a family and pay the bills.

Artemisia lobs a look of disapproval at her father, hating the scorn he harbours for her friend. If she had the chance to choose between them, she knows which she would pick. But Heaven will fall in before she has such a chance.

She watches Piero a while. He has the slate-grey eyes of a northerner, rendered all the more striking by the coal-black curls and tawny skin inherited from his Algerian mother. It is no wonder he is so popular at the cardinal's palace.

Leaving the studio, she climbs the stairs to her bedchamber, where she casts off her clothes and sponges down her body with cool water from the ewer, enjoying the freedom of her nakedness. She recalls her mother, even when she was very small, insisting that she dress and undress in the dark. It had to be achieved by wriggling out of one garment and into the other without exposing any of her body. 'A good woman never shows her flesh, not even to God,' she used to say, and 'The devil can see in the dark.'

When Artemisia had suggested that both God and the devil saw everything anyway, so what difference would it make, she'd told her daughter to take her immodest thoughts to confession and repent of them. Naturally this served only to arouse further her fascination with the human body.

She tries to picture the *Hermaphroditus*, to imagine the fusing of the two bodies, like limpet to rock. The world is so wide, so full of novelty, pressing her with a compulsion to witness it in its entirety. What she would give to paint it all.

She stands in the window from where the undulating rooftops of Rome spread into the distance, roseate against the darkening blue of the sky. Here and there the vast pale domes of the city's many churches rise up above the buildings. It is throbbing with life and art, and she is driven to take her place in it all, to see everything, to be seen. But every part of her – her body, her talent, her true self – must remain hidden from the world.